Also by Lucy Score

LUCY SCORE

Bloom *books*

Published by Bloom Books, an imprint of Sourcebooks
P.O. Box 4410, Naperville, Illinois 60567-4410
(630) 961-3900
sourcebooks.com

Originally self-published in 2019 by That's What She Said, Inc.

Printed and bound in the United States of America.
LSC 10 9 8 7 6 5 4

To everyone who faced an Amie Jo in high school.
Also, to anyone I ever Amie Jo-ed, I am so very, very sorry.

CHAPTER 1

Marley

August

This was what rock bottom looked like.

My childhood room—unchanged except for a new duvet—with the same dark-green carpet, the same dull-yellow walls. The same New Kids on the Block poster I'd defaced with my fourth-grade best friend and a bottle of sparkly purple nail polish.

We'd been too cool to like what everyone else in our class liked.

Yep. That same too-cool elementary school rebel was now thirty-eight, downsized, broken up with, and newly homeless.

I, Marley Cicero, was not winning at life.

My fingers worried at a pill on the peach bedspread while I tried not to think about the fact that everything I owned fit into two suitcases and three cardboard boxes, all tossed in front of the closet where I'd once hidden warm Diet Cokes and pilfered vanilla cigarettes.

I'd given my parents enough of a heads-up that they had time to move their winter wardrobe out of the closet and into my sister's old room, which Dad now used as a calligraphy studio. When Zinnia got married, they'd repurposed her bedroom and left mine alone. I had a feeling it was because they knew Zinnia would never return home with a suitcase and a sob story.

My phone signaled a text, and I held the screen up to my face.

Zinnia: Welcome home, sis! Hope Mom and Dad's retirement sex doesn't keep you awake at night.

I sighed, hating the fact that my perfect, brilliant, beautiful sister knew what a gigantic loser I was. I'd text her back later when I was feeling less like roadkill. Rolling my head to the side took the maximum amount of effort I was capable of. The hot-pink alarm clock informed me that it was 7:05 p.m. Too early for bed. Too late for me to suddenly become a less ambivalent girlfriend or a better director of social media management at my ex-job.

That left only one thing. Smothering by Harry Potter pillow. Mustering the necessary energy, I rolled and pressed my face to Daniel Radcliffe's.

There was a quiet knock on my door. I knew that knock. It was the "tread carefully—my teenage daughter is unstable" knock.

"You aren't in there smothering yourself, are you?" Dad asked through the door.

"Mmph."

Retirement must have made my father braver than he'd been before, because I heard the jiggling of the handle no one had bothered to tighten since I moved out sixteen years ago. Sixteen stupid, wasted, crappy, pathetic years.

Okay. Now I was being a little too melodramatic. It was like the room still gave off the fumes of teenage hormones of despair. It was possible they'd seeped into the drywall and carpet, poisoning anyone who entered…like asbestos. Or lead paint.

The mattress shifted under my father's weight as he settled on the edge of the bed.

"The way I see it, you've got two choices, snack cake." I'd earned the nickname due to my insatiable appetite for the delectable little plastic-wrapped desserts. My preteens were spent embracing the addiction, and then my teen years and early twenties were mostly focused on battling the hold that processed sugar had on me. Now, just the thought of golden cake and butterscotch icing had my mouth watering all over Harry Potter's face.

"You can either wallow in disappointment—which is a legitimate choice—or you can embrace this change as a reboot of sorts." My father, Ned Cicero, had the voice of a Muppet and was a retired computer engineer. A stereotypical one, with plaid, short-sleeved button-downs and thick glasses. He'd been with the local IBM headquarters for thirty years before retiring last year. You could take the geek out of the cubicle, but you sure as hell couldn't take the cubicle out of the geek.

I lethargically rolled to one side. "Dad, I promise that I'm not going to be one of those adult children who move back home temporarily and then never move back out," I said fervently.

"You can stay as long as you like. Did I mention we're opening my calligraphy studio as an Airbnb?" he asked, shoving his glasses up his nose.

I sat up. That was news. My parents were golfing and calligraphying and now starting an Airbnb. And what was I doing? Nothing. Zip. Zilch. Squat. I'd stay here a month tops. Regroup. Refresh the ol' résumé. Try to make the new-job-every-two-years thing look like a benefit. Maybe I'd reconnect with some old friends while I was in town. Okay, maybe not.

I'd land on my feet, dammit. Or at least my hands and knees.

"I don't know what I'm going to do, Dad. But I'm going to do something," I promised.

He patted my knee in that absent, fatherly kind of way. "Sure you are." It was the kind of parental enthusiasm applied to preschooler statements about becoming astronauts and rock stars.

The door burst open, and my mother exploded into the room. Where Ned was calm and contemplative, Jessica Cicero was an effusive ball of energy. She was excited over everything from the first snowfall of the year to front-load washers with windows. This unusual zest for life had served her well in her former career as a first-grade teacher.

"You are *not* going to believe this, Marley! Fate has intervened," she announced grandly. The plastic bangles on her left wrist clanked against tan skin. She was pretty. And not just for her age. She had lovely blond hair that she touched up every four weeks and kept cut short in a face-framing bob long enough to pull back into a stub of a ponytail. She had bright blue eyes that crinkled nicely in the corners because she was always laughing or smiling about something.

I'd spent my entire life wishing I could be either the easygoing girl next door like Mom or the beautiful genius like my adopted older sister. Zinnia was born in India and had grown into a woman who could have easily enjoyed a modeling career had she not been so busy winning grants for worthy causes and changing lives.

"Tell us more, my beautiful angel," Ned said, rolling onto his belly and resting his chin in his hands.

I half wished I'd succeeded in the suffocation. Usually my parents' undying affection for each other was like an anchor in the storm. It was something to depend on, something I could always hold up my relationships to like a measuring stick. None of my relationships ever actually measured up to the great love of Ned and Jessica Cicero. And today, that love just reminded me that I was single, jobless, and hopeless.

"Well, I just got off the phone with Lindsay Eccles. You remember her, don't you, Marley? She worked in the front office of the elementary school when you were in sixth grade. Remember how she went back to school and got her principal's certificate? I still say that surprise party was a mistake. We almost gave the poor woman a heart attack…"

This was typical of Mom's stories. They took the scenic route with nary a shortcut and rarely a punchline.

Dad listened, enthralled. I tuned out.

Culpepper, Pennsylvania, took "small town" and made it microscopic. As much as I would have liked to pretend that I had no idea who Lindsay Eccles was, I was inundated with the unfairly high-definition memory of Mrs. Eccles holding back my hair while I enthusiastically vomited in the trash can behind the front desk in the school's office during the flu outbreak of 1992.

"Anyway," Mom said, taking a deep breath. It was the signal that she was coming to her point. "She told me that Miss Otterbach just turned in her resignation this morning! She and her girlfriend are getting married and moving to New Hampshire to be closer to their family."

My mother paused and looked expectantly.

"Uh. Good for them?" South Central Pennsylvania had come a long way since I'd grown up here. It was no longer the talk of the town to be a lesbian schoolteacher. But I still didn't know what Miss Otterbach becoming Mrs. Otterbach had to do with me.

"More like good for *you*! It turns out the high school is in desperate need of a phys ed teacher *and* girls' soccer coach!"

My dad's feet quit swinging behind him.

"I didn't know Miss Otterbach was the soccer coach."

"She wasn't," Mom said, glossing over whatever she was hiding with a bright smile. Dad cleared his throat. He was picking up what my mother was putting down while I was still miles behind them both.

"Why are you telling me this?"

"She offered you the job, silly!"

"Me?"

Mom nodded, her eyes bright. "Preseason starts in two days. School in two weeks. Aren't you over-the-moon thrilled?"

My mom doled out equal enthusiasm for all things. For instance, Zinnia's straight A-plus report cards and my solid Bs—with the occasional C—both received top billing on the refrigerator and a standing ovation from my mother. It made me feel like a bit of a cheerleading charity case.

"I don't have a teaching certificate," I argued. "And I haven't touched a soccer ball in over a decade." High school had been the bane of my existence. I had not thrived in the captivity of Culpepper Junior/Senior High. I had rebelled and complained and limped my way through the minefields of popularity, academic achievements, and athletic accomplishment. None of those had I any actual personal experience with. At least, not until senior year, when I briefly dated Mr. Popularity and temporarily rose out of the middle of the pack only to be brutally slapped back down.

"It's just for the semester until they can find a permanent replacement. You'd basically be a long-term substitute. The state has emergency contingencies in the case of open teaching positions since they started slashing pay and closing programs. There's a shortage, you know."

Before she could launch into her "sorry state of affairs in education" speech, I held up a hand. "I don't understand. How did Principal Eccles even know I was home?"

"Oh, I have a weekly lunch date with some of my school friends."

"And you told them I was moving home?"

Mom nodded cheerfully. *Great. So all of Culpepper was now aware that the girl permanently banned from Culpepper Homecoming festivities was back, single, and broke.*

"I really don't know anything about gym class or coaching," I reminded her.

"You can learn anything you put your mind to," my mother insisted.

"Let's go out and kick the ball around," Dad chimed in. "You can talk it through with me and wake up some muscle memory." He bounced off the bed and clapped his hands in anticipation.

With great reluctance, I dragged myself away from the safety of my mattress. I could always say no. I could just hunker down, lick my wounds, and start applying for jobs anywhere but here. I could do that.

"I hope you don't mind, but I told them you'd take the job," Mom said brightly.

CHAPTER 2

Marley

While Dad bebopped into the backyard shed—a dusty, spider-filled museum to my childhood—looking for a soccer ball, I sat on the porch steps and dragged on my sneakers.

It was hot. Pennsylvania mid-August humidity hot. The air was thick enough that it felt like sitting in a bland, nostalgic stew. The fence needed a new coat of paint, but the same trees that I'd climbed and fallen out of as a kid were still there. The same garden beds were still as neglected as they had been since Mom's 1988 homegrown-everything experiment. The redbrick patio that I'd scraped my knees open on more times than I could count still cut a jagged swath through the green sod.

Stepping into the backyard was like traveling back in time to when I was eight. Except I was thirty years older. My dreams were dead. And I didn't even own cleats or shin guards anymore. Did coaches need those? Or did they just stand on the sideline yelling like mine had? Were the rules the same? Or had the game evolved into something different with the viral popularity of Abby Wambach and David Beckham?

There was no way I could do this.

"Heads up!" The ball landed with a definitive thud in front of me. It didn't bounce. "Guess it needs a little air," Dad noted, jogging toward me with a bicycle pump in one hand.

He was wearing cycling shorts, leftovers from his three-month spin class obsession. He'd had trouble settling on a new hobby since retirement.

"What?" he asked as he pumped.

"I can't get used to your mustache."

He patted the furry caterpillar above his lip with pride. It was another post-retirement hobby: facial hair growing. "Think I'm going to try a goatee next."

"Can't wait."

He gave the ball a poke. "Nice and firm."

I tried not to watch him handle the ball while he said that. Dad had an uncanny knack for saying inappropriate things without ever trying.

"I seem to recall you were quite adept at juggling balls in high school, snack cake," he said cheekily. "Let's see if you still remember how."

"Jesus, Dad. Listen to yourself." But he was already scampering to the back of the yard.

We kicked the ball and the idea of me being a temporary teacher and coach around.

"What if my team loses every game?" I asked.

"They won one game last season, and that was because the other team's bus got stuck in the traffic when the cattle escaped the auction. It was a forfeit. I don't think the district is looking for a winning season."

"But where do I even begin? Practice starts in two days."

Dad shrugged and kicked at the ball like he was a puppet with wooden joints. His athletic experience had been deferred in favor of the AV Club during his high school career. "What did your coaches have you do during preseason?"

"I don't know. Run until I hated running?"

"There you go. We can start there," he said, winding up for a kick and missing the ball completely.

I laughed. I couldn't help myself. He didn't have an athletic bone in his body, but that didn't stop him from wanting to support me. I didn't deserve him, but I wasn't willing to let that get in my way of appreciating him.

"We can look on the internet after dinner," he suggested. "You can learn anything online."

"Mmm. What about teaching? I don't even know what a gym teacher does besides stand around creepily while students change and then make everyone play volleyball from November to May."

I was by no means in the best shape of my life. Adulthood had taken its toll in the form of happy hours and sodium-laden convenience foods and no time for the gym. I was dehydrated and low on sleep. My shape was soft, round. And I lost my air with a flight of stairs.

"Dad, I don't think I can do this. It doesn't make any sense. I've been working in health care and data mining. Not sports and fitness." I kicked the ball back to him.

He tripped over it and face-planted on the grass. I jogged to his side and pulled him up. "Maybe we should continue this discussion over beers. While sitting," I suggested, picking his glasses off the ground.

"Sounds like a safer plan," he agreed.

There was a loud, strangled honk from the neighbor's fence. I yelped. "What the hell was that?" I was already out of breath just from kicking the ball around. Surprises could explode my already overtaxed heart.

"Dang swan," Dad said without any heat.

"Swan? Did you say 'swan'?"

The honk sounded again.

"Amie Jo thought their yard needed an exotic touch," he said, limping toward the back porch.

Oh, no. No no no no no. Not her. Not the monster from my past.

"Amie Jo Armburger?" I asked as nonchalantly as the lump of dread in my throat would allow.

"Hostetter now," Dad corrected me. "She and her husband, Travis, bought the house next door a few years ago. Tore it down and rebuilt it from the ground up."

My entire senior year came rushing back to me so quickly I got vertigo. Travis Hostetter. Amie Jo Armburger. And I couldn't think of either one of them without remembering Jake Freaking Weston.

This was why I had moved away. Why I rarely came home. And when I did, I didn't make it a big thing. I wore a baseball cap out in public. I refused to go to any local bars or Walmart. I pretended to be a stranger.

"Amie Jo and Travis live next door?" I clarified weakly.

Dad, oblivious to my instantaneous panic, jogged up the back steps. "Yep! I'll grab us a couple of brewskis and check on dinner."

The back door closed, and suddenly I wanted nothing more than to peer over the fence and see what kind of castle the Prom King and Queen had built. It was stupidity and curiosity that had me running at the seven-foot-tall, peeling-paint barrier. My sneakers scrambled for grip as my biceps screamed. I was able to haul my eyeballs above the fence just long enough to catch a glimpse of a huge kidney-shaped in-ground pool surrounded by what looked like white marble. There was a raised hot tub spewing a waterfall of color-changing water back into the pool. The porch had Roman columns holding up the two-story roof.

"A fucking outdoor kitchen and a tiki bar? Are you kidding me?" I groaned.

"Mom! Some lady is spying on us!" The shout came from the direction of the pool, and I realized there were people in the water. Two of them. Towheaded teens with surfer dude haircuts lounging on rafts the size of small islands.

"Shit. Shit. Shit."

11

I dropped to the ground, ducked—for unknown reasons, as I was currently blocked from view by the fence—and ran to the gate. I slipped through into my parents' front yard and stared up at the modern monstrosity McMansion that I'd missed when I'd pulled in the driveway on the other side of the house.

Stately red brick, more white columns, and what looked like a cobblestone driveway. All behind a wrought iron fence that clearly stated that only a certain kind of visitor was welcome. There was a freaking fountain in the front yard. Not just one of those under-stated cement jobs you could get at Lowe's or Home Depot.

No. This had statues in it. Naked ones spitting water at each other.

Honk!

"Oh my fucking God!" I clutched my hands to my heart and jumped a foot off the ground.

A swan waddled past on the other side of the fence, casting a derisive look in my direction. Was it an attack swan? Had it been trained in the art of home defense? Would it swoop over the fence and start pecking at me? Could swans fly?

I had many questions.

The front door of the mega mansion opened, and a man stepped out onto the porch. Even twenty years later and from one hundred feet away, I still recognized him. Travis Hostetter. His blond hair was cut shorter than it had been in high school, but the easy gait, the set of those shoulders was the same. His head swiveled in my direction, and I did the only thing that made sense.

I bolted.

I turned and ran for my parents' front door, diving over the hedgerow of azaleas. Catching my foot on one, I landed hard on mulch and concrete. The wind left my lungs, and all I could do was stare up at the sky and listen to the rumble of the Cadillac Escalade next door as it backed down the driveway.

I'd made a huge mistake coming back here.

CHAPTER 3

Marley

Approximately 1,000 years ago

I wiped my damp palms on my thrift-store-find Umbros. My mom insisted that if I was just going to sweat and roll around in the grass, I didn't need to do it in full-price name brands. So I'd saved up birthday and Christmas money, squirreling it away until our annual end-of-summer outlet trip.

Yep, I was rocking the black-and-white-striped Adidas flip-flops that the varsity first string all had last year, Umbro shorts, and the same Nike T-shirt Mia Hamm, my soccer idol, had worn during the Summer Olympic Games. There wasn't anything about my outfit that they could make fun of, I assured myself.

This year would be different.

I'd gotten rid of the headband they'd cracked jokes about. I'd even shaved the baby fine blond hairs on my big toe that made Steffi Lynn Jerkface gag for ten minutes after she saw me getting taped up before a game last season. I'd grown out my bangs. And I'd spent the last two weeks practicing a new smile. Close-lipped, eyes wide. Friendly, mature.

"Ugh! Your eyes disappear when you smile. Never smile again. It's creepy." My memories of soccer were not fond ones.

The deep breath didn't help settle my nerves. In fact, I felt a little bit like puking. This was the first day of preseason, and it was make or break. I wanted so badly to be one of the sophomores to make the varsity team. I'd practiced over the summer but wasn't sure if it was enough.

The walk from home to the high school was five blocks. Close enough that my parents didn't need to drive me. And in a few short months, I'd have my driver's license. When I had that laminated gold key, I'd back down the driveway just to pick up the mail, I decided. Well, if Mom or Dad would let me use their car.

The high school parking lot loomed in front of me. Pretty, loud juniors and seniors in their very own cars unloaded thermoses of water and tied-high ponytails. They were so confident. So sure of their place in this world. Meanwhile, I was lurking near the entrance to the parking lot and waiting for an engraved invitation to orbit around them.

This would be the year. They would like me. There was nothing not to like, at least according to my annoyingly adoring parents. But they didn't understand. Somehow I'd been gifted with an invisible bull's-eye that marked me as a loser, an undesirable. Sure, I had friends on the junior varsity team. But the older girls? Those juniors and seniors with life all figured out? They hated me.

I wasn't sure what was wrong with me, but I'd hoped I'd changed enough that I'd shed that bull's-eye. I didn't think my fragile teenage heart could stand another entire season of constant ass-kicking.

A car horn beeped. "Hi, Marley!"

My best friend, Vicky—thank God she was on the team—and her mom waved at me. Vicky's family lived outside of town, and her mom took turns carpooling with some of the other JV team moms. Three other girls piled out of Vicky's mom's back seat.

"Ugh, it's sooo early," Vicky complained, scraping her frizz of red curls back in a lumpy ponytail with a scrunchie. It had taken me twenty minutes and half a bottle of Aqua Net to smooth the

lumps out of my own hair. "When I'm an adult, I'm never getting out of bed before ten," she announced.

"Aren't you just a little excited?" I asked. "New year? New start?" Every year, the idea of the first day of school ignited a hard, bright hope in me.

"Please," Vicky scoffed. "Nothing is new. It's the same old assholes doing the same old assholey things. Nothing will get better until we get out of here."

Praying she was wrong, I climbed the hill to the practice field with her. The redbrick prison of the high school building was to the left of the field and parking lot. The entire summer was behind me, and this—the patchy green grass of the soccer field and the glossy, industrial, chemical-scented linoleumed halls—was my foreseeable future.

I couldn't suppress the shudder that rolled up my spine.

"It's not that bad," I said, mostly trying to convince myself. "We're sophomores. This year we get driver's licenses and hopefully boobs."

"I'm going to take that license and my future boobs, and when I graduate, I'm going to drive out of this hellhole with both middle fingers flying out the car window."

I laughed. "How will you steer?"

"With my knee," Vicky said decisively.

"And where will you go?"

"Anywhere but here," she said. "And I'll have a cool job that gives me lots of money and lets me set my own hours. I'll have a stable full of men at my beck and call."

Linking my arm through hers, I thanked my lucky stars for Vicky Kerblanski.

The girls were slowly migrating toward the small set of steel bleachers at the closest end of the field. The coaches, Coach Norman and Coach Clancy, were wearing their standard uniform of seventies-style short shorts and too-tight polo shirts that emphasized

their beer bellies. Coach Norman was barrel-shaped and grizzled.
He smoked like a four-alarm fire. Clancy was short and mostly
skinny with a Hitleresque mustache. Together they coached the
varsity and junior varsity girls' soccer teams. And by coached, I
mean they yelled a lot and took smoke breaks.

But this season would be different. I'd practiced. Hell, I'd even
run a couple of miles over the summer. I was also an inch taller
than last year, and I hoped it was all leg.

None of the older girls had noticed me yet, and I breathed a
sigh of relief. It was probably a bit much to expect them to part
their circle and welcome the new bangless, hairless-toed me.

Vicky and I dumped our bags on the ground and sat to pull
on our cleats.

"Cute socks," Vicky said, nodding at my green striped knee
socks covering my shin guards.

They'd been an impulse buy at an athletic store. I hadn't seen
anyone cool wearing them, but the emerald green had beckoned me.

I kept my gaze down and focused on my fellow JV teammates.

But I heard the whispers start. I hoped, prayed, bargained
with a higher power that they were whispering about someone else.

Hazarding a look, I glanced up. A couple of the varsity girls
were clumped in a tight circle snickering. And they were looking
directly at me.

My dreams, my plans for this season, withered up and died.

"She's so weird," one of them said, not bothering to whisper.
"Like, stop trying already."

"Look at her looking at us with those pathetic puppy dog eyes.
'Please like me.'"

They erupted in laughter as part of my soul disintegrated.

"I can see the summer didn't bring you bitches new personalities."
Vicky snapped her gum and tied her right shoe with some violence.

My desire to be liked and accepted was equal to Vicky's desire
to call assholes. I admired her tremendously for it.

"JV loser says what?" Steffi Lynn asked, batting her mascaraed lashes. Steffi Lyn was a tall, skinny senior and the proud owner of C cups. She was also a terrible person. Her younger sister, Amie Jo, was in my class. As for personality? Let's just say the apple didn't fall far from the other apple. They were both mean as rattlesnakes, taking great pleasure in causing other people pain. Even the teachers were afraid of them. Rumor had it Steffi Lynn had gotten a long-term substitute fired because she didn't like the perfume she wore.

In a few years, she would probably make several husbands very miserable.

It was downhill from there. I tripped over an orange cone halfway through a footwork drill, and they laughed like I'd fallen into a giant cream pie.

When I leaned over to pull up my sock, the senior goalie, a brick wall in braids, sneered at me. "God, you look like a leprechaun. Did your grandpa pick those out for you?"

It was extra mean because my grandfather had died last soccer season. I'd missed a game for the funeral. When Steffi Lynn's estranged great-uncle from Virginia died, the team collected money and got her flowers that they presented in a ceremony during practice. When my Gramps died, they made fun of me for crying when my mom picked me up at practice and told me.

Then came the end of practice scrimmage. The coaches, in their obliviousness, let Steffi Lynn and halfback Shaylynn choose teams.

I waited patiently in the dwindling line as the two seniors picked girl after girl. Until it was down to me and the JV second-string fullback. Denise was in a neck brace.

"We'll take Denise," Shaylynn chirped.

And then there was one.

Steffi Lynn made a show of being disgusted. "Ugh. I guess we'll take her." She pointed at me.

I nodded briskly as if this were business as usual instead of the literal end of my hopes and dreams for my sophomore year and took my place at the end of the line.

I kept to myself on the field and tried hard to fight the burning sensation in my throat. These cutthroat, freckled dictators would not make me cry. Not on the first day of practice, dammit.

Finally, Coach Norman, in need of another cigarette break, blew his whistle, signaling the end of practice.

"Don't get sad. Don't give these dumb fucks the ability to hurt you," Vicky said, dragging me and my gym bag down the hill toward the parking lot. "Get mad. Get even. Call a skank a skank."

I gave her a weak, watery smile.

"It's fine. I'm fine," I lied.

Vicky hissed out a breath. "Come on. Let's walk to Turkey Hill. I'll buy you a French vanilla cappuccino."

CHAPTER 4

Marley

You only get one opportunity for a first impression. Which was why I arrived at the high school at the butt crack of 7 a.m. on a sweltering August morning. Yesterday, I'd had the briefest of meetings with the harried high school vice principal in my parents' kitchen on his way to a yoga class. His only instructions to me on coaching were "Just try to keep them alive."

When I'd asked about the last coach, he'd let out a nervous little giggle and then ran out the door telling my dad he'd see him in calligraphy class on Wednesday.

The high school was a little bigger than when I'd walked its halls thanks to a ten-years-too-late addition to manage the overcrowding. But the student parking lot was the same. It sat at the bottom of the hill the fall sports teams ran in an *S* formation, an exercise that would now almost definitely cost me at least one of my ACLs.

At the top of the hill were the school's expansive practice fields. Two baseball and one soccer with a little extra green space between. I remembered running around the outskirts of the fields during preseason. It had been horrible then, and I didn't see a reason for it to have improved with time.

My *team*, and I mentally used air quotes around the word,

would be arriving for an 8 a.m. practice. And I wanted to be as ready for them as possible.

I had zero money for a new athletic wardrobe, so I settled for old yoga shorts and a T-shirt. I'd tried a tank top since it was seventy-five million degrees already. But I was paranoid about the roll around my middle. I wasn't about to stroll onto my old turf with a visible belly roll. I'd given Culpepper enough to talk about over the years.

"I can't freaking believe I'm doing this."

Talking it over with my parents hadn't helped. Neither had sleeping on it. The only thing that made any difference at all was the fact that I literally had no other options. I could take this job—and the adequate money it offered—and stay in town until the holidays. Or I could wallow in depression in my childhood bedroom, most likely ruining my parents' Airbnb ratings.

So here I was at 7:10 a.m., I noted, checking my phone. I had my freshly printed team roster and the dozen orange safety cones my parents had surprised me with. Wondering how the hell I'd ended up back in the place that I'd felt the most self-loathing and disappointment.

I'd worked some shitty jobs since graduation. There'd been the front desk admin for the concrete company with men in dirty flannel who called me "sweetheart" all day. Then the community magazine that had suffered from so much drama the publisher had called in an HR consulting company to lay down the law before firing fifty percent of the staff. And let's not forget the time I decided that working retail management was what I was meant to do. One Black Friday, and I'd turned in my two weeks' notice.

But none of those jobs compared to how much of a dumb, insecure loser I'd felt at Culpepper Junior/Senior High School. Maybe it was the hormones in the milk. Maybe it was the fact that I couldn't live up to the example my older sister set.

Or maybe—and this was an even worse theory—I just didn't fit here...or anywhere. Whatever the reason, my hands were shaking, and my stomach was queasy.

I was glad I'd turned down my mom's offer of breakfast that morning. Because those burned eggs poured from a carton would have been working their way up my throat right about now.

———

They arrived in minivans and sedans. Some driven by harried-looking parents, others arriving in clumps of gangly teenagers with driver's licenses. We eyed each other in suspicious silence over the row of orange cones I'd set up four times before I was happy with the relative distance between each one.

I stared at the sea of ponytails and bandanas and general sense of disdain and let them look their fill. Diversity-wise, things had changed a lot since I was in school. My sister had been the only "brown kid" in her senior class. It was comforting to see box braids and darker skin, to hear a Caribbean accent and some muttered Spanish. Central Pennsylvania was finally catching up with the rest of the world.

Some of the girls giggled, hunching over to whisper confidences to each other. Others stood tall and unsmiling, waiting for whatever athletic wisdom I was about to unfurl on them. One or two others stood off to the side, and I could identify them as soul sisters.

God help us all.

"I'm Marley Cicero, your new coach," I said. I wanted to play it cool, maybe dazzle them with some fancy footwork. But even in high school at the height of my soccer career, I'd lacked fancy anything. I'd been a midfielder. An endurance player who never scored a goal and rarely did anything but chase my marks up and down the field. It didn't take a lot of skill to just be a body in the way.

A hand shot up in the back. "What do we call you?"

The Asian girl and her artfully messy bun screamed Pinterest Princess. She was tall and confident. I couldn't begin to guess her or anyone else's age. These girls were all in that nebulous twelve to twenty-four age range that I couldn't identify.

"Uh. Coach? Marley? I don't know. What do you want to call me?"

Mistake number one.

"How about Loser Lesbo?" an unfairly pretty brunette suggested. "No offense," she said to the girl with the buzzed short purple 'do on her right.

"Angela," Mohawk sighed. "You can't use it as an insult to one of us and not all of us."

Angela Bitchface rolled her eyes. "Fine. I'm sorry for my insensitivity, Morgan."

"Apology accepted." Mohawk Morgan nodded graciously.

Okay, team peacemaker. Good to know.

A hand on the left side of the pack shot up. She was very tall, very lean, and her hair hung in dozens of pristine braids down to her bra strap. Her skin was dark and impossibly flawless for a teenager. She was dressed in name-brand gear with her cleats and knee socks already donned.

"Yes, um?"

"Ruby," she told me. "What are your coaching qualifications?"

How about the fact that I'm physically present? No? Not an actual qualification? Hmm.

"I played AYSO from second grade on up and then JV and varsity in high school," I told her.

"Nothing in college?" She didn't look particularly impressed.

"Some intramurals." That was a lie. Two games my freshman year didn't count as a college sports career. By college, I'd hated soccer and the drama that came with it.

Ruby's expression told me she was thinking that I sucked. And with my ego in this fragile state, I was inclined to agree.

"Look, I've never coached a team before. So I'm going to be learning right alongside you."

Mistake number two. The eye rolls were audible.

"There goes the season," Ruby complained.

"That's the spirit," I said dryly.

Angela muttered something about "another shitty coach" under her breath, and the broad-shouldered girl next to her seemed to take it personally and told her to shut the fuck up.

"Well, regardless of how you feel about me, I'm here, you're here. Let's get to work."

"Why bother?" a tiny girl with unfortunately large front teeth grumbled, arms crossed over her flat chest.

"I should have played field hockey," another voice muttered.

They were testing me, I realized. I was the substitute teacher that got hazed just to see if she was really willing to send someone to the principal's office. And these girls were nothing compared to the self-righteous whiners, the overinflated egos of middle management that I'd worked with since college.

I remembered my soccer coach in high school yelling until the veins on his neck and forehead looked like they were going to pop.

"Enough chatting. We're going to kick things off with a mile run. Four laps around the field. Anyone finishes over eleven minutes, and we all do it again."

That shut them up. For four seconds.

"Are you serious?"

"Deadly. Everyone line up."

"Aren't you running with us?" Smartass Angela demanded.

"Shut up, Angela," Ruby snapped back at her.

"Bite me, Ruby." Angela's expression was one of loathing. Great. Two varsity players who hated each other. Awesome.

"I'm the coach," I said as if that explained anything at all. Hell no, I wasn't running a mile. I was still sore from vaulting my parents' azaleas. "Three, two, one...go!" Damn. I wished I had a whistle.

I considered it a small victory when they all left the starting line with only a few side-eyes and grumbled "asshole" comments.

Unfortunately, they were faster than I thought they were, or they were cheaters. But what did I care? I was just a temporary babysitter. Ruby crossed the finish line with a gazelle-like stride in six minutes and forty seconds. The next thirty seconds brought four more girls across the finish line.

Dammit. I could have used more time to myself to figure out what we were going to do next.

Ruby gave me an "is that all you've got" look, and I mentally added in another set of sprints. Take that, mean teenagers!

My attention was stolen from my sullen team by a line of short-shorted runners moving at a fast clip up the street that flanked the field. The boys were shirtless and sported zero percent body fat. My team stopped to admire them in hushed silence. They breathed as one. They weren't separate bodies with different goals. They were united by breath and pace.

"That's the cross-country team," the girl on my left told me. She had glasses and a Nike headband. Her wild, curly hair was tamed in a tail.

There was a lone figure at the rear. He was older, more muscular. Tattooed. Sexy AF, in my humble, depressed opinion.

Wait a minute. I recognized that face even under the stubble.

"Holy. Shit," I breathed.

"And *that* is Mr. Weston," Ruby announced.

"*Mr.* Weston? As in *Jake* Weston?" My voice creaked into screeching territory.

"Yep," Nice Lesbian Morgan chimed in. "Why? Do you know him? He's, like, seriously the best teacher in the school."

"I…" What was I supposed to say? I'd kissed him under the bleachers at a boys' soccer game, and then he'd ruined my senior year.

"I think I graduated with him," I said lamely.

CHAPTER 5

Marley

Exhausted already, sweatier than I should have been willing to be in public, I dragged my ass into Smitty's, Culpepper's version of a pub. My T-shirt clung to me in wet, uncomfortable ways. I hadn't even done anything. I'd watched thirty-two girls run a mile and do some sprints.

I was beyond relieved when I noted the very small lunchtime crowd in the bar. I wasn't prepared to pretend to ignore the whispers. "Showing her face around here…" "Ruined Homecoming…" "A disgrace to the entire town…"

No, that could wait. Besides, it was only a matter of time before I did something even more outrageous than ruining Homecoming my senior year.

"You must be Marley." A grizzly bear of a man rose from a high top in the center of the bar. He had a lumberjack beard and a man bun. "I'm Floyd."

He offered me one of his meaty paws, and I accepted. "Thanks for meeting me, Floyd," I said, collapsing onto the stool across from him.

Floyd signaled to the bartender.

"My pleasure. I was hoping to scope you out before you started so I could figure out if I was going to spend the semester working with a weirdo."

The bartender dropped a menu in front of me. "Drink?" he asked.

I steeled myself and looked up. Balding, some extra-long nose hair, knuckle tattoos. Whew. Complete stranger. Awesome. "Uh, yeah. A water and…what's that?" I asked, pointing at the beer in front of Floyd.

"Lager," Floyd answered.

"One of those, too."

"You got it. Good to see you back, Marley," the bartender said.

"Uh. Thanks. It's good to be back," I trailed off, not having a name to put with the stranger.

"His name's Roger," Floyd whispered conspiratorially.

"Roger? Do I know Roger?" I asked. High school was so far back in my rearview mirror, most of those years were a blur of early mornings and unfortunate acne.

"Rumor has it you graduated a year behind him and hung out with his sister, Faith. He claims he could have dated you if he wanted to."

"Roger and Faith Malpezzi? Holy shit!" Faith and I had been friends from elementary school on up through our senior year. Her brother had been a blurry, vague presence farting and scratching himself on the outskirts of our sleepovers.

"Time is not kind to all of us," he remarked.

"Wait, I'm not supposed to know you, am I?" I asked. *Holy hell.*

"Nah. I'm from the Gettysburg area. Landed this gig out of college."

I breathed a sigh of relief.

"Whole town's buzzing about you being back."

I bet they were.

Roger returned with my water and beer. I thanked him by name as if I'd come up with it myself, and he offered a smile that was missing a canine tooth. I skipped the hydration and dove straight into the alcohol. So what if I had a second practice today?

"Is that so?" I finally asked, coming up for air.

He laughed. "Small towns, man. So what's your story? I've heard that you got divorced and are running from your ex. That you got fired from a big, important job for sexually harassing an underling. And that you've decided to come home to find a husband and plant roots even though your eggs probably aren't viable anymore."

"Glad to know things haven't changed that much around here," I groused. "It's none of the above, by the way. I lost my job and broke up with my boyfriend. Culpepper is a pit stop." I was claiming responsibility for the ending of my relationship with Javier though it had been a mutual decision—that he mentioned first—to go our own ways. That happened twelve hours before my job went down the shitter.

"Well, happy to have you even if it's just for the semester. Otterbach was nice and all, but it'll be fun working with the talk of the town for a couple of months."

I wondered if it would be acceptable to order a second beer, then decided against it. My every move was probably being dissected and catalogued.

Roger came back for our orders, and I made an effort at friendly small talk, asking about his sister. He muttered something about nieces and nephews and then wandered away again.

"So what's it like being a gym teacher?" I asked Floyd.

He swiped his beer mustache away with the back of his hand. "Best damn job in teaching. None of that testing bullshit, no homework to grade, papers to read. Just hang out with the smelly little hormones and try to keep them from killing each other during gym class."

Huh. That didn't sound too hard.

"Okay. What exactly does the job entail?"

We talked shop about fall fitness, what to do with the pregnant students, how grading worked.

"Then there's the less physically gifted," Floyd waxed. "Every class has its annoying athletes. Everything is a piece of cake to them. Nothing challenges them. Then there's the ones who stand in the corner of the volleyball court and pray the ball doesn't come near them. I like to think of my job as finding the balance between knocking the piss out of the smartass athletes and giving the wobbly ones a little bit of confidence in their physical abilities."

"That's very Zen of you. So are there any teachers I should watch out for? Any students?"

"Definitely watch out for Amie Jo Hostetter. And the Hostetter twins. Those idiots are God's gift to sports, but they are dumber than a pack of glue sticks. Amie Jo has a tendency to go mama bear on any teacher who tries to actually make them do any real work. She keeps an eagle eye on things at school and won't hesitate to report anything she doesn't like to the administration." He shuddered.

Twins. Of course they were twins. I doubted that Amie Jo would settle for anything less.

"Wait a minute. She's a teacher?"

"Home Economics and Life Skills."

"You have got to be shitting me."

"I shit you not," he promised. "Is this because she stole your high school boyfriend out from under you?"

Floyd was remarkably well versed in ancient gossip.

"Is that what she's saying?" I asked wearily. *How in the holy hell was I supposed to survive an entire semester in the same building as that banshee?*

"She may have brought it up once or seventeen times."

"I only accepted the job yesterday."

He shrugged. "Word travels fast."

"She didn't steal Travis away from me. I broke up with him, and then she ensnared him."

"Interesting. Very interesting." Floyd stroked his beard.

"It's not that interesting," I countered. I needed to find a strategy that would let me fade into the background as a coach and a teacher. The sooner, the better. I didn't want to be thrust into the small-town spotlight. I was going to do my time, collect my meager paycheck, and then move on. Maybe I'd finally find the job, the cause, the meaning I'd been looking for.

"I'm sure you're up on all the Hostetter news," Floyd said expectantly.

"Actually no." When I'd left for college, I'd given my mother a list of people whose names I never wanted to hear again. Travis's, Amie Jo's, and Jake Weston's names were at the top. And while she'd talked my ears off about everyone else in town, she'd honored my request. "I just realized yesterday that they live next door to my parents."

"Did you meet Manolo?"

"Who's Manolo? Their butler?" I asked wearily.

"The swan."

"Yes. I did see something that looked like a swan in their front yard." I didn't add that I'd then proceeded to flop over my parents' azaleas and crash land.

"So, Travis took over the Cadillac dealership from his father. Apparently it's very lucrative," Floyd said, leaning in as if he were imparting secrets. "They bought that lot and tore down a perfectly good two-story to build their mini castle just so the twins wouldn't have to wait at the bus stop anymore because— get this—the elements were ruining the boys' hairdos."

"That seems…extravagant."

"Well, when you spend two hundred dollars per twin every month at the barbershop, I guess you'd look at it as an investment."

30

I wasn't big on gossip. I'd been the target of it enough my senior year that I didn't partake as a matter of principle. Besides, what business of mine was it if someone was screwing their boss or taking long lunches so they could run home and spy on their third-shift husband to see if he was having an affair? However, this piqued my interest.

"Two hundred dollars per twin?"

The air-conditioning vent above me blew a steady stream of arctic air onto my sweaty skin, and I started to feel the chill.

Floyd nodded. "Every month. Rumor has it Amie Jo is pushing to give them both Escalades for their birthday next year. They both drive pimped-out Jeeps that they got when they turned sixteen. Milton is on his second one since he drove the first one into Dunkleburger's pond."

Swans, Escalades, hair.

I shook my head.

"It'll be very interesting to see how you two get along at school." He grinned.

"You seem like a guy who knows a lot about a lot of people," I noted.

He gave a shrug of his massive shoulders. "To be honest, there's not a lot to do around here. And this feels healthier than watching reality TV. So yeah, if you need the dirt on anyone, you just let me know."

I wet my lips and tried to talk myself out of it. What would stop Floyd from telling the entire town if I asked about him? Nothing. But did it really matter? I was only going to be here for a few months, and then I'd be back out in the world forgetting all about Culpepper.

"Jake Weston," I said finally.

Floyd's brown eyes lit up like I'd just handed him a winning lottery ticket.

"What do you want to know?"

31

CHAPTER 6

Jake

The foam roller dug into the hot spot on my quad with a satisfying zing of pain. The first preseason practice was behind me for the day, and I could enjoy a few more hours of summer malaise.

August was bittersweet for me as a teacher.

I loved my summers off. Made great use of them. Taking the bike or the dog on road trips. But there was something exciting about heading back to school. New beginnings. Not that I'd felt that way when I'd been a student. I'd been more "rebel without a clue" back in the day.

"I'm rolling here, Homer. You're not helping."

Homer's wet nose met my bare back. Damn dog did it on purpose. He was practically laughing at me with his shaggy face and lolling tongue.

"You keep doin' that, and I'll dig out the cone of shame."

Homer rolled over on his back next to me, fluffy feet in the air. We'd been enjoying each other's company for five years now, ever since I spotted him in the shame section of the local paper. There was a whole page dedicated to causes we should all be supporting, funds that needed donations, animals that needed homes.

Every once in a while, I picked one at random. It was

atonement for my rabble-rousing days. Or prepayment on any new bad karma I'd attract during my hell-raising summers—which were admittedly more mellow now.

My phone rang from somewhere in the room. In the summers, I had the tendency to ignore it, lose it, forget it existed. I didn't have to be responsible Mr. Weston. I could be Jake the irresponsible badass. Or at least Jake the "sleeps till 11 and wakes up a little hungover" badass.

But with preseason starting today it was probably better to dip a toe back into the responsibility pool.

I found the phone under a stack of books and newspapers. Yeah, I still read 'em. I blamed Uncle Lewis for that. Every Sunday brunch, he'd whip out the "Arts and Leisure" section and read it front to back. And while I didn't have his snazzy wardrobe or his love of the artsy-fartsy, I more than embraced staying up on current events.

"What's up, Floyd? Still on for poker?" I asked. Floyd was the high school gym teacher and self-appointed school gossip. If it happened within the walls of Culpepper Junior/Senior High, Floyd knew who, what, when, where, and why.

"Yeah. Yeah. Wouldn't miss it. I'm feelin' lucky."

"You always say that. Gurgevich is still gonna fleece you," I predicted. Mrs. Gurgevich had been my English teacher in high school, and she'd been ancient then. She'd spent decades terrifying students over diagrammed sentences and dangling modifiers. But get to know her outside of class, and the lady had stories that started with "When Hunter S. Thompson and I were road-tripping to Tijuana…"

"You want me to bring the crab dip this week?" Floyd asked.

"Yeah. The theme's Under the Sea." It was an every-other-weekly game with a bunch of teachers. A while back, we got up the brilliant idea to start serving meals with stupid prom themes.

"Cool, cool. So guess who was asking about you yesterday?" he said.

I couldn't quite work my way up to caring. Gossip didn't interest me.

"I couldn't even begin to imagine," I said dryly, giving Homer's belly a scratch. He grumbled and gave his back leg a lazy shake.

"Marley Cicero."

"Marley 'Graduated with Me' Cicero?" I asked. Now my interest was piqued. I remembered her. At least, teenage her. I'd found her…interesting. Interesting enough to plant one on her, if I recalled correctly. I'd kissed a lot of girls in my time. Still enjoyed a good lip-lock now and then. But yeah, Marley stood out.

"The one and the same."

"She back in town, or are you two Facebook pals?" I tried to keep the interest out of my tone. Floyd could pick up on a shred of something and turn it into a story that would entertain the whole damn town for a month.

"Back in town. She'll be teaching gym with me and coaching the girls' soccer team." Floyd filled me in on Otterbach's lesbian elopement. I scratched out a note to myself to send Otterbach and Jada a wedding present.

"Ouch. Does she know what she's getting into with the team? The old coach?" I said. I wondered what kind of questions she'd asked about me, but showing Floyd any kind of interest now would only lead to the dramas. And I didn't do drama.

"We didn't get into it. Yet. She seemed shocked that you were a teacher."

"I'm full of surprises," I claimed, hinging forward to reach for my toes.

"She was even less happy finding out Amie Jo is teaching."

Amie Jo. Marley. Vague memories of senior year started to click into place.

I believed they'd hated each other in high school. But I couldn't remember if there was a specific reason.

"Oh, yeah?" I said casually. "Doesn't Amie Jo live right next door to the Ciceros?" I asked the question that I already knew the answer to.

"Yep. Marley seemed surprised by that. I got the feeling she hasn't kept up on much news from here," he said.

"Some people move on," I said vaguely.

Homer jolted at the knock on my front door and went into barking terror mode.

"Hey, I gotta go rescue whoever it is at the door from my ferocious dog," I told Floyd. "I'll see you Friday."

I dropped the phone back onto the coffee table where I'd probably forget about it again and jogged to the front door.

I lived in the house my grandmother had left me in her will two years ago. Feisty, fun lady. Terrible taste in home decor. But there was a hell of a lot more room for me and Homer to spread out than at the town house I'd lived in. I kept it, renting it out, and moved my shit and my dog to Grams's.

Judging by the silhouette on the other side of the front door's cut glass, I was about to get yet another lecture on home furnishings and linens.

"Attack, Homer," I said, opening the front door. He launched his curly-furred self at the man on my doorstep. Uncle Lewis made quite the statement with just his existence in Central Pennsylvania. He was black, gay, and, worst of all, painfully trendy. Lewis wore shiny shoes and specially ordered fancy cheeses from the grocery store. But even the most conservative in our community couldn't help but love him. He was the VP of community outreach for a local bank. And outreach he did.

He'd married my mom's brother, Max, in a before-it-was-legal ceremony when I was a teenager. After my dad died and my mom decided she couldn't handle the mess I was, she carted me off to Uncle Max and Lewis's house in Lancaster County. And my life had changed for the better.

Lewis leaned down to give the enthusiastic Homer a big kiss on the cheek, and then he did the same to me.

"Jake, when are you going to turn this flea market find into a home?" he asked, marching inside and eyeing the mess of the living room with hands on hips.

I was a little messy in general and a lot lazy during the summers.

"I'm gonna clean up before poker," I promised.

"You better, because I don't want Max to come home complaining about you needing a wife or a husband to keep you in line again," he reminded me.

Uncle Max joined my poker game most weeks. And Lewis used the husband-free time to host Book and Wine Club, a unisex social event, at their place. My uncles' house, it should be noted, was always immaculate. Even when my cousin, their adopted daughter, Adeline, and I had lived under their roof.

"Want a drink?" I offered, guiltily stacking some of the papers into a neater pile.

"White wine?"

"I've got that grig you like." I may have been a disaster at housekeeping, but I kept my guests' favorites on hand. He followed me back to the kitchen, which was in worse shape than the living room. I'd gotten takeout four nights in a row. Even I knew a rut when I saw it.

"Jake," he groaned.

"I know, I know. Do better. I will. I promise."

I dug out a clean glass and poured.

"It's just this kind of living doesn't look…happy," he said, eyeing the mess of Chinese cartons on the counter. I kicked an empty case of beer in the direction of the recycling bin.

"I'm happy," I argued.

"You're comfortable. That's different."

"Potato poh-tah-toh."

"It's like you're living in some kind of limbo," he observed. "Like you're waiting for something."

"What am I waiting for?"

Lewis shrugged his slim shoulders under his grape-purple button-down. His tie had flecks of yellow and green in it. "That's what I want to know." He sipped, eyeing me over the glass.

"Okay, okay. You didn't come here to tell me to get my act together again."

"Your mother's coming to town for her birthday," he announced. "Good thing she's staying with us since you live like a fraternity. You'll be available for dinner."

It wasn't a question.

"I will be available," I promised, grabbing the back of an envelope and scratching out a note to get Mom a birthday present.

"Excellent. Max and I will cook. You will dress like not a mess. Bring the wine. A few bottles of red and white," he said, rattling off instructions.

"Got it. Wine. Yep." I added it to the list. "Anything else, oh captain, my captain?"

Lewis cupped my cheek and patted it gently. "Next time I come by, I want to see counter top and curtains."

CHAPTER 7

Marley

We did that yesterday," the cocky girl attached to the raised hand announced as if I had some kind of mental deficiency.

"I am aware of that. And now we're going to improve upon that," I told her. Alice? Alex? Alecia? *How the hell did teachers learn names? Would it be okay if I just referred to everyone as "sport" or "hey you"?*

"Is this, like, going to be the same thing every single day?" Natalee with Great Hair asked.

"Why do we always end up with the worst coaches?" one of the girls whined under her breath.

"At least this one is still alive," someone else added.

I wondered briefly what that meant, then decided it didn't matter.

"We're going to run the mile and try to beat our times," I announced, feigning my mother's enthusiasm. I'd painstakingly written everyone's times down from yesterday's run to make it easy for them to compare. But there were no "thank you; that was so nice of yous." Just complaints. Loud ones.

"Wow, I thought whining stopped in elementary school," I quipped. "Line up, ladies! Nobody cares how fast your mouths are."

Day Two was off to a stellar start as the girls plodded off the line, shooting me evil glares.

We'd fumbled our way through a few drills, and I'd asked every girl what position she played.

I had three Morgans, two Sophies, and eighteen girls who wanted to play front line. My high school coach would never have put up with that. He was a pack-a-day smoker who snuck whiskey into his travel mug. He'd never coached girls before, so his tactic was to yell until someone cried. It sort of worked. We had a winning season but missed out on districts. If I could replicate his success, I could leave Culpepper with my head held high.

Thirteen days until school started. Coaching was going to be the hard part, I decided. Teaching would be a breeze. I'd have Floyd—er, Mr. Wilson—to divide and conquer. Really the only scary part would be the locker room. And that was scary for everyone.

I'd yet to venture into the school, deciding instead to fill the water cooler at home and drag it onto the field from the back of my hatchback with the unbreakable lease—believe me, I tried. The locker rooms were open for athletes as field hockey, soccer, and cross-country started their seasons. But I just wasn't mentally prepared for that particular trip down memory lane.

Dammit. Ruby's long legs carried her across the finish line. "Time!" she called.

I read it off the watch. She'd shaved another few seconds off yesterday's time, I noted with annoyance. It was probably the wrong reaction. Here was an athlete who was performing well, yet she was so cocky about it, I kind of wanted her to fail. I wondered how often my teachers or coaches felt that way.

Ancient Mrs. Gurgevich probably had. She'd hated me. She had the uncanny ability to always be standing right next to me every time I did or said something incredibly stupid.

A wisp of a girl whose name I didn't know flew across the

finish line. She looked at me with doe eyes instead of demanding to know her time. I read it off to her and handed her the clipboard so she could write in her time.

Rachel, I observed as she wrote in tiny, precise numbers.

More players returned. I noticed one. A big blond senior who looked vaguely like Miss Piggy. She crossed the finish line and bodychecked Rachel out of the way.

"Oops, didn't see you there, *Raquel*."

Ugh. I *hated* girls like this. They gave me flashbacks to Steffi Lynn and the entire varsity starting lineup.

"Hello! Time?" she said, snapping her fingers in my face.

I told her, purposely adding ten seconds to her time, and shoved the clipboard at her.

"What? You don't know my name yet?" she smirked.

"Should I?" I shot back.

She tossed the clipboard back to me, and I noticed she'd shaved thirty seconds off the time I'd given her. *Asshole.*

Her name was Lisabeth Hooper. But there was something eerily familiar about her horribleness.

Before I could pick it apart, a hush fell over the finish line as the cross-country team, still sweaty, male members still shirtless, jogged effortlessly up the hill next to the practice field.

"Are they a good team?" I asked, already knowing the answer. I was feeling weirdly and unrealistically competitive with Mr. Sexy Bod Weston.

"Won districts last year," Ruby said. She clapped as another player crossed the finish line panting.

Jake was at the front of the pack today, pacing them. He had sunglasses on, but his head swiveled toward me. He had that sexy dark hair buzzed short around the sides, longer on top. His chest was glistening like fucking diamond facets. The corner of his mouth lifted.

"Hi, Mr. Weston," Ruby yelled through cupped hands.

I spun around, breaking the hypnotic spell his sweaty pecs put me under and pretended my clipboard was the most fascinating thing I'd ever seen in my life.

"Hello, ladies," he called back.

Damn it. I remembered that voice. That rough, sandpapery edge to his words. Twenty years later, it was only hotter.

It was the August sun burning down on us that had my cheeks turning fifteen shades of bright red. Heat stroke. Definitely heat stroke.

———

"All right, people. Let's talk sprints," I said, clapping my hands to get their attention. Everyone had had time to rehydrate, wipe the sticky, salty sweat out of their eyes, and start gossiping. Now, it was time to break their spirits.

"Have you guys heard of ball busters?"

Ball busters were the worst invention in preseason ever. Players started on the far goal line and ran to the next white line on the field, then back to the goal line, then on to the next white line. Back and forth until they got to the opposite goal line. It was one long, grueling, miserable pushback. I was going to save these for next week, but their whining was starting to grate my nerves.

"I find that term offensive," Sophie S. announced. At least I thought it was Sophie S. I couldn't tell her and Sophie P. apart. Both fell into the same nondescript brown hair, brown eyes category I was in. One of them had curly hair. But I couldn't remember which one. "We're a girls' team. I think we should name them after female anatomy," she insisted.

"And something more empowering," Morgan W. weighed in. "Busting doesn't sound very positive."

I closed my eyes. "All right. Does anyone have any suggestions?"

"Ovary Exploders!" Ruby suggested. Angela snorted derisively, and Ruby flipped her off. I was going to have to watch these two so their feud didn't bubble over to the rest of the team.

"Vagina Victory!"

"Boob Battles!"

"You guys are idiots," Miss Piggy Lisabeth snapped.

"Oh, for fuck's sake." That last one came from me and was overheard by half of the team.

"Ooh!"

"Okay, okay. Let's think of a name later." I explained the premise to them and gleefully watched most of them look way too confident in their abilities. Ball busters—or boob battles— were miserable. Even the toughest athletes hated them.

"I think you should run them with us," Ruby announced, crossing her arms and cocking her hip.

Hell.

"Ooh," the rest of the team crooned.

The gauntlet had been thrown.

"Motion seconded," one of the Sophies said.

"This is about your endurance. Not mine."

"We've never done them," Ruby said. "You need to show us."

"It's not that hard. You run line to line. Keep running until you run out of lines. Then we all get to go home."

"All in favor of Coach running with us?" Ruby called.

Every fucking hand went up except Angela's. And I knew it wasn't that she was trying to protect me. She just wanted to vote against Ruby. I felt something awfully close to fury well up in my belly. Or maybe that was pre-vomit.

"Fine," I agreed. I could do this. It was only a couple hundred yards-ish. I was really bad at math. "I'll run this one with you if you all promise to actually put some effort into the drills this afternoon."

Yesterday, they'd giggled and sashayed and played their way through every footwork drill I'd dug up online. Pretending it was a party instead of practice.

"If you *finish*, we'll participate," Ruby negotiated.

I would finish this sprint if I had to drag my ass across the line on my hands and knees. They wouldn't break me. At least, not on Day Two.

"Fine. Let's do this."

CHAPTER 8

Marley

It was hotter than hot. My sneaker was going to melt on the line under the morning August sun. At least that was one thing I hadn't screwed up. I hadn't saved the running portion of our practices for the afternoon when temperatures would push into the high 90s.

"Remember, ladies. This is a sprint!" Yeah, right. Most of them wouldn't even be running by the time we got to the far penalty area.

"Ready? Set? Go!" I shouted. I made an effort to explode off of the line to at least make a good show of it. I'd let off as soon as the slower team members started to fall off. There was a point in ball busters when you couldn't physically worry about anyone else. You were too exhausted to care if you were even alive.

There was a blur of legs, the thunder of feet muffled by grass as both junior varsity and varsity teams came off the line. I hid my grin as Ruby and one of the Sophies accelerated past everyone.

Ha. Just you wait, girls. Just you wait.

I touched the goal box line and ran back to the end line. Next was the penalty area line. Easy peasy. I felt a little rusty, but mostly okay. There had to be some muscle memory in this, right?

Ugh. Center circle was next. I should have let them skip the circle and just go to half field. But I was only thinking those thoughts because I was starting to feel winded. Ruby powered past me, and I swear to God she was humming a catchy little tune.

"This is a sprint, ladies! Push harder!" I yelled, channeling my old, beer-bellied coach.

Reluctantly the pack picked it up a little bit.

"Keep going," I gasped as I jogged back to the end line.

I was going to knock myself out with my boobs. These girls could not be harnessed by a simple yoga sports bra. No, they needed to be tamed, smooshed, wrangled into submission.

Oh my God. I could *feel* my heartbeat in my head. I couldn't see—the sweat was stinging my eyes. I swiped at the never-ending river of it with the hem of my shirt. "There's no rest here," I gasped at the stragglers who were trying to catch their breath on the goal line. "Go!"

My world narrowed to the sun, the heat, and the hard ground under my feet. I was plodding. It wasn't even jogging. I wasn't even sure if this qualified as walking. It wasn't just hot. It was Satan's sauna on this patch of crispy fried grass.

I was vaguely aware of girls walking, their breath coming in sharp wheezes heard over the sound of the cicadas buzzing in the trees on the street. This had been a very stupid idea. I might die from this. I might kill one of them from this. I hoped it wasn't one of the nice ones. I looked up, swiped the sweat out of my eyes, and saw Ruby slowing to a jog at the other end of the field.

"Push *harder*!" I yelled.

Out of breath, I felt the words tear through my throat, trying to bring up bile with them. I gagged and slapped a hand over my mouth. *Nope. Nope. Nope.*

"Suck it up," I whispered to myself. I took a deep, shuddery breath and pushed on. My feet were made of lead. I pictured my dad at the end of the field holding a platter of snack cakes and a gallon of ice water.

"Can we quit?" one of the freshmen on the team begged from somewhere out of my peripheral vision.

"You do *not* quit. You cross this line on your hands and knees if you have to," a voice snapped. *Freaking Ruby. How did she still have oxygen to speak?*

I was no longer a coach. I was no longer human. As my foot touched the far end's goal line, I realized that I would die out here on this humid Pennsylvania kill zone. One hundred-ish yards separated me from my water bottle and that bottle of ibuprofen. *Why did I agree to do this? Why would I put myself through this?*

To prove myself. A therapist would have a field day with my constant need to prove that I was at least adequate.

The thought punched me in the sternum as I stared down the field. I'd screwed up or lost everything that had been important to me. On paper, I was a loser. But I didn't feel that way in my heart. I had potential. If I could finish this. If I could put one foot in front of the other, I could do something with my life.

I desperately needed this.

The opposite end of the field wavered in my vision like a mirage. But I forced my feet to move. I was walking, then jogging, then something else. Flailing. Stumbling. Running.

There were still a dozen girls struggling with me on the field. The rest were lying in the grass at the finish line. I wasn't sure if they were dead or recovering. There was only one way to find out.

Get there.

"Come on," I whispered to them, to me. "Come on."

Goose bumps rose on my skin, but I was too hot, too gutted, to pay attention.

My stomach knotted as my breath clogged my throat. I was going to puke. In front of people. In front of teenagers genetically designed to exploit any weakness discovered in adults. But I was going to finish this run first.

Half field. My foot touched the white line, and I swear I felt it zing up my body. Almost there. Almost there.

I chanted to myself.

Oh God. The penalty area. Yes, baby cheeses! So close to the end of this stupid torture. To the end of the only challenge I'd risen to in months. Or years.

I pushed, forcing my wobbly legs to chug faster. Crossing the line on a gasp, a wheeze, a dry heave. I collapsed onto my hands and knees.

"Nice run, Coach," one of the girls said weakly. I think it was sarcasm.

But I was too busy vomiting to respond.

"Well, shit," someone sighed.

Oh God, no. I knew that voice. I knew the man behind that voice. He was the last person on the planet I needed to see me retching my guts out of my body through my throat. A worn shoe, one of those finger sneaker things, came into my line of sight. I gave one last heave before flopping over on my back.

"Hi, Mr. Weston," Ruby said, wheezing from somewhere very far away.

"No, you don't," the voice said as things went blurry and gray. Something hit me in the face. Hardish.

"Coach, what do we do?" a teenage boy squeaked.

"Hey, dumbass. Do you know what heat stroke is?" the gravelly voice demanded of me. I felt another slap. A *slap?*

Someone was slapping me in the face? How dare he!

I struggled against the gray, the stars that were sparkling in front of my eyes. Defensively, I flailed my hands, catching myself in the face.

"Guys, let's drag everyone down to the locker room," the voice ordered. "Take as many bodies as you can."

Suddenly I was airborne. Floating up, up, up. Then I was unceremoniously tossed over something hard and sweaty. I was upside down. My ponytail hung straight down. Everything was still a blur, but was that an *ass* in my face? Wow. A really nice ass. Tight globes of muscle that bunched under shorts.

Hallucination or not, that ass was connected to the finest pair of thighs I'd ever seen in my life. Some women were into the arm porn. Others into the chests or v cuts. Me? I wanted a meaty thigh to sink my teeth into.

"Did you just bite me?" the voice demanded.

Shit.

The grass under those weird shoes changed to sweltering pavement and then... *Oh, God. No.* The industrial tile floor of a high school hallway. It smelled like polish and antiseptic.

I heard a thudding and wasn't sure if it was just in my head.

"Testosterone incoming. Get decent," that voice boomed. A second later, I was facing concrete floor. The smell of cleaner and perfume tickled my nose.

Someone yelped. A barefoot blur to my right shrieked.

"Hi, Mr. Weston," a girl purred.

"Stay covered up, ladies. I've got a few gentlemen with some luggage coming through."

There was giggling. And then my body was floating through air up, over, down. I felt cool tile beneath me and at my back. There was the telltale screech of a twisting faucet. But before I could muster the energy to threaten my attacker, cold water pelted down on me.

"You stay there," the finger in my face ordered. And then those shoes were squishing away from me.

I did as I was told because I had no other options. Besides, the water felt pretty damn good.

There was a ruckus coming from outside the showers.

I heard him triaging my team. "You, shower. You, cold, wet towel."

"Carpenter, you and Kerstetter bring the water cooler down."

"On it, Coach."

One by one, my girls were helped into the shower fully clothed.

It was one of those gross old-fashioned shower rooms so everyone could make uncomfortable eye contact while they tried to wash the sweat out of their genitalia and pray that the popular girls wouldn't notice them.

Angela was propped against the wall in front of me. I raised my hand in a half-assed wave, and she started to giggle. It set me off, and one after another, we all ended up in hysterics.

"I'm so glad you ladies find heat stroke hilarious."

My vision had cleared enough that I got my first good look at Jake Weston looming in the doorway, shirtless and still sweaty. My God, that body had only gotten more delicious with age.

"Let's go, Coach," he said, dragging me to my feet.

CHAPTER 9

Jake

Bedraggled Marley Cicero propped her elbows on her knees in front of me.

"What were you thinking?" I demanded, beyond annoyed. Hell, I was moving into seriously pissed off. "It's ninety-four fucking degrees and a thousand percent humidity, and you decide it's a great day for ball busters?"

"Ovary exploders," she muttered.

"Ha. Hilarious," I snapped. The anger made me antsy. I snatched a hand towel from the neatly folded stack on the shelf and stomped out of her office. In the locker room, I took inventory. My cross-country runners were fanning and rehydrating the girls' soccer team.

My fastest runner, Ricky, was staring into the wide brown eyes of Ruby as he held a wet towel to the back of her neck. That looked like trouble to me.

"Everyone all right out here?" I asked, holding the towel under the sink faucet.

"Everyone's back on their feet, Coach," Ricky reported, jumping back from the girl. He was tall and fast as fuck. Also one of the nicest kids on the planet. And the very pretty Ruby was looking like she might eat him up for dinner.

Good luck, kid.

"Great. Everyone take five and then meet me out front on the steps."

I grabbed a cup of water from the cooler my guys had dragged down.

"Us too?" Morgan E. clarified.

"Soccer team too." I headed back into the office. It had a creepy glass window that looked out on the lockers. There was a big, industrial gray metal desk, a bookshelf with several tomes on physical fitness from the 1980s, and one green-around-the-gills coach. "Here." I dropped the towel on the back of her neck, moving Marley's not-so-perky ponytail out of the way.

"Thanks," she rasped. She took the cup of water I offered and downed it too fast.

"You're gonna puke again," I predicted.

"So thirsty. The girls okay?"

"They're fine. You're real freaking lucky. What the hell were you thinking? First of all, it's too fucking hot to run sprints. The body's main priority is to keep itself cool. Pushing every one like that in Pennsylvania August doesn't build endurance or speed. It makes kids sick."

"I noticed," she said, rubbing a hand over what was probably a big-ass headache.

"For fuck's sake," I muttered under my breath. I dug through the dinosaur desk drawers until I came up with a bottle of expired aspirin. "Here."

When she fumbled the bottle, I took it back, shook out a couple of caplets. She took them, downed them dry.

"I repeat. What the hell were you thinking? These girls went through enough last year. Now you're trying to kill them on the field?"

She didn't answer.

Grumbling to myself, I refilled her cup and brought it back. "Better?"

"Yeah," she nodded.

"You're a real hot mess, you know that?"

She looked up at me for the first time, and I remembered those eyes. The kind of light, warm brown that made me think of brownies and bourbon.

I even remembered what they looked like one second after I'd kissed the hell out of her all those years ago.

Yeah, I remember you.

"I am well aware," she said, snapping me out of my trip down memory lane.

"Good. Now, let's go."

"You're really bossy. You know that?" She made it to her feet, and I had to give her credit for not immediately collapsing back into the chair.

"So I've been told."

"Am I fired?" she croaked.

"How the hell should I know? Come on."

I led the way out of the locker room and toward the glass doors. This was the main entrance for the gym. The girls' locker room was on one side of the gym and the guys' on the opposite. I pushed the door open and surveyed my ragtag bunch of students. "Who wants Italian ice?"

A cheer rose up, and I felt like a damn hometown hero. It was little moments like this that made the hard work and frustrations of teaching and coaching worthwhile.

Marley trudged out of the door behind me sucking on a water bottle.

"Let's go, troops." I hooked an arm through hers to keep her on her feet. We made a pit stop at my SUV for my own water bottle, phone, and wallet.

I fired off a text to Mariah.

Me: Got a small army coming. Ready the electrolytes and pickle juice.

She responded immediately.

Mariah: God I love the smell of preseason.

"Where are we going?" Marley asked.

"To rehydrate."

"Will there be beer?"

The desperation in her voice made me laugh. "Not on the clock, Coach."

We trooped down the hill that the high school sat on, staying on the tree-lined sidewalk to soak up the shade. Mariah's Italian Ice Shack was a glorified shed she'd plopped in the backyard of her row home across the street from the high school. She'd held down some administrative job at a local hospital before being downsized a few years ago. With her fancy severance package, she opened up the shack and supplemented her income with work-from-home gigs. She kept students and faculty cool in the summer with crazy flavored slushies and warm in the winter with the best hot chocolate in the county.

When we turned down the alley, I could see the rows of paper cups already lined up. The bright green of the pickle-juice ices against the red, blue, and orange of the sports-drink ones. Mariah knew how to do preseason right.

"One of each," I told the kids as they descended like sweaty, pimply locusts.

Snagging two of each, I directed Marley to one of the picnic tables Mariah had positioned under the big oak trees that crowded her tiny backyard.

"Here."

She sniffed at the cup. "What is this?"

"Pickle juice."

"No way." I expected her to wrinkle her nose in disgust, but her pink tongue darted out and sank into the green ice. My reaction was instantaneous. It wasn't like I'd handed her a banana and told her to go to town. I was still royally pissed at her total lack of regard for the well-being of her team. But I was also turned on.

Huh. Interesting.

She was less pale now. The summer heat was bringing a pink flush back to her cheeks. She had a dusting of freckles across the bridge of her nose. They spread out more on her cheekbones. Those brown eyes were warier now, less dazed.

"Wards off muscle cramps," I said, gesturing at the sinus-infection-colored ice. "And this one's got electrolytes."

"Mmm, come to Mama," she murmured, scooping the orange-sports-drink-flavored ice into her mouth.

All around us, high school athletes snickered and chatted. I noticed there was a definite divide right down the middle of her team. I couldn't be sure, but it looked like the leader of Team A was Ruby, and Team B belonged to Sophie Stoltzfus. And then there was god-awful Lisabeth Hooper, who worked her demon magic on both sides. I worked my ass off to keep the drama out of my team. A slightly easier feat with the mix of the sexes. I didn't envy Marley with the brewing disaster she had on her hands.

"What's going on with King and Stoltzfus?" I asked.

Marley looked up, brow furrowed. "Who?"

"Ruby making eyes at Ricky and Sophie with the hair." I waved my hand around the back of my head to call attention to Sophie S.'s twisted braid bun thing.

Marley looked in their direction and took another spoonful of slushie. "Hell if I know."

"Look. It's your second day on the job. I'd cut you some

slack, but you coulda put your entire team in urgent care making them run like that today—"

"Your team was running," she interrupted.

"Yeah, but my team is used to this. And in deference to the weather, we took it slow and stuck to the shady route with water breaks," I said pointedly. "What are you trying to prove?"

"Apparently that I'm nothing but a hot mess," she huffed.

"No need to get snippy. I'm just being honest with you. Don't push 'em so hard when it's this miserable outside. You'll get more out of them when they're comfortable. And from here, it looks like you need to focus more on the *team* thing than the training."

Sophie S. was glowering hard at Ruby. If I were Ruby, I'd be feeling around between my shoulder blades for a knife.

Marley gave the girls a long look and sighed. It was the sound of overwhelm. Of utter helplessness.

That Hooper jerk wandered by one of the smaller JV players and slapped the ice out of her hand.

"Hooper," I bellowed.

"What?" she asked, batting her spidery eyelashes.

"Get her another one and don't dick around with it."

The girl stomped off.

"I don't know why I thought I could do this," Marley muttered to herself.

"Because you can. If you get your head out of your ass and start thinking about the good of the team."

"Please tell me teaching is easier than coaching."

I laughed. "Ain't nothing easy about either one. They're just hard in different ways."

"I can't even make easy work."

She had a worry line between her dark eyebrows. There was a tiny freckle next to it.

"Maybe if you spent less time throwing yourself that pity party, you'd be able to figure some shit out."

"Is that Marley Cicero?" Mariah popped her fuzzy head out of the shed window.

"Oh my God. Mariah?" Marley asked, her face lighting up. She slid off the bench and made her way over to the shed.

I watched them share a hug and wondered just what the hell had happened to the Marley I'd kissed a thousand years ago.

CHAPTER 10

Marley

I felt less wobbly and more embarrassed on the short trip back to the school parking lot. Jake walked next to me, making small talk with the students, who all thanked him effusively for the treat. No one thanked me for almost killing them under the scorching summer sun.

What had I been thinking?

"You always disappear in your head like that?" Jake asked.

I blinked, realizing we were standing next to my car, my team dissipating into waiting vehicles. I hadn't even asked them if they were coming back for the second practice. I wouldn't blame them if they didn't.

"Hey. Yo, Coach," Jake waved a hand in front of my face. "You want me to run you by urgent care?"

My stomach rolled at the word "run."

I shook my head. "No, thanks." My feet felt like they were rooted to the spot.

"Do better, okay?" he said, frowning down at me.

The frustration bubbled up without warning. "How? How do I do better? I have no idea what I'm doing!"

"You don't have to know what you're doing. You just have to act like it," Jake shot back, looking amused. "You're holding the wild card. You're the adult. You can bench them or send them to the principal's office. That's all the authority you need. Now you gotta figure out how to communicate with them."

"How did you figure it out?"

"I failed a whole lot and felt like crap. Then I did better. You can do better too, hot mess."

"That is not a nickname I'm going to accept." Even if it were true. Dammit, I had potential!

"Tough shit, Mars." He reached out and booped me on my nose. My jaw dropped. I'd been fireman-carried and booped by this man, and he *still* wasn't wearing a damn shirt.

What a weird-ass day.

"See you around. Stay hydrated," he called over his shoulder as he headed toward his SUV. I blinked and stared after him.

"I'm the adult," I repeated to myself.

Technically, yes. I was an adult. Had been for many years. But I never felt like I'd actually achieved adulthood. Sure, I carried stamps in my purse. And I could cook food that didn't come from boxes. And I understood the importance of eight hours of sleep. But did that make me an adult? I didn't sit up straight in chairs. I still rocked out with the windows down to songs that reminded me of the community pool in the summer.

But I was thirty-eight. I had experience. I'd been through high school and survived it. Barely.

Maybe I could use that? Maybe I didn't have to be the hard-ass that my coach had been. Maybe there was another approach.

———

I headed home and dove straight into an icy shower, scrubbing every inch of my skin and hair to remove all traces of the epic puke-fest fail. I ran the washcloth over the back of my thigh and thought about the four-leaf clover birthmark there. I'd always thought it meant that I'd be lucky.

So far, though, I was still waiting for my dose of luck to kick in. It seemed as though my sister had landed both our shares. Important job with her own assistant. Gorgeous heart surgeon husband who doted on her. Three well-mannered, genius kids.

And here I was, vomiting in front of high school students.

When I got out, I downed another bottle of water and opened my laptop at the dining room table.

"How'd it go, snack cake?" Dad asked, peering into the room.

"I nearly gave the team heat stroke, and then I threw up on Jake Weston's shoes."

Dad's eyebrows winged up.

"Upside, I ran into my friend Mariah when Jake took the cross-country team and my girls out for Italian ice to rehydrate them."

"Um…" Dad wasn't sure how to respond to that. "And how are you feeling about that?"

He'd read a lot of "raising teen girls" books back in the day.

"Embarrassed. Hopeless. A little nauseous."

"Well how about I warm up some Hamburger Helper, and you tell me all about it?" My parents were as committed to convenience food as they had been in the eighties.

"Do you want to watch some sports movies with me?" I asked. "I have a few hours before the next practice. Maybe I can find some inspiration?" It sounded stupid. Really stupid.

But his eyes lit up behind his glasses. "That's a great idea. You fast-forward through the previews, and I'll warm up the leftovers."

We ate and watched while I took notes of anything that seemed remotely feasible. I was not going to encourage my team to spend all night at a strip club or bond against an evil coach, thank you very much, *Varsity Blues*. Nor was I going to get a DUI à la *The Mighty Ducks*. Fun seemed important, and music. The music montages were when everyone got along.

I made a note. I knew I was grasping at straws. But I was desperate. I honestly wasn't sure I could survive another failure. I'd reached for the stars so many times and been smacked back down by the tennis racket of fate. Over and over again. Every time, it was harder to get back up.

Was this my story? Was I just a hot mess?

I yawned and thought about Jake. He was familiar *and* strange at the same time. The twenty years since high school had clearly been very, very good to him. Of course his attitude was brash, and his personality was know-it-all. But he'd treated my entire team to hydrating Italian ice. There was also a good chance he'd run straight to Principal Eccles with a complaint about me. I might be fired before the first day of school. A new record even for me.

I wondered if Jake remembered me. Remembered that kiss…remembered how much I'd despised him after. I obviously didn't hate him anymore. I mean, I didn't want to be judged based on my teenage shenanigans, so it wasn't fair to hold his against him.

An hour later, I woke to an alarm thoughtfully set by my father. There was a blanket draped over me and a sports drink with a sticky note that said, "Drink me and have a good practice, snack cake."

I really didn't deserve such great parents.

Groaning, I sat up and stretched. I could be the first coach in Culpepper history to have an entire team quit on them. One for the record books. But I was at least going to *try* to do something good.

———

This was quite possibly one of the stupidest ideas I'd ever had. Including the time I thought hosting an employee appreciation karaoke event for a bunch of work-from-home hospital billing coders would be great. Introverts, it turned out, do not enjoy karaoke. Or work events.

I unloaded my supplies, closed the trunk of my car, and trudged to the top of the hill. No one was on the field yet. I was still early, but the sense of foreboding was heavy. Would anyone show? Or was this the end of my very brief temporary career?

A human being shouldn't have this many brushes with failure.

"Do better?" Easy for him to say. He had a team that respected him, students who loved him. What did I have? Looking around the empty practice field I had…not much. I had my water bottle. Two of them actually. A full cooler for the girls, who probably wouldn't show up, and my mom's genius idea of a food storage bag full of cold, wet paper towels for sweat mopping during breaks.

Plopping down on the hot metal bench, I waited. The sky was full of dull, gray, humidity-laden clouds. We could use a good rainstorm. My parents' yard was turning brown. The Hostetters' lawn was still a brilliant emerald green. Either their lawn service worked mid-summer miracles, or swan shit was the caviar of fertilizers.

Enough wallowing and whining, I decided. It was time to count the ol' blessings.

I had a car that ran and cooled and heated—even though I couldn't afford the payments. I had my parents and my sister. My health, such as it was, I thought, pinching the flesh at my waistband. I hadn't been unceremoniously fired this afternoon. I was kind of like a human version of Schrödinger's cat, both fired and unfired. Employed and unemployed. But in this exact moment, I was okay.

A car door slammed in the parking lot, and I perked up. Another door slammed, and my heart burst into a hopeful little ditty. Was that a giggle? God, half my team was the giggling little sister from *Pride and Prejudice* that I'd wanted to punch in the giggling face. But I could forgive them for that since they were showing up.

One by one, they wandered up the hill. In groups and twosomes, gabbing as if I hadn't almost put them all in the hospital this morning.

All was forgiven.

CHAPTER 11

Marley

Nothing was forgiven. They lined up in front of me and eyed me suspiciously in that way only teenage girls can. With disgust and pity and annoyance in their mascaraed eyes. *Ah, youth.*

"Since we had such a rough morning—" I began.

"You mean puke fest," one of the girls interjected helpfully.

Ha. Hilarious. I was already well aware of the fact that I'd committed the ultimate faux pas when it came to being in charge of teenagers. I'd shown my weakness, exposed my underbelly.

"Anyway. I thought we'd have a little fun this afternoon with a scrimmage." Were those actual smiles on their judgmental little faces? It felt like a very small, very satisfying win. I'd loved scrimmaging when I played. We got to let loose and forget about drills and just play the damn game. For fun. And I'd hoped that feeling was mutual with this generation.

"I'd like to see you all play your assigned positions and be open to moving around the field a bit to see what you can do. Oh, and I brought some music." Fishing the phone out of my pocket, I queued up the playlist, and the Spice Girls warbled to life through my Bluetooth speaker.

Those were full-fledged grins now, and I patted myself on my already sweaty back.

"Line up and count off," I instructed. I thought I was being smart not letting them choose their own teams. However, Sophie S. ducked behind one of the Morgans and made herself a 2 instead of a 1. Putting her on the team opposite Ruby.

So they didn't like each other. They didn't have to. They just had to play together. I'd let it go for now, I decided.

Ruby and Sophie S. were immediately nominated team captains, making me swear under my breath.

I started play with a clap of my hands since I was still a coach without a whistle.

The Spice Girls gave way to Pitbull and then Macklemore as the JV and varsity girls' soccer teams danced, skipped, and jogged their way down the field. They weren't taking it seriously, but at least they were playing. I could determine who had footwork, who had speed, and who was a brick wall to get around. Who just wasn't very good.

And who was the Marley of the team. It seemed to be the small-statured, quiet sophomore named Rachel. She hunched her shoulders when she ran as if she were warding off the spiritual blows of unpopularity. I watched that damn Lisabeth with her curly ponytail hip check Rachel after the play, sending the much smaller girl to the ground.

"You!" I shouted.

"Me?" Lisabeth pointed to herself innocently.

"Laps." I hooked my thumb over my shoulder, mentally switching her from first string to bench warmer for the first game.

"For what?" She crossed her arms over her chest, challenging me.

"For being a shitty team player and having a craptastic attitude. Newsflash, you want to act like a jerk, do it at home to your parents who made you this way. Now, run."

The rest of the team was staring at me open-mouthed as Lisabeth lumbered off under a cloud of rage. Damn. That felt good. Really good. I felt like I'd finally stood up to my own bullies.

"What are you waiting for?" I asked the rest of the team. "Play!"

I took notes on my clipboard and swiped at the sweat as it beaded my forehead. I'd spent the last few years in Illinois and Colorado and had forgotten how oppressive Pennsylvania summers could be.

There were some hoots and cheers from each team as two of the girls tangled for the ball. They laughed it off and high-fived. Nice sportsmanship, I noted. But there was no communication. No camaraderie. It was like the teams were made up of two- and three-person cliques. Ruled from a distance by dictators including Ruby, Sophie S., and Lisabeth. I wasn't sure what to do about it.

I let them play another ten minutes before calling them back over. I really needed to get a whistle. The yelling was hell on my throat. We took a drink break, and I shuffled around a couple of players on the field. Sophie S. had the fast footwork to strip the ball from the defense, but her shots on goal were weak. Juggling her to fullback, I realized my mistake five minutes into the game.

Ruby's long legs were eating up the field as she dribbled toward the goal. She'd shown signs of deadly accuracy straight on in the penalty area. Sophie S. was aware of this and hunkered down and charged. She took the ball and Ruby in a slick sliding tackle that had her team whooping it up.

The tangle of limbs started to flail as Ruby rolled and mounted Sophie. They grappled and clamored, and I was in a dead run. By the time I crossed the fifty yards, I had to push my way through the team of girls encircling the fight. Sophie S. had Ruby by the hair while Ruby worked some weird WWE wrestling move on her.

"I hate you!"

"I hate you more, you pathetic, extra bitch!"

The rest of the team watched, horrified and enthralled at the violence. Wading in, I grabbed Sophie first, since she'd worked her way back on top. I shoved her in the direction of Team Sophie and pulled Ruby to her feet. Ruby tried to get around me, and I saw stars when her bony elbow connected with my cheek.

"Knock it off, or you're both benched," I yelled. Sophie broke free of her friends and tried to climb over my back to get at Ruby. It was my turn to throw an elbow, right into her stomach. She deflated like a popped beach ball. Ruby laughed with a taunting grin.

"Both of you to the damn bench!"

"But coach, she started—" Sophie wheezed from the ground.

"Do I look like I give a rat's ass who started it? You're both acting like..." Teenage girls who haven't yet learned women are on the same team. "Idiots."

"Why don't you do us all a favor and quit?" Ruby said to Sophie.

"Why don't *you* quit? Then you'll have more time to chase after Milton like the pathetic loser you are," Sophie shot back.

"Do not even tell me this is over a guy named Milton," I said. "Both of you. Bench. Now. The rest of you, let's finish this game without the drama queens."

The rest of the team seemed relieved to get back to the scrimmage and jumped back into play. I kept a wary eye on the two girls pouting on the bench. I couldn't believe they stayed. Didn't they know there was nothing stopping them from getting in their cars and driving off? Was this the perceived authority Jake told me about?

I slapped a damp paper towel over my throbbing cheekbone and cursed my life.

Me: OK, Ms. Psychology Major. I've got two girls on the team battling it out over the same boy. How do I fix it?

Zinnia: I do not miss those teen years. We were so dumb.

Me: Come on. You never stooped to the normalcy of obsessing over a boy. You were too busy being brilliant.

Zinnia: Don't be a jerk.

Me: Sorry. Rough day. I vomited in front of my team, was carried off the field by a very attractive cross-country coach who ruined my life in high school, and earned a black eye from breaking up a girl fight.

Zinnia: Apology accepted. And I'm definitely going to need the full story. Call me Tuesday? In the meantime, I'll send you some resources on team building and the scarcity mentality.

Me: Thanks. I need to find out if this Milton is worth the There Can Be Only One shit show. Everything good with you? How are the kids?

Zinnia: The usual craziness here. Think we're going to squeeze in a quick trip to Paris over Christmas break. Edith is really doing well with the violin. First chair in the children's orchestra! The other two are drowning us in A's and accolades. And Ralph is being wooed by a shall-not-be-named medical center in NYC for a department head position.

Me: ...

Me: ...

Me: Wow. Congratulations.

Me: Teen boy named Milton. Go.

Floyd: I can only assume this is regarding Ruby and Sophie S. and their catfight today. How's the eye?

Me: Cheek. And I don't even want to know how you know. It's bruised and they're benched. Milton?

Floyd: Teenage stud. Starter on the varsity boys' soccer team. Floppy Harry Styles hair. Shot up six inches last year. Rumor has it he dumped Sophie S. for Ruby this summer and then dumped Ruby for half the field hockey team.

Me: Great. So they're fighting over a guy neither of them is dating?

Floyd: It's the hormones in milk. It makes them all insane.

CHAPTER 12

Marley

"You look adorable," my mother announced.

"Thanks." I glanced down at my outfit. Khaki shorts and a polo shirt. I'd sent pictures of both to Floyd the night before to make sure it was gym teacher approved.

As long as they weren't booty shorts, he'd given me the thumbs up. They weren't booty, but they were shorts. I couldn't remember the last job I'd had that encouraged shorts.

On the bright side, the last two weeks of sweating my ass off on the soccer field had resulted in the shorts fitting less snugly around my ass and midsection.

"I made you lunch," Mom said, holding out a brown paper bag with my name scrawled across it.

"Aw, Mom." For some reason, it went straight to my heart, and I wanted to cry. Even though the food would be something like soggy leftover fish sticks, my parents' support was both a security blanket and an oppressive reminder that I'd yet to do anything to really earn their love. I felt like they were just making down payments on being proud of me for a time in the future when I'd actually earned it.

This was my first "first day" of school in sixteen years. Holy shit. I did the math again. Yep. I'd been out of college for a whole person who could drive.

But this was by far the scariest first day of my entire life. I couldn't handle thirty-two teen girls on a soccer field for two hours at a time. We'd barely survived preseason as a team. What the hell was I going to do with who knows how many of them I'd be juggling over the course of the next six hours? Oh, and then there was after-school soccer practice. Also known as ninety minutes of pure torture. The divide between Team Ruby and Team Sophie was Grand Canyon deep since their fight. And there was bully Lisabeth lurking around being a straight-up dick.

The girls hated me. I disliked them intensely. They questioned everything I did. I yelled at them until practice was over. It sucked.

My dad trotted into the kitchen, a big grin on his face. He handed me my car keys. "All gassed up and washed for your big day," he said.

The school was five whole blocks away.

There was that stinging behind my eyes again. "Dad, you didn't have to—"

"Just want to make your first day as great as it can be," he beamed.

"Thanks, Dad," I said, hugging him hard.

I really needed to not fuck this up.

———

My office was…depressing. I hadn't paid much attention to it when Jake hauled my ass in here. But now that I wasn't dying of heat exhaustion, I took a good long look around. I didn't have any office knickknacks or supplies to move in. It was just me and my brown bag lunch.

The bell rang, signaling the start of first period. It was a freebie for me. I didn't have a class until second period, so I had forty-odd minutes to hyperventilate or peruse the Jane Fonda VHS tape collection neatly arranged on one of the bookshelves.

"Yo, Cicero!" I heard Floyd call through the gym door.

I exited my office and stepped out into the gym. The floor gleamed with its new coat of wax, and the HVAC system groaned in the rafters above us.

"You ready for this?" Floyd asked, bouncing a basketball at me.

I caught it and dribbled without enthusiasm. The lump of dread in my stomach had unfurled into a large, winged dragon.

"You look like you're gonna hurl again," Floyd observed.

"Very funny," I said, passing the ball back to him.

He dribbled to the hole, tongue out like Jordan, and made a peppy layup.

"You can be nervous, but don't be palpably nervous," he advised, sending the ball back to me. "Miss it, and you have an H."

It was 7:45 a.m., and I was playing HORSE. Not a bad gig if I could rescue myself from my own terror.

"Palpably nervous?" I drove in, nearly tripping over my own feet, and heaved the ball at the backboard. The gods were smiling on me because the ball dinked off the backboard and swished neatly through the net.

"Don't let them smell the fear."

"How does this team-teaching thing work. Good cop, bad cop?"

"Ooh! Dibs on bad cop! Nah. We just tag team two classes at once. You grade your students, I grade mine, and we both get to yell at all of them."

I was good at yelling. I could do this.

Second period was off to a bang-up start when sixty percent of the kids didn't show up with a change of clothes. "It's like the first day of school," a girl in a purple bodysuit and high-waisted jeans complained. "We're not, like, supposed to *do* anything."

We weren't asking them to do anything. We were asking

them to stand around in the gymnasium and take the pieces of paper we handed them that listed suggested clothing and shoes and laid out the fall curriculum. Floyd introduced me to the class. Two of my players were in the class. Two who didn't totally hate me. I felt good about that.

A guy with floppy blond hair and a dark tan purposely shouldered another small, less surfery-looking student out of his way to get his paper. "Watch it, Amos," Floppy said in an excellent imitation of Keanu Reeves in *Bill & Ted's Excellent Adventure*. He looked vaguely familiar.

Amos hunched in on himself as if he was used to the douchebaggery.

Floppy snatched the paper out of my hand, spun around, and shoved his face into Amos's. "You got a problem?"

"Start running," I said pleasantly. The entire class and Floyd gasped.

Floppy turned around and looked at me. He pushed the hair out of his eyes. "Say what?"

"I said start running. Laps. You know. In a circle." I made the shape with my finger in case he'd flunked *Sesame Street*.

"I'm not dressed to run," he said, waving a hand over his pink checkered polo and pressed golf shorts.

"Should've thought of that before you displayed the manners of an entitled toddler. Go forth and run, Floppy."

"Floppy?" He didn't find it funny, but the rest of the class did.

"You heard the lady," Floyd said, clapping his hands. "Hit the court, kid. Blue line. No cutsies."

I rolled my eyes at the "Ooooooh!" that arose as Floppy kicked off his flip-flops and sullenly jogged to the edge of the court.

Floyd held up his clipboard in front of his face. "That's Milton, by the way."

I held up my clipboard to join him in the cone of silence. "You've got to be shitting me."

He wiggled his eyebrows at me. "Milton Hostetter."

Hostetter. As in the son of my ex–high school sweetheart and his horrible, perfect wife. As in owner of Manolo the honking swan. As in stirrer of shit between Ruby and Sophie S. Just freaking great.

Some of the kids were taking video of Floppy Milton. "Are they allowed to have phones?" I asked Floyd. He shrugged.

"They're supposed to leave them in the locker room. Can't pry 'em out of their carpal tunnel, selfie-taking hands otherwise."

"O-M-G, look at this Snapchat filter," one of the kids said, and the rest of the class crowded around him.

———

We went through the same thing two more times in a row, and then, according to my schedule, I pulled early lunch duty. Gross. There was something nauseating about a hundred bodies simultaneously going through puberty in one room that already smelled like hot dogs and milk. I found my way to the cafeteria, which was remarkably unchanged since I graduated.

Same rickety folding tables with red and blue stools. Same jukebox, which had appeared during my junior year. It had been enjoyed until it became tradition for some joker to play "Cotton Eye Joe" on repeat every day. I wondered if the administration had removed that particular song from the playlist.

Kids were pouring into the space, talking at full volume, jockeying for spots. The lunch ladies and gentlemen, I noted, were unveiling the day's culinary specials. Spaghetti, salad, and dinner rolls.

"Excuse me, Ms. Cicero?" A woman in a cat sweater and dangly cat earrings approached.

I glanced over my shoulder. "Huh? I mean, yes?" I was Ms. Cicero. I was a teacher. Not a troublemaking student.

"Principal Eccles would like to have a word with you," Miss Kitty said.

Okay, maybe I was also a troublemaker.

"Me?" I squeaked.

"She said it would only take a minute. I'm Lois, by the way. I work in the front office."

"Nice to meet you, Lois."

Lois led the way into the office and pointed at the long wooden bench that I remembered was for troublemakers. "You can have a seat right there. She'll be with you in a minute."

Reluctantly, I sat. I tried to keep my focus on the floor. But the door opened, and I looked up. Jake was wearing nice-fitting khakis and a polo shirt somewhere between silver and blue. He'd shaved, trimmed his hair. But the ink down both his arms still said nothing but "bad boy."

"Hey, Lo. Got anything in my mailbox?" he asked, juggling a cup of coffee and a file folder.

"Welcome back, Jake," Lois said, hopping up from her desk to paw through a mailbox on the back wall. "Kids giving you a hard time yet?"

"Nah."

He glanced my way and flashed me that dirty, bad boy grin. "Well, well. I'd say I didn't expect to see you here, Mars. But I'd be lying."

Lois handed him a few papers. "Oh, leave her alone. It's her first day," she clucked.

"I wasn't sure if I was doing this right," I said, gesturing at the bench. "You had a lot more experience than me in the day."

"Maybe sometime we can compare experiences," he said

with a wink. He left, and Lois picked up a fund-raising flyer and fanned herself.

"If I was twenty years younger, not married, and more flexible…"

I knew the feeling.

CHAPTER 13

Marley

D r. Lindsay Eccles was a far less terrifying figure than I imagined. Instead of a stern dictator in a suit, she wore cargo pants and a sleek black shell top with purple reading glasses on top of her salt-and-pepper curls.

"Marley." She greeted me with her hands extended, and I didn't know what to do, so I took them both and made a weird little curtsy. Had I lost the ability to people? "So good of you to stop in. I just wanted to have a quick chat."

"Sure, no problem," I said, wiping my palms on the seat of my shorts.

Following her into the office, I was hit with a subtle citrusy scent. There were houseplants on every flat surface and a small fish tank crammed in a corner next to shelves holding books, art, and knickknacks.

It didn't feel like the stern disciplinarian space my principal, Mr. Fester—who looked exactly as he sounded—had occupied. He was old-school and of the belief that any expression of creativity was one step away from mutiny. I remember running into him at a trampoline park a few years after graduation and being shocked to realize that he had a family and grandkids… and a smile.

Principal Eccles sat behind her desk and gestured for me to do the same.

My bare thighs touched the vinyl upholstery of the chair, and I wondered if this was a trap to prove that my shorts were too short.

"I wanted to see if you had any questions or concerns for me with this being your first teaching position?"

First and last. I didn't know a lot of things for certain, but this was one of them.

"Oh, um. Not so far," I said. "Floyd has been really helpful."

"Good," she nodded, stirring her tea. "I heard that there was a small issue or two during your preseason practices." She looked pointedly at the mostly faded bruise I'd covered up with foundation on my cheek.

I swallowed hard. Yeah, I almost gave thirty-two girls heat stroke, then vomited in front of them. Oh, yeah, and I got a black eye breaking up a fight that I didn't prevent.

"It's been a steep learning curve," I said evasively.

Dr. Eccles smiled. "As long as you're putting the safety of your students first. We can deal with just about anything else *temporarily*."

I nodded, not trusting myself to say the right thing.

"So you will?" She was looking at me, eyebrows raised expectantly.

"I will make their safety my priority," I parroted. *Somehow.*

"I appreciate that. Along those lines, I believe that everyone deserves a second chance. And I'm assuming there won't be any repeats of Homecoming 1998, will there?"

Most people weren't brave enough to bring it up to my face. Most of them just whispered behind my back. Twenty years later, and you'd think the town would have something better to talk about. Damn Culpepper.

"There won't be any repeats," I promised.

"Excellent. One more thing. Milton Hostetter."

I bit my lip. News certainly traveled fast in these walls.

"Yes. I met him this morning."

"He's not used to being disciplined. His mother might try to have a discussion with you. She's quite protective of her sons. Don't let her scare you off."

My head was bobbing again. Now probably wasn't the time to admit that she'd scared me off once already. "Thank you. I won't," I said.

There were miles between me and the old Marley. I'd shed most of my people-pleasing tendencies by the time I hit thirty. But I'd be lying if I said the idea of Amie Jo didn't still terrify me. She'd been a holy terror at eighteen. I doubted that knocking on forty would have mellowed her.

"Great," Dr. Eccles said with a smile. "I'll let you get back to your first lunch duty. Good luck."

I returned to the cafeteria feeling like I'd somehow just dodged a major bullet.

"You must be Marley Cicero." A man in orange corduroy pants and a plaid shirt approached. His thick-rimmed glasses made his already thin face look longer and leaner. He was definitely one of those cool, hipster nerds.

"Yeah. Hi," I said, shaking his offered hand.

"I'm Bill Beerman."

"Beerman," I repeated.

He flashed a shy smile. "Yeah, it's a real hit with the students. Computer science, by the way."

"Ah. Gym."

"Right, right. How's it going so far?"

The cafeteria was full. Mostly recognizable food was either being inhaled by growing teenage athletes or pushed around plates while its students were too busy talking at full volume.

There were two cash registers buzzing away as kids purchased lunches, snacks, and slushies. Barely controlled chaos.

"So far so good," I said.

"You look like a deer in headlights," Bill offered.

"I feel like a deer that's been hit by a school bus," I confessed.

"It'll be fine. Just make sure they know you see them."

Okay, that was new advice. "See them?"

"Your attention is the best and worst thing you can give them. Either they need to know someone out there sees them. Or they need to know they're being constantly monitored so they shouldn't stuff that freshman in their locker."

"Were you the freshman in the locker?"

"Sure was," he said cheerfully.

"I was the 'waiting to be seen' one."

Bill stuck his hands in his pockets and eyed a table of what must have been mostly basketball players. There wasn't a student under six feet tall.

"You graduated from here, right?"

"Yeah. A thousand years ago."

"Think of this as a do-over," he suggested. "Remember everything that you hated about high school and see if you can do anything about it from this side of things."

I wasn't a touchy-feely kind of person. But something had me reaching out and putting my hand on his shoulder. "Bill, that's the best advice I've gotten since I came back."

He turned six shades of tomato.

"*Ooh!* Mr. Beerman has a *girlfriend*," a boy in ripped jeans and an eyebrow ring crooned.

"Oops. Sorry," I said, dropping my hand.

"It's better than when they spent a week asking me if I took my sister to prom."

Reflexively I made the sign of the cross. I wasn't even

Catholic. But I'd take every layer of protection I could get against these adolescent monsters.

"I don't suppose you'd want to be a girls' soccer assistant coach?" I'd been thinking my adult-to-teenage-athlete ratio was too slim. My dad had volunteered to help out, but I couldn't put him through that. Plus, I worried about him breaking a hip or saying something inappropriate while lugging a bag of balls.

Bill's neck was breaking out in hives. "I don't really have a background in the sports. Besides, my role-playing group is gearing up for a big festival at the Renaissance Faire in a few weeks. I'm pretty busy. Besides…" He leaned in closer. "Teenage girls are terrifying."

"You're not wrong, Bill."

We split up to make sure no one was making out in the corners or sticking chewing gum to the bottom of the table. I had a sudden, intense flashback to seeing Jake Weston strut through the cafeteria, leather jacket thrown over his shoulder, sunglasses on. That right there was a benchmark. When a woman stopped finding sunglasses indoors sexy, she could go forth into this world and choose a respectable mate. Maybe I could impart some of these pearls of wisdom on my team. After all, I'd been them. I'd suffered through everything they were currently suffering through.

I spotted my Mean Girl Angela at a table with six other sleek brunettes. They were all in coordinating blouses and plaid skirts. She shot me a glare.

I waved cheerily back at her and wondered if this desire to embarrass her publicly was what parents felt on a daily basis.

CHAPTER 14

Jake

Ah, that industrial cleaner smell on the first day of school. Everything was clean, sanitized, and the air quality was high. There was a buzz in the building. Kids excited to catch up with friends. Teachers anxious for a regular paycheck.

It would be all downhill from here.

I surveyed my new fourth-period American History class and prepared to dazzle them.

The teaching of history was, traditionally, one of the most boring things ever invented. We whitewashed our country's doings, painted a bunch of white dudes as heroes, and swept everyone else's good deeds under the rug of gender and race.

When *Hamilton* came out, I fucking cried. Okay, it was only *a* tear. Still counts. But if I ever see Lin-Manuel Miranda on the street, I'm gonna kiss that guy on the mouth for what he did for American history. With the popularity of the musical, some of the curriculum shackles fell off. This district in particular—our superintendent was a huge *Hamilton* fan—embraced the idea of teaching *real* history. As long as my students could still pass the tests.

I picked up the plastic tote I used every year and began my trip up and down the aisles collecting cell phones. I wanted every ounce of their attention. I also didn't want them capturing me burping the first line of the Declaration of Independence and putting it up on Snapchat or whatever the fuck.

"Let's talk about why you are going to end up caring about American history," I began. I could *feel* the freaking eye rolls and embraced them. "Quick. Someone gimme the definition of insanity."

"Making us learn history." A blasé motherfucker in the back row smirked, his size 14 sneakers stretched out insolently into the aisle. On the spot, I made it my mission for the semester to turn him into a history freak.

"Funny guy, Chuck." He blinked when he realized I knew his name. "But that's not the definition I'm looking for."

A girl in the front row waved her hand. She wore glasses and one of those thick headbands to keep her curly hair scraped back from her face, a total Hermione. "Chelsea," I said, snapping my fingers at her.

She blushed. I was aware of my manly appeal, but I ignored reactions from the under thirty crowd. "Doing the same thing over and over again while expecting different results," Chelsea said primly.

"Bingo." I pulled the five-dollar Starbucks gift card out of my pocket and tossed it to her.

Her face lit up like Times Square billboard, and the rest of the class, including Size 14 Chuck, sat up a little straighter.

I dropped fifty dollars a month on gift cards just to keep these guys engaged. I didn't need every single one of them leaving here with a burning passion for American history, but they would sure as hell know shit.

"We study history so we don't make the same mistakes over and over again. So we can grow. Do better."

"Mr. Weston, man, aren't we already the greatest country in the world? Why wouldn't we want to keep doing the same stuff?" This kid's dad still drove around with a MAGA sticker on his Maserati.

"What makes us the greatest, Perry?"

He looked confused like he was walking into a trap. It totally was.

"Our military."

"Our military that leaves roughly forty thousand veterans without a roof over their heads?"

"Okay. Then wealth."

"Qatar, Singapore, Brunei. Hell, the U.S. doesn't even crack the top-ten-richest-countries list. I know what you're going to say: education. Twenty-one percent of our adult population reads below a fifth-grade level."

Perry was searching for some random Fox News "fact" to back up the line.

"Let me tell you a secret, something no history teacher has ever told you before. Are you ready?"

They were all leaning forward in their chairs.

"You've been lied to your entire educational career. But guess what? You're old enough for the truth."

Kids loved salacious gossip. They loved scandal. And thankfully, American history was chock full of both.

I taught American history. Black history. LGBTQ history. Feminist—or womanist—history. I taught what actually happened to get us to where we are today. If someone did something or said something that contributed to turning this country into what it is today, I taught it.

"You know that Thomas 'All Men Are Created Equal' Jefferson fathered six children with his slave, Sally Hemmings. But did you know that before President George Washington fought the British, he fought for the British? How about that he was in love with his best friend's wife? Did you know that Elizabeth Cady Stanton, who launched the women's rights movement, said some really racist crap?"

I dumped the phone bin back on the desk I rarely sat at.

"We're going to learn *real* history this semester. If you know what really happened, who the real heroes are, then you can go be better Americans. Because maybe we're not the greatest country in the world. But we've still got potential. Our strength comes from our diversity, our willingness to change, to fight inequality, to explode scientific advancement."

They were all sitting there blinking at me like I'd lost my damn mind. I loved it.

"So…" I rubbed my palms together. "Let's get ready for your first assignment."

Groans went up, and I heard the whispered "But it's the first day" complaints. Poor babies. Summer was over. It was time to embrace it.

"Break up into teams of four or five. You're going to work together to write a gossip blog exposing the truth behind any of the historical figures on that list." I pointed at the board. "Due on Friday."

They hopped to, shifting their desks around.

This little exercise did more than get the students excited about history. It showed me who had friends. Who was left out. Who was willing to get creative and put some effort into the assignment.

I thought of Marley sitting on the bench in the front office. I hoped she had some creativity, some effort to put forth. Because that would make her even more interesting.

CHAPTER 15

Marley

Half of my first day was officially behind me without any major trauma. Punishing my nemesis's teenage son, having Jake Weston witness me in my principal office shame, and being warned to take my students' safety more seriously notwithstanding.

It was lunchtime, and I planned to respond to my family's texts in the sanctity of my dungeon-like office.

> **Dad:** I bet you're the best gym teacher the district has ever seen! LOL!

I really needed to finally break the silence and tell Dad that LOL does not mean lots of love.

> **Mom:** Hope you're having a great first day! I'm making pancakes from that box mix you like tonight to celebrate!
> **Zinnia:** Best of luck today.

I was just getting ready to compose a cheerful thank-you when my phone buzzed again.

> **Floyd:** Come on. I'll take you to lunch in the teacher's lounge so you can finally peer behind the curtain.

As a student, I'd assumed that the teachers ate their teacher food and discussed appropriate teacherly things. That is until one day I'd gotten a hall pass to get my geography book out of my locker and walked past the lounge to hear the Spanish teacher telling a punchline with the f-bomb in it to a shop teacher and an algebra teacher who laughed so hard I thought she was going to spit out her tuna sandwich.

After that, I never looked at them in the same two-dimensional, just-an-educator way again. And now I was being granted behind-the-scenes access? I grabbed my bagged lunch and headed for the door.

The teacher's lounge that Floyd led me to was on the other side of the school. There was a closer one to the gym, but Floyd insisted this one was better. He opened the door to raucous laughter, and I stopped short. Mrs. Gurgevich, my ancient English teacher from seven thousand years ago, was unwrapping what looked like jalapeño poppers at one of two battered tables.

She lifted her gaze to me. Her gray hair was pulled back in the severe bun I swear she slept in. The glasses, giant acetate frames, looked like the same ones she'd had when I was a student. The skin on her cheeks sagged in a fascinating, rippled texture. Her lips were painted a pearlescent pink that never seemed to smudge or smear.

She was wearing polyester slacks and an ivory cardigan set. She'd had one in every color of the rainbow and rotated them out with brown, black, and navy pants.

"Everyone, this is Marley Cicero, the new gym teacher," Floyd said, pulling out the chair next to Mrs. Gurgevich. He hefted his lunch tote onto the table. It was the size of a tailgating cooler.

"Well, well, Ms. Cicero. Back to grace our hallowed halls again," Mrs. Gurgevich said.

Was that a smoker's rattle I heard?

"Don't bust her balls, Lana," Floyd said, elbowing Mrs. Gurgevich in the arm.

Lana? Mrs. Gurgevich had a first name? And a sexy one at that.

"Hello, Mrs. Gurgevich," I said weakly. "It's nice to see you again."

She gave me a brisk, no-nonsense nod. Floyd thumped the seat next to him. "Come on, Cicero. Take a load off."

I sat and opened my lunch sack, finally noticing that there were other teachers in the room. Two of them were loudly debating a Fortnite strategy by the refrigerator. There was a round table with three women who were chewing in silence and scrolling through their phones. One by one, they called out introductions, names, and positions. And I retained zero of them. I was going to need a yearbook or something if I was expected to remember kids' names and teachers'.

"Well, hello, everyone! How's your first day?"

My heart beat out a frantic SOS as a short, curvy bouffanted blond strolled in on four-inch heels.

Amie Jo Armburger.

She looked as though time had frozen her in the 1990s. Which, in Culpepper, had been the equivalent of the late eighties. We didn't get the trends here until a decade after things were popular. Her hair was big, her makeup was thick, and she was dressed like my childhood Office Barbie in a pink pencil skirt and suit jacket.

"Marley Cicero?" Amie Jo's raspberry glossed lips parted in the perfect O. "Well, bless your heart. I heard you were back living with your parents after you got fired and dumped. You poor thing." She batted seventeen-inch lashes and pretended to look concerned.

The entire lounge shut up and opened its ears. All eyes pinned me down.

It was good to know that she was consistent. Still a shitty human being out to make herself feel better by belittling everyone else in her path. It was familiar territory for me, and it no longer scared me. "Ally Jo? Is that you?" It was mean. I knew it was mean. But she really was a horrible human being.

"Amie," she corrected. "But I wouldn't expect you to remember that. We ran in *such* different crowds in high school."

Our graduating class had 102 students in it. Ninety-six percent of us had known each other since preschool.

"Really?" Floyd piped up. "I heard you two had quite the history. Didn't she date and dump your husband?"

There were a few titters of laughter from the cell phone table.

"It's nice to see you again, Amie," I interrupted, intentionally dropping the Jo. "What do you teach?"

She flounced into the room in a cloud of suffocating perfume and dropped her bento box on the table across from Floyd. My eye caught on a diamond the size of a cafeteria tray riding her hand. I wondered if her left bicep was significantly larger than her right with all the hefting it had to do.

"Only the most important subject we offer: home economics and life skills."

Mrs. Gurgevich snorted and dragged a popper through her puddle of raspberry jam.

"Oh?" When I'd taken home ec, I'd learned how to burn brownies and balance a checkbook.

"I'll have to tell my husband, Travis Hostetter, president of Hostetter Cadillac and Trucks, that I ran into you today. Why, just yesterday we were talking about you. Travis said, 'Amie Jo, what *was* the name of that girl I dated before I fell in love with you?'"

I had a pet theory that narcissists had an overwhelming desire to hear their own names and tended to use it themselves in conversation. So far, Amie Jo was proving my hypothesis.

I gave Floyd a look that clearly asked what the hell was wrong with the *other* teacher's lounge. But he was too busy shoveling his second bologna sandwich into his beard.

"Everyone surviving?"

I looked away from Amie Jo's Aqua Net masterpiece to see Jake standing in the door, a curious aluminum foil triangle in his hand.

"Hey, Jake," everyone said.

His gaze skated to me, and I saw his lips quirk. "How's the first day, Mars?"

"Hi, Jake," Amie Jo purred with a flutter of those spider lashes. "You're looking nice and tan. Our pool's still open if you ever want to go for a dip."

Well, well, well. It looked like Amie Jo was still holding on to a bit of a high school crush despite being married to Travis Hostetter, *president of Hostetter Cadillac and Trucks.*

"Thanks." Jake took the seat at the foot of the table next to me and unwrapped two neatly stacked slices of pizza. Amie Jo pouted.

Floyd sang something under his breath that sounded like "evil queen."

"How's the first day?" Jake asked me again, his voice lower.

I gave a shrug and finally unwrapped the sandwich my mom had made me. White bread, marshmallow fluff, and peanut butter. I needed to take over my parents' kitchen. Their culinary skills had frozen sometime in the mid-eighties. "Good, so far."

"No troublemakers?" he pressed. Amie Jo's pale blue eyes burned into my flesh.

Shaking my head, I answered, "Nope."

I pulled a box of animal crackers and another of raisins out of the bag. It was the breakfast of junior high champions unconcerned with diabetes and belly fat.

A yellow sticky note fluttered out.

Have the best first day in the history of first days. I love you.

Love, Mom

Jake's eyebrows winged up in amusement. Embarrassed and touched, I stuffed the note in my shorts pocket.

Our feet were inches apart under the table. My sneakers near his comfortable loafers.

"Gurgevich, you coming to poker this week?" Jake asked.

I blinked.

Mrs. Gurgevich shifted in her seat. "You can keep your money this week. I have tickets to that nudie acrobatic art show they're putting on in Lancaster."

"Nice. You taking the Harley?" Jake asked.

I'd entered a parallel universe. One in which Mrs. Gurgevich rode a Harley and went to burlesque shows.

I ate quietly and listened to the conversations around me. Disconnected, out of place, but not uncomfortable. It was how I always felt in new work situations. But at least I knew this situation was just temporary.

"Five-minute warning," one of the teachers announced, and everyone groaned.

"We better get going, Cicero. It's a long walk back," Floyd said, packing up his food pantry.

"It was nice meeting everyone," I said. Jake winked.

"Whew. I thought Amie Jo was going to tear into us about Milton," Floyd said when we were in the hallway. "She rarely eats in this lunchroom."

"Marley, do you have a minute?"

Floyd's face drained of color. "Shit. Evil Queen alert."

Amie Jo tottered out of the lounge on her heels. Seriously,

how did she even teach in those? My feet would have been bleeding by second period.

"I know you're new here, but I really think you need to understand that my boys are angels. They are handsome, athletic, popular boys, and there is *never* a reason to discipline them."

"He was being a dick, Amie Jo," Floyd intervened.

She held up a manicured hand. "Zip it, Floyd. Never. A. Reason." She poked me with her Barbie Corvette pink talon to emphasize every word. "Got it?"

I was working up a response somewhere between "get your weird bird hands off of me" and "your son is a moron who's too entitled to treat people nicely" when the bell rang.

The hallway instantaneously flooded with bodies and BO. I could hear the staccato click of Amie Jo's stilettos on the industrial tile floor as she marched back to whatever ring of hell she occupied.

CHAPTER 16

Marley

Lunch duty *and* parking lot duty?" Floyd asked when I headed in the direction of the student lot. "Somebody hit the jackpot this semester."

Grimacing, I bumped the exit door with my hip as I shot him pistol fingers. "Lucky's my middle name." The late-August swelter took my breath away when I stepped down onto the asphalt. I could bake a frozen pizza on this slab of parking lot.

Parking lot duty, as it had been mirthlessly described to me, entailed making sure students didn't light up their cigarettes or run each other over on school grounds. Apparently there was something about liability insurance. I was to report to the top of the practice field hill that overlooked the student lot and yell disciplinary phrases if necessary.

There was a teacher in a flowy skirt and T-shirt already waiting at the top of the hill. I huffed and puffed my way to her.

"Hey," I said, wheezing a bit.

"You must be Marley," she said, holding out a hand to me. "I'm Haruko Smith. French teacher."

I shook and tried to catch my breath. "Nice to meet you."

She tucked her blunt bob behind both ears. "How did it feel to discipline that Hostetter punk?"

I laughed.

"Does he really get a free ride?" I asked.

"He and his brother, Ascher."

"Ascher?"

Haruko sighed. "Yep. Named after Amie Jo's favorite diamond cut. You're the unsung hero of the day. We're all terrified of her, but you had the guts to tell that wannabe surfer moron where to stick it."

"Technically I just made him run laps." I didn't need some overblown story of my Amie Jo defiance blowing up in my face.

"Still," Haruko said. "It's more than most. Rumor has it you put her in her place in high school, too."

A blaring horn in the parking lot captured our attention and saved me from having to answer.

"Blaire Elizabeth! Get away from that Camaro!" a woman yelled out of her open minivan window.

A girl in denim shorts and a Katy Perry tour T-shirt stomped away from a much-older-looking boy leaning against a rusted-out Camaro, its body panels a variety of colors including primer, red, and orange.

"Mooom! You're embarrassing me!"

"Embarrassment is better than teen pregnancy! Trust me!" There was something vaguely familiar about that voice. A Pennsylvania twang wrapped around expensive education.

I peered down the hill trying to see through the glare on the windshield.

The horn honked again as the girl climbed in through the sliding passenger door. "Marley Cicero? Is that you?" The driver was hanging out of her open window and waving at me.

"Holy shit, *Vicky*?"

I jogged down the hill. Vicky Kerblanski—now Rothermel—my best friend through all twelve years of Culpepper schooling, popped out of the van, arms open.

She was wearing pajama pants, a tank top, and a baseball cap over her fire-engine-red hair.

"I can't freaking believe you're here!" she said, yanking me into a violent hug. Vicky always had been largely unaware of her freakish upper-body strength. "Mariah said she saw you at the ice shack, and now here you are. You look gorgeous by the way. You obviously haven't ruined your body giving birth to three ungrateful kids."

"Mom! Are we *going*?" the grumpy teenager demanded from the van.

"Shut up and eat your snack," Vicky said cheerfully. "We need to catch up."

"Yes. Please." I was suddenly desperate for a friend. Hmm, a friend who had played soccer with me. "Hey, what are you doing in half an hour?"

"Yelling at these bozos probably," she said, shooting her thumb at the van behind her. "Why?"

"I need an assistant coach—"

"Yes. Oh, my fucking God, yes." Vicky said, taking me by the shoulders and shaking me. "I got laid off from the hospital two months ago, and if I don't get out of my house to do something besides sell bullshit wrinkle cream to 'all my closest friends,' I will die."

"Are you serious? I could really use the help. Like desperate measures."

"Let me get these ungrateful wombats back home, dump them on Rich, and I'll meet you back here."

One of the ungrateful wombats was a sticky-looking toddler waving a plastic dinosaur at me. I waved back, and he burped.

"Thank you, Vicky. You have no idea how grateful I am."

Vicky rubbed her palms together. "This is going to be amazing," she predicted. She grabbed me one more time, placed a smacking kiss on my cheek, and ran back to the van. "Peace out, Girl Scout!"

She revved the engine and took off, tires squealing.

I shook my head and started the climb back up the hill. Vicky had been the ridiculous sidekick to my boring self. She brought fun and adventure to everything we did. Even if it was just sitting in class together. I'd missed her and hadn't even realized it. Judging from the van full of kids, she had an entire life I wasn't even aware of.

"Did I miss anything?" I asked Haruko.

"Eh, just a knife fight and an FBI van rolling through. I see you, Mr. Aucker! There's no need for you to take your shirt off just to drive home," she yelled to a scrawny, trucker-hat-wearing boy. "They're basically animals, you know? Without us, they'd be not showering and wandering around naked just licking things. We're goddamn superheroes."

The parking lot slowly emptied, and Haruko and I went our separate ways, she to her classroom to grab her cross-stitch and Kindle to head home, me to the locker room to change for practice.

School was out, but with fall sports, there were plenty of students loitering in and around the gym. I didn't have the energy to yell at them to stay off the climbing ropes, so I ducked into the hallway.

And ran smack into a wall of male muscle.

"We meet again," Jake said.

His hands were like warm, sexy vices on my biceps. What was it about this guy? I wanted to stare at him, follow him around, dissect his appeal. If I understood it, I could avoid it.

"At least I'm not vomiting this time," I said.

His lips quirked, and his eyes crinkled. Hot damn. Crinkly eyes. Add that to the list of Things That Turn Me On.

"You seem to be holding up."

"Made it through preseason, my first day of school, and I just hired an assistant coach. I might just survive this semester."

"That's the spirit." His fingers squeezed my arms once before letting me go. My flesh sizzled from his fingerprints. "Hey, if you need any teaching or coaching tips, I'm your man."

I'm pretty sure I wet my lips in that stupid "I'm fantasizing about licking every inch of your body" way, because his eyes narrowed just a little bit, and he snagged his bottom lip with his teeth. Then he was winking and walking away.

My face was flaming when I walked into the chaos of the locker room. There were girls everywhere in various states of undress. I averted my eyes and ducked into my office. I needed to change, too. But I wasn't going to do it in front of students. I'd already puked in front of them. They didn't need to see my mismatched bra and underwear, too. I grabbed my gym bag and hustled back out of the locker room to the nearest restroom. I wrestled my way into my sports bra, knocking my elbow into the stall wall and seeing stars. Dressing quickly and clumsily, I hurried back out. I cut through the gym and headed straight to the practice field.

Our first game was coming up in two days, and we were not ready. I didn't know how to make us ready. Hopefully Vicky would have a suggestion or ten to get us on track.

I took the concrete stairs to the practice field in hopes that they'd be less steep than the hill itself. No such luck. At the top, I found half of my team staring down what looked like the better part of the boys' soccer team.

"This is *our* field time," Angela announced.

A man wearing shorts that were entirely too short and a very shiny whistle leaned into her face. "Too bad, sweetheart. They're reseeding our field, and *we* need to practice. So you can take your PMS and get off my field."

Angela looked like she was one second away from kicking him in the balls.

"Excuse me," I said, using my most authoritative voice.

"You're excused," he said dismissively. "We're gonna start with a header drill, men."

"No, you're not," I said, stopping in front of him.

"No you're not," one of the boys mimicked in a falsetto. It was that fucking Milton kid.

"You feel like running some more laps, Floppy?" I asked.

Ruby's jaw dropped, and Sophie S. looked like she couldn't decide if she was going to laugh or cry.

"You don't have any authority over my players," Short Shorts announced, sticking his hairy-knuckled finger in my face.

"Ooh," I winced. "Actually I do. I'm a teacher, and this is school property, sooo..." I wasn't sure if my authority carried over to after-school hours. But this asshole was trying to steal my field.

"Bull. Shit." He enunciated.

"Is *that* what I smelled?" I asked sweetly. "You're not taking our field."

"Why don't we ask an administrator? Who do you think they'll side with? A temporary, no-experience coach and her loser girls or last year's district champs?"

Milton moved to stand beside his coach. "Why don't you ladies go prance around with the cheer squad?" he suggested.

Sophie S. made a dive for his face, but Ruby caught her and pulled her back. Milton gave them both a little finger waggle.

"Take a hike, ladies," Short Shorts snapped.

"There a problem here?" Vicky, in her athleisure glory, marched across the field.

"How about this? Coaches Challenge. Half-field sprint. Winner's team gets the field," Short Shorts said, snapping his fingers.

Vicky sidled up to me. "Listen, I hope you're fast, because the last time I ran, it was after an ice cream truck, and I peed myself a little."

CHAPTER 17

Marley

"I can't believe you didn't even try," Morgan E. complained.

Our entire team was mid–walk of shame up the street to commandeer an elementary school field, having lost our field to the guys' team.

"You've seen me run. I have that vomiting problem."

"You should have at least tried," Angela put in.

"Me losing to Short Shorts wouldn't have done any of us any good," I insisted. Thank God Lisabeth hadn't shown up for practice today. I could only imagine the nastiness my giving up would have provoked.

"Come on, ladies," Vicky barked, rounding up the stragglers like she'd been a coach all her life.

I looked over my shoulder to where Ruby and Sophie S. were walking in sullen silence next to each other. "Okay. I gotta ask. What did you two see in that floppy-haired idiot?"

They glanced at each other and away again quickly.

"Come on. I need to know."

The girls' cleats made a hollow clacking noise on the asphalt.

"He was cute," Ruby said finally.

"He had a pool," Sophie added.

"Don't settle for cute boys with pools when they won't treat you with respect," I told them, pointing a knowledgeable index finger at them.

"Amen, sister," Vicky piped up.

"You're like fifty and single," Angela the Jerk reminded me.

"I'm thirty-eight and not in a relationship with a disrespectful dummy," I countered.

"You sound like a guidance counselor. 'It's better to be happy alone than miserable with someone,'" one of the girls mimicked.

"Do you think we're BS-ing you?" I asked.

Her "duh" expression translated flawlessly.

"Ladies, we're not trying to keep you from having fun," Vicky insisted as we trooped onto the elementary school playground. "We're trying to save you years of agony."

"We've been in your shoes," I added.

"Yeah, right," one of the Morgans groused. "You're just trying to keep us celibate."

Okay, we were tiptoeing into dicey territory. I didn't think the girls' parents would appreciate me talking to their teenage daughters about sex.

"I'm not talking about sex," I said evasively. "I'm talking bigger picture. Don't waste your time in relationships that lack respect."

"Is that why you're single?" one of the JV players piped up.

My mind jump-started a black-and-white reel of relationship highlights culminating in Javier telling me that my lack of passion had dried up what little chemistry we had. And then me telling him that I didn't find him interesting enough to be passionate about. After we'd finished sniping at each other and decided to amicably call it quits, I'd felt a swift rush of relief. Unfortunately, it had dried up twelve hours later when I'd lost my job at the startup that had folded as quickly as it had launched. The startup I'd sunk every dime of my savings into.

"I'm single because I haven't met the right guy yet," I said stiffly.

"Maybe you should practice with a few of the wrong ones," Ruby suggested.

"We're not talking about me here," I argued.

"What about Mr. Weston? He totally carried you around, *and* he yelled at you," Phoebe said. "My dad yells all the time. It's how he shows he cares."

"There is nothing happening between me and Mr. Weston," I insisted, dumping the ball bag in the grass. Even if he was spectacularly good-looking and interesting and funny. I'd been there. Kissed that. Bought the T-shirt. "Let's practice some controlled dribbling around these rocking circus animals."

"Didn't you kiss Jake senior year?" Vicky mused out loud.

I picked up a ball and threw it at her.

"What?" the girls shrieked together.

"You and Mr. Weston?"

"No way."

"Were you prettier in high school?"

I hated teenagers.

"No way."

"Two lines," I shouted. "When you get to a circus animal, use a dodge. Let's see some footwork."

They lazily made their way into two sloppy lines, making kissy noises.

"Go!"

As my team juked and jogged their way around the playground equipment, I felt myself slip a little deeper into the misery I'd been holding at bay.

"Do I really look like my prime years are behind me?" I asked Vicky.

"Oh, sweetie." She tucked a stray lock of limp hair behind my ear. "Yes. But that doesn't mean they are."

We adapted to our unfortunate circumstances and practiced corner kicks trying to arch the ball over the tube slide. For the header contest, we paired the girls off on either side of the monkey bars. "Head it over the bars, not under, Leslie! Stay on your toes. Don't take balls to the forehead with your heels on the ground!"

I was starting to sound like my father.

"Ugh. This sucks," Ruby said, snatching the ball out of the air and punting it in the direction of the kickball field.

"Look, I appreciate your frustration. I'd like nothing more than to go back over there and—"

"Throw up on Coach Vince's shoes?"

"Har. Har. Hilarious."

Vicky elbowed her way into the conversation. "You girls might not know this, but Coach Marley was quite the prankster in high school. She once convinced our entire trigonometry class to speak only in lines from *The Princess Bride*."

My lips quirked. *Yeah, that was a good time.*

"Oh, and how about the time you snagged Coach Norman's car keys out of his bag and hid his truck in the adult store parking lot?"

"Yeah, yeah. I was a real rebel. Let's at least pretend we're interested in soccer."

"You stole a car, *and* you kissed Mr. Weston?" Angela demanded. She was wearing her dark hair in two buns on top of her head. They looked like horns.

"Badass," Natalee said.

"If only there was something we could do to get back at Coach Vince and the boys' team," Vicky mused.

I eyed her suspiciously.

"Let's prank them!" a sophomore with braces said, hopping up and down.

"Yeah!"

Vicky wiggled her eyebrows at me. "What do you say, Coach?"

"Aren't you supposed to be an adult, a mother, a respected member of society?" I demanded.

"Come on, Coach. It'll be like a team-building exercise," sneaky Morgan W. begged.

"You guys, I could lose my job, and you could get suspended."

"Not if we don't get caught," Vicky announced.

"Are you kidding me right now, Vic?"

"Tell me you don't have at least three ideas floating around in that devious brain of yours," she insisted. I actually had four working concepts that I could build on. "They took our field. They humiliated us. They forced you to back down with shame!"

"You are taking this very seriously for only joining the team an hour ago."

"We are on an elementary school playground because a bunch of zero-body-fat buffoons chased us off of our turf," Vicky reminded me.

"Come on, Coach!"

"Yeah, please!"

"We *need* this."

"They took our field."

I groaned and scratched a finger over the bridge of my nose.

"I know that look," Vicky sang.

"I refuse to dignify that with an answer." I had a great idea, and I was pretty sure I was absolutely going to go through with it. But I didn't need my team getting arrested with me or suspended after I got fired.

A collective groan of disappointment rose up.

"*We* are not retaliating. Now, don't tempt me to make you run," I warned them.

"Old single ladies are so mean," one of the girls complained.

CHAPTER 18

Marley

"What in the hell are you guys doing here dressed like freaking ninjas?" I was standing at center field in the high school's soccer stadium at 9 p.m. facing almost the entire varsity team—Lisabeth Hooper was missing, thank God—and Vicky. All of whom were dressed in head-to-toe black.

It was dark except for the flashlight apps on our phones.

"When you and Coach Vicky whisper, you're not nearly as quiet as you think you are," Phoebe announced.

"Where do your parents think you all are?" I demanded.

"My parents think that I'm studying at the library with Morgan G., Morgan W., Sophie S., and Leslie," Angela said.

"Mine think I'm at a stage crew meeting with Ruby," Natalee said.

"My parents are getting a divorce. They don't really care where I am as long as I don't come home pregnant or with tattoos," Chelsea chirped.

I sighed heavily.

"All right, ladies," Vicky said, rummaging around in what looked like a diaper bag. "Since you're here, let's go over the plan."

This was quite possibly the worst decision I'd ever made as an adult. Involving high school students in trespassing and vandalism. It was a wonder I wasn't already fired.

"Fine," I said. "But if I get arrested, you all showed up here to stop me, not participate."

They nodded solemnly.

"So, what we're doing is inserting these baggies of dye in the head of each sprinkler," Vicky said, pulling out a small plastic bag. "Do *not* puncture the bags until you've installed them in the sprinkler heads."

"Try not to get any dye on you. It's not permanent, but we don't want anything tying us to this," I insisted as the girls collected the bags.

I watched them jog off into the dark, giggling.

Vicky grinned at me and held up two red packets. "Ready to have some fun?"

We tackled the closest sprinkler head, unscrewing the cap, inserting the baggy, and carefully poking a hole in the very top of the bag.

"Should we be wearing gloves? You know, fingerprints?" Vicky asked, wiggling her fingers.

"Not unless the sheriff's department budget quadrupled since we were in high school," I said dryly.

We moved on to the next sprinkler head and repeated the process.

"Come on." Vicky nudged me. "You're enjoying this. You don't have to be all Droopy the Clown."

"Droopy the Clown is my new persona," I insisted.

Vicky put her hand on my arm. "Babe, we all go through shitty periods. I'm the mother of three. Rich and I haven't had sex in four months. I am so far behind on the dishes that I gave up and we only eat off of paper products now."

I dropped my ass onto the ground while she screwed the sprinkler head back on.

"I lost my job when the startup I worked for shut down, taking all of the savings I invested with it. That was the day after Javier gently told me I wasn't passionate enough for him and that he wanted something more than a lukewarm relationship. Meanwhile, Zinnia was just named a 40 Under 40 to the Do-Gooders annual list. Her youngest is a violin prodigy. And her husband operated on the Speaker of the House last month."

"I really want to hate your sister," Vicky said, flopping down next to me.

"I know. But we can't because she's so…"

"Good." She patted me on the back. "Look at this as a fresh start."

"Really? Because this feels like more of the same. Another place that I don't belong. Another job I'm not good at."

"Uh, I realize this is contrary to the example set by your robot sister of perfection, but most people have to work really hard to get good at something. There's a lot of work that goes on behind the scenes before anyone gets any good at anything."

I tightened my ponytail, scrubbed a hand over my nose. "By the time I get even marginally better at this, the semester will be over, and it'll be time to move on again."

"There's a lot of time between now and December. Don't you think it would be good for you to leave a job on good terms? Maybe with a few glowing references? What if you find out you like education or coaching? What if this is the start of something instead of the end?"

I eyed her over the glow of my cell phone. "When did you get so good at pep talks?"

"When I had a thirteen-year-old daughter who looks at me like I'm the dumbest human being on the face of the planet. I had to step up my advice-giving game. Even if most of it is ignored."

"Coach!" A group of girls rushed up, giggling. "We finished that side of the field."

"Good work, ladies." I rose. "Finish this side off, and I'll go reprogram the timer."

Thanks to a lengthy article in last year's *Culpepper Courier*, I knew exactly where the controller was. I patted the pocket of my cargo shorts, making sure my tool kit was still there.

I jogged around the bleachers, the gravel crunching beneath my feet. The field house was a big, blue brick tower built into the back of the home-team bleachers. At the top was the announcer's booth. On the ground level was a maintenance room. A locked maintenance room.

And beneath those bleachers was the spot where Jake Weston kissed me until my knees gave out.

"How's she going to get in?"

I whirled around on the whisper to see the team gathered behind me.

Sigh. "Forget you saw *any* of this," I cautioned, pulling the toolkit out of my pocket. It was bad enough that I'd involved them in vandalism. Now they were accessories to breaking and entering.

"What's that?"

"What's she doing?"

Vicky cracked her gum and smirked. "Shh."

I pulled the tiny tension wrench and pick out of their holders and inserted them both into the lock. "Can I get a little light over here?"

A flood of cell phone flashlights lit my way. So much for covert ops. We could land a plane here.

"What is she doing?"

"She's picking the lock."

"No way. Only people in movies do that."

"Let her concentrate."

"Five bucks says she can't open it."

I felt the last pin give and turned the knob. "Ha. In."

Their jubilation was hushed but enthusiastic.

I ducked inside. It was a large room with block walls and

a dirt floor. There was a collection of groundskeepery imple-ments and industrial-sized trash cans on the far wall. And there, wired into the block next to the light switch, was our pretty little irrigation system controller.

The boys' practice started at 3:30 p.m. tomorrow. We'd already be on the bus to our first away game, far away from the accusing fingers. It was diabolical, if I said so myself. I keyed in the required changes, double- and then triple-checked it, and then locked the door and stepped outside before pulling it closed behind me.

"Well?" one of the girls whispered.

I gave them a thumbs-up.

"No, no, no. This is cooler than a thumbs-up," Sophie S. insisted. She made a heart shape with her fingers, holding them over her chest. One by one, the other girls followed suit. A silent, heart-shaped salute. Damn if I didn't feel a little teary.

"Shit! What's that?" Vicky hissed. She pointed in the direc-tion of a single light bobbing in the dark. Bobbing *our way* in the dark.

"Crap. Okay, everyone go over the fence at the end of the field. Quietly! Go!"

They took off, a roiling mass of adrenaline and good old-fashioned teenage fear.

"Vicky! Go," I said, shooing her with my hands.

"No way. What if it's a murderer? I'm not leaving you here to be murdered! What kind of a friend and assistant coach would I be?"

The answer to that would have to be debated later because the bouncing light was getting closer, and it was attached to a fast-moving, muscled form.

"You have *got* to be kidding me," I breathed.

"What?" Vicky asked, batting at me as I tried to push her into the shadows of the bleachers.

"Out for a stroll around the maintenance room, ladies?"

Jake Fucking Weston slowed to a stop in front of me. He was sweating, shirtless, and smiling. A combination I found perilously attractive.

"What are you doing here?" I asked, crossing my arms over my chest. "I'm starting to think you're following me."

"Clearing my head with a night run," he said as if it were the most natural thing in the world.

"Huh. Us too," I said.

"Yeah. Us too," Vicky said, mimicking my stance. He eyed us with amusement and suspicion.

I heard the jingle of chain metal and a distant giggle.

"Uh-huh," Jake said. "Sure."

Shit.

"Okay, Weston. What's it going to take to get you to forget you saw us here?" Vicky asked.

Hands on his hips, he studied his feet for a beat. He was still wearing those dorky shoes. "You still make those salted caramel cookies?" he asked Vicky.

"Hell yeah, I do. I make 'em good." Apparently, Vicky took her baking very seriously.

"Two dozen of those babies and, providing you didn't commit a felony, your secret is probably safe with me."

"Deal," Vicky said.

We heard another giggle in the dark. I coughed loudly to cover it and looked everywhere but Jake's sweaty torso.

"I guess we'll be on our way," Vicky said slowly.

"Yeah. I guess we'll be going."

"I'll just finish my lap around the field," Jake said.

"No! I mean, you should walk us to our car?" It came out as a question. "I mean, since it's dark and nighttime." Those things meant the same thing.

"It *is* both of those things," he agreed, clearly enjoying himself.

"Ugh. Just come on," I said, spinning his sweaty body around and pushing him in the direction of the stadium entrance.

"Getting a little handsy there, Mars."

"Funny. Move."

He walked us to our cars, and while Vicky listened to the four voice mails her family had left for her with a variety of small emergencies, Jake opened my car door.

"I take it you'll be behaving from here on out," he said, leaning into my space.

I held up a couple of fingers. "Scout's honor."

"I don't think that's quite right," he said, adjusting my fingers into the proper formation. *Zing!* My blood wasn't just sludging its way through my veins. Now it was simmering. Had I ever felt that zing with Javier just from his hand touching mine? Yeah, that was a solid no.

"You look like you've got a lot going on in that head of yours," he observed.

"Nothing out of the ordinary," I told him. Just a mild case of lust with a side of self-doubt, insecurity, and…hope.

He reached around me, and for a second, I thought he was going to wrap his hand around the back of my neck and pull me in for a kiss.

Instead, he tugged the end of my ponytail.

"See ya around, Mars."

CHAPTER 19

Marley

"You must be Miss Cicero."

I jumped out of my skin and bobbled my insulated lunch bag. I was standing in the hallway, debating whether to brave the teacher's lounge for lunch or if I should just hide in the locker room and eat my salad alone in my dungeon. If it helped me avoid Amie Jo, it would be worth it.

"Uh, yeah, hi," I said, recovering slightly. "Marley."

"I'm Andrea." She was medium height, medium build, with brilliant red hair and really nice pale skin. I felt like I was staring at a Disney character. "I'm the guidance counselor."

"Oh, it's nice to meet you," I said, executing a sloppy handshake and wondering if I'd been busted. Had someone figured out I'd tampered with the irrigation system last night? Was she really a guidance counselor, or was she an undercover Culpepper cop?

"I've been meaning to meet up with you, but floating between the elementary school and here makes it hard," she told me. "You wouldn't happen to want to have lunch with me in my office, would you?"

I didn't care if the woman had bear traps on the floor of her office. If it kept me away from Amie Jo, I'd happily gnaw my foot off. "I'd be happy to," I told her.

She brightened, and I looked around for the cartoon deer and birds that should have flocked to her.

"Great! Follow me!"

Andrea's office was a cramped but cozy space with two armchairs in front of a desk that held an ancient computer and a chrysanthemum in a pot painted by some toddler artist. She immediately earned my trust by kicking off her heels at the door and slipping her feet into comfy slippers.

"Do you try to get to know all the new faculty?" I asked, unpacking my lunch—a chopped Niçoise salad with lemon vinaigrette. After Tuesday night's frozen fish sticks, I'd begged my parents to let me take over the grocery shopping and meal prep.

For dinner, we were having marinated chicken breasts that were currently cooking away in the Crockpot Mom had never used and a new green bean recipe I'd found while I should have been studying soccer drills.

"I do," she said, pulling a foil-wrapped sandwich from her lunch bag. "And your mom is one of my good friends."

I paused, mixing the hard-boiled egg and tuna into the lettuce. I smelled a setup.

"And my mom asked you to talk to me," I guessed.

Andrea smiled, and I blinked when she didn't burst into a song. "Maybe. She's been concerned about you for quite some time."

"Why ever would that be? Because I showed up on her doorstep unemployed, single, and homeless?" I took a big bite of salad. It tasted bitter on my tongue.

"Actually, she was worried before that."

"When I was gainfully employed and in a steady, monogamous relationship?" I clarified.

"She sensed you weren't happy."

I sighed. This was very much like my optimistic,

everything-has-a-silver-lining mother. She didn't want to have the conversations that could upset someone. She'd just enlist a stranger to do it.

"I'm fine. I was fine then. I'm fine now. I'll be fine at the end of the semester."

"Is that what you want out of life? To feel fine?" Andrea asked innocently. She nibbled at the edge of her sandwich and stared at my salad.

I was suddenly tired of all the things I never said. All the things I told myself to stop feeling.

"Has she told you about my sister?"

"Zinnia? Yes, of course."

"Can you imagine what it's like to grow up being average when your sister is blazing a trail toward being the best at everything she does while you're busy dealing with puberty and trying to be, at the very best, average?"

I took another bite of salad. Andrea watched the fork on its way to my mouth. "Do you want some of this?" I asked.

"Normally, I'd pretend to be polite and say no. But I was running late this morning and accidentally packed myself a mayonnaise and lettuce sandwich. So yes, I will be your friend for life if you share that delicious-looking salad with me."

She threw the soggy sad mess of sandwich in the trash, and I scooped half of my salad onto her foil. She pulled a plastic fork out of her bottom drawer and dug in. "Okay, this is delicious. Who knew salad could taste good?" she moaned.

"It's a pretty simple recipe."

"I'm going to come back to this salad thing because I have an idea. But first, let's finish the thought on your sister," Andrea said, taking care to layer tuna, egg, and black olive on her fork.

"It's not really anything. My sister is great at everything. I'm not."

"And how does that make you feel?"

"I don't know? Fine? It's not like I can hate her for being so great. She's also annoyingly nice."

"It would be easier if she were an ass about being so great," Andrea guessed.

"Exactly. But she's all humble and 'I feel blessed, now let's talk about you.' So really, there's no thing. I'm me. She's Zinnia."

"You feel like you're not as good because your sister is an extraordinary person."

"And I'm just ordinary. Only I can't even seem to get that right." I credited Andrea's innocent fairy princess sweetness as the reason I was hurling my entire childhood worth of insecurities at her. "I've lost every job I've ever had. I've never had strong feelings for any of the guys I've dated. I can't seem to do what everyone else does. It's like I'm missing an important piece of my DNA or I missed an entire semester of school when they taught everyone how to adult."

Andrea leaned back in her chair and smiled. "Excellent work."

"On the salad?"

"Yes, but also on the deep dive of where you feel you are in life. I have a proposition."

"This is going to involve salads, isn't it?"

"I propose we meet for lunch once a week. You provide the delicious meal, and I'll provide free therapy. Have you ever talked to a therapist before?"

"You think I need therapy?" More like *my mother* thought I needed therapy.

"I think we could all use an independent third party to talk to, to say the things you can't say to people with a vested interest in your life," Andrea said diplomatically. "And I could use some actual food to get me through the workday."

"What if I think I'm a lost cause?" I asked.

"You don't," Andrea said, finishing the last scrap of lettuce on her foil. "And neither do I."

"What does my mom say about my sister?"

Andrea grinned. "Oh, she's worried about Zinnia, too. Thinks she's too focused on success and the outward appearance of it. But we decided to tackle you first."

———

I left Andrea's office feeling unsettled and nearly walked right into Jake's broad chest. Too bad it was covered by a sexy button-down today. Damn. He had the sleeves rolled to the elbows. I liked that.

"Long time, no see, Mars," Jake said, hitching an eyebrow.

What was he expecting? A confession of what he'd nearly caught me doing last night?

"Uh, yeah." My verbal abilities were failing me.

"Missed you at lunch," he said.

"Are you flirting with me?" I asked.

"If you have to ask, then I'm not doing a very good job."

Everything that came out of Jake's mouth sounded like it was suggestively threatening. No wonder his female—and some of his male—students were in a constant lather.

If I had to sit in a classroom and watch him—

"Hello? You in there?" He tapped me on the forehead.

I swatted his hand away. "Uh, yeah. I was just wondering what kind of teacher you are."

"You have a free period next, don't you? Why don't you swing by? Do some observing?"

Hmm. Tempting.

"I have an away game today. Rain check?"

"Soon then," he said with a flash of dimple. "I'll save you a seat."

CHAPTER 20

Marley

I forgot how much I hated school buses. The vinyl seats smelled like farts, and the suspension made me feel like I was enjoying a leisurely cruise in a tank over desert boulders. My internal organs were bruised, and I felt queasy. But at least the girls were in good spirits.

Vicky was sound asleep in the seat across from me, her mouth open, daintily snoring.

Natalee slid into the seat behind me. "Okay, so we didn't want to miss all the fun, so Leslie's cousin Brad is at the stadium, and he's going to record it."

"I thought we weren't going to tell anyone about this." I glanced around the bus before remembering that Lisabeth had been on the absentee roster today. Apparently, she had parents who felt she didn't actually need to attend school.

"Brad isn't going to tell anyone. He hates Tyler on the varsity team because Tyler told Mr. Vandish that Brad was copying off of his trig test when really it was Tyler copying Brad." Natalee was extremely well informed, and I was probably already fired.

"I hope he's at least subtle about it," I said dryly, but I moved closer to peer at Natalee's phone. It was 3:29. My fingers danced on the clipboard that held the first quarter's lineup. We were playing the Huntersburg Bees. A warm, fuzzy name for a team that systematically dismembered its opponents. The Huntersburg Bees were from an all-girls private school. To get to them, it was a forty-five-minute drive through Amish country. But the peace-loving Amish weren't enough to dilute the Bees.

They were as evil as teenage girls could get. At least, that's how I remembered them after they trounced us on the soccer field every time.

Was I nervous about my very first game as a soccer coach? Hell yes. Did I think there was a possibility that this prank would get me fired? Definitely. Especially since everyone was waving their phones around talking about vandalism and breaking and entering. High school–aged girls were not good at keeping secrets.

Was I also still thinking about Jake telling me he was flirting with me? Yes. A lot.

Someone squeaked toward the back of the bus. "It's Brad," Leslie said, brandishing her phone. "He said 'It's starting'!"

The excited squeals woke Vicky. "Huh? What's going on? Where am I?"

"You're halfway to Huntersburg, and the sprinklers just went off."

Vicky bolted from her seat and ran down the aisle screaming, "I wanna see!"

"She's super weird," Natalee confided.

"Aren't we all?"

Phones started dinging all up and down the bus aisle.

"I got video! I'm sharing," Leslie announced.

Natalee's phone signaled a message.

She pushed play, and I watched with satisfaction as the sprinklers erupted, arcing red water into the air. The varsity team was on the field, running some complicated footwork drill. There were the usual noises of surprise and then panic when they realized this wasn't just water.

Ah. Nothing felt as good as watching a plan come together. Perfect execution. And we were miles away from the scene of the crime. Even I was impressed with myself.

The girls were celebrating with a cheery "Suck it" chant. I hoped the bus driver wasn't taking notes for the administration. But he was a beefy guy with a bologna sandwich in his shirt pocket and earbuds in his ears.

My phone vibrated in my pocket. I pulled it out and saw Jake's name on the screen. I'd been given access to the teacher's directory, which included phone numbers. I may have plugged Jake's name and number into my contacts just in case.

Jake: I had a hunch there might be some excitement up here today.

Attached was a picture of a snarling Coach Vince waving his arms in the air while his players scrubbed their faces on their shirts. They were all cherry Kool-Aid red.

I debated replying. But I couldn't help it.

Me: Huh. Imagine that. They must have really pissed someone off.
Jake: It's not permanent is it?
Me: If I had to guess—seeing as how I have no personal knowledge of the situation—I'd say it was one of those semi-permanent prank dyes. It can hold up to water for a couple of days, but baby oil will strip it right out.
Jake: I don't feel inclined to share that information right now.
Me: I like that about you.
Jake: Good luck today, Coach.

I felt a smile spreading across my face. If we could take

down the entire boys' soccer team and their shithead coach, maybe we had a chance today. Starting out the season with a win? Now, that would be pretty great.

—————

We lost.

So badly that the Bees' head coach apologized to me when he shook my hand after the game.

7–0. And the last two goals had been scored by the Bees' junior varsity second string.

We hadn't been able to string passes together. Our communication was nonexistent. And while our defense worked harder than they should have had to, the offense couldn't get anywhere near the goal.

The team mood had gone from jubilant over our secret revenge plot to dejected in ninety minutes of terrible play.

Even worse, my parents had surprised me and stood in the bleachers with a handmade sign that said *Coach Marley* in glitter and calligraphy. After halftime, I wanted to climb up into the stands and rip the sign into pieces. How many more ways could I disappoint them before they gave up on me completely? How many more ways could I fail before I gave up completely?

We trooped back on the bus in silence, except for Vicky, who was doling out pep talks like a panicked life coach on espresso.

"Rome wasn't built in a day, ladies!"

Ruby and Sophie S. were back to ignoring each other after the two had gotten into an argument at center field. They had to be separated by the ref, and I'd benched them both.

We really could have used Lisabeth's beefy aggression on the field.

It felt like we were missing something. Some key component. Even worse, I worried that whatever tools I was missing in my personal life were exactly what the team was missing. It was my fault. I had a gap in my leadership. I could tell them to run and dribble all day long. But that wouldn't lead to a W.

I had the distinct feeling that, until I figured out what was wrong with me, I wouldn't be able to fix what was wrong with them.

Vicky flopped down in the seat next to me. "Well, that was a shit show," she said cheerfully.

"I don't know how to fix this, V," I told her.

She patted me on the leg. "Some things aren't fixable. Maybe you should just quit while you're behind."

"Are you kidding me right now?"

She smirked and yanked her hair out of her crooked ponytail. "Babe, it's gonna be fine. You're not the first coach to lose a game."

Yeah, but I had a feeling I was the first coach who had no clue how to win.

———

We stopped for a fast food dinner, which I skipped. The recent progress around my middle and the fact that I no longer felt like I needed a nap every day at noon and again at two felt like a move in the right direction. I had Crockpot chicken waiting for me at home and a beer. A big one.

The mood on the bus lightened a bit by the time we got back to the school. Apparently news of the now bright red boys' soccer team had spread far and wide. The girls gleefully took turns sharing pictures and Snapchat videos of the aftermath.

"There's a rumor going around that it was Middletown's team that did it," someone reported from the back of the bus. "Their school colors are red and white."

"Do you think Coach did that on purpose?" someone else asked.

I sighed and stared out the dark window. The loss was a distant memory to everyone but me.

We got back to the school, and I waved the girls off. The parking lot slowly emptied, and I loaded the balls and my gym bag into my hatch. The night was warm, and I couldn't believe I had to be back here in less than twelve hours. Who knew teachers worked so much?

A vehicle pulled into the lot, and I was suddenly aware that I was all alone at night in a poorly lit parking lot.

The windows were down, and I could hear Bon Jovi wailing through the speakers.

Jake Weston.

CHAPTER 21

Jake

S he looked dejected, tired. Like someone who had been knocked down one too many times. I wanted to fix it. To work the kinks out of those slumped shoulders, tell her everything would work out.

"What are you doing here?" she asked.

"I thought you might want one of these," I said, holding up the six-pack I'd pulled out of the fridge.

Marley nodded solemnly. "I do. I really do."

I pulled in next to her car and popped the hatch on my SUV. A little late-night tailgating in the high school parking lot with a pretty girl would go far in reminding me I hadn't entirely lost my rebellious ways.

She finished stuffing things into her car and joined me. I sat, patting the lip of the hatch next to me.

Marley obliged. I twisted the top off a beer and handed it to her.

"Did you bring me pity beer because you feel sorry for me?"

"Why would I feel sorry for you?" I asked, incredulous.

"Because we lost. Badly. They put the second-string JV in against us. And we still lost."

I winced. "Them's the breaks in sports. You should be celebrating."

She looked at me skeptically with those pretty brown eyes. "Celebrating what?"

"Right now, Coach Vince is standing in a shower that's gone cold and scrubbing his misogynistic skin."

That brought a ghost of a smile to her face, but it was gone just as quickly.

"Do you know what my sister does for a living?" she asked.

"I have no clue. Macramé shit and sell it on Etsy?"

She laughed, and I decided I wanted to hear the sound again.

"She works for a human rights organization and applies for grants to bring refugees to the U.S. for lifesaving surgeries."

"Cool."

"I hypothetically dye teenagers red."

"I don't think you're grasping the pure poetic justice of what you just pulled off...if it was indeed you. I still haven't heard an actual confession."

"I'm admitting to nothing," she said, taking a sip of the beer. "But tell me more about this poetic justice."

"Vince Snavely is a sniveling, steroid-eating weasel. The only thing he cares about is winning, and he imparts that lovely wisdom on impressionable teenage boys."

"Huh. He really does look like a weasel," Marley said.

"Come on. Admit it. Tell me you did it. It'll make you feel better," I told her, nudging her with my elbow. I liked the way it felt when our skin brushed. There was something chemical there. A reaction every time.

She sighed. "When am I going to learn that pranks never make me feel better?"

I had a feeling she was thinking back to Homecoming our senior year. People still talked about it. "Still waiting for a confession."

"How do I know I can trust you? Are you a narc?"

"I brought you beer that I'm drinking on school property," I pointed out.

"Yeah, but maybe you're wearing a wire," she joked.

"Do you want me to take off my shirt?" I offered.

She paused mid-swallow and coughed.

"Because I'd be willing to do it. If it convinces you to trust me."

"Keep your shirt on, Flirty McGee."

Playfully, I tugged at the hem of my T-shirt and watched her eyes follow the movement.

"Marley, do I need to remind you that you're not the only one with prankster cajones? Remember junior year when I built a ramp and jumped the principal's car with my bike?"

She cocked her head to the side. "Oh, that was you?" she asked innocently.

Damn right it was me.

She looked me up and down. "You don't look much like that guy anymore. You look…well behaved. Like a Boy Scout."

It was an insult, and we both knew it. "I may portray myself to be an upstanding adult during school hours. But I assure you, after school I'm a little rougher around the edges."

"Hmm." She considered me, then shook her head. "Nope. Don't buy it. There's no sign of the teenage rebel."

Challenge accepted. "Allow me to reacquaint you with him." I leaned into her space, happy when she didn't retreat. I remembered that about her. She didn't back down or give up.

"Oh, so you're going to kiss me?" she asked. Her tone was lighter now, her eyes sparkled.

"Yeah. Get ready."

"I'm ready. Impress me."

I started to lean in, slow. Building the anticipation. She parted her lips, and I could hear that little intake of breath. Almost like a whisper. Oh, I was going to enjoy this. Marley put a hand on my chest, and I stopped just an inch shy of her mouth.

"You're going to be better at this than you were in high school, right? I mean, I assume you've had some practice since then."

I laughed softly. Yeah, I liked this woman. She was sneaky funny, and there was something a little sad about her. Both were my personal kryptonite when it came to women.

"I think I was pretty damn good in high school," I argued.

She smiled at me, and I felt my heart take a nosedive right into my gut. I *really* liked that smile.

"What does this mean?" she asked suddenly.

I didn't pull back; instead, I held my ground. We were so close I could feel her body vibrating.

"What does what mean?"

"You showing up here, with a beer, a kiss? Is this a pity thing? Is this a onetime thing? Are you gonna suddenly give up your bachelor ways and fall head over heels for me? We work together. I'm only here for the semester. And given our history, you'll forgive me for wanting a clarification."

"You worried I'm gonna want to put a ring on you, Mars?" I asked, reaching out to take her long, slim fingers in mine. I let my thumb trail over her ring finger. "Get my heart broken?"

Her breath hitched, and I felt my heart rate kick up a notch.

"I just want to know what I'm getting into."

"How about we start with a kiss and see what happens?"

She hesitated. "Okay. As long as you make it a good one."

"Hey, it takes two for a great kiss. You better hold up your end," I teased.

I set my beer down and took hers, placing it next to mine. Taking my time, I cupped her face in my hands. I could feel the tension in her, the impatience, and that delicious little sliver of nerves. This was a pretty stupid move on my part. We worked together. I never dated anyone I worked with.

But I really wanted to kiss her. And I didn't like not doing what I really wanted.

I let my thumbs stroke her jawline, noted the way her bottom lip quivered. Her neck was soft, smooth, warm. It made me want to sink my teeth in. But I was knocking on forty. That was a little too old for hickeys.

"Why aren't you kissing me yet?" she asked.

Our mouths were so close. Her lip brushed mine when she spoke.

"Because sometimes it's more about the journey."

"I'm more about getting there—"

I closed the distance, cutting her off.

Her lips were ridiculously soft and inviting beneath mine. I had to bite back the urge that rose up and took me by the throat to deepen, to take, to chase.

Forcing gentleness, I moved my lips over her mouth in a caress. She was trembling against me, and every cell in my body was lighting up and paying attention. Just a kiss, I reminded myself. Just a freaking kiss. But I wanted more.

Her hands were on my chest, fisted in my T-shirt, and our hips and legs were pressed up tight against each other, seeking flesh. The way she responded to me was fucking mind-blowing. I was painfully aware of everything. Every breath, every tremor, every whimper that worked its way up her throat.

I was hard. Like "welcome to puberty, you have no control over your body" hard.

"Jesus, woman. Where did you learn to kiss like—"

But she didn't give me room to finish the question. Marley was pulling me back to her mouth and sinking her teeth into my lower lip. That little nip of pain was all it took to shove me right over the edge of civility.

I pushed one hand into her hair and hauled her into my lap with the other. If the kiss made me want more, this position with her sweet round ass centered on my uncomfortably hard cock made me want to set our clothes on fire and howl at the fucking moon.

I wasn't into overthinking things. I liked her. I was attracted to her. Very, very attracted to her.

But there was one tiny sliver of my brain that wasn't fully dedicated to sexual pleasure, and it was beating out an emergency message in Morse code reminding me that I was in the school parking lot with a woman I wanted to get to know a bit better before I stuck my needy dick in her.

"Mars." I drew back and then dove in again, raining kisses down her throat.

She wiggled against me, and the friction made my vision go black around the edges. Fuck.

I gripped her hips and tried to hold her still. "Marley," I said again. My voice was rough.

"Hmm. What do you know? Maybe there is a little bit of teenage rebel in there after all," she said. She nipped my bottom lip one more time and slid off my lap. "Thanks for the beer, Boy Scout."

———

Vicky: Please tell me you guys made out after I left.

Me: How did you know??? Were you lurking in the shadows with night vision goggles??

Vicky: I saw him pull in as I was leaving. Figured his lips had a homing beacon on you. Was it just as good as the first time?

Vicky: Don't even try to go radio silent on me. The last time Rich and I had sex, he kept his socks on.

Vicky: I need to live vicariously through your swinging singlehood.

Me: Fine. There was a kiss. It was nice.

Vicky: *Hulk smash meme*

Vicky: NICE?? JAKE WESTON LAYS ONE ON YOU AND IT WAS JUST NICE???

Me: Go tell Rich to take his socks off.

CHAPTER 22

Marley

A millennium ago. The Kiss.

I *don't know, V. I'm just not happy. I mean, Travis is great."*

"So great," Vicky agreed, digging into the Styrofoam cup of chicken corn soup, a staple at cold weather soccer games. "But?"

"But I don't know. I feel, like, ungrateful saying it out loud."

"Ungrateful like you owe him a debt of gratitude for dating you?" Vicky looked at me like I'd just declared that Russia had invaded Pennsylvania.

"Well. Yeah. Kinda. I mean, look how much nicer everyone has been to me since we started dating."

"And by nicer, you mean Amie Jo stopped calling you Zit-Faced Loser to your face. I told you the fastest way to shut her up is to punch her in her goddamn mouth and call it a day. She comes after you because there's no consequences. You don't freak out on her. You don't defend yourself. You just wilt like a pretty little flower."

Vicky was annoyingly right. I just didn't have the weaponry to defend myself from mean girls. As far as I could tell, Amie Jo wasn't human. She'd named me an enemy on the playground in kinder-garten and had dedicated her life to being an awful person to me. Dating Travis had been the only respite from her bitchy nastiness.

"Can we get back to the Travis thing?" I asked. The action

on the field stopped with the whistle, and we watched twenty-two long-legged guys jog off the field for halftime.

"Fine. Tell me why you're having doubts about breaking up with Prince Travis, the mostly okay boyfriend."

Vicky had been involved in a relationship with Rich Rothermel since the end of tenth grade. She said she just didn't want to commit the time to a decade or two of dating, so she was going to marry her high school sweetheart. But not until they were thirty and done with their two-year backpacking trip around Europe.

With her future already planned out, she was more than willing to help me shape mine.

"He's nice," I said. "And sweet and thoughtful."

"Uh-huh. How's the sex?" Vicky was skilled at cutting to the heart of an issue and then poking it in the eye.

"It's...okay."

I'd held on to my virginity until senior year, not liking any of my short-term boyfriends enough to hand it over to their clumsy, sweaty hands. But when Travis Hostetter swept his blond hair out of his blue eyes and flashed me that all-American dimpled grin on the first day of school—miracle of miracles—I'd all but stuffed my v-card in an envelope and addressed it to him.

I liked him. I really did. He was a great guy. But...

"I don't have anything to compare it to," I reminded her.

"Trust me," Vicky said, jabbing the plastic spoon at me. "You'd know if it was good."

"Ugh, I feel like an ungrateful ass. So the chemistry isn't really there for me. Is that a good enough reason to break up with him? And is being moderately more popular a good enough reason to not break up with him?"

"You got yourself a real conundrum there," she told me. "Bottom line, are you happy?"

"No, but—"

"No buts. There's your answer."

I knew she was right, but it didn't alleviate the guilt I felt for not being more grateful that the guy picked me from obscurity and had done all the right boyfriendy things. Travis Hostetter was a great guy. He just wasn't my great guy. He'd make some lucky girl an amazing boyfriend if I could lady up and release him back into the wild.

I felt eyes on me and looked up to see Travis waving to me from the bench.

I raised a hand back and cursed myself for not swooning. The feelings I had toward the blond Adonis in his heroically grass-stained socks were friendly, not lusty. And that made me defective.

"You ready to go back?" Vicky asked, jutting her chin in the direction of our rowdy circle of friends. Together, we were an island of misfits in the middle of the shark-infested waters of high school.

"I think I'm gonna grab a hot chocolate," I told her. I didn't actually want the gritty, powdery crap. But I did want to be alone with my thoughts.

"Okay," Vicky said. "I'll see you back on the bleachers." She meandered off, eating her soup while she walked. I headed back toward the concession stand and then veered off behind the bleachers. Here I was separated from the action, the people, the lights. Here I was all alone even with a few hundred people crowding the stands, lining up at the restrooms, and stuffing their faces with fake orange cheese nachos at the concession stand.

"Hey there, Mars."

I recognized the voice before I turned around.

There, leaning against one of the bleacher supports all James Dean-y, was Jake Freaking Weston.

My heart gave a little pitter-pat somersault in my chest.

"Hey, Jake," I said lamely. I was in a committed relationship. I shouldn't be having a physical reaction to the very non-Travis guy before me.

He was wearing a leather jacket and jeans. A flannel shirt

131

was tied around his waist. And he had a chain peeking out of his pocket. His hair was a little longer than fashionable. Like he was too cool to care about things like haircuts and grooming.

"Thought you'd be watching your boyfriend play," he said with that sexy rebel smirk.

Jake had worked his way through an impressive portion of the female sex in our class and last year's graduating class. Rumor had it a substitute teacher had her eye on him.

"Just needed some air," I said. Well, that was a stupid thing to say. We were outside. There was nothing but air out here.

"You know what I think?" he asked.

I shook my head. I should have walked away, but my feet were moving toward him as if he were using some kind of Star Trek tractor beam on me. It was the facial hair, I decided. It drew me in like a platter of chocolate-covered doughnuts.

I'd known of him for a few years since he'd transferred to Culpepper from New Jersey in the middle of our sophomore year. We were in the same class in a very small school. But he remained an enigma in a way the guys I had gone to kindergarten with couldn't.

He walked different. Talked different. Carried himself different.

"What do you think?" I asked, stopping a careful two feet away.

Jake pushed away from the support and took a step into my space. He was taller than me. I liked that too.

Nervous, I took a short step back and found a metal post pressing into my back.

He advanced on me slowly like a lion prowling toward a fat, sick gazelle. Jake rested a hand above me and leaned in. "I think you're with the wrong guy, Mars."

Yeah, I was imagining this. I was standing in line waiting for my brown sugar water from Sue Clempet, Booster Club president, who wore not one but two crosses around her neck should anyone fail to notice the first one. I was not under the bleachers, breathing

132

in the clean, naughty scent of the class rebel while my very nice boyfriend was probably scoring another goal on the field.

I blinked. Then I worked my mouth closed when my jaw started to hurt.

"Uh. What?" I asked.

He had really pretty lips. For a guy. They quirked up in one corner, amused by my gazelleness.

"I don't think Travis is the guy for you," Jake said, running a thumb over my jawline.

My heart was hammering against my ribs so hard I worried they might crack and puncture a lung. That would not be cool. "What makes you say that?" I asked mechanically. I was a robot needing input.

"You're the highlight of English class," he said, rubbing that thumb over my lower lip. Danger! Danger! Warning bells clunked and clanged to life.

"Go on."

He grinned, and my knees nearly buckled. This was what I was missing from Travis. This insane physical reaction. The sweaty palms. The ragged breathing. The dark pleasure of knowing I was about to make a huge, amazing mistake.

"See? That right there. You entertain me."

Entertain like a puppet-show kind of thing or a sexy exotic dancer slithering down a pole? There was an important difference.

"I entertain you?" I repeated.

"I think we'd have fun together."

Travis talked about our future. Applying for the same colleges. Whether or not we could talk our parents into letting us go to the beach together this summer. Asking me what I wanted for Christmas.

Jake talked about fun.

Like I was one of those girls who would let him into her jeans and then cheerfully wave him off when the fun was over.

"I'm not really a fun kind of girl," I said stiffly.

"Hmm." He dipped his head in close. I could feel his breath on my cheek while my own caught in my chest. "I think I'm going to kiss you."

The hell you are, sir!

"Okay." Damn it! Betrayed by my mouth. I should have pushed him away. Kicked him in the kneecap. Called him a dirty temptation.

Instead, I stood perfectly still while he pressed his lips to mine.

They weren't Travis's lips. They didn't move like his, didn't taste like his. And, good Lord, when his tongue swept into my mouth, I knew without a doubt that this irresponsible, heady rush of lust was what I was looking for.

He kissed me thoroughly and didn't pull back until the crowd on the bleachers exploded over some play on the field. Jake looked at me and smirked.

"Think about it," he said with a wink. And then he turned and walked away, leaving me trembling against the metal support.

It was then that I noticed Amie Jo glaring at me. Her hands were on her hips, pom-poms sprouting from them.

I was a dead woman.

CHAPTER 23

Marley

I didn't dare turn on my vibrator when I got home. Not in my bedroom with my parents and that Airbnb guy from Seattle just down the hall. So I'd settled for a quick dance with the shower head before going to bed and dreaming about dry humping Jake in the high school parking lot. I'd need six showers a day at this rate.

I passed out cold on my bed, the lousy game a distant memory replaced by some very pleasant flashbacks to Jake's mouth.

The next morning, I walked into school and came to a full stop when a boy with dark curly hair and a magenta face walked past me. Holy shit. I'd forgotten about the tomatoing. Pranking deserving victims was one of my reasons for living. But a well-executed kiss from a U.S. history teacher had me forgetting about my diabolical plot and its success.

"Cicero!" a voice snapped.

I had to bite six holes in my lip to keep from laughing. Coach Vince stormed toward me. Half of his face was his usually brawny tan. The other half looked like it had suffered an unfortunate fruit punch explosion.

"What can I do for you, Coach?" I asked innocently.

Morgan E. and Angela stopped a short distance away.

"I want to know what you know about this," he said, gesturing at his own face.

"Well, we only met that one time. I've gotta say you really didn't make a good first impression. But keep at it. I'm sure you can do better."

He snarled at me, but any fearful effect was ruined by the red stain. "If I find out you or your team of losers had anything to do with this, I will make your life a living hell. Do you hear me?"

His volume was high enough that I was pretty sure everyone in a hundred-yard radius heard him. The students in the hallway were gawking at us. Teachers were poking their heads out of the classrooms.

"My advice, Coach Vince, is to get your finger out of my face and lower your voice. My team and I were at an away game yesterday. My guess is I'm not the only one in this town who thinks you got exactly what you deserved."

"Ooooooh!"

Morgan E. and Angela stepped up to flank me, their arms crossed over their chests like sassy teenage bodyguards who were not amused.

Our audience was thrilled.

"Uh, Coach?"

Vince turned, and I caught sight of Milton Hostetter... or his brother. His face had been spared for the most part, but that pretty blond hair was now a lovely shade of pink. Oh, Lord. Amie Jo was going to kill me.

I was a hell of a lot more afraid of her than the overgrown jackass in front of me.

"I'll get to you in a minute, dumbass," Vince roared at the kid.

I felt a little bad for him. I mean, he didn't choose to have Vince as an authority figure. "Coach Vince, I'm going to suggest that you back up out of my face and leave school property until you can control your temper." The asshole wasn't even on the faculty here. He was a sales guy for a cabinet factory out of Lancaster.

"I'll leave when I'm good and ready."

That fat finger was in my face again.

"What are you laughing at, Haruko?" Vince demanded. "Didn't my country bomb the crap out of yours a few years back?"

"Is there a problem here?" a voice snapped.

The cavalry had arrived. Jake and Floyd worked their way through the crowd to stand next to me. Angela and Morgan stepped to the side.

"I was just explaining to Cicero here that if she had anything to do with that prank yesterday, she'd be hearing from my lawyer."

"Are you sure it wasn't your lawyer who did it?" Jake offered.

"Yeah, I heard that you didn't pay him after you lost that suit against your next-door neighbor and their hedgerow," Floyd added.

"Guy's got a lot of enemies," Haruko said from her classroom doorway. She scratched at the corner of her eye with her middle finger.

Vince glared at her before turning his attention back to me and stabbing his finger in my face.

"Careful there," Jake said, his voice low and controlled.

"I know you did this!" Vince hissed.

"Like I said. I had an away game yesterday," I reminded him.

"What about the night before?" Vince demanded.

"She was with me," Jake said.

"Ooooooh!" The gathered students *really* liked that.

"Is that so?" Vince snarled.

"Are you calling me a liar?" Jake asked calmly. He sounded amused, almost bored. He was way scarier than the tantrum-throwing Vince. I liked it.

"If either of you think you can mess with me or my team again, you'll be hearing from my lawyer!" With a parting growl, the man turned and stormed out, knocking Milton out of his way.

"Well, that was fun," Floyd said, watching him go.

"All right, everyone. Show's over. Get to class," Jake said, herding students toward classrooms and hallways.

"Marley Cicero!"

Jesus, what was with people sneaking up on me?

Amie Jo stormed down the hall under a full head of steam. "Did I hear Coach Vince accuse you of doing this to my poor sweet boy?" she demanded, yanking Milton's head down so I could see the pink cast better.

"Oh, shit. You're on your own," Floyd hissed and turned tail into the gym.

"Coward," I called after him.

"We were at an away game yesterday, Mrs. Hostetter," Morgan E. reminded her. "We weren't even here."

"How convenient," Amie Jo hissed, eyeing me like a mangy raccoon. "But I seem to recall you being mean and violent in high school."

I scoffed in her face. "I was mean and violent in high school? Are you forgetting the time you tried to run over Shelly Smith in the parking lot?" Shelly had made the unfortunate mistake of running against Amie Jo for class secretary our junior year.

Of course the entire town was always happy to forgive Amie Jo for her bad choices. Mine, however, still lived on.

"I know *exactly* what you're doing," she hissed at me. "You're pretending to be innocent, but I know what you're capable of."

I'd once broken into her locker and filled it with a dozen of the largest pairs of granny panties that I could find at Walmart. It had cost me two weeks of lunch money, but it had been so worth it. They'd fallen out at her feet between classes and been waved as flags by hilarious classmates.

It occurred after she'd called me an ugly whore during gym class when I missed her set in volleyball.

And then there had been Homecoming 1998 when I'd taken things way, way, way too far.

The warning bell rang, and students reluctantly left the scene of what was shaping up to be a girl fight.

"Go on to class, Milty," she told her son. "I'll take care of this." She waited until the hallway was mostly empty before sidling closer to me.

"Now you listen to me, Marley Cicero. I know you. And I know you had something to do with this. Maybe you're just jealous that I got Travis and you got nothing. Maybe you feel bad that your life is so pathetic. Maybe the only joy you get in life is by staging these childish pranks. I get it. I wouldn't be able to stand myself if I were you either. All alone in life. You're a what not to do. A human Pinterest fail. But don't you *ever* do anything to my sons' hair again." Her voice screeched higher.

I absorbed the words. Used to the verbal weapons Amie Jo and people like her employed.

"A human Pinterest fail? I feel like that's uncalled for."

"Admit it. You're jealous of me." Amie Jo was turning an unnatural shade of red, and I worried about her blood pressure. She was like one of those Instant Pots. You didn't want that bursting open.

"Whoa. Let's hang on there a second," Jake was back at my side. "Amie Jo, I don't know what you were told, but Marley couldn't have had anything to do with that prank."

"It was her! I know it was," Amie Jo insisted. "If she didn't tamper with the sprinklers yesterday, she did it the night before."

"She was with me the night before. All night. Speaking of," Jake said, sliding his arm around my waist. It was an incredibly inappropriate time for my nipples to go hard. "Do you mind if we do dinner at my house tonight. Last I heard, dining naked is frowned upon at Cashews." He leaned in and nibbled at my ear.

I could hear him. He was speaking English. But my brain was inserting the *word* salad for what he must actually be saying. Jake Weston was not telling Amie Jo that he wanted to get me naked for dinner. *Was he?*

I looked at her. She had an expression of horror, revulsion.

Okay, maybe he actually said it. "Baby?" he asked. He pinched me, hard.

I made a yelping noise and then recovered. "Uh. Yeah. Fine. Naked dinner at your place is...fine."

Amie Jo's perfect pink lips worked their way through what looked like several four-letter words before any noise came out.

"I'm sorry. I don't think I heard you correctly. Are you two—"

"Dating," Jake filled in. "Yeah. One look at Marley here during preseason, and I remembered all of those high school feelings that never went away."

Amie Jo looked like she was trying to say a word that started with "f." Her front teeth were wearing off all that sparkly lipstick.

"I'll make your favorite," Jake said, leaning down to give me a peck on my cheek before hurrying off.

The bell rang, and I decided it was just smarter to leave Amie Jo standing there eating her own lipstick. I ducked into the locker room and, as a precaution, threw the deadbolt. What in the holy hell had just happened?

One kiss and...and what? He'd swooped in, riding to the rescue with first Vince and then Amie Jo.

"Yo, Cicero!" Floyd the Coward called through the gym door.

I yanked it open. "I didn't know you could run that fast, Floyd."

"No shame, man. That woman terrifies me."

"Why's she so mad anyway?" I asked.

Floyd pointed over his shoulder into the gym. There was a velvet backdrop set up.

"It's Picture Day."

CHAPTER 24

Jake

Principal Eccles," I said, stepping into her office. "How goes the molding of young minds?" I was pouring on the charm. It was a leftover from my youthful indiscretions. Trips to the principal's office still made me a bit uneasy.

"Jake, I never thought I'd see the day," she said with a small smile.

"What day?" Okay, I was definitely nervous.

She held up a neat stack of papers and waved it at me. "This day."

"Sorry I'm late." Marley barreled in the door out of breath and pink-cheeked in a way that made me immediately envision her naked on rumpled sheets. My rumpled sheets. "One of the freshmen put their combination lock on backward, and well…" Her torrent of words slowed when she spotted me making myself at home in the chair.

"This will just take a quick minute out of both your days," Principal Eccles said, sliding matching paperwork toward us both. "I heard the news that you two have entered into a personal relationship."

Marley's face went an even brighter shade of pink, and her brown eyes widened. "Oh, uh, that isn't exactly—"

"Have a seat, Mars," I insisted, tugging her into the chair

next to mine and kept her hand in mine once she was settled. She looked at me as if I'd gone and lost my damn mind. Maybe I had.

"As I was saying to Jake here," Principal Eccles continued, "I never thought I'd see the day when he'd be signing one of these contracts. But I guess we all grow up eventually."

"Contracts?" Marley repeated. She yanked her hand out of my grip.

Oh, this was going to be good.

"Here in the Culpepper School District, we don't like to do things like forbid staff from dating." Principal Eccles launched into her HR speech. "What we do ask is that teachers who enter into relationships continue to set a good example for the students."

"Naturally," I said.

Marley's head whipped in my direction. The look she shot me telegraphed a loud and clear "WTF?"

"We, uh. That is, Jake and I haven't exactly defined what this thing is," Marley said weakly.

"And that's exactly why we have this contract. We certainly don't expect our staff to give up their romantic lives just to be teachers. But we do require you to set a standard. One-night stands and short-lived, volatile relationships teach these hormone-addled teens that monogamy is, for lack of a better word, lame." She slid two pens across the desk at us.

"It's up to you to prove the opposite. So all I ask is you date exclusively for the remainder of the semester. Preferably the entire school year. But given both your histories and the temporary aspect of Ms. Cicero's position here, that would be rather lofty."

"You want me to sign a contract to be in a monogamous relationship with Jake Weston for the rest of the semester?" Marley looked pale like she'd just been given three months to live.

"Great summary, honey," I said, cheerfully patting her bare knee. The woman was going to need CPR from the looks of it. "We're happy to sign the contract," I told the principal.

She looked relieved.

"Thank God. When Amie Jo sprinted in here purple-faced with the news, I was worried I'd have a problem on my hands," Principal Eccles sighed. "She seemed rather insistent that there was no way the two of you were actually dating."

"I can't imagine why she'd think we weren't being honest." I was the epitome of innocence. "Can you, sweetheart?"

Marley didn't answer to the endearment, so I kicked her.

She jerked out of her shock coma. "Oh. Uh. No. I can't imagine, dear? Babe? Jake."

I reached out and took her hand again. From all appearances, it looked like a sweet gesture, but I applied a little more pressure than necessary.

"Great. Because I have zero tolerance for adult drama in this building. Got it? I get enough of it from students and parents all day, every day. I'm going to do what it takes to keep this ship sailing smoothly. And if your relationship blows up or either of you gives Amie Jo the tiniest excuse to go batshit obsessive over this like the Ninth-Grade Class Trip Fiasco, I will not hesitate to take it out on you."

I was basically crushing Marley's hand, grinding her bones into a fine dust.

Faced with losing to Amie Jo, she recovered admirably. "We understand, Principal Eccles. I know that Amie Jo and I haven't always seen eye to eye, but you can count on Jake and me to maintain our..." Marley glanced at me, "decorum."

"Wonderful. Now, if you'll both just sign here and here and initial page three, you can be on your way."

"What the fuck was that?" Marley hissed as soon as we exited the inner sanctum of the front office.

"Uh, you're welcome," I said, crossing my arms over my chest and leaning back against the trophy case.

"I'm welcome?" Her brown eyes were a little crazed, and I was enjoying the show. "Do you think you just rode to my rescue or something?"

"Yeah. I do." Not only had I rescued a damsel in distress, I'd also fibbed to an authority figure. Both sides of my personality were pretty damned pleased.

"I don't need rescuing!"

"Said the woman who could have hospitalized her entire team," I reminded her.

"Not that again."

"Now you pick on Coach Dickweed and the boys' varsity soccer team, who are as close to Jesus as you can get in Central Pennsylvania. And then you piss off Amie Jo 'Evil Queen' Hostetter. Do you have any idea what that woman is capable of?"

"Yes!" Marley shrieked. "For fuck's sake, yes! Of course I know! And Culpepper knows exactly what I'm capable of."

Classes were in session, and the lunch ladies were staring at us, so I pulled Marley to the closest exit. Outside, it was warm and sunny with just the slightest edge to the air. A sliver of the scent of autumn rode the breeze.

"You need a goddamn keeper. It's like you're trying to make terrible choices," I told her.

"You're not *my* teacher or my keeper, and my choices are mine to make. I just signed a contract under duress without even reading it! And now we're, what? Fake dating? For the rest of the semester? What happens if we fake break up? Do I get real fired?"

Damn. I really liked this girl. Even furious, she was funny.

"Pretty much. There's something about an ethics clause or

145

some shit. I think you can go before a review board in case of emergency."

She was pacing, and every time she turned away, I couldn't help but admire the shapely curve of her ass under her khaki shorts. Marley Cicero had a really nice ass.

"Why does this shit keep happening to me?" She wasn't talking to me anymore. She was communicating with a higher power.

"Look. Let's face it. You need me. I can help you with coaching, teaching. Whatever. You said it yourself. Your life's a mess. Use me as a resource. I guarantee I can turn your life around by December."

"So you're a life coach now? Jesus, Jake. Why are you even doing this?"

"Maybe I hate to see potential wasted."

"Don't bullshit me. I remember you once stole a goat and locked it in the vice principal's office over the weekend. You don't do things out of the kindness of your heart. You do it for the entertainment value."

"Oh, yeah. I forgot about that," I said, appreciating the fond memory as it arose.

"Why, Jake?" she asked again.

"I'm not exaggerating when I say Amie Jo would have made it her life's mission to ruin yours, and she would have made the rest of us miserable in the process. She's a terrible, terrible human being."

"Uh-huh. You expect me to believe that you've willingly labeled yourself my boyfriend for the next four months so you don't have to witness Amie Jo destroy me."

"And there's the other thing."

"What other thing?"

"We've shared exactly two kisses now. Both of which have resulted in some serious brain frying. I liked it. Both times."

"I don't want a pity fake boyfriend," she insisted, her jaw tightening.

"There's no pity, and stop being a dumbass. I've been doing some thinking recently, that maybe it's time I settle down... sometime. In the future. Eventually."

She closed her eyes and then opened them. I liked the inky line of her lashes. "I don't think you're speaking English."

I gave a little shrug. "I don't know. I mean, maybe if I help you with your teaching and coaching, you could help me navigate a monogamous relationship. Like a practice run."

"You want me to help you practice being in a relationship?"

"Yeah. You've done long-term relationships before, right?"

She stared at me for a long minute and then nodded slowly.

"Good! See? It's a mutually beneficial fake relationship. I keep Amie Jo off your back and help you not suck as an employee here, and you can get me into relationship shape."

"I can't decide if this is the stupidest idea I've ever heard or if it's marginally less terrible than letting Amie Jo publicly crucify me at the next pep rally."

"Your choice, sweetheart. Though I should warn you, the district takes their contracts pretty seriously. If you go back in there and tell Eccles it was all a lie, well, let's just say neither one of us can afford an unpaid suspension."

She mouthed a string of four-letter words, and I tried not to laugh.

The bell rang inside.

"Dammit." Marley trudged up the steps toward the door. She paused, her hand on the handle. "Jake? How many of those contracts have you signed?"

"Counting this one?"

"Yeah."

"One."

CHAPTER 25

Marley

Thanks to a mishap with the field hockey equipment in the storage room, I was late for practice. I'd managed to get my foot stuck in a volleyball net and fell into the cage, knocking the door open. Sticks and balls went everywhere. I fell two more times before I managed to wrangle everything back into its home.

Sore, battered, and psychologically exhausted from the day, I climbed the concrete steps to the practice field.

I don't know what I expected to find—perhaps a wrestling match between disgruntled teenage girls or a homicide in progress—but it sure wasn't my team lined up and applauding me.

The surprise was so sharp that I turned around and looked over my shoulder to see who they were clapping for.

"Let's hear it for Coach Cicero," Vicky shouted through megaphone hands. She had a voice that carried whether it was in study hall or the library or across fifty yards of grass. She could have made a living out of announcing sports for teams that couldn't afford audio equipment.

The girls whooped it up, and I approached cautiously, not trusting their enthusiasm. They encircled me, and I braced for an attack or at least some spitting and pointy elbows.

"Did you see Austin's face today? It was like Hawaiian Punch red," one of the girls squealed.

"You should have seen Coach stare down that ass Coach Vince this morning. He came at her like a bull in a field, and she was all 'ho hum, you bore me,'" Angela said with…was that respect or sarcasm?

"And then Mr. Weston is all 'let's calm down now,'" Morgan E. said, doing a decent impression of his rumbly baritone. "You guys are, like, dating, right?"

"He's so gorgeous," Phoebe swooned.

"I really am, aren't I?" This time it wasn't someone impersonating the baritone. It was the real deal. Jake strolled into our circle.

Vicky elbowed me so hard in the gut that I lost the air in my lungs.

"Mr. Weston, are you and Coach dating?"

"Can we be your bridesmaids?"

"Mrs. Hostetter did *not* seem happy today. Do you think it's because her son's hair was pink for picture day or because Coach stole her crush out from under her?"

"Shh! We're not supposed to talk about the red thing!"

"She can't have a crush! She's *married*!"

"My mom has a list of celebrities she's allowed to sleep with if she ever runs into them."

"For the love of God, everyone shut up, or you're all going to run laps," I said. I really needed to get a whistle. The giggles and peanut gallery comments quieted. "You," I said, pointing at Jake. "What are you doing here?"

"My team has a long run on their own today. Ends back here. Thought I'd observe you in action." He winked at me, and I wanted to punch him in his smug face.

"Ooooooh," the team squealed with delight.

"We have a lot to talk about later," I warned him.

The "Ooh" was now more "someone's in trouble" tinged.

"I'm all yours, Miss Cicero."

Vicky fanned herself while I rolled my eyes so hard they nearly popped out of my head.

"Okay, everybody line up. We're going to practice throw-ins and corner kicks," I snapped.

———

"Well, that was probably our best practice yet," Vicky observed, slinging a bag of balls over her shoulder as we waved the girls off. The sun was getting a little lower in the sky, and it was almost cool enough for the warm-up jacket I had in my back seat. Jake was huddled with his cross-country team, doing whatever it was that a cross-country coach did.

"Yeah. Not horrible," I agreed. It hadn't been the usual disaster of in-fighting and bitching and moaning. I doubted that we'd made any real progress on moving the ball back into play, but at least there hadn't been any fistfights. Lisabeth had sauntered in twenty minutes late with a bogus "I was at the gynecologist" excuse and a bunch of snide comments. I hadn't realized until she'd arrived how nice those twenty Lisabeth-free minutes had been.

The scrimmage at the end of practice still highlighted our complete lack of offensive strategy. But at least we were starting to communicate on the field. Jake had been taking mental notes, and I was maybe a little interested in hearing what he had to say.

"Sooo…" Vicky did a little shimmy with her shoulders. "Heard you and Jake had to sign the 'We Promise Not to Be Dirty Little Whores' contract."

"Jesus, V! How did you hear that?"

She shrugged. "Eh, there was an email that went out. Bet Amie Jo shit a brick."

"An email?" Of course there was an email. When I was in

school, neighbors would run door to door to spread the word because our dial-up internet was too slow. Now, thanks to fiber optics and high-speed internet you could blast an entire school district in a matter of seconds. "And yeah, she wasn't exactly thrilled."

"Knew it," she sang. "Doesn't it feel good? All of these years later, you're finally getting back at her."

"Yeah, over something she shouldn't even have an opinion on. How can she care who Jake does or doesn't date? Isn't she, I don't know, *married*?"

"Amie Jo stakes her claims on what she wants, and it's up to the rest of us to respect those claims."

"Um. That's bullshit."

Vicky peered over her blue lenses at me. She looked like Penny Lane from *Almost Famous* today. "You know what a nightmare she was in high school. It follows that, with a fat bank account and no authority figures brave enough to stand up to her, she'd become an even bigger monster."

"She's *married*."

"Jake's *hot*."

"We're not really dating," I confessed.

She clapped her talonlike hand around my wrist like a slap-on bracelet. "Those words had better never be uttered aloud again, Marley Cicero!"

"What? Why? We're not. It's totally fake. He came to my rescue with that buffoon boys' coach and Amie Jo when she was ready to claw my eyes out over the dye incident."

"You are Culpepper's hometown hero right now. You stood up to the Hell Beast and lived to tell the tale."

"Amie Jo or Vince?"

She ignored my question. "Plus, you land Jake 'Never Had a Relationship Longer Than Three or Four Orgasms' Weston."

"Fake, Vick. It's fake."

She slapped her hand over my mouth. "You will not speak that word again in my presence. You kissed him. You have a history with him. He waltzes into battle to make sure you don't get your face punched in by a steroid-swilling orangutan or your eyes clawed out by Evil Barbie. Then he willingly signs a contract saying he will date only you for the rest of the year. A contract that he could get fired over if he defaults."

"Semester," I cut in. I was only here until December. Let's not prolong this into something it wasn't.

"There's a lot more real than fake in that chain of events," she pointed out.

We both turned to watch Jake as he walked his team through a cooldown of foam rolling. Some of my girls had joined them and were drooling over his meaty thighs. I couldn't blame them. Part of me wanted to snack on those thighs.

"I can't be in a relationship with Jake Weston," I insisted. I felt the panic rising in my throat. "I'm a mess. A hot mess. You date guys like that in your prime, not twenty years past it." Jesus, when was the last time I'd had a bikini wax? Or a freaking haircut? Besides, the man couldn't be trusted. He'd thrown me over for something blonder and shinier before.

"No. Nope. This can't be real. He's just helping me out."

"Why? Marley, why would Jake just help you out?"

"We have a deal. He's going to keep Amie Jo off my back and help me brush up on my teaching and coaching."

"And in return you have dirty, dirty sex with him?" she prodded.

"In *return*," I elbowed her hard, "I'm going to teach him how to be in a relationship."

"Why would he want to know what that's like?" she asked.

"He says he's ready to settle down."

Vicky sucked in a breath and choked on her gum. I thumped her on the back until she started breathing again.

"You say that like it's not the most momentous thing that's ever happened in Culpepper," she wheezed.

"What's the big deal? I'm thirty-eight and have never been married either."

"But not for lack of trying. You've dated. You've lived with men. You've been on that track."

I winced. I'd been on that track and then fallen off of it. Repeatedly.

"Jake's never shown *any* interest in doing anything resembling a relationship. Do you know how many bridesmaids and flight attendants have been spotted leaving his house at all hours of the night?"

"So he changed his mind. Big whoop."

Vicky pinched the bridge of her nose. "How can I put this so you'll understand? It's like if Hostess snack cakes came out with a fat-free, calorie-free Twinkie that was good for you. But only one person in the world could have them."

"I'd annihilate the competition," I breathed, staring off into the distance, imagining such a beautiful thing.

"Jake Weston is the fat-free, calorie-free Twinkie. And only one woman can have him."

CHAPTER 26

Jake

I flopped down on the couch and kicked my feet up on the coffee table. Homer rolled onto his back on the cushion next to me to give me better belly-scratching access. I obliged, scruffing his tummy.

"You need another haircut, fur face." He was part goldendoodle, part who the hell knows what, and his pretty little curls had the tendency to get unruly. Homer grumbled at me in agreement. He had a crush on the lady who ran the groomers. I'd drop him off before work, and he'd follow her around, mooning after her with his dopey brown eyes for the day.

My phone dinged from somewhere, and I went digging for it, finding it between the couch cushions.

Marley: We need some ground rules if we're still doing this thing.

I laughed. "Women, am I right, Homes?" His tail tapped out a beat against the armrest.

Me: Whatever pleases m'lady.

I could hear her rolling her eyes across town.

Marley: I'm serious. What are we doing here? How are we going to pretend to be together for an entire semester? Are we supposed to make out on lunch duty?
Me: We should definitely do that.

The dots appeared, signaling she was replying, and then disappeared again. They did twice more before my phone rang.

"Hey, girlfriend," I answered cheerfully.

"What are we doing, Jake? This is stupid." Her voice was husky, grumpy. A unique combination that I apparently found very attractive.

"What's stupid?"

"This scheme. We're adults. Adults don't pretend to be in a relationship."

"You're operating on the assumption that there's a standard adulthood that we all subscribe to. You think it's grown-up to go tattling to the boss over a coworker relationship? Is it grown-up to throw your weight around and steal some other team's practice field? We're all just overgrown teenagers running around trying to be happy."

There was silence for a beat on her end. "That's oddly deep."

"What can I say? I'm a deep guy."

"No, you're not."

"I can have deep thoughts," I argued. "What's the real problem here, Mars?"

She sighed. "I thought I'd have it figured out by now."

"It?" I knew what she meant, but I wanted her to talk it through.

"Life. Job. Relationship. I never thought I'd be in this situation this close to forty. I'm supposed to know what I'm doing by now."

I could tell she regretted the confession and the vulnerability it exposed.

155

"You feel like you're failing?" I asked, sneaking the question in before she could rebuild the walls.

She was quiet and then, "Yeah. Over and over and over again. Jobs. Relationships. Personal accomplishments. It's like I missed the day in school when they told us how to be an adult."

"I'm gonna throw something out here that's probably going to melt your mind. Are you ready?" I asked, stroking a hand over Homer's silky ear.

"Hang on—let me get a notebook and a pen," she said dryly. Man, I was so into her.

"What if none of those things were right for you?"

"What if *I* wasn't right for any of those things?" she shot back.

"What's the difference? If a job or a guy didn't fit you or you didn't fit them, the problem's the same. The fit was wrong."

"No. It's not. Because if it's not them, it's gotta be me. Maybe I don't fit anywhere. Ugh. This is stupid. I'm stupid. I don't know why I called."

"Because you wanted to talk. So talk, Mars. There's no judgment here. You think I've got my shit together? I've got my feet up on a three-week-old box of pizza. And it just moved on its own. I've never been in a relationship. I've had a few one-night stands that extended into a week or maybe a month. But I've never met a girl's parents. Hell, I've never even bought a woman I wasn't related to a Christmas present."

"You ever think that maybe you just don't want that?" Marley suggested. I imagined her lying on her bed, staring up at the ceiling, kicking one of those nice long legs up.

"I didn't. Now I'm not so sure." I glanced around my grandmother's living room—*my* living room. Maybe it was her ghost that was pushing these new, weird feelings at me. She wanted her grandbabies settled, married, pumping out their own babies and organizing car pools and bake sales.

"Do you feel like you're missing out?" she asked.

Did I? "I don't know. Kinda. But I don't know where it's coming from."

"I feel the same way," she admitted. "But now I'm starting to wonder if I'm just meant to bounce from job to job, boring monogamous relationship to boring monogamous relationship."

"Sweetheart, our monogamous relationship might be fake, but I can guarantee you it won't be boring."

She laughed softly, and it made me smile.

"Back to this fake relationship," she said. "What does it entail?"

"I don't know. What does a real relationship involve?" I asked, picking up a tennis ball that I used to work out shoulder kinks and tossing it in the air. Homer eyed it lazily.

"Dates. Dinner. Movies. Lazy Sundays. Spending time together."

"Sex?" I asked.

"Usually."

"Cool. Sign me up for that."

"We're not having sex in a fake relationship, Jake," she groaned.

I tossed the ball up again and caught it one-handed. "Would it matter if I told you that I actually like you?"

"Why wouldn't you? I'm a catch." The sarcasm was strong with this one. "I think we're complicating things enough with a scheme that we have to perpetuate until the holidays. Let's not add a bigger mess to it," she continued.

I let my gaze travel the perimeter of the living room. Speaking of messes. Maybe it was time I stopped living like I was a transient teenager.

"Let's keep it simple then. Friends who occasionally have to hold hands and make out in public," I suggested.

"That sounds…acceptable."

"Good. We got a deal? I'll give you some pointers on coaching and teaching. You be my relationship guru. And we hang out."

"You're not going to throw me over for Amie Jo again, are you?" She said it lightly like it was a joke, but there was something serious in her tone.

The tennis ball nailed me in the forehead, and Homer grumbled when it bounced onto his belly. "Throw you over for Amie Jo? When did that ever happen?" I demanded, doing a quick history search in my memory banks.

"Never mind. Got any actionable words of wisdom when it comes to coaching?" she asked, changing the subject. "I can't for the life of me figure out how to get them to get along."

I laughed. "Well, you did kinda get them at the worst possible time for a team or a coach."

"What do you mean by that?"

"They didn't tell you?" I knew the district had been in a hurry to fill the position, but I didn't think they'd intentionally leave something like that out. I mean, a new coach deserved a heads-up.

"Tell me what?"

I could hear the dread in her voice.

"Their old head coach died of a heart attack halfway through the season last year."

She was quiet for a moment. "Eesh. I had no idea."

"He died during a game," I added.

"That's horrible!"

"An away game. They watched him turn blue and quit breathing on the sidelines and then had to ride home with just the bus driver because their assistant coach went to the hospital with the head coach."

"Are you fucking kidding me?"

"And if that wasn't traumatizing enough, one of the team moms took over coaching for the rest of the season, and she went all Hitler on the team. Dividing them right down the middle into favorites and undesirables."

"That's beyond horrible," she said. "But it's also making me feel a little better. I thought I was the problem."

"Mars, believe me, you ain't even half that team's problem."

She blew out a breath.

"So how do I undo an entire season of disaster that happened before I got here?"

"One practice, one game at a time," I suggested.

Marley sighed. "Thanks for getting me up to speed. I can't believe no one mentioned this before. This is Culpepper. There are no secrets."

"Well, now you know. Besides, that was last school year. We have the attention span of mosquitos."

"Everyone still remembers our Homecoming," she pointed out.

"Well, that was worth remembering."

She groaned. I found it oddly endearing that the event that she felt some level of guilt over was the event that made her a town hero.

She yawned into the phone. "Look, the Airbnb guy just got out of the bathroom. I'm going to take a shower."

"Airbnb guy?" I asked, intrigued.

"It's a long story. Goodnight, Jake."

"Night, Mars. Sweet dreams."

CHAPTER 27

Marley

I was standing there in front of my entire senior class wondering how in the hell I'd left home without pants while trying to cover my nether regions with my biology binder when I was rescued by a distant ringing.

"'Lo?" I breathed into my phone.

"Up and at 'em, girlfriend."

"Jake?" I sat up in bed feeling a combination of relief at knowing I had not just been naked in front of half of Culpepper and annoyance at his chipper tone.

"That's me, baby. Come on. Your life lessons start right now. Get dressed. Running clothes. Meet me outside."

"You're here?" I was horrified. I flew to the window and yanked back the curtains. And there in his shirtless glory stood Jake Weston on my parents' front lawn.

"Cute jammies. Hurry up, peaches. I ain't got all day."

"It's 5:30 in the morning."

"And if you try to crawl back into that bed, I'm going to ring the damn doorbell and wake up your whole house."

My parents' first Airbnb guest would probably protest with a bad review. Byron from Seattle. He had glasses and a briefcase and began every sentence with "I don't know if you know this, but…"

"I hate you," I told Jake.

"Get your ass down here."

I hung up and spent thirty seconds debating whether or not to crawl back into bed before dragging on a pair of clean shorts, a sports bra, tank, and sneakers. I slothed my way out of the house to where Jake was stretching his really spectacular quads.

"What are you doing here?"

"Meeting my girlfriend for an early run," he said as if it was obvious.

"How is torturing me like this going to keep She Who Shall Not Be Named at bay?" I yawned.

"You'll see. Besides, your health should be your number one priority. If you're gonna coach a team of girls in a sport that's ninety percent running, shouldn't you know how?"

"I know how. Move legs. Stop breathing. Puke. Repeat." I was hilarious at the ass crack of dawn.

"Come on, Mars. I'll go easy on you the first time."

Oh, that devil may-care grin. I might have been mostly asleep, but even I wasn't fully conscious, that bad boy smile was lethal.

"Whatever. Just tell me what to do," I said pretending not to be enthralled with those really nice muscles peeking out of his shorts. V cuts, I believe those delectable lines were called.

"Submissive. I like it," he teased, jogging in place.

"You're disgusting."

"We're gonna warm up for ten. A nice light jog," he said, jerking his head toward the sidewalk. "Come on, pretty girl."

I was annoyed by the warm appreciation that coated my stomach like honey at the nickname.

Following him down the sidewalk in the predawn light wasn't the worst early morning experience I'd had. His legs chugged along in front of me hypnotically. The muscles in his back bunched and tightened. Too bad my lungs were burning as if I'd just inhaled ammonia.

"I can hear you puffing like a chain-smoker." He slowed his pace until I gasped my way to his side. "Lesson One: The Breath."

"Teach me, Obi-Wan," I wheezed, mustering the energy for an eye roll.

He shoulder-checked me, and I tripped, landing in Mr. and Mrs. Angstadt's pink flamingo flower bed in their front yard. I took a beak to the gut and made one hell of a racket.

"Christ, Cicero. You're a freaking disaster," Jake snickered. He pulled me to my feet.

"You pushed me, you jackass."

"As I was saying, the breath is important because if you don't have that, you ain't got nothing."

"Did you ever think of teaching English?" I asked, righting a dented flamingo.

"Shut up and run."

We took off again slowly. The beak break had been good for my breath. I had some now.

"Good girl. Now, breathe in for three steps. Nice and steady. And out. In for three. Out for two. This is called rhythmic breathing."

Sucking and gasping, I survived his thorough scientific explanation on footfalls, breath, and stabilizing core muscles on the exhale. We navigated a few more blocks, and I was moderately pleased when the side stitch never made it beyond a vague nagging in my right side.

He was sweating, little beads that formed on his chest and shoulders before melding together in sexy little salt rivers. I had a good sweat on too, and I hated to admit it, but I felt...okay.

We turned back onto my parents' block.

"Three houses to go. Sprint it out," he said, not even remotely winded.

Mainly just to save face, I let my legs unspool and listened to the whistle of wind in my ears as I eked out a respectable medium speed. I arrived at my parents' walkway several steps behind him and bent at the waist to gulp in air.

"Don't do that," Jake told me, pulling me up. "Walk it off. Let your heart rate come down naturally. Don't ask it to come to a screeching halt."

Hands on hips, I paced the sidewalk, trying to control my breathing. I'd gone through the couch-to-5K program about four times in the past seven or eight years. Well, technically I'd never actually finished it. Or run a 5k, come to think of it. But every once in a while, I tried to talk myself into becoming a runner.

However, the torturous misery of it guaranteed my failure. But this hadn't been awful. I felt awake. And maybe just a little bit alive. The birds in the maple tree were chattering about something, and the sky was getting lighter.

"Is that a smile?" Jake asked, amused.

I used the hem of my tank to mop at the sweat that was stinging my eyes. "Okay. So maybe it wasn't horrible."

He grinned at me, and my heart rate that had started to slow skyrocketed again. Jake held up a hand, and I slapped it. But his fingers closed around mine.

"Nice job, Mars." He was pulling me in, reeling me like a fish. My legs were too jelly-like to fight it.

"What are you doing?"

"I'm congratulating you," he said.

We were standing toe-to-toe, our bodies not quite touching. There was a buzz between us. Blood thrumming through primed veins. Awareness shimmered on my skin, mingling with the sweat. I wanted him to touch me, to kiss me. But…

"Jake. This is fake," I said quietly. It was more of a reminder to myself. I didn't want to get swept up in this and forget that all of this was only temporary. Only pretend.

He traced a thumb over my lower lip. "Hmm."

"Jake. Focus."

"I'm very focused."

"You don't have to put on a show at six in the morning," I told him. "Let's not complicate things."

"Mars, I don't know if you know this about me, but I really like complicated."

"Why is it that everything that comes out of your mouth sounds like a come-on?"

"It's a gift."

I shook my head and took a step back. "You're a lot to handle before dawn."

He grinned. "Baby, don't I know it."

My running shorts spontaneously combusted.

"Now, be a good girl and make yourself a protein-rich breakfast. I'll see you at school," he said.

"Thanks for the run," I said.

"Anytime, Mars. Anytime."

I turned toward the house and whooped when he slapped me on the ass.

"Later, pretty girl."

I shook my head and watched him lope off. He raised his hand in front of the mausoleum next door. "Morning, Amie Jo," he called.

And there she was in pink silk pajamas, gaping after him with a tiny espresso cup in her hand. The swan waddled past on her side of the fence.

We both watched Jake's retreating figure until he disappeared into the morning shadows. Amie Jo and I made uneasy eye contact for a long minute before I turned and went inside.

CHAPTER 28

Marley

Mars,

Now that you're contractually obligated to be my girlfriend, I decided to thoughtfully provide you with a Honey Do list. Quit whining. You need this.

1. Daily run. Thirty minutes minimum. I'm happy to run with you when I can and show off my superior prowess. Helpful Hack: Do it in the morning like we did today and get it out of the way so you're not dreading it and making excuses. Trust me you'll feel better.

2. Teaching. The walls have eyes at Culpepper Junior/Senior High. And those eyes are reporting that you're a disinterested mess in the gym. Despite what the administration may have told you upon your hiring, you are there to do more than just make sure no one gets injured and sues the district.

The most important thing about teaching is breaking through the anti-adult barrier that exists in every teenager's brain. They're smarter than they look. Don't pander. Don't try to be their friend. Do remember their names and use them. Don't just yell at them.

Give unexpected compliments like, "Nice back

handspring into a roundoff, Julio." Or "You really bounced back from impaling yourself on that hurdle, Tina."

Your job is to engage them. Get them to focus on what's happening in class. Stretch out their phone-wielding hunchback posture. Give them the time and space to move and be present. Find ways to get them to want to do that.

Please see the helpful video links in the appendix.

3. Coaching. This is like teaching, only in more concentrated doses. You have a group of human beings who are trying to get better at something specific. Help them get better without making them feel like shit. Again. Names. Compliments. Attention. Those are more important than imparting the fine art of whatever the hell soccer is. Kicking and falling down? Whatever.

The secret to being a good coach is figuring out how to make your team function like a—you guessed it—team. It should be easy, right? They all like the same activity: soccer. They all have the same goal: winning. Wrong! A high school sports team, especially one of the female variety, is a wartime microcosm of popularity and belonging. These people have been programmed to think that there can be only one prom queen or only one dreamy teenage boyfriend. (Side Note: Only in the graduating class of 1998 did that prove to be true. It was me. Dreamy teenage boyfriend, not prom queen.)

You have to use your powers to unite them. Some coaches feel like their teams should be united against them, but that's when you wake up with a jockstrap dipped in itching powder. Find a way to force them to get along long enough for them to realize they like each other. I could tell you a couple of ways to do it, but it's more character-building to figure it out yourself.

Yours Romantically,
Jake

CHAPTER 29

Jake

Dear Jake,

Thank you for your very thoughtful, humble take on how to be better, like you. I appreciate the time you took complimenting yourself. Someday, I hope to be as blindingly confident in my awesomeness as you are in yours.

Since you were so helpful with your 8,000-item list on ways for me to improve, I thought I'd return the favor and give you some basic ground rules of relationships.

1. Don't honku your partner's breasts in public. It's never appropriate and rarely as funny as you think it will be.

2. Do work to memorize the important information about your partner as quickly as possible:

A. First and last name. Bonus points for middle.

B. Birth date.

C. Current pets, names.

D. Personal preferences in the following areas: bed, dishwasher loading, movies and TV viewing, restaurants/ diet (don't take a lactose intolerant person out for ice cream before sex), politics, relationship guidelines (e.g., Are stripper boobs touching your face considered cheating or just sad?).

3. Do learn to show an interest in the words that come out of her mouth. You will earn a stupid amount of bonus points for using a callback and asking for an update on that issue at work last Tuesday involving the bad chicken salad and Keith from accounting.

4. Learn the difference between venting and asking for advice. Hint: We're very rarely asking for advice.

5. Don't stop your pursuit of physical perfection just because you've landed the future Mrs. Weston. She'll still deserve your six-pack abs and hypnotic pec dance even after you've been married for twelve years. Put down the cheesesteak. Do it for the children, Jake!

Let's start here and work our way up to things like discussing whose family to spend the holidays with (answer: whoever has the best food) and when flowers are appropriate (answer: always, but the best ones are no reason flowers).

Yours Contractually,
Marley

CHAPTER 30

Marley

September

Inhale. Exhale," I gasped to myself as my feet carried me in a slow jog toward the empty practice field. Running and I were still not friends, but if I was being totally honest, the relationship was a smidge less contentious than it had been at the beginning of the week.

Stupid sexy Jake being right about form and breathing and stuff. He was an annoying know-it-all.

I glanced at the screen of my phone. Fifteen minutes left. Crap on a damn cracker, this was the longest forty minutes of my life. Had time stopped? Was my phone's clock broken?

Running was a lot less fun when shirtless, sweaty Jake wasn't with me. It gave me too much time to think. I'd had lunch with guidance counselor Andrea again today and asked her opinion on the whole coaching-a-traumatized-team thing. I still couldn't believe Floyd or one of the girls or even Vicky hadn't thought to mention that the last coach died during a game and that the substitute coach had been the devil incarnate. Probably some woman working her way through old high school trauma...only not in a healthy way like *I* was doing.

Andrea seemed to think I could make things work with the

team. I just had to tackle the biggest problem—the bad relationships on the team—and everything else would fall into place.

A slow, rhythmic thunking distracted me from my labored breathing. I used the hem of my T-shirt to wipe the sweat out of my eyes. There was a kickboard between the soccer field and the baseball field with a yellow soccer goal painted on it. In front of it, a spritely girl juked, jived, and kicked the shit out of a soccer ball. She pegged the board in the lower left corner, a perfect shot that would challenge the best goalkeeper.

I came to a screeching halt. Okay, maybe not screeching. More like meandering to a stop.

She faked left, nudged the ball right, and lined up another shot. It curved gracefully into the upper right corner.

"What's your name?" I called.

She eyed me suspiciously between the hoop in her eyebrow and the stud in her nose. "Morticia."

Cautiously, I approached. "Har. Super funny. I'm serious. What's your name?"

"I wasn't doing anything wrong," she said stubbornly.

"Uh, you were doing something super right, and now I'm trying to recruit you."

"Into what? A cult?"

In her black cargo pants, combat boots, and gray hoodie—it was almost 80 freaking degrees still—she already looked like she belonged in one of the underground bunker ones.

"My soccer team."

"Aren't you a little old to be playing soccer? Shouldn't you be worried about breaking a hip or something?"

Sometimes I really hated kids.

"I'm the girls' team head coach. We could use your feet."

"Not interested." She turned back to the ball and kicked it. It sailed up in a graceful arc, pegging the board in the upper right corner like a postage stamp. "I'm not really a team person."

"What would it take to make you interested?" Lord, now I sounded like my father. "In joining the team," I added hastily.

"I guess you haven't heard about me yet," she said, her face devoid of any emotion. But I saw something simmering in those bright green eyes.

"Look, Morticia, I don't care if you spent last semester clubbing baby seals." That was a lie. I wouldn't feel great about bringing a seal clubber onto the team. But at this point I was desperate. We'd lost our second game of the season by a respectable four goals. Lisabeth called all of the midfielders dumbass hick bitches, and the boys' team had mooned us when we left the stadium. "I'm interested in what you're doing this semester."

"I can't play," she said, rolling the ball up onto the toe of her boot and flicking it into the air. She caught it with her knee.

"Why not?"

"First of all, you're a complete stranger. How do I even know you're a coach? You could be some sweaty creeper trying to lure me into a van."

"It's a hatchback actually."

I saw a glimmer of humor in her eyes.

"Secondly, team sports cost money. I don't have any."

I warmed up my argument. "If the only thing standing in your way of joining the team is money and not an outstanding warrant or the fact that you're in the witness relocation program, then I have several solutions."

"Don't need your charity." She was freaking juggling the ball back and forth from foot to thigh. I needed this girl and wasn't above groveling.

"No, you don't. But I need you and your magic feet."

With a clean nudge, she sent the ball sailing at me. I trapped it with my foot and thanked God when I didn't fall on my face. I scooped it up and managed a back and forth between my knees before awkwardly knocking it back in her direction.

She took it from foot to knee to forehead. "Look, lady—"

"Coach," I interjected.

She stopped, caught the ball. "I just moved here. I live in a foster home with an overworked foster mother who's too busy working two jobs and being responsible for five kids to run me to practice and games. Happy?"

"Where do you live?"

She gave me a "not happening" look.

"I can give you a ride."

"You're working really hard for a stranger trying to convince me to get into her kidnapping hatchback."

"I have candy."

"They let you be responsible for students?" she asked with the ghost of a smile playing around her bare lips.

"They were desperate. But they're starting to really appreciate my awesomeness." *Lies!*

She was quiet for a minute, her teeth working her bottom lip.

"Look, I can drive you to and from stuff. I have no life. We're coming off of six years of losing seasons, and we're off to a stellar shutout start. You could help. Uniform's free. You'll just need cleats, and I'm sure we can figure something out there."

"I don't like charity," she repeated.

"I don't blame you. But look at it this way, you'd be doing me a favor. I have a lot to prove because I think the boys' coach is a misogynistic wiener and no one expects much of me."

She swiped the back of her hand under her nose. "No one expects much from me either."

"Maybe we can surprise them. Together. With the candy in my kidnapper van."

She sighed.

"Look, just come to practice tomorrow. Three thirty right here. See what you think. We're enthusiastically not good. But you might have fun."

"I don't like mean girls," she warned me.

I mentally worked out a plan to have Lisabeth Hooper kidnapped.

"Good thing your BFF the coach has the power to make mean girls run until they throw up."

"Hmm."

"Think about it," I told her. "Three thirty tomorrow. Free candy."

She nodded and bounced the ball on the grass. "Libby, by the way."

"Nice to meet you, Libby. I'm Coach Cicero. You'll probably see me lurking around the gym, too."

"Not creepy at all," she said, that sort-of smile still hovering.

I decided to leave before I got down on my knees and begged, terrifying her into cyber school or something.

"See you around." I gave her a wave and with great reluctance jogged back to the road. I had fifteen more minutes to go on this torture run, and I was going to spend it praying that Libby would show up tomorrow.

CHAPTER 31

Marley

What's this?" Dad asked that night, his already high-pitched voice cracking in eager anticipation as he lifted the lid on the slow cooker.

"Pork roast," I told him, checking the broccoli roasting in the oven.

My tiptoe onto the scale this morning revealed a mind-boggling, four-pound weight loss. My first not credited to the stomach flu or bad hangover in years. Not since I did that low-carb, lettuce and carrot diet for my coworker's destination wedding five years ago had I seen a purposeful drop like this.

Who knew chasing after a shirtless bad boy hunk in the predawn hours could be such great exercise? Oh, right. Literally everyone.

I was feeling…gosh, what was that warm, bright feeling in my chest? Indigestion? No. It was more glowy, less burny. Was that *hope*? It had been so long since I'd felt it, I didn't even recognize it. I'd lived the last decade or so in constant fear of losing jobs, health insurance, the security of a relationship. I'd forgotten what it felt like to feel hopeful about the future.

Dad poked his head in the pantry and pulled out a bottle of wine. He waggled it at me. "You look like you're in a good mood," he squawked. "Should we celebrate?"

"Why not?" I said, pulling down two dusty wineglasses from the cabinet. My parents' kitchen had been updated once. In the early eighties when Zinnia and I were rambunctious toddlers. The backsplash was a yellow-and-orange tile mosaic that absolutely did not match the brown Formica countertops. But as displeasing to the eyes as it was, it was the place I felt most at home.

Dad pulled the cork out with an enthusiastic pop and poured to the rim. I laughed and sipped without picking the glass up so as not to spill it.

"Oh, hello." Byron the guest poked his head into the kitchen. He was close to seven feet tall and very, very pale. His hair was the color and texture of straw. It stuck out at odd angles, at least from what I could see without breaking my neck. His glasses were red, and his pants were three inches too short.

"Hey there, Byron! How's your stay?" my dad squeaked.

I couldn't imagine this scarecrow of a man was very comfortable in Zinnia's double bed. His legs probably hung off the mattress up to the knee.

"It's quite lovely. Thank you." He stared pointedly at the slow cooker. We all did.

"Would you like to join us for dinner?" I offered.

"Oh, I couldn't possibly intrude," he said, now eyeing the bottle of wine. I recognized that look. Hope.

"It's no problem," I told him.

———

My parents shoveled the pork roast and vegetables into their faces as if their last meal had been Styrofoam six days ago. Apparently none of their retirement hobbies had translated into any skills in the kitchen.

Byron ate daintily with a fork in one hand and knife in the other, looking up every bite to gaze lovingly around the table.

"So, Marley," Dad said around a mouthful of broccoli. "How's the soccer team coming?"

"We're doing okay. We still have no offense to speak of, but I think I might have solved that problem this afternoon."

"Did you go Tonya Harding on the opposing team's offensive line?" Mom asked.

"No. But I did find a ringer. Fingers crossed she shows up tomorrow."

Byron immediately crossed his pinky and ring fingers and smiled broadly.

"Good for you," Mom said. "Now, when were you going to tell us that you're dating Jake Weston?"

I choked on my wine. Tears glassed over my eyes as the merlot burned its way into my lungs.

"And for God's sake," my mother plowed on as she shoveled more pork onto her plate, "why didn't you at least invite him in for breakfast this morning?"

"I, er…" I couldn't tell them the truth. Neither one of them could keep a secret. They'd practically handed Zinnia and me itemized inventories of our Christmas presents in November because they were too excited to keep quiet. By the time Christmas Day rolled around, the wrapping was purely ceremonial.

Byron was stuffing dainty bites of pork into his mouth and watching the conversation like a tennis match.

"Jake Weston?" Dad asked. "Is he the one with the mustache or the one who covers the rust spots on his Volvo with NPR bumper stickers?"

"Neither," my mother said. "He's the one who got caught making out with a substitute teacher in the darkroom his junior year."

"He's the cross-country coach, Dad," I said, pointedly reminding them that some of us grew up. "And history teacher."

"Oh. Who's the guy with the Volvo?" he asked.

My parents and Byron, weirdly enough, insisted on handling cleanup. So I packed up a dish of leftovers for lunch tomorrow and headed upstairs to work my way through Jake's Coaching Appendix videos and some of the volumes of team mentality that my sister had sent in drips and trickles since the weekend.

Before I could boot up my laptop, my phone rang.

Zinnia. I hated the fact that just my sister's name on my screen dulled the good feelings that had bloomed inside me.

I accepted the call, and Zinnia's beautiful face filled the screen. She wore her dark hair long and straight in a glossy curtain. Her lips were painted a shade of ruby that I could never in a million years pull off. Her thick eyebrows were waxed and groomed into perfection.

"Hey, sis," she said.

"Hey, Zin. How's life?"

She gestured around her, and I could see that she was still in her office. The Washington, D.C., skyline stretched on behind her through the windows of her thirteenth-floor corner office. "Considering I feel like I haven't left this place in three weeks, good. Rumor has it my husband and children are still alive. How's Culpepper? Are you settling in?"

"Everything's fine," I told her. I hated giving Zinnia the details of my day. It all seemed so trivial compared to what she spent her time doing. "Save any war-torn orphans lately?" I asked.

"Ha. Some. I hear you and Jake Weston just signed a relationship contract."

I flopped down on the bed. "How in the hell did you hear that?"

"The Culpepper grapevine is as deep as it is wide," she laughed. "So what's that all about?" It dented my feelings just a bit to know that Zinnia knew me well enough to know that me and Jake dating was a little too good to be true. But at least she could keep a secret.

"It was kind of an accident. There was some drama with the boys' soccer coach and another teacher, and Jake got involved, and one thing led to another, and we told the administration that we're kinda sorta dating."

"Only you, Marley," Zinnia laughed.

Yeah. Only me.

Zinnia was my older sister. By nine months. However, her unfair brainiac advantage and maturity had leapfrogged her ahead of me in school in the fourth grade. As much as it had chafed, it had also been a relief. Not having to share the same playing field with her. Not comparing apples to apples.

"Is he still gorgeous?" she asked.

"Oh my God. Take senior year Jake and multiply him times one thousand. Stubble. Tattoos. More muscles."

Zinnia spooned up something exotic from a takeout container and chewed thoughtfully. "I'm going to need some photographic proof," she decided.

"I'll try to snap a picture of him running shirtless," I promised.

"You are a marvel, sister dear," she said.

"That's what I keep telling people. So how's Ralph? Still surgery-ing his ass off?"

Conversations with my sister were odd. I didn't want to share the pitiful details of my life with her, and she didn't seem to like talking about how amazing her life was to me. Presumably because she didn't want me to feel worse about myself.

"Darling Ralph has very little ass to lose," Zinnia said fondly. Her husband was a genius and a talented surgeon. But he had the build of a two-by-four.

Byron poked his gawky head into my room. "Thank you

again for dinner," he said with a toothy smile. "I'll keep my fingers crossed for your ringer."

"Thanks, Byron," I said, getting up and closing the door.

"Uh, who was that?" Zinnia demanded.

"Oh, your room is now an Airbnb," I told her.

CHAPTER 32

Marley

Was there anything sexier than a shirtless man with a doofy dog? I pondered that thought while Jake and I muscled our way through another early morning run. Homer, the goldendoodle something or other, was lazy and grumbly and kept stopping to pretend to pee. I admired his strategy.

When we got back to my parents' house, I invited them both in for breakfast and got to see the legendary Jake Weston almost swallow his tongue.

"Breakfast? With your parents?" he choked.

"Yeah, probably. And Byron. He's staying another night."

"Mars, I can't meet your parents like this." He spread his arms wide and forced me to take in his godlike proportions.

"Are you nervous?" I laughed.

Homer flopped against my leg and slid down to the ground on a groan.

"Nervous? Me? Ha."

"You look like you're going to throw up. They're just regular people. Mostly."

"I wasn't kidding when I told you I've never met a girl's parents before," he said, swiping his hand over his mouth. "I'm not gonna do it like this."

The disappointment was swift, surprising, and totally

uncalled for. "Oh. Yeah. I guess it would make more sense for you to give a real girlfriend the honor of your meet-the-parents virginity," I said, leaning over to scruff Homer's belly.

"No, dummy. I mean I *should* meet your parents. But even I know it isn't smart to show up at the breakfast table in just shorts and say, 'What's up? Can my dog have some bacon?'"

"That's quite considerate of you," I said, biting my lip to keep the smile from making my eyes disappear.

"I'm serious, Mars. I wanna do this right. I'm giving you good advice. I need you to do the same for me. Introducing your parents to me when it would look more like I just spent the night getting sweaty with their daughter and then expecting free breakfast? Even I know that ain't good."

"But you *do* want to meet them?" I pressed.

"Hell yeah, I do. They're your parents. I assume you like them? They're important to you?"

I nodded.

"Cool. Then let me know when and where and how to prepare for it."

"Okay," I said, feeling my mouth stretching into a smile.

Before I knew it, he was leaning in and pressing a kiss to my salty cheek. "See you at school, pretty girl," he said.

"Bye, Jake."

He pulled the reluctant Homer to his feet, and I watched them jog off.

————

Gym classes should have been reasonably not horrible. The girls were on a field hockey kick while the guys played flag football. All Floyd and I had to do was divvy up teams and make sure no one got too hurt.

Unfortunately for all of us, Rachel, the quiet junior varsity forward from my team, had the misfortune of being in class with Lisabeth, the mean big girl from the varsity team.

Lisabeth was like a bull shark lurking in the shallows with her rows of nasty teeth and her bad sharky attitude. I was watching as Rachel made a breakaway toward the hockey goal. And Lisabeth, running faster than I'd ever seen her do at practice, thundered in and slashed the girl right across the shins with her stick. Rachel crumpled to the ground like a piece of tissue paper. Lisabeth's cronies, three girls with teased hair and too much bronzer, nearly fell over laughing.

I was so fucking done with this.

"Enough!" The rage gave my voice a boost, and not only did the hockey game stop, the flag football game came to a screeching halt in the middle of a touchdown run.

I stalked onto the field. "Rachel? Are you okay?" I asked in a quieter, calmer tone of voice.

"I'm fine," she whispered, wincing.

"Angelika, can you help Rachel to the nurse to get some ice?" I asked nicely.

Angelika nodded, looking nervous. "Sure."

"Great. You," I said, pointing at Lisabeth, feeling the rage bubble back to life.

She shot me a "what are you going to do about it" look, and I gave myself a satisfying second to envision me making her eat her hockey stick.

"Everything good, Cicero?" Floyd asked nervously behind me.

"Can you watch the hockey game for me?" I asked him without looking away from Lisabeth's smug face.

"Sure. Yeah."

"Great. Let's go, Hooper."

"Where are we going?" she sassed.

"To have a little chat."

Under a full head of steam, I marched Lisabeth into my locker room office. "What's your problem now, Coach?" she asked, examining her fingernails like she was bored.

But she underestimated me. I had experience dealing with girls like her at that age and every other age.

"That's funny. I was going to ask you the same thing. See, I'm new here. I don't have the benefit of knowing you for your entire high school career. So let me tell you what I see."

"Goody," she said with an eye roll.

"I see an entitled, insecure bully trying to make herself feel good by tearing other people down."

"You can't talk to me that way. It's against the anti-bullying policy," she snapped, her face turning crimson.

"Oh, and what's hitting someone with a hockey stick?"

"An accident. She got in my way. I was going for the ball."

"I don't get it. Do your parents fall for this? Your teachers? Or are they all just biting their nails and clinging to the hope that maybe you'll get into college and move far, far away and make a bunch of strangers miserable?"

Lisabeth was gaping at me. "*Excuse* me?"

"You heard me. Do you think people like you because you're an emotional teenage terrorist? Do you think that makes you popular? Worthy? Do you think whispering mean little lies to people makes you better than them? Because let me tell you what it actually makes you. Pathetic. And I've seen a hundred girls like you graduate and go out into the real world and get chewed up and spit back out."

Okay, that part wasn't necessarily true. Some of them married Cadillac dealership owners and lived happily ever after in their mansions.

"You can't talk to me like this. I'll go to the school board."

"And what? Get me fired from my temporary job? Or is this finally the excuse that all your teachers and your so-called

183

friends have been waiting for? A reason to finally take away your power. What would you be if you weren't popular? What do you have left as a human being?"

"I have my friends!"

"You have people you gossip about behind their backs. You know, the acoustics in here are really good. What do you think Morgan W. would think about you telling the bronzer triplets that you think she's a slut for going to second base with the guy you have a crush on?"

"You're a shitty coach and an even shittier teacher!"

"Ooh. Now you're swearing at me, and I feel kind of threatened," I said, crossing my arms. "Do you know where you'll be in five years? Sitting in a divorce lawyer's office because your fifty-thousand-dollar wedding was the beginning of the end to some poor idiot who thought he loved you. But you can't hide mean forever. And that's what you are. A sad, mean girl whose only joy in life comes from inflicting misery on others. I feel sorry for you."

"I fucking hate you!"

"Yeah, the truth hurts. And guess what? I don't care if you were the high scorer last year. You're off my team. I don't have room for bullies."

"My mom is going to sue you and ruin your life," she shrieked.

Culpepper must have turned into a litigious community. This was the second time I'd been threatened with a lawsuit. But it was amazing how freeing it was to have nothing to lose.

"She can do that. As soon as you report to the principal's office."

"I'll tell everyone that you dyed the boys' team red!"

I shrugged even though her threat made me uneasy. "Your word against mine, and I'm feeling pretty lucky today. Besides, you're the one acting like a vindictive jerk chasing down a sophomore during gym class. I'm just the concerned coach and teacher looking out for my students."

"I HATE YOU, you crazy bitch!"

"Lisabeth, this is your wake-up call. It's not too late for you to be a better person."

"Fuck. You. You're just jealous because you're old and ugly."

Well, at least I tried.

I whistled as I followed her down the hall to the principal's office.

———

"What steaming hot mess did you bring me?" Principal Eccles asked, thumbing open a bottle of aspirin.

"Lisabeth Hooper," I said.

The principal eyed me as she shoved the aspirin back in the bottle and swapped it for a prescription migraine medicine.

"What did our lovely Ms. Hooper do?" she asked.

"Other than being just a shitty human being?" I was still mad. Really mad.

Eccles washed down a tablet with water. "This is where I'm supposed to tell you that teaching is not an opportunity for you to right the wrongs of your teen years. That you can't insert yourself into student politics and hierarchies because it's a more valuable learning experience when they live through it themselves."

"I'm not so sure that Rachel will survive Lisabeth," I interjected. "Lisabeth hit her with a hockey stick as hard as she could. On purpose. If her tibias aren't fractured, I'll be surprised."

"This is me insisting that it's imperative that students figure out their own way through social situations, the good and the bad," Principal Eccles said, pinching the bridge of her nose. "And this is also the part where I encourage you to understand that many students who exhibit negative behavior, including bullying and general assholery, are struggling with serious issues that we may not be privy to."

"Look. I know I'm new to all of this. But I've been Rachel, and I've known Lisabeths. And sometimes an asshole is just as asshole."

Principal Eccles looked toward the closed door and sighed. "Off the record, Lisabeth Hooper is an entitled asshole, and none of the staff and faculty can stand her. Her mother, by all accounts, was the same kind of nightmare. And still is."

Relief coursed through me.

"I can't do much about having her in my class. But I don't want her on my team."

"Are you prepared for the fallout of punishing her? It'll be ugly."

"Principal Eccles, I'm only here for the semester. Who better to deal with this than someone who doesn't have to worry about any long-term effects?"

CHAPTER 33

Marley

I felt like a teenager waiting for her prom date to show up, worrying that she was going to be stood up.

"Would you stop pacing?" Vicky demanded from her vantage point on the practice field bleachers. The team was running a warm-up lap around the field, and I was getting ready to start gnawing on my fingernails like an animal caught in a trap. "You're making me anxious, and I don't like to be anxious without my medication."

Vicky's medication was as many rum and Cokes as a bartender could mix during happy hour.

"What if she doesn't show? I just kicked the only chance we had at scoring a single goal this season off the team, and if Libby doesn't show, how am I not going to hold that against her and fail her in gym?"

"Desperation is not a good color on you," she said, stuffing her hands into the pocket of her hooded sweatshirt. In true Pennsylvania fashion, summer had abandoned us abruptly and without warning.

"Oh my God. There she is!" I grabbed Vicky's arm and squeezed as a dark head bobbed up the steps in our direction.

"She could be David Beckham's twin," Vicky said dryly.

"Just you wait," I said smugly. "I didn't screw this up."

Libby approached slowly, her hands drawn up into the sleeves of her no-brand, off-black sweatshirt.

"Morticia," I said, giving her a nod.

"Potential kidnapper."

"This is Vicky, my assistant coach," I said.

"'Sup?" Vicky said, cracking her gum.

"Hey."

"So you wanna practice?" I asked, trying to keep the desperation out of my tone.

Libby shrugged. "I guess. But just because I practice doesn't mean I'm joining the team."

"Understood."

"Are you okay playing with all that metal in your face?" Vicky asked, peering at Libby's piercings.

"We'll check the rule book later," I said. "Just try not to get kicked in the face today."

The faster runners returned, and after another minute, the rest of the team was sucking wind in front of us.

"Everyone, this is Libby. She's thinking about joining the team."

They eyed her with teenage hostility and suspicion.

Libby stared back, seemingly bored and unintimidated.

"Is she Lisabeth's replacement? Is this why you kicked her off the team?" Angela demanded.

"Lisabeth wasn't kicked off the team. She was asked to leave. Nicely," Vicky lied.

"I kicked Lisabeth off the team because she was a toxic presence. She might have had a big foot, but her attitude was holding back the entire team. Libby here is a coincidence. A really good one, so I suggest you not act like a pack of rabid wolverines for once. Anyone have any problems with that?"

Over a dozen hands raised. "Tough crap," I said. "I'm the boss. And I need you all to know that the decisions I make are what I think is best for all of you. Not just some of you. We're a team. Remember that. We've got common ground, common goals. And we're basically awesome human beings. Does anyone have anything they'd like to talk about?"

I didn't really want to delve into the whole "sorry your coach died on the sidelines" thing, but it was my job to make these girls a team.

"Can we talk about why the only makeup you wear is mascara and ChapStick?" Natalee asked.

"No, but if someone wants to discuss how they were affected by their head coach's death last year, we can talk."

There were blinks and shrugs around our little, sweaty circle.

"Ugh. Not this again. We already sat through guidance counselor therapy last year," one of the girls groaned.

"Nope. We're good," Ruby announced.

I was relieved. "Great. Now, let's line up for super fun shots-on-goal drills."

On Libby's first shot, a fast-moving grounder, she sent it sailing into the far upper corner of the net and jogged to the end of the line like it was no big thing.

"Lucky shot," one of the Sophies grumbled.

Libby wiggled her eyebrow ring at the girl.

They got really quiet on her second shot. Libby trapped the air ball under her foot, executed a neat little 360, and put the ball in the lower right corner.

"Who the hell is this chick? Carli Lloyd?" one of the girls grumbled.

By her third turn, everyone was watching with bated breath. I decided to give Libby a little room for the dramatic and floated a ball to her. With a precise snap, she banked it off her forehead, directing it under the crossbar and into the back of the net.

That earned some applause from the easier-to-please members of the team.

I shot Vicky a smug look, and she tipped an imaginary top hat at me.

I'd designed the entire practice to play to Libby's strengths. Her controlled dribble was the fastest, her footwork the cleanest, and, by my count, she was twelve for twelve in shots on goal. The entire team was taking notice, and the muttered bitchiness was quieting.

"She's so fucking good," Vicky hissed at me. "Do you think she likes us?"

"God, I hope so. Is it legal to bribe high school athletes?" I wondered. There was just one more test. "Okay, gang. Let's scrimmage for the last fifteen minutes before we turn you lose to wreak whatever havoc you wreak on a Thursday night."

I divvied them up varsity vs. JV and put Libby on the JV team. In less than five seconds, Libby had snagged the ball from forward Natalee and was running toward the goal as if she were being chased by an army of zombies. The fast ones. Not the limping ones.

"Holy shit," Vicky whispered next to me.

Libby juked, jived, and danced her way through the varsity defense until it was just her and the goalie. One graceful little nudge from her foot sent the ball sailing past Ashlynn. The whole run had taken less than fifteen seconds.

Angela was speechless. Morgan E. offered Libby a high five as she jogged back to center field.

I restarted them with a kickoff and kept my fingers crossed. There was one last thing I needed to see from Libby. One essential piece of the puzzle. This was my team, and there was one thing I valued more than talent and skill.

The varsity team kicked off and worked their way down into the JV's penalty box, but a sloppy move by Ruby gave the defender a chance to clear the ball. She cleared it to center field, not exactly ideal, but Libby plucked it out of the air and turned toward the other end. Again, she systematically beat her way through the midfielders and started picking apart the defense.

Vicky and I watched, holding our breath, Vicky's fingernails digging into my arm.

Just when I thought Libby would dodge her way around the last defender, she passed the ball to little, speedy Rachel, who was hovering just outside the play. Rachel was so shocked she reacted purely on instinct and nailed the ball into the back of the net.

"Yes!" Vicky and I were jumping up and down hugging each other. We would have made quite the spectacle of favoritism, but the JV team had already tackled Rachel and Libby to the ground in celebration.

"Oh, shit. Guys, try not to celebrate so hard," I called. "Did you see that?" I slapped Vicky's arm.

"Teamwork makes the dream work," Vicky said, still jumping up and down.

———

"Sooo…" I said, trying desperately to play it cool. I was driving Libby home after her victorious debut as a Culpepper Barn Owl.

She looked out the window, the picture of teenage boredom. "So?"

"What did you think of the team? Do you want to play?" I held my breath while she took her sweet time answering.

We were getting closer and closer to her house, and I didn't want to let her out of the car without an answer. But that might be considered abduction, and if I had two civil lawsuits pending, I should really keep the felonies down.

"It was okay," she said.

"You're killing me, Morticia," I said, losing my facade of cool.

"Look. You should probably know that I was kicked out of my last foster home for being violent."

I blinked. Considered. Culpepper High had been desperate enough to hire someone banned for life from Homecoming. I too was that desperate. "Eh. Doesn't matter," I decided. Besides, she didn't read dangerous or violent. Libby read too smart for her own good. I liked that about her.

"You're so weird."

I snorted. "Libs, you have no idea."

We rode in silence for a minute.

"I wasn't actually violent," she confessed finally. "My seventeen-year-old foster brother kept *accidentally* walking in on me in the shower until I told him if he did it again I would pin his ears back with a staple gun. The kid had gigantic ears. And overprotective parents."

"That sucks." I knew what it was like to bebop through life with a dark smudge of judgment against me. Sometimes people only saw the smudge, not the person. "I still want you on the team."

"I believe I was promised candy," Libby reminded me.

"Glove box."

She shot me a look of suspicion and then opened it. A stack of Taco Bell sauces and a Reese's Peanut Butter Cup fell out.

"Well, since you held up your end of the bargain, I guess we have a deal," she sighed.

"Yes!" I pumped my fist into the roof of the car. "Ouch!"

"You're so weird."

"Yes, I am."

"So, I wasn't kidding before. I don't have any money."

"Leave that to me." My first direct deposit was burning a hole in my checking account, and I couldn't think of a better use. "Do you want me to talk to your foster mom about the team and stuff?"

"Nah. She's not around much. She'll just be happy that I'm entertaining myself. She's nice. Just busy," Libby added. She pointed to the right. "It's the second one on the right. The white one."

It was a small ranch house with a more-dirt-than-gravel driveway and an entire toy store in the front yard. A little boy was chasing a young teen girl with a hose while a toddler rode a Big Wheel at max speed around the side of the house.

"Did their last coach really die?" Libby asked.

"Yep. And then their substitute coach played mind games with them for the rest of the season. You can be my spy and let me know how deep the damage goes."

"Fun," Libby said dryly.

"No game or anything this weekend," I told her. "Practice on Monday and a home game on Tuesday."

"Okay."

"Thanks for showing up today, Libby."

"Thanks for the candy, Coach."

———

Me: I kicked a jerk off the team and landed a new star player. I'M INVINCIBLE.

Jake: *wipes a tear* My girlfriend's a superhero! I bet you can rock a cape.

Me: I'm going to celebrate with Taco Bell. You in?

Jake: Nothing but the best for my girl. Homer loves the soft tacos. Pick me up in ten.

Vicky: Did she say yes? Does she like us? Is she going to carry us to victory?

Me: SHE SAID YES!! And she called me weird.

Vicky: Win some. Lose some. Hang on. Rich just walked into the bedroom in his socks...

CHAPTER 34

Jake

Poker nights were my favorite nights of the month. I gathered my closest mostly teacher pals, plied them with beer, and gabbed about shit we didn't dare say within students' hearing. All while trying not to go bankrupt to Mrs. Gurgevich, card shark extraordinaire.

I opened the bag of chips and tossed it on the poker table.

I wondered what my grandmother would think of me turning her formal dining room, the room that had hosted generations of family for holidays and special events, into a man cave with a green felt table and velvet *Dogs Playing Poker* reproduction.

At least I had a cover for the table in case I ever tried to use it to eat food off of.

Luckily, Grams went for cremation. Otherwise, she might roll over in her grave.

Uncle Max was the first to arrive. In juxtaposition to his husband, Lewis, Max was lily white with a fluffy beard and absolutely zero fashion sense. He was wearing elastic-waist cargo shorts and a Queen T-shirt that had seen so many washings part of the "n" had worn off, making it look more like an "r."

He poked his head into the living room as he handed over the covered plate he was carrying. "Kentucky bourbon beef jerky for the Anything Goes theme," he said without preamble.

My gay uncles and their refined palates were a very bright highlight of my life. And they were both horrendously disappointed that I'd never developed an interest in creating the food, only eating it.

"Gimme," I said, reaching for the plate.

"You know, you'd really be doing me a favor if you'd clean some of this up before poker nights," he said, eyeing the mess that had migrated off the coffee table and onto the far end of the couch, floor, and one of the end tables.

Was that a six-pack in the bay window? I'd looked for that thing for three days before giving up and buying another.

"I'll get to it," I promised. And I meant it. The mess was starting to annoy me. Or Grams's ghost was haunting me into annoyance.

The doorbell rang, and the front door opened as Floyd, gym teacher and gossip, let himself in. "What smells like meat and whiskey?" he asked, scenting the air like a bloodhound.

"Let's move it along," Mrs. Gurgevich grumbled behind him. "I got a half ton of sashimi on clearance. If we don't eat it in the next thirty minutes, the parasites will start growing." She maxed out at five feet tall with a frizzy nest of salt-and-pepper hair and severe black-rimmed glasses. Tonight, she was wearing a black caftan with metallic threads. Work Mrs. Gurgevich was wildly different from Outside of Work Mrs. Gurgevich. She'd been married three times, knew three presidents well enough to call them by their first name, and a Saudi prince owed her a favor.

"Where's my great-nephew?" Max asked.

"Homer's watching Animal Planet upstairs," I told him. My four-legged roommate would make his way downstairs to scam some table scraps from the guests during a commercial break.

"Gurgevich, I'm coming for your money!" Bill Beerman

was timid everywhere but the poker table. The mild-mannered computer science teacher who got tongue-tied around pretty substitutes was a trash-talking riot after a light beer and one hand of Texas Hold'em. Since his shocking loss last time to Gurgevich, he was ready for battle in a neatly pressed golf shirt and shorts.

"All right, gang. You know the drill," I said, leading the way into the kitchen. I'd at least made an effort to shovel some of the trash and old leftovers into the garbage can before everyone arrived. Bill dug out my ever-present stack of paper plates and doled them out.

Why use dishes if you just have to wash them? I was basically the Mark Zuckerberg of kitchens.

"I really thought you'd clean up your act now that you have a girlfriend," Mrs. Gurgevich mused, unwrapping the sashimi and shooting a side-eye at the overflowing trash can in the corner.

"If you haven't tamed me yet, how can you expect any other woman to?" I teased.

"Do you think she'll survive the Hooper Horror?" Floyd asked, grabbing a spoonful of the pulled pork that I'd picked up from the barbecue joint.

"I just got a royalty check in the mail. I'm willing to use it to pay her legal fees if it gets that sociopath out of my fifth period," Mrs. Gurgevich said.

"Royalty check for what?" Bill asked.

"Marley can't really get into trouble, can she? I mean, from what I hear, Lisabeth basically assaulted another girl. How's that going to blow back on Mars?" I asked, stuffing a piece of jerky in my mouth.

"Never underestimate the power of parents who think their children are perfect and special," Mrs. Gurgevich snorted.

Uncle Max was staring at me open-mouthed.

"What?" I asked, dumping the plastic utensils on the counter.

"You have *a girlfriend?*" he demanded. "Like an actual human woman who agreed to be in a relationship with you?" Uncle Max was not good at keeping up with gossip. I took after him in that aspect.

"No, she's a blow-up doll I met at a porn store," I said. "Yes, a human woman. Is that so hard to believe?"

"Yes," they all answered in unison.

"Funny. Real funny. We gonna play cards or gossip all night?"

———

"You should invite her over," Uncle Max said, reorganizing the cards in his hand.

"Huh? Who?" I asked, eyeballing my pair of ladies.

"Marley," Floyd said. "Does she play?"

Christ. They weren't letting this go. Even after Homer came down and did his table and lap surfing for scraps, they were still talking about me having a girl.

I threw my chips in. "I dunno."

"How do you not know if she plays poker?" Bill asked.

"Because we just started dating. We're taking things slow. She hasn't even been inside the house yet," I said. She'd picked me up last night for celebratory Taco Bell, but I'd been waiting outside. I may have been used to the mess. But that didn't mean I was comfortable with it.

"Slow?" Gurgevich sat with an unlit cigarette dangling from her posy pink lips. "You? Ha!"

"Yes, me. Jesus, you guys make me sound like a manwhore or something," I grumbled.

"I think you should invite her over tonight," Uncle Max insisted.

"You're just saying that because then you can tell Uncle Lew that you met her and he didn't."

"I see no problem with that," he sniffed.

"She's a cool gal," Floyd said. "Seems like the kids are warming up to her a bit. I mean, except for when she got red eyes and a cloud of smoke came out of her nose at Hooper yesterday."

"Are you protecting her from us or us from her?" Mrs. Gurgevich asked me.

"Fine. Geez. I'll text her. Okay?" I yanked my phone out of my pocket.

Me: You don't maybe want to come over so my asshole friends and nosy uncle will get off my back about why my girlfriend isn't here at poker night, do you?

"There. I texted. Happy now? Can we please get back to playing?"

My phone dinged.

"What did she say?" Bill asked.

"Did you see me pick up my phone yet, genius?" I muttered. Having a girlfriend was turning out to be a pain in my ass.

Marley: What the hell kind of an invitation was that?

"What did she say?" Uncle Max asked.

"She wants to know what the hell kind of an invitation was that."

"How did you say it?" Mrs. Gurgevich asked.

"I told her you guys wouldn't get off my back and she could maybe come over so you'd shut the hell up."

Uncle Max stroked a hand through his beard. "You're not very good at this," he observed.

"It's my first relationship! What do you want from me? Jeez!"

Mrs. Gurgevich was shaking her head sadly. "I really thought you'd be better at this."

"And I really thought I'd be playing poker tonight, not sitting through some henpecking party."

Floyd let out a chicken squawk.

Me: Please come over and hang out with my stupid friends. I'd love to have you. There's bourbon-flavored beef jerky.

"What did you say back to her?" Bill asked.
"Is she coming?" Floyd asked.

Marley: You're lucky my only other option was laundering the bed linens for my parents' next Airbnb guest. Be there in ten.
Me: Bless you. P.S. They all think this is real so, you know, dress sexy and get ready to French-kiss the hell out of me.

She responded with a middle finger emoji.

"Well?" Uncle Max demanded.

"Joke's on you, jerks. Now we gotta quit playing so you can help me clean up."

CHAPTER 35

Marley

I don't know what kind of place I expected Jake to live in. But it wasn't the pretty brick two-story with big windows and wraparound porch. My curiosity had been piqued when I picked him up last night. And now I was going to get to see behind the curtain. See how Jake Weston, former teenage rebel and current history teacher/cross-country coach, lived.

There was a tidy front lawn with a big maple tree and actual flower beds. Sure, they looked a little neglected, but the whole package still said "family home." This was a place where people would gather for Thanksgiving and a girl would make an entrance on the stairs in a poufy dress on prom night.

This was not a bachelor pad designed to debauch women. Not a Jake Weston residence.

There was a freaking welcome mat at the front door. Next to it rested a pair of those five-finger running shoes that must have been too smelly to make their way inside.

I reached for the bell but paused when I heard a noise from within. It sounded like someone was dragging something heavy across the floor.

"We don't have enough time to actually dust," I heard Jake yell. "Just kinda blow the bigger dust bunnies under the furniture."

"Hey, yo! What do you want us to do with the lo mein that's stuck to the sink?"

Was that Floyd?

"Just chisel it off as best you can! And hurry up. She should be here any second!"

"You have any nudie magazines that need hiding?"

"If I knew I was going to be playing janitor, I would have stayed home tonight."

"Just shut up and try to get some of the smears off the kitchen table, okay?"

What the hell was I walking into?

I pushed the bell, and several voices yelled "Come in!" at the same time.

Before I could turn the knob, the front door opened, and the foyer beyond filled with a mob of people.

"Um. Hi," I said.

"Hey, Mars," Jake said, muscling his way through their ranks to give me an awkward and out of breath peck on the cheek. He had a wet, dirty rag in one hand, and when I eyed it, he tossed it over his shoulder.

The bearded man behind him wearing a T-shirt that said Queer caught it in mid-air.

"Come on in," Jake said, reeling me in like a fish. "I believe you know everyone except for my uncle. Uncle Max, this is my girlfriend Marley. Mars, this is—"

The bearded man yanked me out of Jake's grip and gave me an enthusiastic hug. "You have made me so happy," he said. "Now, I just need to take a quick selfie with you."

"Oh, I, uh…"

Jake broke Max's hold on me. "Uncle Max, let's let her breathe for five seconds before you go rubbing Lewis's nose in this."

"He always thought you'd go gay in the end, but I knew

all you needed was a special woman to get you to settle down," Max said, tapping away smugly on his phone.

"My uncles are gay. They always assume everyone else is too," Jake explained. "They were heartbroken when my cousin Adeline married her husband."

"It would have been so much fun to have lesbians in the family," Max sighed.

"Definitely." I had no idea what to say to anything. I wasn't even sure why I'd come over.

"What's up, Cicero?" Floyd waved. "Still have a job?"

"Hi, Marley," Bill Beerman spoke up, his voice barely a squeak.

"Hi, guys. Oh, Mrs. Gurgevich. I didn't recognize you." Mrs. Gurgevich looked…ravishing? She was decked out in sparkle from her fancy caftan to the very large diamonds on her fingers. "Wow, those are some rings."

They looked like hefty engagement rings. Four of them. I'd seen the woman every day of my junior year of high school and didn't recall her wearing a single piece of jewelry.

Mrs. Gurgevich wiggled her fingers. "Let Ms. Cicero in, gentlemen," she said, clearing a path through the testosterone.

"What's going on?" I hissed at Jake as everyone peeled off to the right of the—I knew it—prom dress–worthy staircase.

"The teachers want the dirt on what went down with Hooper, and my uncle wants proof of monogamy so he can blab to his husband about it."

"Why does it smell like Lysol in here?"

He skated a hand over the back of his head. "You probably don't want to know."

I heard a galloping coming from upstairs, and we both watched as a blond furball launched itself down the stairs.

"Homie!" Homer planted his front paws on my chest and shoved his cold nose into my face. "Hey, buddy! Wow. Are greetings like this why people have dogs?" I asked.

"Geez, I wouldn't know. He just kind of grumbles at me and then pushes his food dish around when I come home," Jake said, eyeing his dog.

"You have a nice place," I said, glancing around the foyer as I gave Homer a good scruff. The trim work was dark, the hardwood original, and the ceilings high. There was a living room with a lot of glass and a lot of built-ins to one side of the staircase and what looked like a dining room turned poker den on the opposite side.

"You should've seen it ten minutes ago," Floyd piped up from the dining room.

"Har har. Very funny. Are we playing or what?" Jake growled. "Come on in, and don't mind the inquisition."

———

I played, poorly. It had been a long time since my college poker days. And as in all other areas of my life, Lady Luck was not on my side. But it was fun to kick back and listen to the razzing. To hear Mrs. Gurgevich drop fascinating nuggets about a life that sounded nothing like that of a high school English teacher.

She knew Tony Bennett from her backup singing days?

She had a lover in Greece who was twenty years her junior?

Jake sat next to me, his knee pressing into mine as he man spread in his chair. He didn't look like he belonged to this house. Except for maybe the velvet *Dogs Playing Poker* art. That definitely was his style.

We played. We ate pretty great beef jerky. And I dodged questions like a skinny, spectacled seventh grader dodged balls on the playground.

Mrs. Gurgevich wanted to know if Lisabeth Hooper was finally someone else's problem.

Floyd wanted to know if I was getting fired.

Bill had questions about Coach Vince blaming poor little

innocent me for the red dye incident. I didn't have answers for any of them. Next week would be early enough for me to face whatever legal trouble I may have stirred up.

And Uncle Max had seventeen thousand questions about what kind of life partner Jake could expect out of me.

It was awkward, amusing, and somehow even a little bit fun. Mrs. Gurgevich took me out with a full house, and one by one everyone else fell to the reigning poker queen until it was down to her and Jake, eyeing each other across the green felt and trash-talking.

I was still having trouble believing that my high school English teacher who dressed in catalogue-ordered monochromatic polyester was a devilish, delightful, worldly woman who once dated a music star. We had it narrowed down to Neil Diamond, John Mellencamp—in his Cougar days—or Billy Ray Cyrus.

"I call," Mrs. Gurgevich said. She sounded so blasé as if she hadn't a care in the world or a worry over the seventy-five-dollar pot in front of her. "Full house."

Her smile was feline, like a lion ready to rip her prey's face off.

"Huh," Jake said, looking down at her cards. "That looks like a winning hand to me." He started laying his hand down one card at a time. Carefully. Precisely. "I mean, it would be if I didn't have these four gentlemen jacks."

The rest of the losers and I crowed at the showmanship. Mrs. Gurgevich raised an expertly sketched on eyebrow.

"Your lady friend is a good luck charm," Uncle Max observed.

"Yeah, she is," Jake said, looking in my direction and winking.

I tried to dissect exactly why his cocky attitude and overly confident persona were so appealing to me. Normally, I went for a different type. Nonthreatening. Easygoing. Maybe just a little preppy leaning.

Jake was rough enough around the edges that I could get splinters. Maybe it was just the fact that he was a damn good kisser.

With the game officially over, everyone set about cleaning up and packing up leftovers. It was a mass exodus of yawns and "see ya Mondays," and before I knew it, I was alone with Jake Weston in his house. I debated going home. I glanced his way and noted the very nice flexion of his ass muscles as he bent to pull the trash bag out of the can. Yeah. Going home was smart.

"You want a beer?" he offered.

"Uh. Sure." I wasn't in any danger here. This was a fake relationship. I wasn't going to fall prey to his charms, rip my pants off, and tackle him. And let's be honest. Would that be so awful? My last relationship had been, shall we say, lacking in the *bow chicka wow wow* department for quite some time.

Could wild sex with Jake Weston really do me any harm?

CHAPTER 36

Marley

Jake pulled a pair of beers from the fridge and popped the tops all one-handed and sexy-like. "Come on," he said, nodding toward the back door. "I'll show you the porch."

It sounded like a euphemism. And along I went, willingly.

"Oh, wow." Okay, I was a little disappointed that it wasn't a euphemism, but the disappointment was tempered by the fact that we were standing in a cool-ass screened-in porch. The seating was of the cozy, wicker, old-lady variety. But the cushions were deep and inviting. There was a tiki bar crammed in the corner with a half-dead palm of some sort in the other corner, and the lighting was soft and glowy from an actual table lamp, and a few strings of lights hung from the ceiling.

"This is my favorite thing about the whole house," he said. "Thinking about doing a grilling patio over here." He gestured into the dark yard.

The crickets were loud, the lights were soft, and my beer was cold. Life felt pretty damn good.

I sat down on the couch, relaxing into the cushions. Jake ignored the chair and crowded me on the couch. He kicked his feet up on the coffee table and took a long pull of his beer. "You mind?" he asked, pulling a cigar out of his pocket and rolling it between his fingers.

"Not at all," I shrugged. My shoulder was squished against his, and I missed the contact when he leaned forward to light the cigar. When he relaxed back, he looped his arm over my shoulders. His body heat took the chill out of the night air.

The smell of cigar smoke was sweet, pungent. Blue rings of smoke floated lazily to the ceiling.

The crickets lulled me into a relaxed trance.

"You cold?" he asked.

I rubbed my arms. "A little."

Jake reached behind us and pulled a quilt off the back of the couch and arranged it neatly over us. I pulled it up to my chin and let my head tip onto his shoulder.

This felt...good. How long had it been since I'd felt like this? Everything was always such a battle. A constant, overwhelming wave of anxiety. Always afraid of losing the job, the man, the security. But right now, in this moment, on this pretty little porch, I felt good.

"How did you end up with this house?" I asked him.

He tilted his head and blew a gauzy cloud of smoke upward. "It was my grandmother's. She died a year or so back and left it to me."

"That explains the family feel," I said. "You haven't changed it much, have you?"

"I've added a superficial layer of mess to make it feel more like mine," he joked.

"Mmm. I know all about waiting," I told him.

"Waiting?"

"You know. Having all these plans but waiting to do anything about them until something is right or the timing is perfect."

He scratched at the stubble on his jaw. "Huh. Is that what I'm doing?"

"You're too busy. You'll get to it after the holidays. You'll carve out some time for it after you're done binge-watching

Riverdale. You'll wait until you meet the right person, have the right job."

"I still feel like a visitor in the house," he admitted. "It still feels like Grams's house."

"If you were going to start with one thing, what would you change?" I asked.

"You want?" he held the cigar out, and I took it from him, puffing lightly on the end. "I think the living room. It's my couch, but everything else is still hers. The curtains," he decided.

I handed the cigar back. "Good call. Gingham isn't your style."

"I don't know what it is. But as soon as I moved into this place, just me and Homer roaming around with all those bedrooms, all that square footage, I started thinking that maybe it's time to try the whole relationship thing. To be honest, I'm a little afraid Grams's spirit is haunting me. She wanted me settled down for a long time."

I smiled at the idea of a Grams Ghost. "Is that why you came up with this arrangement?"

"I know it's stupid. To be thirty-eight and have no idea what a relationship is supposed to be like. And maybe I won't like it. But I feel like I gotta try, you know? I got the house. I got a great job. Who knows, maybe I'll like being bossed around, having to check in, making decisions with someone." He squeezed my shoulder. "You're making it pretty easy on me so far."

"I guess I didn't really think you were serious about it," I admitted with a yawn.

"Well, I am. And I'm counting on you, Mars, to whip me into relationship shape. I want to give it a go. I figured relationships probably take practice, just like sports. Right?"

"I guess you're right. I'll take it more seriously," I promised.

"Good." It was quiet for a while. A comfortable silence,

both of us lost in our own thoughts. "What do you want? Out of life, I mean," he asked. "I was embarrassingly honest about tryin' out the whole boyfriend-to-husband track. What kind of plans do you have?"

I blew out a slow breath. "I don't know the specifics, but I want to do something big. Something important. I want to be important, essential. My sister is…amazing. She's always been larger than life. Crazy smart. Freakishly beautiful. But the good that she does in this world is kind of mind-boggling. I want to do that. Be that."

"Okay, so define big," Jake pressed.

"It's stupid," I told him.

"Nobody's dreams are stupid," he countered.

I sighed. "I want people I don't even know to have heard about me. And not in the loser, jobless, homeless, pity party way. I want to be impressive. I want to do important things, not just collect a paycheck or wait to get downsized again. Do you know how many times I've been let go, downsized, laid off, or fired?" I shifted my head to look at him.

"How many?" he asked, passing me the cigar again.

"Six. Since college. It's like I've developed this radar. As soon as there's the tiniest hint of trouble, my clock starts ticking down. Waiting for the inevitable. I've never been important enough to keep. I've never survived the first round of layoffs. I'm dispensable. Replaceable. No one misses me when I'm gone. I want to see what the other side is like."

"Damn, Mars," Jake said. "That would really mess with a person."

I gave a sad laugh. "It's hard not to feel like a loser. And this job isn't making me feel much better now that I'm physically losing."

"That's because you're looking for outside validation."

I lifted my head off of his shoulder. "Okay, Dr. Phil."

"I'm serious. I've spent the last fifteen years working with teenagers. I'm practically a life coach. You need to figure out what would make you more confident in yourself. No amount of 'attagirls' from other people is going to give you that swagger you're looking for. You're a hell of a girl, Mars. Start acting like it."

"And how would you suggest I make myself more confident?"

"Set some goals. Things you wanna accomplish. Then go out and crush 'em. Start with some small ones, things you can definitely do. But don't be afraid to put bigger, scarier shit on that list. Every time you cross one of them off, you just proved to yourself that you can do something good."

"Wow." Okay, maybe I was tired. Or maybe it was the intoxicating pheromones of cigar smoke and sexy man, but that actually made sense. "You really are like a life coach."

"Stick with me, pretty girl. Stick with me."

———

I woke up to birds chirping, a crick in my neck, and someone else's body pressed up against mine. When I opened my eyes, I still wasn't sure where I was and who was breathing softly into my hair. I was outside. Sort of.

Oh my God. The screened-in porch. Poker. Jake.

I tried to sit up, but strong arms banded tighter around me. "Nope. Five more minutes," he mumbled, rubbing his chin over the top of my head. I used my hands to pat myself down. I was still fully clothed. I'd had two beers last night, but I wanted to make sure I hadn't stripped down in my sleep and mounted the man.

"Relax, Mars. We just fell asleep."

"Shit. I didn't tell my parents I wasn't coming home."

"I texted your mom from your phone. She instructed you to have a good time with about six winky emojis. Now be quiet and let me enjoy waking up with a girl."

210

I was warm, comfortable, and extremely well rested. And apparently accommodating.

"Okay. Five more minutes," I conceded. "And then tonight you're taking me out on a practice date."

"Cool," he said, his mouth moving against my hair.

We both heard the grumble from the back door.

"Damn dog," Jake groaned. "Why can't he learn to let himself out?"

I yawned and pried my way out of his embrace. Fake or not, this was not a bad way to start the day.

CHAPTER 37

Jake

I stared at the front door before me and rolled my shoulders. "No big deal. Just picking your girl up for a date," I muttered under my breath. I'd followed Marley's instructions to a tee and even gone a step farther. I had not one but *two* bouquets of flowers since my girlfriend lived at home with her parents.

I stabbed the doorbell and let out a long, slow breath. It was embarrassing that I was nervous. I'd gone on dates before. Real ones. I could totally do this. Marley wasn't here to judge me. She was here to teach me. And I was a willing student.

The door opened, and I found myself staring up at a very tall, very broad black man. He was wearing a suit with a bow tie and tortoise shell glasses.

"Uhh…" Instinctively, my gaze slid to the house number and then to the next-door neighbor's house. Yep, monstrosity of a mansion with a swan. I was at the right place. "Hi. Is Marley in?" I asked.

"You must be Jake." His voice boomed, and I could feel the sound waves in my bone marrow.

"I am."

"Are those for me?" Bow Tie demanded, checking out my flowers.

"Uhh—"

"Hey, Jake." A breathless Marley in jeans and a cute button-down appeared next to the giant paragon of fashion. "This is Dietrich," she said.

"Dietrich. Nice to meet you."

"We'll see. What are your intentions toward Marley?" he asked.

"Well, um. Mostly honorable."

Dietrich's pearly-white smile blinded me. "I'm just messing with you, man. Come on in."

Relief coursed through me, and I crossed the threshold into Marley's childhood home.

"Thanks for getting the door, D," Marley said.

"Anything for you, cupcake." He shot her the pistol fingers and bounded up the stairs three at a time with the grace of an NFL receiver.

"What the fuck was that?" I breathed.

She laughed. "I'm sorry. Little prank. He's my parents' Airbnb guest for the week. He's in Lancaster for business and wanted a homier atmosphere than a hotel."

"He scared the hell out of me."

"Yeah, he did." She grinned, and I found that I really liked it when she did that.

"Here," I said, shoving the flowers at her.

She cleared her throat and gestured at her outfit. "Don't forget your Dating 101 notes."

"Oh, right." I took a moment to give her an appreciative look. I was really into button-down shirts. There was nothing I looked forward to more in this world than undoing that long line of buttons to reveal the treasures beneath. This was a girlie flannel, which checked another box for me. "You look gorgeous, pretty girl."

"Nice delivery," Marley said, accepting the flowers.

"And these are for your mom," I said, brandishing the other bouquet.

"Wow. Someone's going for extra credit," she said.

"Is that Jake?" a woman called from the back of the house.

"Yeah, he's here to sweep me off my feet and hopefully feed me," Marley called back.

"Don't let him leave!"

There was something that sounded like a scuffle, and then Marley's parents both appeared in the hallway. They got tangled up in their rush to get to us. Her dad tripped and knocked a family photo off the wall, but he recovered quickly.

"Jake, so nice to see you again." Jessica Cicero and I had crossed paths every once in a while on in-service days when she was still teaching. She was a looker. Her blond hair was pulled back in a perky ponytail, and her smile reached her bright blue eyes. She held out a hand, and I shook it.

"It's nice to meet you, Mrs. Cicero," I said, holding out the flowers. "These are for you."

"Oh my! They're just beautiful," she said, sending Marley a what-a-doll look. "And please call me Jessica."

"I'm Ned," the man in the canary-yellow polo and silvery mustache said, extending his hand. His voice was unusually high.

"Ned, good to meet you." I shook and let him win the grip war. It was a perfunctory introduction. We'd all known of each other for years. Had probably exchanged pleasantries in the grocery store produce aisle or when one of us was backing out of a parking space as the other one waited patiently. It was Culpepper. Everyone knew everyone.

"Did you bring me anything?" Ned asked, looking hopefully at Marley's and Jessica's flowers.

"Uh, no, sir."

"Strike one!" he screeched. He put his thumbs into the

waistband of his Dockers and yanked them up as if spoiling for a fight.

"Dad, don't tease him. I already had Dietrich open the door and demand his intentions," Marley said.

"Ooh! That's a good one," Ned said, giving his daughter the double thumbs-up.

———

"So where are you taking me, Mr. Boyfriend?" Marley asked as I held the passenger door open for her.

"Okay, so check this out. We're going to Smitty's for dinner and drinks. Keeping it light, casual, and public."

I caught her wince.

"What? Is that a bad first date?"

She shook her head. "No. Sorry. That's just my knee-jerk reaction to socializing in Culpepper. It's a good, solid first date plan for a future girlfriend."

Smitty's was always busy on Saturday nights, but I wrangled a small table in front of the window overlooking Main Street. Marley hopped up on the stool, putting her back to the room, and opened the menu.

"So? How am I doing so far?" I asked, taking the seat across from her.

"You picked me up, were nice to my parents, complimented me on my outfit, brought my mom and me flowers, and didn't run screaming from Dietrich. I'd say you're nailing this date."

"When you say nailing—"

She smacked me over the head with her menu. "Funny guy."

I picked up my own menu and browsed. I wasn't a "same thing every night" kind of guy. Mixing it up was more fun to me than being consistent. One night it was hot wings. Another night it was beef and broccoli. Sometimes, for the hell of it, I went for a salad or threw caution to the wind and ordered the greasiest pizza I could find.

Marley was looking around us at the Saturday night crowd. Tentatively, she raised her hand at someone across the bar and smiled awkwardly. Then looked away just as quickly.

"This is weird. I actually know half of these people," she whispered, picking up her menu and hiding her face.

"Welcome to small-town America."

"You know, there's something to be said for being a stranger to everyone," she said, dropping the menu again.

"You're nervous."

"I'm not nervous. I just feel...exposed."

"Why?" I was intrigued.

"Because most of these people remember my horrible, awkward, humiliating teenage years."

"What was so horrible, awkward, and humiliating about your high school career?" I wondered.

She gave me a long look. "Homecoming our senior year? Does that ring any bells?"

"I think I remember Homecoming differently than you do. I remember a scrappy senior who had been pushed around one too many times and took things into her own hands by—"

Leaning across the table, she slapped a hand over my mouth.

"You know what? That's not first date conversation. Make some small talk." She removed her hand.

Women were strange. Pretty, smooth, fascinating, and strange.

"How 'bout them Steelers?" I asked cheerfully. Marley rolled her eyes.

"Hey, guys." A waitress materialized next to the table. "Can I get you something to drink?"

We ordered beers, and I threw in an appetizer request for a

basket of onion rings. When she left, Marley carefully avoided making eye contact with me and everyone else in the place.

I covered her hand with mine. "Look, for what it's worth, I'm sorry if I did something that hurt you in high school."

She looked at me like words were clawing their way out of her throat. But she reined it in, kept a lid on it. "We all did incredibly stupid things in high school," she said quietly.

"Okay." I waited. She stared at her menu for a solid minute.

"So, on a first date," she finally said, "you want to focus on getting your date to talk about herself and file as much of the information away as possible. You can tell a lot about a person by how they talk about themselves."

"So, Marley. Tell me about yourself. If you won the lottery, what would you do with the money?"

She laughed approvingly. "Nice question."

I tipped my head all princely like.

"I'd pay off my mountain of debt," she decided.

"Student loans?" I asked with a frown.

She shook her head. "It's embarrassing. My last job was a startup that offered buy-in options. I could be a partner in the business, and I liked the idea of that. I dipped into my savings, then drained it trying to ride to the rescue. Before I knew it, my savings were gone, and so was my job. The company folded, and I had to take out a personal loan just to cover expenses."

Our beers arrived, and we clinked bottles.

"That sucks," I told her. "Say your debt is magically gone. What's the most frivolous thing you'd spend your lottery winnings on?"

She took a long pull on her beer and closed her eyes. "I always wanted to road-trip across the country. Stop and see all the biggest balls of twine. Live off of beef jerky and convenience store snacks."

"Road trips aren't lottery expensive," I pointed out.

"No, but taking the time off from work is. I've never had a job with more than two weeks' paid vacation. And most of that got sucked up by holidays."

"You're a teacher now. That gives you the entire summer for your beef-jerky-fueled adventure."

"I'm a teacher until Christmas. Then it's hasta la vista, Culpepper."

"What do you want to do after?" I asked, leaning in, not really loving the idea of her packing up and moving on again.

She shrugged. "I have no idea. Nothing's ever been a good fit."

The *V* in her flannel kept drawing my eyes. I liked seeing that long line of her throat, the subtle curve of her breast when the shirt gaped open.

"Hey, no cleavage staring on the first date, buddy. Eye contact only," she said.

I snapped out of my hypnotic state.

"Sorry. Old habits."

"What would you do if you won the lottery?" she asked.

"That's easy. I'd buy Homer a diamond-encrusted collar."

CHAPTER 38

Jake

This dating deal wasn't half bad. Mars and I ate our way through the standard getting-to-know-you practice questions. Either I was totally nailing the charming and delightful thing or she was an excellent faker.

We dealt with the attention from curious onlookers by pretending not to notice it. I understood the interest. Though a Culpepper native, Mars was technically new in town and creating a stir. And then there was me, the perma-bachelor who allegedly took one look at grown-up Marley Cicero and decided to change his wild ways.

I snagged the check off the table while Marley boxed up her leftovers. "What should we do for dessert?" I asked wolfishly.

She raised an eyebrow at me. "Why do I think you're not talking about ice cream?"

I leaned in flirtatiously. "Why, Ms. Cicero, are you coming on to me?"

She mirrored my move and rested her elbows on the table. "In your dreams."

"Well, seeing as how we already slept together, my dreams are your dreams," I pointed out.

She slapped a hand over my mouth and glanced around. Culpepper had sensitive ears and big mouths everywhere.

I nipped at her palm with my teeth, and she narrowed her eyes. "You're bad news, Weston."

"Don't I know it," I said, pulling her hand away from my mouth and holding it.

"Oh, shit," she breathed.

But she wasn't reacting to my expert-level flirting. She was looking over my shoulder.

"What's the problem?" I asked, twisting on my seat to see who was stealing my thunder here.

Amie Jo Hostetter, in ice-pick heels and fashion-forward baby blue sweatpants that probably cost more than my property taxes this month, strutted in. Her hair was big. Her makeup was troweled on. And she had a hand wrapped around her husband's wrist.

He glanced our way, and I saw the second he recognized Marley.

"Figures he'd age well," she muttered, pretending to be enthralled with the table top.

"That the type you usually go for?" I didn't much care for that. Travis was a clean-shaven, ironed-clothes kind of guy. He got his hair cut every three weeks and spent a small fortune on hair products and custom-tailored oxford shirts to fit his narrow frame. His only hobby was golf. Talk about a snoozefest.

High school me would have—and probably had—referred to him as a pretty boy. He was soft and smooth. Nice guy, but a schmoozer. And I couldn't imagine someone like Marley ending up with someone like him. She'd be bored to tears within a week.

"Are you forgetting the fact that I dumped him in high school for *you*?" she hissed.

"You did not," I argued. "You broke up with him because you were bored to death."

"Just shut up and stop looking at him—them. Oh, God. Here they come. They're coming over!"

I squeezed her hand. "Chill out. You're here with me, your *boyfriend*, remember?"

She straightened. "Right. Okay. Good. I forgot."

She forgot she was dating me. That was a kick to the ol' ego.

"Well, don't you two look cozy?" Amie Jo cooed. She reeled Travis in and tucked herself under his arm, painting a picture of a happy couple right in front of us.

"Hey there, Hostetters," I said, giving Marley's hand a hard squeeze.

She snapped out of the deer-in-the-headlights expression and pasted on a smile as phony as Amie Jo's tone.

"Travis, you remember Marley from high school, right?" his wife asked. Judging by his expression, he definitely remembered.

"It's good to see you again, Marley," he said pleasantly. "I heard you were back in town."

"Uh. Hi. Yeah, I'm back for a little while," she said, the words coming out in a rush. "I, um, I like your swan."

I shot her a WTF look, and her eyeballs went half-dollar sized.

"Isn't he just divine?" Amie Jo asked, laying a possessive hand on Travis's stomach. "I saw Lady Gaga had swans at her Hamptons estate and just had to have one. Travis made it happen. He spoils me! Isn't that right, sweetie?"

"Aren't swans supposed to have a mate?" Marley asked suddenly. "I mean, don't they get lonely when there's just one of them?"

I slid off my stool and pulled Marley to her feet. "Well, we'll leave you two to your dinner. We've got some private dessert plans," I said with a suggestive eyebrow wiggle. "Great seeing you, Travis."

Pulling Marley behind me, I wove my way through the high-top tables to the front door. In seconds, we were outside, and Marley breathed a sigh of relief.

"I like *your swan*?" I said when we were halfway down the block.

She covered her face with her hands. "Oh my God. I really said it? I didn't know what to say to him! I haven't seen him since high school graduation. He didn't speak to me after Homecoming. After that whole broken leg thing."

"Are you still into him?"

"No! I don't know! I don't think so. *I* broke up with *him*, remember?"

"Yeah, and one look at him at Smitty's, and you're wondering if you'd be in Amie Jo's shoes if you hadn't dumped his ass." I didn't like that it annoyed me.

"I'd never wear those shoes," she quipped. "I'd spend more time falling down than walking."

"Be honest. You didn't see those two together and wonder?"

"Isn't that natural?" she dodged the question.

I slid my arm around her shoulders and guided her toward my SUV.

"How the hell should I know?"

"Haven't you ever run into an ex-sex partner and wondered what it would be like if you were still with them?"

"Nope."

"God, this is why I never showed my face in town after graduation," Marley complained. "It's like holding up a mirror to every single mistake I ever made."

"Like breaking up with Travis?"

"You sound mad," she said, looking up at me with a frown.

"Mad? Ha. I'm not mad." I was totally mad. Illogically mad.

"Annoyed? Irked? Filled with rage?"

"Are you supposed to make a guy feel like second fiddle on a first date?" I asked.

She opened her mouth and then closed it. "Ouch."

"Yeah, ouch."

She winced. "Okay. That's fair. If this were a real date, I'd definitely owe you an apology."

"Why don't you demonstrate one for me right now so I'll know the real thing when it comes along?" We were in front of the library, a squat, yellow brick building that also housed the police department. My car was just a few spots down, but I pulled her to a stop.

"Fine. Jake?"

"Yes?"

"I'm sorry for making you feel like second fiddle. It wasn't my intention, and I was just kind of shocked to see him tonight. I wasn't mentally prepared to face the past when I was having such a good time with you, and I'm sorry."

"Apology accepted," I said.

"Do you forgive that easily?" she asked, eyes narrowing.

"Let's find out." I dipped my fingers into the *V* of her shirt and yanked her up against me. I'd been thinking about it since I woke up with her this morning. Feeling the weight and heat, the press of her body.

Before she could complain or take a swing at me, I crushed my mouth to hers.

I told myself I was just doing a little PDA duty, putting on an act. Maybe making her forget all about Travis Hostetter and his alligator shirts.

But then her tongue danced around mine. Her hands gripped my shoulders. Her hips rocked into me. Blindly, I stumbled over to one of the library's pillars at the foot of its stairs. I pressed her against the brick and tasted her. She made my blood sing with those sexy little moans.

I went hard in the blink of an eye and shamelessly thrust against her. My dick demanded to be let loose, and I had trouble remembering where we were. My hands were everywhere.

Skimming her sides, teasing the undersides of her breasts. I wanted them bare and crushed against me. I wanted to rut inside her and hear her say my name, breathless and needy.

Loud throat clearing yanked me back to reality. I stopped kissing Marley but couldn't bear to step away from her and give her some space.

"The library is *not* for necking," Mrs. Ritter, the head librarian, said crisply. She was dressed in schoolmarm brown. Brown clogs. Brown dress. Brown cardigan. Disapproving look on her face. When I was a teenager, I'd been a little obsessed with wondering whether letting her hair out of her tight bun and taking off her nerd glasses would transform her into the sexy librarian. I never got my answer, but I liked to think at home Mrs. Ritter would let her hair down and do naked Pilates or something.

"Sorry, Mrs. Ritter," I said sheepishly.

"Ms. Cicero, I would have expected better from you," Mrs. Ritter sniffed before toddling off with her tote bag that said *DON'T INTERRUPT ME. I'M READING.*

"Sorry," Marley croaked after her. She turned her attention back to me and punched me in the arm. "What the hell was that?"

"I kissed the hell out of you, and then we got yelled at by the librarian," I recapped.

"You're a jerk."

I stuffed her into the passenger seat of my car. "Do swans really need a mate?"

CHAPTER 39

Marley

It was our first home game under the lights in the stadium, and the dozen or so spectators, mostly parents, spread out in the stands trying to look like a bigger crowd. The opposing team, the Blue Ball Blue Jays—Lancaster County had some weirdly named towns—arrived caravan-style with parents and friends pouring out of cars behind the team bus. We Barn Owls were officially outnumbered on our home turf.

It was not an auspicious start.

My parents were there holding a *Coach Cicero Is Our Snack Cake* sign. I waved weakly at them, and Dad held the sign over his head.

Libby tugged her new socks into place over the shin guards I'd sweated over for thirty minutes before making the decision to buy. I was trying to weigh the expense of name-brand sports equipment with the nasty snark that came from generic second-hand stuff.

"Is this normal?" she asked, nodding toward the nearly empty stands.

"Got me. I'm new." When I was in high school, the girls' team didn't draw the crowds that the boys' soccer teams did. But I didn't remember it being quite this dismal.

"They don't have a reason to come see us," Morgan E. said, threading her fingers through her purple mohawk.

"Yet," Vicky corrected her from her bottomless well of delusional optimism. "They don't have a reason to come see us *yet*."

"New girl's playing varsity, isn't she?" Angela asked, sticking her chin out in Libby's direction.

"Name's Libby," Libby corrected.

"Whatever," Angela grumbled. "Just don't embarrass us."

"Nice attitude, Suzy Sunshine," I told Angela.

I sent the varsity team, with Libby, up to the stands to spread out and make it look like there were actual fans present. The JV game went reasonably well. In a year or two, they'd be a solid team since they hadn't had as much time to be scarred by the varsity assholery of Lisabeth.

At the end of the first half, we were down 1–0, but I'd seen a lot of potential on the field. I took Rachel, the shy forward, aside while everyone else was taking the field for the second half. "Listen, you've got everything you need. Speed, footwork. Go out there and put the ball in the back of the net."

"I'll try, Coach."

"Don't try. Just do it."

Rachel nodded and jogged out onto the field.

"You're mixing your *Star Wars* with your Nike slogans," Vicky observed.

"Shut up. I'm new at this rah-rah shit."

The ref blew the whistle, and the second half began. Twenty seconds in, one of our midfielders stripped the ball from a Blue Jay and fired it up the line to Rachel.

Vicky and I grabbed each other and started shouting. "Go!"

Rachel took off, her little feet a blur as she drove down the field. "TAKE THE SHOT!" I screamed. I was going to need to drink a jar of honey after every game to soothe my throat.

In slow motion, Rachel cranked her right leg back and fired away.

Vicky and I held our breath with the rest of the team and the five or six people in the stands who were paying attention.

The ball soared through the air. The Blue Jay goalie dove for it. I swear, even from fifty yards away, I could still hear the victorious swish of ball meeting net.

I was screaming. Vicky was screaming. The JV team was on its feet. The varsity players were pounding the bleachers. And Rachel was standing on the field frozen as if she couldn't believe what she'd just done. And then her teammates tackled her.

"My daughter taught her to do that," my dad howled from the stands.

———

We won 3–2. Rachel had two goals and an assist and couldn't wipe the dazed smile off her face. I wanted to cry happy tears and eat celebratory chicken corn soup and nachos. But I still had an entire varsity game to get through.

"Yo, Coach!"

I turned my attention away from the varsity's warm-up on the field. Floyd waved from behind the field's fence. Guidance counselor Andrea and French teacher Haruko Smith were decked out in Barn Owl gear next to him. I waved back, grateful for their support and hoping they weren't going to witness anything humiliating.

They took their seats near the JV team, which was busy squealing and giggling their way through a recap of their first victory of the season.

"Not much of a crowd, Coach." I heard another voice call. This one immediately raised my hackles.

Coach Vince, flanked by a couple of his players, stood behind my bench, smugly taking in the empty bleachers. The red had faded to a dull pink on their hair and complexions. Now they just looked sunburned.

"Nice of you to show your support," I said dryly.

"Support?" he scoffed. "I'm here to witness your humiliation."

Nice job, universe, bringing my greatest secret fears to life.

"Be sure to buy some soup and hot chocolate to support the Booster Club," I said, rubbing my eye with my middle finger. Like a toddler with a temper tantrum, he kicked gravel in my direction and stormed off.

"Good luck tonight, ladies," Milton said to Angela and Ruby.

I couldn't tell if he was being sarcastic or just a dumbass. But I collared both girls and pushed them back toward the field just in case they were feeling particularly bloodthirsty tonight.

I sent Vicky to round up the team to go through the lineup and snagged Libby from the circle. The field lights banged on overhead.

"You ready?" I asked her.

"Relax, Coach. It's just a game."

I heard a wolf whistle and turned around. Jake—looking studly in jeans, a thermal, and a down vest—waved from the middle of most of the cross-country team. "Lookin' good, Cicero," he called.

I sent him a weak wave before turning back to Libby. My heart had kicked up a notch, and I couldn't tell if it was pregame jitters or "Jake Weston looks fine" hormones.

"I really want to win," I confessed to Libby.

"Then tell the team that," she suggested.

I huddled everyone up on the field and eyed the clock. "Okay, guys. This is where I'm supposed to tell you to play hard and have fun and be proud of yourselves."

They looked at me skeptically.

"This is also the part where I'm going to tell you I really, really want a win tonight. Coach Vince and half of the boys' team is here ready to watch us implode. I don't want to give them the pleasure. So I'm asking you, selfishly, unfairly, to do your very best out there tonight so I can rub this in his face. Make me look good tonight, and I won't make anyone run tomorrow."

"Well, I do hate running," Ashlynn the goalie said, clapping her gloved hands.

"Then let's go out there and kick Blue Ball's ass—butts," Vicky said. "Hands in, ladies."

"Three, two, one. Go, team!"

"Go, team!"

"We need a way cooler call to action," I said as the first string took their positions on the field.

"How about 'destroy the enemy'?" Vicky suggested as we walked back to the bench. The stands were still mostly empty, but the number of spectators was growing, slowly.

"How about 'fuck off, Coach Vince'?"

Jake was sitting with my parents, and it looked like Dietrich had made it out tonight too. I gave them all a little wave and tried to swallow the nerves that were turning my stomach into a roller coaster.

I felt a shiver run up my spine. Evil was near. Turning around, I spotted Lisabeth Hooper, flanked by the bronzer triplets and... "Is that? It can't be?" I murmured.

She was still blond. Still had a terrifying resting bitch face. She was fifty pounds heavier but still annoyingly attractive.

"Steffi Lynn?" Vicky supplied. "Yeah. Didn't you know she's Lisabeth's mom? After she flunked out of cosmetology school, she moved back in with her parents and took a job as an assistant to an insurance agent in Centerville. She got knocked up by her boss, which was a shame, because he was married.

Anyway, she's been married and divorced, like, three times. She was a massage therapist until she got sued when her essential oil blend ate the skin off of a couple of her clients. Still lives with her parents. She's broke and going through another divorce."

"Wow."

Steffi Lynn took a step closer to the fence and glared down at me. "Once a loser, always a loser," she said snidely.

There was something less monstrous, more sad about her than I remembered. Had I somehow cursed Steffi Lynn all those years ago at our showdown, or was it just cumulative karma?

Lisabeth stared me down coldly and mouthed "Fuck you."

"Thanks for coming to show your support," I said, giving them a little finger wave.

"Didn't she get suspended? Should we call security?" Vicky whispered out of the side of her mouth.

Stadium security consisted of a seventy-year-old partially deaf man who carried a walkie-talkie and napped in the ambulance.

"It was a day of in-school suspension. And let's just rub her face in our victory," I said grimly.

CHAPTER 40

Marley

My heart was pounding away in my throat when the ref blew the whistle to start the game. I'd always felt like this before my own games. Nerves. Anticipation. The hope that I'd somehow magically unlock my untapped athletic ability and be the team hero.

I guess twenty years wasn't quite long enough to dull the muscle memory of a home game under the lights. And now I had even more riding on the game. I had three enemies in the stands and a point to prove to everyone else.

I watched the Blue Jays mount a credible offense and move the ball into our territory. We were nervous, clunky. The team's collective horror was palpable as, pass by pass, the Jays advanced on our goal. A tall forward trapped the cross and lined up her shot.

"Please no. Please no. Please no," I chanted helplessly from the sidelines.

She fired a wild shot on goal, and Ashlynn dove and rolled. "Did she—"

Vicky's question was cut off by the roar of the crowd. Okay, more like approving murmur. Ashlynn climbed back to her feet, ball safely clutched in her hands.

"Oh, thank God!"

I wondered if most coaches were on anxiety medications or if they just played fast and loose with potential heart attacks.

The Jays dominated the next run and the next, but every time they crossed half field, our defense got tougher. They were warming to the challenge. In both of our previous games, we'd been down by two goals already. This was improvement. However, I greedily wanted more than improvement.

I wanted victory.

The ball rolled out of bounds at half field, and I felt my phone vibrate against my hip. I pulled it out and glanced at the screen.

Jake: You look crazy tense. Chillax. Be encouraging.

I responded with a thumbs-up emoji and took the time to roll out my shoulders, shaking out my arms. He was right. Taking a deep breath, I did my best to relax. I high-fived the midfielder who came out of the game on a substitution and shouted words of encouragement and athletic brand slogans.

Little by little, our offense started to come to life. Natalee mounted our first attack on the Blue Jays' goal. We came away with a corner kick. Something we'd practiced hundreds of times. But never under the lights during a home game. Never in front of an audience.

Our midfielder paced off the ball, eyeing the goal. My front line had forgotten our practiced formation of starting at the penalty box and running at the goal. Instead, they stood flat-footed and nervous in front of the goal, jockeying with the defense for position.

"MOVE, LADIES!"

"Get your rears in gear!" Vicky echoed.

As if awakening from a trance, the girls backed off the goal.

"We're going to have to run that drill a million more times," I grumbled.

"Or give up and drink margaritas after school every day."

"That plan has merit."

The whistle blew, and the midfielder booted the ball up, up, up. My line was moving.

"Get a head on it!" I shrieked.

It looked like a clump of Jays were going to come up with it, but then I saw Libby's dark head moving gracefully through time and space.

Everything went silent in my brain except for the laborious *ca-clunk ca-clunk* of my heart. I saw forehead meet ball. I saw the goalie jumping, arms outstretched, and then—

"What the fuck just happened?" Vicky screamed.

"I don't fucking know!" I was screaming too. So was the rest of the stadium.

"Holy shit! She fucking scored!" Vicky howled.

"Watch your mouth, Coach," the linesman said as he jogged down the sideline.

"Can't fucking help it, Clarence," Vicky squealed.

The players were off the bench and on their feet. Libby was jogging back to midfield blasé AF, like she was just out for a stroll under the lights.

One by one, the girls on the field approached her for dignified high-fives.

It was 1—0, and we were *winning*.

She did it again five minutes later. When her left purple cleat sent the ball into the lower corner of the net just inches from the goalie's gloves, I peeked a look over my shoulder. Steffi Lynn was glowering from her seat in the bleachers. Next to her, Lisabeth brushed her hair over one shoulder and took a duck-lipped selfie and ignored the world around her. Coach Vince looked constipated.

The celebrations were slightly more enthusiastic this time. Slaps on the back and fist pumps ensued.

At halftime, we were tied up 2–2. But it felt like a win to me.

"Sophie G., really nice tackle last quarter. 87 keeps beating you down the field. If you need to, swap coverage with Angela on number 43. Ruby, great job getting open in the middle. Offense, keep an eye out for her. See if you can feed her the ball," I said, guzzling water for my sore throat. I wasn't used to forty-five straight minutes of shouting.

They were all looking at me like I'd just ridden up on a unicorn.

"What?" I asked.

"You're being really coachy," Phoebe observed.

"Well, you guys are being really teamy. You're working together."

Vicky put her arms around me and two of the players. "We're working as a team! Isn't that exciting?" she squealed.

"Don't make this weird, Coach V," I warned.

The Blue Jays' coach must have given one hell of a halftime pep talk because they came out swinging. Their offense was tighter and more bloodthirsty. But damn if our defense didn't rise to the challenge. We were scoreless for another twenty minutes, each side battling for domination. Back and forth. Both defenses were getting tired, and I subbed in some fresh legs.

The clock was ticking down. Ties meant overtime, and I didn't know if we had it in us. At least the crowd was more invested this half, and the attention seemed to feed my players.

Angela executed a sliding tackle with the precision of a pro and did a little celebratory shimmy when she popped back up. The crowd hooted its approval.

There was one minute left in the game, and I had no fingernails left to chew.

"One minute, ladies," I yelled, clapping my hands.

It didn't look good for us. A Blue Jay snaked her way around our midfield and started charging for the goal. I slapped a hand over the heart, which was trying to explode out of my chest. Angela must have heard my fervent prayers. She stepped in front of the runaway forward and got mowed down.

I was already halfway to her when the ref whistled me onto the field.

"Angela! Are you alive?" She was crumpled on the grass, but her eyes were open. She had two perfect cleat marks on her cheek.

"Did I stop her?" she asked, rolling onto her side.

"Like a brick freaking wall," I said.

One of the EMTs huffed and puffed over to us. She dropped a medical bag on the ground. The team huddled up a short distance away while we made sure Angela wasn't concussed or missing any limbs.

There was a good-natured cheer when we got her back on her feet to hobble off the field.

Angela stopped and faced the team. "Don't let my sacrifice be in vain. Win this, bitches," she said.

Ruby approached and put her hand on Angela's shoulder. "We will win this for you, Cleat Face."

"Oh my God. Let's just finish the game, okay?" I said, slapping an ice pack on Angela's face.

The ref awarded us an indirect kick for the foul with twenty seconds left on the clock.

I dumped Angela on the bench, where she received a hero's welcome, and returned to Vicky's side.

"This is it," she said.

"Yep."

"Do you want a drink?" she asked.

"I don't think water is going to calm me down."

Without looking away from the field, Vicky unzipped her fanny pack. "I got tequila minis in here. For emergencies."

I laughed, loud and long. I was still laughing when our defense took the kick. One of our midfielders got it and fired it up the field to Libby.

"Holy shit," I whispered. Ten seconds.

Libby worked her fancy footwork around a defender and snuck closer to the goal. I grabbed Vicky's arm, my fingers stabbing into her flesh. She had me around the neck in a choke hold.

Libby looked up at the goal and then away.

"What is she doing?" Vicky screeched.

Five…four…three…

She kicked the ball, sending it straight to Ruby's feet at the top of the penalty box. Ruby didn't bother trapping it, she just swung away with that long-ass leg of hers.

The buzzer signaled the end of the game and warred with the shouts of the crowd. I didn't hear either. I was too busy screaming my freaking head off because the ball—that glorious, glorious ball—was in the back of the net. The Barn Owls had their W. I had my victory.

Vicky and I charged the field with the rest of the girls. The JV team jumped the short fence and joined us in our ecstatic sprint. We collided, a big, blue pile of screaming estrogen on the goal line. Varsity, JV, first string, second string, coaches, players. For that moment, that shining, victorious moment, we were all one.

Somehow we made it to mid-field and lined up to high-five the Blue Jays.

"Nice game, Coach. Girls looked great out there tonight," the Blue Jays coach told me.

"Thank you," I said. I couldn't wipe the grin off my face if I tried.

Then I was being turned around and lifted off the ground.

"You did it, Mars!" Jake swung me around under the stadium lights, and everything was just about perfect.

On our way out, we were stopped every ten feet by fans. My players were thrilled, their parents were ecstatic, and according to Haruko, the faculty was happy that I finally shoved a W in Coach Vince's face. He'd left abruptly in the third quarter when it became apparent that a blow-out was not going to happen.

I didn't know when Lisabeth and Steffi Lynn ducked out, and I didn't care enough to ask.

"This is so great!" Vicky said, strutting toward the concession stand to see if they had any leftover nachos. "I mean, not only did you get to shove this in that Neanderthal's face, you also got to show Steffi Lynn how to coach."

"Why would she care?"

Vicky stopped in her tracks. "No one told you?"

"Told me what?" I looked over my shoulder for Jake. He was in conversation with one of his students.

"She's the one who took over coaching when their coach died last season."

"Steffi Lynn is Hitler?" Once again, I realized too late that I needed to have my epiphanies more quietly when a dozen heads swiveled in my direction.

Vicky clamped a hand on my arm and dragged me a few steps away.

"I thought you knew! She went all dictator on them and made Lisabeth the queen of the evil universe."

"Why doesn't anyone tell me this shit?" I whined. "I could have done a lot better with this whole 'Hey, I'm your new coach. I swear I'm not an ass' thing!"

"Hey, Coach!"

I turned around and found the varsity team lined up behind me making the heart sign with their fingers.

"I think they know," Vicky said, slapping me on the back.

CHAPTER 41

Marley

We won our next match, an away game that Thursday. The girls were clicking on the field, and that was as gratifying as seeing those very nice final scores.

It was a different kind of bus ride home after a win.

I basked in the 4–2 victory to the sounds of happy teenagers who, for once, weren't at each other's throats. Things were going well for me. It was a new experience. And while I expected a shoe or a brick wall to drop on me at any moment, I was determined to enjoy it while it lasted.

The cheerleader coach had paid me a visit to ask if I minded if she let her squad get a little more creative with their cheers at our games. The boys' team had been throwing garbage at them during games. They were more than happy to switch to cheering for the girls. I was all for it.

Then there was the cute little wrapped package I found on my desk the day before.

It was a whistle engraved with the words *Coach Marley*. Courtesy of Jake. I had to give him credit. The man was an excellent gift giver.

I tapped out a text and attached a picture of the scoreboard.

Me: Another W in the books.

Jake: Nicely done, Coach. I'm thinking I should take my girl out to celebrate. Bonfire Saturday?

Oh boy.

Culpepper had two kinds of bonfires. The high school kind where underage drinking and sex happened. And the adult kind where overage drinking and bullshitting occurred. I'd never actually been to an adult bonfire here. It was one of those moments when I had to take a mental step back and wonder when the hell I'd turned into an adult. And when the hell I would start feeling like one. Inside, I was still an overgrown, wounded teenager who had no idea how to function in the real world.

"Are you texting your boooyfriend?" Phoebe asked, peering over my shoulder.

"Maybe," I said.

She screwed up her nose and studied me. "Have you ever thought of, like, I don't know…trying?"

"What?"

"You know, like makeup, hair, shoes that don't have to be tied? Something above and beyond moisturizer and deodorant?"

"Is Phoebe talking to you about making an effort?" Natalee's head popped up over the seat.

"Hey, we were going to tag team this. Remember?" Morgan E. groused, sliding in next to the sleeping Vicky.

"What are you guys talking about?" I asked, not sure I really wanted an answer.

"Okay. Obviously Mr. Weston is into you, and that's great. But you're still kinda sad circling around." Natalee said, brushing her fringe of glossy black hair back from her face.

"Sad circling?"

"Remember that antidepressant prescription commercial with the sad circle?"

"Yes," I said carefully. Was I a cartoon frowny face with a rain cloud over my head?

"That's you," Angela said, appearing one seat back in the aisle.

"Look. We know in the nineties, it was cool to be all apathetic and stuff. But that was a *long* time ago," Morgan E. explained.

"Yeah, like a hundred years," Angela snorted.

"Thank you for that, Angela."

She smirked at me.

"What are you trying to say?"

"We think if you made an effort with your appearance, you'd be happier," Phoebe insisted.

I wasn't a stranger to makeup or hair products. It wasn't *that* long ago that I'd dressed in nice pants and pretty shirts and worn mascara every single day. But it had all seemed pointless given my current circumstances.

I was just passing through. Just filling in. My fake boyfriend didn't care what I did with my hair.

"Isn't this sending the wrong message? Making yourself artificially prettier to be more attractive to other people?" I argued.

Natalee scoffed. "That's adorable. And so wrong. You don't make an effort for other people. You do it for yourself."

"Duh," Morgan E. added.

Okay. That was a lot different from my high school days. Everything everyone did back then was for the approval of other people.

"Wait, wait, wait." I waved a hand in the air and then pointed at Natalee. "You're telling me you don't spend forty minutes every morning on your hair and makeup to look good for boys?"

She rolled her eyes. "I don't even know where to begin with that erroneousness."

I wondered if *erroneousness* was a word.

"First of all, it's closer to an hour. Looking my best makes me *feel* my best. Guys don't notice whether you have a smoky eye or the right shade of lip liner. They notice when you're confident. Which serves a two-fold purpose," Natalee instructed.

"If you're confident," Ruby said, popping up in the aisle, "you're more attractive and interesting, and it's harder for assh—jerks to mess with you."

"True story," Angela agreed. "If you're confident, you're not an easy victim."

I had a blinding and horrible flashback of my entire high school career compressed into one montage of victimology. I felt a little sick.

"Where are you guys learning this stuff?" *Was there a new class that schools started teaching after I graduated? And could I audit it?*

"On the gram," Morgan E. announced.

"The gram?"

"Instagram. You know, 'doin' it for the gram'? Hashtag true self. Hashtag beautiful you."

"Instagram. YouTube. They're full of role models. You want to learn to contour your face? How to get the best clothes haul at Target for back-to-school? How to respond to bullies without losing your soul? It's all there," Natalee said.

The rest of the girls nodded.

"Basically, we've been talking, and we think you can do better," Morgan E. said, laying a hand on my shoulder.

Vicky snored.

"Better than Jake?" I asked.

Their raucous laughter woke Vicky. "Whaz happening? Whaz going on?"

"We're making over coach," one of the girls explained.

"Oh, thank God. I was going to start stuffing makeup samples in her gym bag," Vicky announced.

"Not better than Mr. Weston," Phoebe clarified to me. "There *is* no better than Mr. Weston. Better than what you're doing now for yourself." She bounced on the seat and grinned at the rest of the girls. "Sooo…"

"You're going to meet us at Ulta Saturday morning, and we're making you over," Natalee finished, clapping her hands.

Libby poked her head up between two of the girls. "Did someone say Ulta? I have coupons." She grinned wickedly.

My phone buzzed in my lap.

Jake: I'm taking your silence as a "Yes, Jake, I'd love to go to the bonfire with your handsome face and hot body. I'm looking forward to it so much that I'm going to buy you a present just for inviting me."

"I think she should get a haircut," one of the girls said, pulling my brown, blah, nothing-special tresses out of their ponytail prison.

"I've got a board on Pinterest with some potential styles."

"Ooh, let me see," Vicky demanded. "Do you think she could pull off bangs?"

CHAPTER 42

Marley

I sucked wind through three whole miles and felt like an Olympic champion when my parents' house came back into view. Autumn descended with its traditional unpredictability. Pennsylvania entertained a very long winter and summer punctuated with a day or two that could be considered a life-affirming spring and cozy, crisp fall. Some of the leaves were starting to change color on the maples, but other trees had already surrendered, dumping their still green foliage to the ground.

Pumpkin spice and baggy sweaters were everywhere even though the temperatures were volleying between the 40s and the 70s.

I hosed off quickly in the shower, grabbed the closest clean clothes, and then stopped and glanced in the mirror.

Effort.

Okay, fine. I could make some. I didn't have to dress like I was always ready for a nap or a workout.

I dug out a pair of jeans and did a happy little shimmy when I realized they were loose around the waist. Unless I was mistaken, this was the pair I'd had to lay down on the bed and zip myself into last winter.

And here I was standing up and not choking like a stuffed sausage. Huh. Imagine that.

Rifling through the clothes I'd shoved carelessly into the closet when I'd unceremoniously crash-landed back here, I found a cute cashmere blend sweater with three-quarter sleeves. I'd treated myself to it when I'd gotten my last job. The job that was going to be my big break into adulthood and importance. I winced at my naivete and dragged the sweater over my head.

Dang. Not bad. Was it my imagination, or was my back fat a little less noticeable now?

Fully in the spirit now, I found a pair of ankle boots that made me think of tough chicks who rode motorcycles. I nodded at my reflection. *Not bad at all.* Maybe my team was on to something.

Speaking of, I had a makeover to get to. God, I hoped they wouldn't talk me into dyeing my hair pink or something.

———

The entire varsity team greeted me at the door of the cosmetics store, and I had a moment of unadulterated panic. What if this was some kind of cruel joke? What if they were going to shave my eyebrows off and make me up to look like a new drag queen. New drag queens didn't have the deft touch that experienced ones did.

"You ready for a new you, Coach?" Natalee asked gleefully.

"Uh, maybe?"

Morgan E. gave me the once-over. "Solid effort on the clothes," she said. It sounded like a compliment.

"Thanks."

I was surprised and a little relieved to see Libby there. I considered hers to be a friendly face. I felt I could trust her. If she was here, that probably meant the team wasn't about to exact some complex, humiliating revenge.

"How'd you get here?" I asked her as we trooped inside.

She stuffed her hands into her sweatshirt pockets. "Angela picked me up."

My face must have given me away.

"Don't start getting all dewy-eyed. We're on the same team. She lives a couple blocks away. We're not BFFs and braiding each other's hair, so relax."

"I'd like to point out that we're not on school property, and you can't give us detention for swearing or not listening to you," Ruby announced, leading the way toward the back of the store.

"Understood." Did that mean I could swear too? I definitely did not have the vocabulary of someone shaping America's future. "I'd also like to point out that please remember I'm low maintenance."

"Low maintenance doesn't have to mean absolutely zero fucks given," Morgan E. shot back.

———

There were aisles and aisles of makeup, skin care products, hair tools. Artful displays of charcoal face masks and fake lashes caught my eye.

I was officially in over my head. At their mercy.

Ruby stopped at the entrance to the in-house salon and faced me. "Do you trust us?" she asked.

I looked around the circle. No one looked like they were choking on laughter or trying to cover up nefarious intent.

"Yeah. I guess so," I said finally.

"Good," Angela said. "Because we've picked a haircut for you."

"Lemme see." Oh, God. Was it a pixie cut? I didn't think I had the bone structure or the hair product to pull one of those off.

Sophie S. crossed her arms. "We want you to trust us with your hair."

I swallowed hard. It was just hair. It would grow back. Unless they used some kind of next-generation Nair that ate through my scalp. *Oh, my God!*

My team wanted to know that I trusted them. Hair grew back.

"Okay," I decided. "I trust you."

They went from serious negotiators to giddy teenage girls in a heartbeat, clapping and squealing.

"Coach, this is Wilma. Wilma, this is our coach. We want you to do this to her," Natalee said, holding up her phone to the six-foot-tall South American beauty sporting purple eye shadow and one skinny silver braid in a sea of thick, highlighted curls.

Wilma studied the screen, then me, and then the screen again. Her eyes narrowed.

"This is doable," she decided.

She looked like she could be an authority on things like not ruining a person's psyche with a bad haircut, so I decided to just go with it. "Let's get this over with," I sighed.

Wilma whirled the cape around me and pushed me into a chair.

"We're going to get started on your makeup look," Phoebe announced, and the girls dispersed.

"Oh God. This has the potential to go horribly wrong, doesn't it?" I asked Wilma.

"Darling, you will leave here better than you arrived. Now, how do you feel about defuzzing these caterpillars?" she asked, running a pink-tipped fingernail over my eyebrows.

———

Wilma spun me away from the mirror, presumably to prolong the torture. But at this point, it wasn't necessary. I was resigned to my fate. I'd never had a relationship with my hair. It existed. I existed. We were two separate entities that were completely apathetic toward each other. There wasn't much Wilma could do that I would either (a) notice or (b) really, truly care about.

My main concern at the moment was paying for this. I

was still flat broke. I'd earned a few paychecks, but nearly every dime had gone to late fees on my credit cards and personal loans. The rest had gone to my parents and groceries and my athletic support of Libby.

I had a feeling my $500 emergency fund was about to be depleted to nearly nothing.

"Uhh. That looks like a lot of hair," I observed, watching very large, very long chunks of my brown hair detach from my head. My eyes were still stinging with involuntary facial hair-waxing tears.

"I'm defining a shape," Wilma said. "You have no shape. Just blah. Blah is not a shape. When was your last haircut?"

"A while ago." I was afraid what she'd do with those scissors if I admitted that it had been close to a year and a half. I'd been busy. Then broke. I wasn't going to spend money on a mane when there were bills to pay and alcohol to buy to numb my pain. It was thick, brown, and, well, that was it. Even when I worked in an office, I wore it in a tail or a knot. Elastic bands were my only accessories.

She continued violently snipping, and I tried to tune it out.

As long as it was long enough to pull back, I'd be fine. I comforted myself with that thought. When the scissors stopped, I breathed a short-lived sigh of relief. Then it was on to color or highlights or God knows what. I'd never had my hair professionally colored. The few times I'd been desperate for a change, I'd grabbed a box off the grocery store shelf and thrown it in my cart. That's how I'd ended up with burgundy hair that one Thanksgiving.

"This isn't a weird, punk rock color is it?" I asked Wilma. "I kinda have to set an example for students and not get fired by the school board."

"Your example will be a much more attractive one," she said. I noticed she hadn't bothered answering my question.

I submitted to the foil, the heat, the rinsing, all the while listening to my girls pick up and comment on every single freaking product in the store. And I vowed that no matter what it took, someday I would be in a position where I didn't have to freak out over every expense.

Wilma turned on the hair dryer and drowned out my internal pity party.

Slowly, the audience around my chair began to grow. The girls were grinning smugly as Wilma worked her long fingers through whatever was left on my head.

"Are you ready for the reveal?" Wilma asked.

She didn't wait for an answer. My chair was spinning, and the mirror was coming into view. *Please don't let it be awful. Please don't let it be awful.*

I did a double take. And then a triple one. The person in the mirror looked like me. Sort of. Except her hair was now a choppy shoulder-length cut. It was full. There were coppery highlights shimmering in the gentle waves.

"I gave you face-framing layers so you can have some visual interest when you pull it back," Wilma said, demonstrating by gathering my hair at the base of my neck in a fist. The layers cut across my forehead and curled gently around my jawline.

"It makes my forehead look normal-sized," I observed. Zinnia, in a fit of PMS, had once called my forehead a fivehead. She wasn't wrong. There was a lot of acreage above my eyebrows. And it had given me something else to be paranoid about for the rest of my life.

I tilted my head side to side and watched in fascination as those loose waves moved and caught the light. I didn't want to sound like a shallow girlie girl, but this was probably worth my emergency fund.

"Well?" Phoebe demanded. "Do you love it?"

"You better love it," Angela said.

They all chimed in, demanding my opinion.

"I do. I do love it," I admitted. "You guys definitely did not screw me over."

"She means 'thank you,'" Ruby said smugly.

I laughed and pushed my fingers into this strange hair.

"Here are three ways to wear your hair. Two of them should take under ten minutes to style. And these are your products," Wilma said, holding up a paper and a trio of bottles. "For frizzies between washing. For volume at the roots. For style hold."

"Oh, I can't afford—"

"It's all been taken care of," Wilma said. "Including the tip."

"By who?" I demanded. Had my dad stormed the store this morning, waving a credit card?

Wilma pointed to the team. "Them."

"You guys!" I stared at the girls, floored.

They grinned.

"I can't accept this. It's too much. It's probably illegal," I pointed out.

"You believed in us. You're making us better. We're just returning the favor."

"We took up a collection."

"I guilted my parents into a donation."

I was humbled. Embarrassed. Deeply touched.

"I don't know what to say," I confessed. Self-consciously, I held up my hands and formed a heart with my fingers. Grinning, my girls repeated the gesture.

"Now let's move on to makeup!"

CHAPTER 43

Marley

I didn't recognize the person in the mirror. She was tall and leanish. Her hair was artfully choppy in a careless "I rolled out of bed looking gorgeous" way that I prayed I could replicate on my own. Her normal, boring brown eyes were two times bigger thanks to a very nice neutral palette and some excellent mascara. Her lips were painted a subtle nude that shimmered a bit. Her eyebrows were waxed and glossed to perfection. And she had a mountain of cosmetics neatly lined up on her childhood dresser.

She looked like she could handle spending an evening at a bonfire with a bunch of people who would only remember how her revenge plot had ruined an entire Homecoming celebration.

She was supposed to be me. Only a better version that involved actual effort.

I couldn't help myself. I snapped a selfie and sent it to my sister.

> **Zinnia:** What the hell happened to you, and can you make it happen to me too? If this is a photo filter, I need it.
> **Me:** My team made me over. I don't recognize myself.
> **Zinnia:** You look gorgeous! Tell me you're not wasting that look on Saturday-night leftovers with M&D.

Me: Actually, Jake's taking me out.

Zinnia: You can't hear me, but I'm squealing right now. Okay. I'm squealing internally because I'm at Edith's violin concert. Where are you going? Will there be sex?

Me: Uh. Yeah. Fake relationship. Remember?

Zinnia: He's single. You're single. He's gorgeous. You're gorgeous. I'm not seeing the problem.

Me: Sex would complicate EVERYTHING.

Zinnia: Your willpower is laudable. And annoying. If you loved me at all, you'd have sex with Jake and then write up a detailed report on it for me.

Me: You're ridiculous.

Zinnia: Gotta go. Miss Edith just strode on stage in epic resting bitch face. She's about to rock this place with the Suzuki rendition of "Itsy Bitsy Spider."

Ah, precocious child protégés.

Me: Break a leg, Edith

I glanced at the time and realized Jake was picking me up any minute. I gave myself a last once-over, reveling in the fact that "oh well, whatever" didn't echo in my head like it usually did. I'd kept the jeans, changed into a cute green sweater I'd stolen from my mom's closet, and added a puffy vest for warmth. I looked…good.

My confidence was further reinforced when I answered the front door.

"Hi—" Jake's greeting cut off abruptly as he took in the visual glory of the new me.

Was there an odder pleasure in this world than having a man bowled over by your attractiveness?

"What?" I asked innocently as his gaze traveled from my

boot-clad toes to caramelly new hair. Those green eyes paused an additional second in the boobal region.

"You look…different," he mused. "Are you taller?"

"That must be it," I said, rolling my eyes. "Are we ready to go?"

"Hell yeah, pretty girl." He grinned. His eyes crinkled at the corners, and I reconsidered Zinnia's demand that I have awesome sex with Jake.

I followed him down the walkway toward the street and came to a halt. "Where's your car?"

He held out a helmet to me and stroked a loving hand over the seat of the motorcycle parked at the curb. It wasn't the crotch rocket he'd ridden in high school that had mothers warning their daughters to stay away from "that Weston boy." This was something bigger, beefier. Sexier.

"You're not afraid of a little fun, are you?"

Jake wouldn't understand that my hesitation wasn't fear. This moment was straight out of a dorky high school loser's fantasy. *The* Jake Weston was picking me up at my house on a motorcycle. I was sure I'd fantasized about this exact scenario. Today I was living out a high school ugly duckling turned swan movie. I'd had the makeover. Bonded with the cool kids. And now the cutest guy in school wanted me to climb on a bike and wrap my arms around him so he could drive us off into the sunset.

"I figured we could ride to dinner and then grab my SUV before the bonfire," Jake said, wiggling the helmet.

I took it, praying that Wilma's miracle hair spray could withstand helmet head.

"Let's do it," I said. *See? I could be cool. I was totally cool.*

"You okay? You sound kind of like you're going to hyperventilate."

I jammed the helmet over my beautiful hair. "Fine. Everything's fine."

"You ever ride before?" he asked.

I shook my heavy, helmeted head.

"I'll get on first, and then you climb on behind me. Make sure you hold on real tight," he said with a devilish wink.

Ugh. I had a crush on my fake boyfriend. This was not good.

I waited until he swung a long leg over the seat and pulled on his helmet before awkwardly climbing on behind him.

"Hang on, pretty girl," he said over the roar of the engine.

Grown-up Jake wasn't into the stupid speed that Teenage Jake had been. We cruised out of Culpepper, and I clung gleefully to his back.

I, Marley Jean Cicero, was on the back of a motorcycle, hugging the hottest boy in town. It probably wasn't healthy, but I felt that on some level, I had just healed an old wound.

Who knew having Jake between my thighs could make me feel so good? Oh, right. Everyone.

I wondered idly how many women he'd charmed the pants off of with a motorcycle ride. Then I decided it really didn't matter. I was here now. And for however long this lasted, I was going to soak it up.

We drove for another few miles, passing horses and buggies to the outskirts of Lancaster and then into the city itself. Jake took his time maneuvering the streets until—too soon in my opinion—he backed us into a spot on the street. He cut the engine and pulled off his helmet.

"We're here."

I slid off the back and yanked off my own helmet. I shook my hair out and heard a thunk and a muffled curse.

An early twentysomething had tripped over an easel sign in front of the frozen yogurt shop. He set it back up and hurried off, casting glances over his shoulder.

"She's all mine," Jake called good-naturedly after him.

"Jake!" I hissed.

"What? He saw you do the slow-motion hair toss out of a helmet and walked smack into the sign. It was fucking hilarious."

I shoved a hand into my hair. It still felt appropriately poufy, and I hoped it wasn't standing on end.

"He did not."

"Totally did," he argued. He took the helmet from me and lashed it to the bike. "You hungry?"

Looking at him in his leather jacket, his boots, his well-worn jeans, I was suddenly starving.

"I could eat."

He reached for my hand and pulled me into him. His eyes were more serious than I was used to seeing them. "You look real good, Mars."

"Thanks," I said lamely. "So do you."

He grinned and leaned in nice and slow. When his lips landed on mine, it was with a slow, sexy burn that had me insta-melting. Yeah, this Jake Weston wasn't worried about getting anywhere fast. He was more interested in having fun along the way.

He pulled back, a cocky grin on his handsome face. "Come on. I'll feed you."

He fed me tacos from a truck parked in a courtyard between a coffee shop and a music store. We laughed and flirted our way through a couple of gourmet tacos and split a cold soda on a park bench. Food gone, we walked a few blocks around the downtown. A lot had changed since I'd lived in the area. A revitalization had slowly but surely claimed entire city blocks. Now there were coworking spaces and kitschy clothing stores nestled between farm-to-table restaurants and hip small businesses.

"You're good at this," I told him after he negotiated with a guy selling flowers from a sidewalk stand.

"Here," Jake said, shoving the fall bouquet at me. "Appreciate these before we get back on the bike. Good at what?"

"Dating," I said. "A motorcycle ride, a taco truck, and now flowers? A-plus."

"It's not as hard as I thought it would be," he admitted, taking my hand. The sun had dipped behind the buildings, and the streetlights were flickering to life. "I just did what you told me. Thought about what you'd like to do and then did it."

God, he was so...*everything*. He walked down the sidewalk with a sexy swagger like he owned the city. He looked like a model out for a casual, sexy bad boy photoshoot. Don't think I didn't notice every double take from every woman and several of the men we passed.

And now he was being thoughtful and sweet?

I came to a halt on the sidewalk outside of a yarn store when the realization hit me. I was grooming Jake to be the perfect man. For someone else.

I'd go back to frantically polishing my résumé, landing jobs that weren't quite the right fit, dating guys who also weren't the right fit. Meanwhile, Jake would meet a nice girl, fall in love with her, and spend the rest of his life making her very happy.

I wanted to throw up my tacos.

"Something wrong?" he asked.

"Nope," I lied. "Everything's great."

"We should probably head back. Bonfire'll be starting soon," he said. "You done appreciating those?" He nodded at the flowers.

I took one more sniff. "Done."

He plucked them from me.

"Excuse me," he said, dragging me up to a woman in her fifties chattering away on her phone. She was wearing sweatpants and clutching a grocery bag in her free hand.

She stopped mid-sentence, her jaw working as she took in the gloriousness of Jake Weston.

"Yes?" she breathed.

"These are for you," he said with that damn devastating grin.

"Oh my! Oh, thank you!" she gushed.

"Have a nice night, gorgeous," he said, shooting her a wink.

We left her there on the sidewalk staring open-mouthed after us. I had a feeling she was feeling what I was. Unbelievably lucky and unreasonably jealous at the same time.

CHAPTER 44

Jake

Back in Culpepper, we traded my bike for my SUV and headed south out of town toward Dunkleburger's farm. Chaz Dunkleburger, who graduated two years ahead of us, took over his parents' farm when they moved to Boca and, being a nostalgic Barn Owl, preserved an acre or two of the back pasture for good old-fashioned bonfires.

Of course these were no half assed teenage bonfires.

No, we had seating and kegs and snacks. Good snacks. There was still the usual small-town drama to be had when large groups got together and started reminiscing. Overall, a bonfire on a Saturday night in Culpepper was the place to be.

Marley was quiet, and I found myself wondering what was going on in that pretty head of hers. Where some women would blab your ears off about how they were feeling about every damn thing, Marley Cicero was quieter, more mysterious.

It made me want to pry her open like an oyster.

"You sure you're up for this?" I asked, easing through the gap in the fence.

"Sure," she said.

She was definitely lying.

I pulled to a stop between a tractor and a rusted-out pickup truck. When Marley reached for the door handle, I hit the lock button.

"Jake."

"Marley."

"Let me out."

"I need your guidance first," I insisted. "Dating question."

"Okay."

"What should a guy do if his date is acting all weird and not talking? Should he pretend everything's fine? Should he force her to tell him what's wrong? Should he give up and go home and watch porn for the rest of his life?"

She was not amused.

"Come on, Mars. You're here to make me good at this. What do I do? One second you were totally fine and eating tacos, and the next you're like a sexy iceberg."

"An iceberg?"

"A sexy one," I reminded her.

"You're ridiculous."

"Come on. Spill. What's the problem?"

She ran a hand through her hair and then stopped herself. "It's embarrassing and stupid."

"You probably shouldn't discount your feelings like that."

"I'm about to spend an evening with a whole bunch of people whose main memory of me is getting suspended over antics that ruined Homecoming."

"*That's* what you're worried about?"

"Don't say it like it's ridiculous."

"Well, Mars, you grew up in a small town. You know how it goes. People talk about the last ridiculous thing you did until you give them something else to talk about."

"I destroyed Homecoming, not just for the Homecoming Court but also the soccer team. I ruined Travis's college sports career."

"First of all, I wouldn't say you ruined it. I'd say you made it interesting. You unmasked a villain."

"And then injured the soccer team's star player," she added.

"You know there's two kinds of people in this world," I began.

"You mean the kind who divide all of humanity into two groups and the kind who don't?"

"Har. Hilarious. There are people who take too much responsibility for everything and the people who don't take responsibility for anything."

"Which one are you?" God, she was pretty with the moonlight filtering in through the windshield. Her eyes were big and sad, and all I wanted to do was kiss that mouth into a smile.

"I'm one of the perfect ones who only takes credit for what I'm actually responsible for," I said smugly. "Now, it sounds to me like you've been carrying a lot of baggage around with you for too long."

"Everyone hated me," she said in a small voice.

I was surprised by her statement. But a few things started to fall into place. "No, they didn't. Maybe you're only remembering Amie Jo and her inner circle of demons, but you were a hero to half the school. You don't think you were the only person that girl tormented, do you?"

She shrugged, but I could tell she was listening.

"You weren't hated," I promised her. "And you're certainly not hated now."

She wet her lips, drawing my attention back to the mouth that fascinated me. "I just hate being judged on my eighteen-year-old self."

"Honey, we all do."

Marley looked at me, her wheels turning. "But your antics were a lot more fun."

"Do you think I like having every class of students know that a substitute teacher got fired and could have gone to jail because I talked her into a makeout session in the copy room?"

She made a noncommittal noise.

"You really think I like that attention?" I poked her in the shoulder, and she grinned.

"Maybe I made a few unfair assumptions."

I reached out and twirled a strand of her hair around my finger. "My point is, none of us are who we were at eighteen. Not even Amie Jo. And especially not you. You know what people remember more than a salacious story from our teenage years?"

"What?" she asked, resting her cheek against my hand. I felt something warm slide through my belly.

"How you make them feel now."

"You definitely aren't the same guy you were twenty years ago," Marley admitted.

"So let's go out there and erase a few old memories tonight," I told her, nodding in the direction of the bonfire.

She bit her lip and studied me. And then she was leaning across the console and placing a soft, sweet kiss on my mouth. That warmth in my belly turned molten. This was something different from the fun and familiar tug of lust. This was something more. Marley was something more.

She pulled back, that smile I wanted on her lips.

"Thanks, Coach."

———

We joined the crowd that ringed the tall flames in the middle of the star-lit field. I'd always found comfort in my history with Culpepper. I'd known the same people for decades now. And they knew me. We were part of each other's memories. There was something to be said for sharing that kind of intimate knowledge of each other.

We understood each other.

I knew that it was apple cider in Wes Zimmerman's cup because he'd quit drinking after a DUI six years ago. I also knew that as much as Heidi and Elton Pyle joked around about how hard raising triplets was, they thanked their lucky stars every moment of every day after a seven-year battle with infertility. I knew that Belinda Carlisle—not that one—needed a longer hug tonight because her mom was in hospice care and not expected to make it to the holidays.

I watched Marley join in the horseshoes game by the fire with Andrea, the guidance counselor, Faith Malpezzi, and our classmate Mariah. She was welcomed into their group like a long-lost friend. And really, that's what she was. Marley had extricated herself from Culpepper. She'd left after senior year and never looked back. So it made sense that she was frozen in everyone's mind as the girl who had been pushed too far in senior year.

"Hey, cuz!"

My cousin, Adeline, popped up next to me looking not a day over fourteen. She credited her Vietnamese heritage and Uncle Lewis's lessons on skincare.

"Hey, Addy." I looped my arm over her shoulder. "Long time no see."

My cousin might look like she was too young to drive, but she was a successful sales rep for an alternative energy company and spent a lot of her time traveling.

"I'm back for the rest of the year," she said with a happy sigh.

"I bet Rob is happy to have you back," I predicted. Addy's husband, Rob, worked from home. Together, with their four kids, they achieved a delicate balance of work and family life.

"He kissed my feet when I got off the plane," she joked. "So is that your girl?" Addy pointed her cup in Marley's direction.

"News travels fast," I said dryly.

"Spare me your social commentary on small-town gossip. Are you guys serious?"

I thought about our arrangement. Our *temporary* arrangement. And I thought about those wide, brown eyes looking up at me.

"Maybe a little more serious for me," I admitted.

"Well, well," she said smugly. "It's about damn time. What do my dads think?"

"I've been putting off their family dinner invitations."

She laughed. "Your mom's birthday is next week. You have to bring her to the party, or they'll riot."

I sighed. "I know. I will. Unless she has a game."

"Then we'll reschedule," she said helpfully.

I put her in a headlock and gave her glossy black hair a brotherly scruff. "Enough about me. What's new in your life?"

"I'm pregnant with surprise baby number five, and Rob is getting a vasectomy tomorrow."

I laughed loud and long. "Tell me this is the kid you're finally naming after me."

"Baby Jake O'Connell due next May," she said, waving at her husband, a tall Irish-looking guy who was trash-talking a neighbor in Baltimore Ravens gear. He blew her a kiss and raised his beer at me.

"Tell your dads yet?" I asked, raising my beer in response.

My uncles had the best good-news reactions.

"Saving it for your mom's birthday dinner."

"She'll love that."

"Give your girl a heads-up," Addy said, nodding in Marley's direction. "Does she even know what she's getting into with the Weston clan?"

"Now, what's the fun in warning anyone in advance? If memory serves, you didn't even tell Rob you had two dads," I mused.

She grinned. "Yeah. And he stuck, didn't he?"

"Maybe a fifth kid will push him over the edge?" I teased.

"How about I go get my baby maker, and you introduce us to your very pretty lady friend?" she suggested.

"Fine. Just don't get your fertility all over the two of us."

CHAPTER 45

Marley

Three months ago, if someone had suggested I'd be hanging out at a Culpepper bonfire enjoying myself, I would have called them a drunk and a dirty liar.

Yet here I was, slinging horseshoes at a barely visible stake plunked in the uneven pastureland.

Andrea, my new friend and part-time counselor, was looking cozy in a puffy jacket and headband that covered her ears. Mariah and Faith, my old friends, were bundled up against the fall chill reminiscing about back in the day.

Mercifully, no one had said a word about Homecoming. Yet.

"So you have how many kids?" I asked Faith.

"Three. They're exhausting, and I feel like a failure every day," she said chipperly.

"Preach, sister," Mariah agreed. "I have two kids and work part-time, and I still can't get a grocery list made or the Halloween costumes bought."

"To bad moms!" They clinked beers. Andrea giggled.

I liked their honesty. There was no white-washing or one-upping. They weren't trying to prove who was the best. And it felt refreshing.

"What about you, Marley? What's life outside of Culpepper like?"

I could have told them lies. Could have spun real life into something that sounded exciting and respectable. But, damn it, I was tired of trying to paint a fucking picture.

"It's busy. There's never any time for anything but the absolute necessities. I've been meaning to go to the gym for six years now," I confessed.

They laughed like I was doing a stand-up routine.

"Oh, you always were the funny one," Faith sighed, wiping at the corner of her eyes.

"I was?" I asked. "I always thought I was the mousy, sad one, hiding in the corner waiting for someone to like her."

"Nope. That was me," Mariah insisted.

I blinked. Mariah had been artsy and smart and, to my recollection, rather popular.

"Uh, no way. I laid claim to Sad Mousy One," Faith argued. She had been in every stage production Culpepper Junior/Senior High put on. And she made it to the semifinals in the state spelling bee when we were in the fifth grade.

"Guidance counselor secret," Andrea said, leaning in. "Ninety percent of people remember high school as a miserable experience."

"What about you, Disney princess? I bet you were prom queen and captain of the volleyball team," I guessed.

Andrea snorted. "I had braces until I was nineteen and didn't get breasts until I was twenty-one. And I was really into graphic novels. I got into the guidance counselor thing so I could tell kids like me that, usually, life after high school is a lot better."

"Now, there's someone who remembers high school fondly," Mariah said, raising her cup in the direction of the fire.

Amie Jo strolled through the crowd, greeting people like a sash-wearing beauty contestant. She was wearing a pink parka and yet another pair of Uggs, also pink. She'd probably throw them out after an evening in a cold, muddy pasture and break out the next pair in her inventory, I guessed.

Travis was behind her. If Amie Jo's outfit had a train, he'd be carrying it.

"She's wearing fake eyelashes and hair extensions to a bonfire," Faith observed with a head shake.

"I admire the effort, but I'd rather gouge my eyes out with bacon tongs than spend my free time locked in a bathroom in an endless search for perfection," Mariah claimed.

"We only have one bathroom," Faith laughed. "If I tied it up for an hour at a time, my husband would break down the door with the sports section in one hand and his Sudoku in the other."

We laughed, and I turned my back on the picture-perfect Hostetters. They didn't need any more attention.

I saw Jake coming. He had a pretty girl and a gangly redheaded man in tow.

"Marley Cicero, meet my cousin Adeline O'Connell and her husband, Rob," Jake said, taking my empty cup and handing me a fresh one. "Adeline? Rob? This is my girlfriend, Marley."

I felt my cheeks warm at the "girlfriend" introduction. I *liked* having that designation with Jake. I *liked* being attached to him in that way. And, if I were continuing with the whole honesty thing, I would be forced to admit that I liked just about everything associated with Jake.

As if reading my mind, he gave me a slow wink. There must be something in the smoke here, casting its spell of attraction. Or maybe it was the cold beer, enjoyed under a crisp autumn sky. Whatever the source of the magic, the "fake" in our relationship was becoming less and less important to me.

We made small talk, shooting the shit. Interweaving old memories with new stories. And I didn't hate it. Not with Jake's arm around my shoulders. Not with old friends, once forgotten, reminding me that childhood and high school hadn't been quite as bad as I remembered it.

It was too good to last.

"Oh. My. God," Amie Jo screeched as if seeing me for the first time. "What happened to your hair? Did you demand your money back?" She shouldered her way into our happy little circle, carrying a glass of wine. Only Amie Jo would show up to a bonfire with her own crystal.

"Oh, you don't like it? Darn," I said, lightly.

"*You* don't like it, do you? I mean, I don't see how you could. If you need someone to fix it, I'd be happy to recommend my stylist. But she books out months in advance. She's very popular." This clearly was not Amie Jo's first crystal goblet of wine.

"Amie Jo," Travis appeared behind her and laid a hand on his wife's shoulder. He sounded embarrassed.

"What? I'm just offering to help," she said batting her lashes, the picture of innocence.

"That's very sweet of you," I said as Jake reeled me in closer. "But I'm happy with everything just the way it is."

Her eyes narrowed, and I could hear her run through her long list of barely veiled insults. I didn't necessarily blame her. I'd taken a crown away from her senior year. I'd embarrassed her and ruined her senior year as much as she'd ruined mine.

"Hi, Jake," Amie Jo chirped.

Ah, she'd settled on the "flirt with the enemy's date" route.

"Hi, Hostetters," Jake said cheerfully. He ran his hand through my hair, an intimate gesture that had his cousin's eyebrows skyrocketing.

"You should have gone blond," Amie Jo said to me, fluffing her platinum mane. "I always have more fun."

"I prefer brunettes," Jake said, winking at me lecherously.

I didn't know if he was standing up for me, slapping Amie Jo down, or complimenting me. Whatever it was, it made my intestines feel like they were full of molten Hershey's chocolate. In a good way.

"If you'll excuse us. I think I need to make out with my lady in the shadows," Jake said. He led me by the hand out of the group, away from the crackle and heat of the bonfire.

I laughed. "Well, *that's* an exit everyone will be talking about," I said dryly.

But he just pulled me deeper into the night until it was just the two of us and the dark.

And then he was kissing me. Slow and deep. Thoroughly. Like he wanted the air I was breathing. I wrapped my arms around his neck and held on for dear life.

He'd kissed me before. I'd kissed him. But this was the first time that I felt like our agreement, the premise of our relationship, was disintegrating under newly applied heat.

This felt real.

It didn't feel like a game or a joke or pretend.

I kissed him back, pouring myself into him. Letting myself go. For once.

He pulled back and ran his thumb over my lower lip. "I loved looking across the fire and seeing you smile at me," he said gruffly.

Oh crap. There was nothing fake about that declaration.

"Maybe we should talk about this," I suggested. If we got a bit of air, if we talked it through, maybe the terrifying edge of these feelings would wear down. Maybe I could manage them. Survive them.

"I have a better idea than talking," Jake said softly.

He shoved one hand into my nice, new hair and used the other to drag me against him.

CHAPTER 46

Marley

"Come home with me." Jake wasn't asking or begging. It wasn't even a question, an offer. It was a statement. A direct order.

And I had no intention of arguing with him. Not even for posterity's sake.

I *wanted* to be wanted. Even just for one night. And especially by him.

I was throbbing everywhere for him. The pulse between my legs had gone beyond noticeable to life-threatening. I wanted his touch on every square inch of my body. Even the parts I wasn't totally fond of. I wanted him to blaze a trail from my scalp to my toes. Kissing and licking his way over me until we were both satisfied. Or dead.

I kissed him again, reveling in the scrape of his stubble against my jaw. The pressure of his mouth against mine, the heat that he was pouring into me.

I'd had half a beer, but my head swam as if an entire bottle of tequila had found its way into my bloodstream. *This* is what Jake Weston did to a woman. And he was doing it to me. Finally.

Without breaking our hold on each other, we fumbled through the tree line that skirted Chaz's pasture, tripping and stumbling back to Jake's SUV.

And when his hands slid under my sweater and cupped my breasts through my bra, I knew we weren't making it home.

Still kissing him, still making needy little groans, I wrestled the back door open.

"Are you kidding me right now, Mars?" he asked, his teeth nipping at my earlobe.

"Do you want to wait until we get back to your place when I've had a whole car ride to come to my senses?" I asked, scooting onto the back seat.

"No. No, I do not," he said, jumping in behind me. "Take off your shoes."

"Huh?"

"Shoes, Mars. Lose 'em," he said, shrugging out of his coat and dragging his shirt over his head. Oh, Lord. The ink. The muscle. The chest hair.

Jake Weston was all man. And, for tonight, he was all mine.

I kicked off my boots, and then his nimble fingers went to work at the fly of my jeans. Hypnotized, I watched his hands as they competently worked my pants down. I lifted my hips to help while he wrangled them past my knees and stripped them off completely.

"Turn around, Mars," he said. His voice was ragged like a gravel road. "Hands and knees."

That would put my ass in his face. I didn't usually like to shove my very round, rather full posterior in men's faces.

"Why?" I asked. I sounded like I'd just run up the practice field steps sixteen times.

"I gotta do something, baby. I've been dying to."

The vagueness of his statement should have resulted in a color guard of red flags. But the lust zinging through my blood like a drug made me stupid.

I did what he said. Before I could worry about what he was

seeing up close, he was yanking my simple cotton briefs down and then—

"Did you just bite me?" I yelped.

His teeth were *definitely* on my ass.

He groaned without releasing my flesh from his mouth. I felt him suck and lick hard enough that I cried out. It felt *good*. Wrong and delicious and wonderful.

Then he was kissing the abused inch of flesh. "I've been thinking about doing that since I threw you over my shoulder. I wanted it to be my knee," he rasped.

Could I orgasm just from his voice? Low, guttural, dirty. Okay. No. But still.

He licked over the spot he'd bitten and, at the same time, shoved two fingers into me without warning. "Oh, fuck me, Mars," he breathed, pumping his fingers into me. "Jesus, baby. You are so fucking ready."

I would have answered, but I'd smashed my face against the window. Letting it cool my skin. I bucked against him. Never in my wildest dreams had I imagined that my body had the capacity to feel all this. I'd held on to a library of rote fantasies that I dutifully used to orgasm during sex. But this? With Jake? I couldn't hold a thought in my head other than, "Oh God, yes!"

He worked me mercilessly, and I heard him lower his zipper.

Masterful womanizer that he was, Jake released his cock from the confines of his jeans one-handed while his other hand busily destroyed me. He levered up on the seat situating himself behind me. And then I felt the drag of the smooth head of his dick on my ass cheek. It was wet.

He was grunting softly, and I imagined him stroking himself with one big, hard hand while using his other to drive me fucking insane.

I needed to see. I needed to watch him jerk himself off to me. That would be the new permanent installation in the Marley Cicero Spank Bank Hall of Fame.

My muscles quivered around his talented digits, and I realized I was seconds away from death by orgasm. I was on my hands and knees. Nothing had so much as grazed my clitoris. My boobs were still covered. He was a maestro of the female orgasm. And he was using his powers for good tonight.

"Baby, you're so close," he groaned. "Don't you fucking come."

"What?" Oh my God. He wasn't one of those alpha asshole orgasm withholders, was he? I was *not* into that.

"I need to see you. I need to be in you when you come."

I thought about swooning and decided against it. I wanted this orgasm more than I wanted to live into my eighties.

"Jake, hurry the fuck up, or one of us will die."

He laughed and slapped at my hip. "Roll, baby."

"Condom, Weston."

I rolled onto my back as Jake dug through his console. He pulled out an entire strip of condoms as if his console was a safe sex dispenser. I rolled my eyes as he used his teeth on the first one.

He looked so *dirty*. His chest was bare, the veins in his tattooed arms stood out. And that cock. That magnificent, long, thick cock jutted out of his jeans proudly. I felt light-headed. And desperate. He rolled the condom on, and I hit myself in the jaw with my knee while I wrestled my underwear off of one leg.

"Do you have any idea what you do to me, Marley?" he asked, shards of glittering glass in his voice. I would have rolled over those shards if it made him touch me.

"If it's half of what you're doing to me, I'd say you're in deep shit," I guessed.

His green eyes softened for a beat, and then he was leaning over me and pressing a kiss to my mouth. It wasn't hurried or frantic, but it still had the same effect. His erection prodded at my entrance while his lips gently ravaged my mouth.

He pulled back, still hovering over me. His expression soft, affectionate. He looked like he was going to tell me something I'd treasure for the rest of my life. Something about my under-the-radar beauty or my womanly charms. How I'd hypnotized him with my wit.

"Lose the sweater," he said gruffly.

I blinked, then laughed. To Jake, that probably was romantic. And I'd take it. With his help, I pulled Mom's sweater over my head. He threw it into the front seat and then made quick work of my bra.

My usually sensitive nipples were already on high alert, and when the cold night air hit them, I felt them pebble into tight buds.

"Oh my God," he breathed.

"What? What's wrong?" Were they lopsided? Did I have weird underwire marks on them?

"I've been thinking about your tits since I dumped you in the locker room shower."

Reverently, he cupped them both. I couldn't think of anything in this world that could compete with the feel of Jake's palms on my boobs. Not a litter of golden retriever puppies. Not world peace. Not even triple chocolate fudge brownies with ice cream.

"You're going to kill me," he murmured.

I couldn't tell if he was talking to me or my tits. But we were all good with it.

"Can I?" he asked, still staring at them. I could feel the hair on his hard thighs against mine. Yeah, he could pretty much have his way with any body part right now.

"Yes," I hissed.

And then his mouth was closing over one pert nipple. I nearly launched myself off the seat. Yeah, sensitive nipples. I mentioned that before. But sensitive nipples with a man who knew what he was doing and wasn't afraid of really enjoying himself? GAH! Sweet baby cheeses, I wasn't going to live through this, and I didn't even care.

"Jake, if you want to be in me when I come, then you better get moving now," I said desperately. He wasn't even fucking me with his fingers, and I was still ready to explode.

He pulled back from my breast, leaned in, gave the other one a lick, and growled his approval. "Just so you know. Once isn't enough. I'm just getting started, pretty girl."

"Less talking. More orgasms," I begged.

I watched him fist his cock in one hand. Even wrapped in latex, it was a sight. The Eighth Wonder of the World: Jake Weston's Erect Penis.

And then he was lining himself up with my entrance. "You sure?"

I nodded. There were a lot of things in life I wasn't sure about. Should I register independent or choose a political party? Would I have better luck landing a dream job in a big city or a smaller suburb? How did the remote start on my car work?

But wanting Jake inside me. That was as clear of a yes as I ever had.

"Hold on to me," he said, and then he was easing into me inch by spectacular inch.

CHAPTER 47

Jake

So this was what Heaven felt like.

S   I was buried inside Marley Cicero and trying my hardest not to explode. I thought about Homer and my grandma. Homer eating my grandma's broccoli casserole at Thanksgiving. I thought about the gas bill I'd left lying on a flat surface somewhere in the house.

Anything but the woman under me, around me.

Damn it. I was thinking about her again. I could feel my pulse in the tip of my dick and knew I was one jerky thrust away from coming so hard my fillings would pop out.

"Are we good?" she panted under me.

"Baby, don't take this the wrong way. But if you say another word or move a muscle, this is going to be really embarrassing for me and really disappointing for you."

She gave the tiniest laugh, and it almost put me over the edge.

Homer. Grandma. Broccoli. Gas. Did the Steelers have a shot at the Super Bowl this year? John Quincy Adams.

The old white guy did it. I felt the biological need to hose Mars down with my ejaculation dull just enough that I could start moving again.

I pulled out slowly, reveling at the drag of her flesh gripping me. She wasn't just tight. She was holding me like she'd been specially made for me. And her muscle strength down there was impressive.

"Fuck. Mars. You feel amazing," I said, sliding back into her.

"Jake, I think I'm going to…" She interrupted herself with a long low moan, and I felt it echoing in the eager quivering around my dick.

"Yeah, baby. Let me have it. Give it up for me," I said, lowering myself onto her. Her breasts smashed against my chest, and I wished I had a few days just to suck on those perky, rosy nipples. I wished I had months to make love to her. Years to explore her body until there were no secrets left.

She was there. I could feel it even through the layer of latex that I was currently cursing. I wanted to feel her climax up close and in person.

"Come with me," she breathed.

Women have no idea the turn-on and stress statements like that bring. First of all, it's really fucking hard to time your own orgasm with a woman. But when you do it right, hot sex turns into a spiritual experience. And for Marley, I was willing to minister or preach or whatever the fuck the right metaphor was.

I pulled out again, but this time I slammed into her and growled when I felt her grip me like a glove. *Fuck. Fuck. Fuck.*

I thrust again, harder and faster this time.

"Yes, Jake! Yes!" She was yelling now, and I fucking loved it.

She had one foot on the window behind me and one hand on the one above us. Condensation coated the glass as I pistoned into her like a machine. And there it was, boiling up in my balls, working its way to the base of my spine.

She was coming. I felt the first wave. The clench and release, and that was all it took. My orgasm exploded up my cock and burst free.

I made some kind of unintelligible grunting groan. Half wild animal, half desperate man. It abraded my throat coming out. I pumped into her, wishing that I was coming into her depths, mixing with her release. I wanted to paint her from the inside out as she wrung me dry with each heaving sob of her own orgasm. Her muscles choked me, making sure I'd lost every single drop of come to her. I was wrung dry, and it still wasn't enough.

I collapsed on her, loving the feel of Marley trembling under me.

"Wow. Wow. Wow," she whispered, her lips moving against my neck.

I grunted my agreement.

My pants were still on. My cock was still in her. And we'd just fucked in a field like a couple of stupid teenagers. I was beyond happy. Beyond satisfied. Beyond wanting to do it again.

"Wow," she said again.

My lips curved. "Am I crushing you?"

"You're holding me on the surface of the planet, because what we just did destroyed gravity," she said.

"Do you have any idea what you're saying?" I asked, nuzzling her hair. It smelled like vanilla and cinnamon. And I wondered if I'd ever be able to smell those scents again without going porn-star hard.

"Words are just bubbling up like lava. I have no control. Lipstick. Penalty kick. Casserole," she said. Her hands found my hips, and she squeezed me there. I liked that, too. I wanted to fold her up in my arms, hold her tight against me. But we were crammed into my back seat. And I didn't do shit like that.

"Do you usually have this effect on women?" she asked, giving a little laugh.

The laugh had her tightening around me again, and my cock stirred. It was a little too soon for Round Two, especially after that orgasm that had ripped through me and flayed me.

"Are you still hard?" she asked on a gasp.

"Getting there. Like I said, Mars. I don't think one time is gonna be enough. And I *really* hope you're cool with that."

I could feel her thinking, so I picked my head up to stare down at her. She was chewing her lip, considering.

I dropped a kiss on her mouth. It was supposed to be sweet and soft, but she opened her damn mouth for me, and my tongue was plundering like it was his job. Marley brought her knees up around my hips, drawing me in deeper.

"Baby, I need more. I want you in a bed. My bed."

"Jake?" she whispered, tracing a finger over my jaw and then pressing it to my lips.

She was going to tell me I was a stallion. The best lover she'd ever had. That she'd fallen in love with me and was going to spend most of her waking hours naked with me. "Yeah, Mars?"

"Will you help me find my pants?"

I laughed at my own stupidity, and she grinned up at me.

God, she was beautiful. Her brown eyes were warm and heavy. Her hair was a freaking mess. And the smile that played on her swollen, abused lips was angelic. I so wasn't done with her. With us.

"If I help you find your pants, will you come home with me?"

She nodded, and that sweet smile did something weird to my chest region. It felt warm. Like heartburn, only nice.

We fumbled for clothes in the dark.

"I can't believe we had sex in a back seat in a field," Marley scoffed as she worked her way back into her jeans.

"I'll make it up to you on a nice king-size," I promised.

"Oh, are you talking about your dick?" she teased.

Well, fuck me sideways. I was in love.

I stared at her as she wiggled into her sweater. When her

head popped through the hole, her hair was standing up in all directions. Her makeup was smudged, and she was happier than I'd ever seen her. I did the only thing I could do. I tumbled off my bachelor pedestal face-first, hitting every step on the way down. This was going to be a freaking disaster.

––––––––

I probably should've tried to pump the brakes, not maul her on my front porch. But Marley was irresistible, and I was powerless. All I knew was that my cock wanted to be buried inside her again—lasting longer than ten minutes this time, thank you very much—and that I wanted to wake up to that sweet, sleepy smile.

"Text your mom," I insisted, raining kisses down her throat. I had to pull back, careful not to leave any marks. I wasn't a seventeen-year-old hornball with no finesse. No, I was a nearly thirty-nine-year-old hornball with decent skills. And more self-control than I was displaying currently. "Tell her you're not coming home tonight."

"Okay," she breathed. "Let me find my phone."

She dug for it with one hand while cupping my aching hard-on through my jeans with the other.

"What are you doing?"

"Multitasking."

I unlocked my front door and unzipped my jeans in the span of 1.7 seconds before pushing her inside. She was more interested in wrestling my cock out than finding her phone, so I took charge.

I slammed the door and dumped her purse on the floor and kicked through the contents. She knelt down, and I thought she was going to pick up her phone, but then her mouth was on the crown, and her tongue was doing evil, beautiful things to the very sensitive underside.

"Mars! You gotta warn a guy before you—oh, fuck."

I lost my balance and crashed back against the front door. The thump had Homer hurling himself down the stairs in a lather of barking and growling. From past experience, I knew it was dangerous to wave my wiener around when my dog was stirred up.

He wasn't a biter by nature, but I'd had a couple of close calls after Uncle Max had bought Homer a flesh-colored hot dog toy.

"Marley, baby," I pulled her to her feet and picked her phone off the floor. "I'm going to let Homer out. Text your parents. You're not going home tonight."

She nodded, looking a little dazed and a lot happy. "Okay."

I jogged to the back of the house and sent Homer on his way into the backyard. "It might be a while, buddy," I warned him.

Homer trotted outside, tail wagging, not a care in the world.

And I ran back inside to my lady.

CHAPTER 48

Marley

Me: Don't wait up tonight!

Mom: Wait up for what?

Me: Me to come home.

Mom: Why would I do that? You're almost 40.

Me: I'm just saying I won't be home tonight, and you shouldn't worry.

Mom: Why won't you be home tonight??? Did something happen??? Are you okay?

Me: Mom, I just said don't worry.

Mom: TELL ME WHAT NOT TO WORRY ABOUT!

Me: I'm having sex with Jake. Okay? There. You made me say it. It's your own fault, and now we can never make eye contact again. Don't tell Dad.

Mom: Have fun at Bible study, sweetie.

Me: ???

Mom: Just kidding! I'm a cool mom. Condoms are fun. Make good choices!

"Everything all right?"

I jumped, and my phone and purse slipped out of my grasp and landed on the floor in the pile of tampons, loose change, and other bottom-of-the-purse rubbish. *Was that a whole candy bar or just the wrapper?*

Jake was standing at the foot of the stairs looking all kinds of sinful with his jeans still undone. His dark hair was a mess. His sleeves were pushed up, and there was a wild look in his eyes.

He'd let Homer out into the backyard. It was just the two of us. Alone. Horny.

The primitive, sexy time part of our brains must have taken over because, instead of picking up my phone or cleaning up the purse debris, I launched myself at him. He caught me in the air and crushed me against his chest, winding my legs around his hips.

I decided I could cling to him permanently. His hand was in my hair, pulling it just hard enough for sparks to ignite on my scalp.

"You drive me fucking crazy, Marley," he said, pelting me with wild kisses. He used teeth and tongue as weapons, and I was only too happy to surrender. "I want to go slower this time," he said.

There was nothing leisurely about the way he was looking at me.

"But?"

"But I don't think I can this time. Maybe the third or the seventeenth time."

"I'm good with that." My lipstick was on his mouth, and it was freaking hot.

"Bed?" he asked.

"Yeah. Hurry."

He didn't put me down, merely jogged up the stairs with me clinging to him. I was no waiflike flower. I was solid with healthy curves and muscle. And being handled like a package turned out to be an incredible turn-on.

So did being tossed on the bed like a suitcase. I was working my jeans free on the first bounce.

"Strip. Everything," he insisted, standing at the foot of the bed and tearing off his shirt. I obliged, and we both raced for nudity. He won and celebrated by tackling me to the mattress.

I couldn't be bothered to look around and take in the scenery, even though I was in the forbidden paradise of Jake Weston's bedroom. Not with his foot-long sub staring at me.

We tangled with each other, rolling and gasping for breath. Our hands were everywhere. Our mouths were fused. My heart raced. I was galloping into heart attack territory with the adrenaline coursing through me. And I didn't care. All I wanted was an orgasm like the one I'd had less than an hour ago. I wanted Jake to chase it down for me and present it to me on a silver platter.

"Your tits are perfection," he groaned, pressing his face to my chest and nuzzling in.

I'd had him pegged as a boob man. He latched on to a nipple, and I writhed next to him. Reaching between us, I found his cock ready and waiting.

He pumped himself into my hand as he devoured my breast. I threw a leg over his hip and angled the head of his penis against me. Every time he thrust into my hand, he nudged against that needy bundle of nerves that had never been more alive.

It was more than enough stimulus. In seconds, a ninja orgasm snuck up and blindsided me.

"Jake!"

"Mmph."

The world went cotton-candy-colored with glitter and rainbows as I dry humped him to victory. I was so wet I worried about long-term damage to his mattress. It was like the rainy season in Costa Rica down there.

"Need you," he groaned, releasing my breast.

We rolled closer to the side of the bed. I was on top of him, kissing the ever-living shit out of him. Blindly, he reached into his nightstand. The drawer crashed to the floor but not before he grabbed the tail end of another roll of condoms.

"Stay right there, baby," he said, sliding me down his thighs far enough that he could roll the condom on.

I helped. And by "helped," I mean I stroked his shaft with the desperate violence of the sex-starved woman that I was.

Then he was grabbing my hips and lifting me up. With eager fingers, I gripped him, lining the head of his erection up with my desperate-for-another-orgasm greed hole.

Notched in place, Jake stared up at me and gave one swift thrust.

I probably screamed. Why else would Homer start barking in the backyard? But it didn't matter if the neighbors were waking up to screaming and barking. If they called the cops and reported us for disturbing the peace and unmarried sex, I assumed that was still a law on the books somewhere—it didn't matter if Jake and I were sentenced to death by stoning.

The only thing that did matter was how beautifully full I was, impaled on his stone-hard cock. We froze like that for long seconds before I started to move. I wasn't a reverse cowgirl—my quads weren't strong enough—butthole-waxing, walk-in-closet sex-toy-having kind of woman. I was experienced but not expert level.

But something about Jake Weston groaning beneath me turned me into a wanton sex goddess.

And this wanton sex goddess was riding the stallion beneath her as if they'd both die if she—I—didn't.

His hip thrusts hammered into me rhythmically as I rode him. Two bodies united in purpose. His fingers dug into my hips, and for once, I wasn't concerned with how much flesh was there to hold on to. Or whether my boobs were bouncing too much or if I should have done more than just shave my nether region.

No, I was too busy ravaging and being ravaged.

Nothing had ever felt this good before. And I guessed nothing ever would. I could accept that. I could accept the fact that my sexual experience would peak at age thirty-eight at the hands—and penis—of Jake Weston. I was willing to have nothing but mediocre sex for the rest of my life if I could have him like this now.

His hands were at my breasts now, cupping and stroking, busy thumbs rubbing over my at-attention nipples.

I dropped my head back and released a long groan from my throat. Perfect. Everything was perfect.

"You were made for me, baby," he gritted out.

"Don't make this weird." I gasped for breath.

"*You* don't make this weird," he countered.

"Stop talking."

On a dirty, guttural growl that had my vagina standing up and applauding, Jake shoved and rolled. He came up on his knees. "I want to have you every way possible," he said, pushing me onto my belly.

Grabbing my ankles, he pulled me back against him. I scrambled eagerly to my hands and knees. "Is this good with you?" he asked. I felt him teasing me just outside my entrance. The tip of his shaft nudging, waiting for permission.

"God, yes."

Carefully, slowly, enticingly he sank into my flesh. "Oh, yeah, Mars. Yeah, baby."

He pulled out and just as slowly thrust back in. His hands, those broad palms, caressed my back, my hips, my ass cheeks. And all the while, he fucked me.

It felt like…poetry. The perfection of my body welcoming his, embracing his. I was better because he was inside me.

And the way he moved in and out of me. It was like worship, obsession.

I could feel sweat forming on our skin. Hear our ragged breaths as we embraced a more reckless speed. He rolled his hips against me on a long, deep thrust, and I pushed back against the mattress to take all of him.

He leaned forward, hinging over me, one hand gripping my hair. His lips moving against my ear.

"I love this, baby. You're perfect," he whispered. He was losing the steadiness. Abandoning the finesse. Now, he was a beast in rut, and I was the object of his lust.

He released my hair and grabbed my breast, palming it as it bounced and wobbled from every hard thrust.

"Touch yourself," he ordered on a rasp. "Touch yourself for me, Mars."

I obliged, circling my clit with eager fingers. Dipping my head, I looked under me. I saw his hand working my breast. Watched his dick tunnel into me, his balls slap against my thighs. Over and over. Faster. Harder.

His grip on me was punishing, and I fucking loved it because I was coming apart at the seams. My fingers blurred at their work, and I couldn't hang on any longer. I was going up in flames.

"I feel you, baby. Let it happen," Jake breathed.

I let go, flinging my body into the epicenter of the explosion. My body was light and heat. I could feel the orgasm in my fingertips and toenails. Those deviously talented little inner muscles clamped down on him so hard he groaned.

I rode it out, spiraling out of control.

"Can I come on you?" The question was far away but desperate. I could hear the clench in his jaw, the rawness in his throat.

Oh, God. Yes! YES! HELL YES!

"Yep."

He pulled out of me, but before I could complain, Jake shoved two fingers back inside me. He grunted, and on one long, sinful groan, I felt him come across my back. Hot ropes hit my skin, branding me.

"Fuuuck," he rasped. I squeezed his fingers with my muscles and was rewarded with more of his orgasm. He kept coming, kept fucking me with his fingers. I don't know if it was the same climax or a surprise second one, but it rolled through me, and I pushed and jerked my way to Heaven against his hand, covered in his release.

CHAPTER 49

Marley

I feel like I should apologize." Jake's voice was muffled by my hair. His face was pressed into my neck. I hadn't moved except to collapse onto my belly. He'd gotten a warm, damp towel from the bathroom and cleaned us both up while I languished like a limp piece of lettuce on his sweaty, tangled sheets.

"Apologize for what?" I said to the mattress.

"I feel like that's kind of a big no-no, making an ask like that the first time you have sex," he said.

"An ask like what?" I smiled to myself, knowing exactly what he was talking about.

"Uh, you know. The, uh, coming on you thing."

"Technically it was the second time," I said, holding up two fingers and nearly blinding him.

He kissed my fingers and rolled me onto my back.

"I'm serious. Did I fuck up?"

I gave him a lazy smile. Every muscle in my body was loose and happy.

"I think you clued in on our compatibility and went with it."

"Marley," he said. "Manspeak, please."

"Me liked."

"You sure? I didn't want to take the gift of sex and piss all over it."

"Gross. That wasn't piss, was it?" I joked.

"As long as you're sure I didn't take it too far. I got a little carried away," he confessed.

I cupped my hand to his face, delighted by the stubble I found there. "I'm sure," I promised.

"Good." He dropped a kiss on my bare shoulder. "You hungry?"

Those truck tacos were long gone, lost to the calorie furnace of sex. "Starving," I admitted.

He slapped me on the ass. "Meet me downstairs. I'll whip up something for us. And by whip up something, don't get your hopes up too high. I mostly microwave and dump things out of a can."

"Good enough," I told him.

Whistling, he pulled on a pair of gray sweatpants—hallelujah, Lord—and disappeared with a wink.

I lay there, still lettuce-limp, enjoying the way my body felt after a thorough round of sex. Downstairs, I heard Jake open the back door and the scrabble of doggy toenails on the floor. They had their own conversation while Jake made a ruckus opening and closing cabinet doors and drawers.

I took my time looking around his room. High ceilings in here like on the first floor. The same fancy wood trim. Same hardwood floors. He could do with a rug in here, I thought. Oh, hell. And drapes. I hoped there weren't any peeping eyes beyond the windows because if there were, they'd gotten one hell of a show.

The window bowed out and was framed in by a dusty window seat. Its bench could use a thick cushion.

The room looked as though he'd plopped furniture into it and decided to worry about the rest of it later. There was a dresser pulled slightly away from the wall on one end as if something had rolled behind it and been retrieved.

Where the giant pile of dirty laundry resided in the corner, I pictured a deep chair and side table. A quiet place to read or nap on winter days.

The only other thing in the room was a very large picture of a crucified Jesus hanging on the wall next to the door. I had a feeling that had come with the house.

I got up and stretched before beginning my quest for the bathroom. One door led to a walk-in closet. There was more clothing on the floor than hanging up. I found a bathroom through the other door and cleaned myself up. The toilet had a pull-chain flusher. The vanity, a coating of dust.

Grinning, I combed my hair with my fingers, trying to reform Wilma's shape and style. Jake Weston wasn't so perfect after all. He really was a slob.

I gave up on my hair and went in search of clothing. I didn't want to put Mom's sweater back on my recently sexed body. I mean, I was already going to have to buy the woman a new one to make up for debauching the old one. So I helped myself to a floor T-shirt that passed the smell test.

I padded downstairs and headed into the kitchen.

Jake was still shirtless and stirring something on the stove. Homer was snarfing down his dinner. He paused to grumble and wag his tail at me before diving back into the kibble. A domestic scene that caused my lady heart to pitter-pat.

"What's cooking, Chef Weston?"

He looked up and skimmed me from head to toe. "Now, that's a pretty picture," Jake said.

The man was good with flattery. I had to give him that.

I pulled out a barstool and sat across from him, resting my chin in my hands.

"I hope you like SpaghettiOs," Jake said, pulling the sauce pan off the stove and dividing its contents between two bowls.

"SpaghettiOs?" I asked in wonder. "I don't think I've had a can of SpaghettiOs since college."

"I got some Lebanon bologna, too. Other than that, your only choice is some kind of furry Chinese takeout that's so old I don't remember ordering it."

"I'll stick with the Os and the bologna."

"A wise choice. We can eat on the couch," he said, pushing one of the bowls toward me.

We dined on childhood favorites on his couch while watching reruns of *Cheers* and *Parks and Rec* on his gigantic flat screen.

"So how am I doing so far with this dating thing?" he asked, taking my empty bowl and adding it to his on the coffee table. I guessed they'd sit there for a week or two.

Oh, right. We weren't *actually* dating. I was just grooming him to date someone else. He'd be coaxing orgasms out of a new woman and making her canned food by Valentine's Day, I predicted.

I ordered the canned pasta to stay in my stomach and not projectile vomit across the room.

I cleared my throat. "Good." *Great.*

Homer trotted in and shoved his head in my lap.

"You're in his spot," Jake explained and slid me a couple of inches closer to him. Homer hopped up onto the couch, circled the cushion, and flopped down with a heavy sigh.

"You're doing great," I admitted. Eh. I'd worry about the stickiness of our consummated fake relationship later. I snuggled up against his side and rested my head on his shoulder.

He pulled a throw off the back of the couch and handed it to me.

"I think I'm ready to meet your parents," he said while I was busy spreading the blanket out.

"You already have," I pointed out, baffled.

"No, I mean like dinner and talking. Not just picking you up and being charming for five seconds."

Okay, it was one thing for me to get a little wrapped up in our *arrangement*. But I didn't want my parents falling for the guy only to have us fake break up right before I left town.

"Seriously?" I mean, I guess I owed the guy the complete girlfriend experience. Even if it hurt to deliver.

"Yeah," Jake said. "I want this to go the distance."

He didn't realize how real he was making us sound, I told myself.

"You know I'm not an expert on relationships, right? Obviously, none of mine have worked out," I reminded him.

"You're more experienced than I am."

"Meet the parents. Got it. Anything else?"

"Okay. What about gift-giving?" he said, pausing the show on Ron Swanson's frowning, mustachioed face.

"Gift-giving?"

"Yeah, like, how do I know what to buy you and when? What's the budget for birthdays and holidays? How does being a couple at Christmas work? Do I buy your family presents?"

"Uh. Those are valid and very specific questions. And that's all going to depend on the relationship. For instance, you and your girlfriend might decide that she buys for her family and you buy for yours. The main thing to remember is it's important to talk about things like that in advance. You don't want to go all out and buy her diamond stud earrings for Valentine's Day when she just gives you a coupon book for massages and hugs."

"It all comes back to communication, doesn't it?" Jake asked with a yawn. His fingers stroked my arm under the sleeve, leaving the skin deliciously sensitive.

"Pretty much. Yeah."

He was quiet for a minute. The silence was punctuated by

Homer's nasally snores and the beat of his tail as he dreamed good dreams.

"Why are you leaving, Marley?" Jake asked.

I blinked and shifted to look at him.

"Because I don't belong here. I want something bigger. Something more than Culpepper can offer."

"Do you like teaching? Coaching?" he asked.

I thought about it. About the wins. The makeover. The girls. Most of the rest of the students. Floyd. Vicky. Haruko. Jake. "Yeah. I do," I decided. "But it's not the plan."

"And there's no way this could, I don't know, end up being what you want?" he asked.

I snorted. Find what I've been looking for in Culpepper? The place I couldn't wait to leave as soon as that diploma was in my hot, little hand? "Trust me. Culpepper and I are better off apart," I told him. "Why do you ask?"

I wanted it to be because he liked me. Because he'd miss me if I were gone. But he'd replaced me once. What were the odds that he wouldn't do it again?

He gave a shrug. "No reason."

He hit the play button, and we turned our attention back to Leslie and Ron.

CHAPTER 50

Jake

I woke from the best night of sleep of my life to an empty bed. My bliss instantly evaporated, and I bolted from my cocoon. She'd been here. She'd gone to bed with me. We'd argued good-naturedly about the quality of my linens and pillows. To be fair, she had a point. I was nearing forty with a good job, and these cheap-ass sheets were rough enough to exfoliate.

It was time to upgrade.

Uncle Lewis was going to fucking love Marley if her influence got me into a store with sheets and curtains and shit.

I heard a clunk from downstairs and a short bark followed by a laugh.

She was here.

I dragged my sweats on and noticed, possibly for the first time, the giant mound of laundry in the corner on the floor. Maybe it was time I did a little growing up elsewhere too.

I found a laundry basket in the closet and filled it to the brim. Whatever didn't fit I threw back into the closet and closed the door. I'd deal with that later.

I found Marley and Homer deep in conversation in the kitchen. There were grocery bags on the counter, and Homer was eying a new bag of dog treats every time he surfaced from wolfing down his breakfast.

"Good morning," Marley said, beaming at me from across the island.

Well, shit. So that's how it felt. Knowing you wanted to do something every day for the rest of your life. That's what I wanted right now. And it was incredibly inconvenient, seeing as how the object of my affection had just reiterated her desire to blow this Popsicle stand once her obligations here were finished.

"Morning," I said, dropping the laundry basket on the kitchen table and swooping in for a long, hard kiss. She wanted to leave? Fine. But I wasn't going to make it easy on her. "What are you doing up so early?"

She laughed and pointed at the clock with a spatula. "It's 9:30."

"On a Sunday," I pointed out. "For teachers, the weekends are little slivers of reprieve."

"Homer woke me with his cold nose and a very insistent demand to go outside," she said, returning to the pan on the stove.

My dog was an asshole. But a cute one.

"Usually I can get a couple more hours of sleep after his demands are met," I told her.

"Well, since I was up and you didn't have anything edible in the house, Homie and I took a quick ride over to the grocery store, and I got some necessities."

I felt...cared for. Spoiled. Cherished.

"Really?" I asked, clearing the emotion out of my voice.

"Yeah. Cheesy omelets are almost done. Wanna pour the coffee and get the bacon? I put it in the microwave so it wouldn't get cold."

She made me breakfast. Bought me groceries. Took my dog for a car ride. *Fuck. Fuck. Fuck. Fuck. I was truly fucking sunk.*

And Homer was basically laughing at me with his doggy smirk.

"Sure. Awesome. Yeah," I said, digging out a pair of mugs and trying not to think how domestic this all was. Forget haunting. Grams had taken control of my mind. I needed an exorcism.

"It's kind of warm outside and not as unclean as in here. Want to eat on the porch?" Marley asked.

I followed her through the back door, juggling plates and mugs and utensils that she must have washed herself, since I'd been using plastic ware for weeks now.

We sank onto the wicker couch and dumped our breakfasts on the little coffee table. Fall was in the air, but summer was pushing back, clinging to the late September Sunday. It would be a good day for a leisurely run.

"Think you could go for a few miles today?" I asked Marley.

She forked up a bite of omelet. "Sure. It'll have to be this afternoon though. Uh, were you serious about meeting my parents?"

"Yeah. Definitely," I told her. I shoveled a bite of cheesy eggs into my face. "Whoa. What magic did you work here?"

She smiled prettily. "It's all in cage-free eggs and good cheese," she confessed. "Anyway, you're invited to dinner tonight. At my parents'."

I chewed thoughtfully. Sipped my coffee. "Cool. What kind of hostess gift should I bring?"

"You're really into this gift thing, aren't you?" Marley teased.

"I am. Stick around, and you'll be showered in thoughtful trinkets."

She grinned, and I decided this was my favorite Sunday morning in recent history. "Why?" she asked.

"Why what?"

"Why do you like giving gifts?"

I bit into a crisp piece of bacon. "Dunno. I like finding something that I know someone will love. You know, put thought into it. Show them I care, I guess."

"What's the last gift you bought?"

"Mmm. I got this painting for my mom. A custom job of her dog. Got it framed and everything. Her birthday's coming up. She's coming out from Jersey for a weekend. We're doing up a dinner party at my uncles'."

"Do you and your mom have a good relationship?" she asked.

By going to school with me, Marley would have a general knowledge of my messy teenage years. My dad dying. My mom not being able to handle a rebel without a clue. Being shipped off to bumfuck Pennsylvania to live with my uncles I didn't know well. It had been the best thing she ever could have done for me. But it had taken me some time to come to that conclusion.

"Yeah. We're good now. Things were rocky back when I first moved here. But honestly? I can't imagine not growing up with Max and Lewis. Those guys took none of my teenage shit and made sure I turned out to be someone they could be proud of."

"I like how you talk about them. Like you can just tell how much you love them," Marley observed.

"Come to the birthday thing," I said. "Meet my mom. Meet Lewis. My cousin'll be there."

"I liked Adeline," she admitted. "And her husband."

"Max and Lewis decided they did such a good job with me that they'd adopt. They ended up with Adeline. Now we've got a full house for the holidays with her four kids."

"Is it nice? Having family nearby?" she asked.

"Oh, yeah. I mean, you go on vacation, you've got a cousin's kid to cut your grass. You're under the weather, you've got an uncle bringing you chicken soup and Gatorade. Your birthday rolls around, and even just dinner turns into an instant party."

"That sounds nice," she admitted, focusing on her plate.

"Sometimes I wonder if it's hard for my parents that Zinnia and I both moved away. You know?"

"I'm sure they miss you," I told her, trying real hard not to push the big, shiny red button I was seeing. "But there's the family you're given and the family you choose. They don't have to be sitting home alone on Thanksgiving if you're not around."

She nodded and scooped up another forkful. "Right. Yeah. You're right." She sighed. "It's just, I think maybe they're a little lonely. They're both retired now, and they don't have their office and their school friends every day. I think that's part of why they decided to do the Airbnb thing."

"You think they're lonely?"

"Yeah. A little."

"What about you, Mars? Are you lonely?"

She didn't answer right away. Instead, she picked up her coffee and took a contemplative sip. "Yeah. I am."

I laid a hand on her shoulder. "Me too, pretty girl. Me too. But you know what?"

"What?"

"We have each other now."

She gave a soft laugh.

"I'm serious, Mars. We're dating. We're banging. We're basically in a real relationship."

"Yeah, until Christmas," she scoffed.

We'll see about that.

"Well, what's wrong with not being alone until Christmas?" I prodded.

"Nothing," she sighed.

"Exactly."

"So, seeing as how it's a lazy Sunday morning and we just had an incredible breakfast, what do you want to do?"

Her face lit up, and she leaned in close. "I have an idea."

Her voice was husky, and my dick was already standing at attention.

"Why don't you explain this idea in graphic detail?" I suggested.

"You and I are going to go inside and..." She leaned in closer and nibbled at my jaw.

"And?" I demanded, practically breathless with anticipation.

"And clean your kitchen."

CHAPTER 51

Marley

This was probably a terrible idea. Bringing Jake into my parents' lives like this. Getting their hopes up that their wayward daughter was finally getting her life in order with an extraordinarily good-looking guy who had eluded other hopeful bachelorettes for nearly forty years.

I was painting a "look how special and great I am" picture when I knew I'd just be snatching this reality away from them in a few short months. I was officially the worst.

The doorbell rang, and I rocketed out of the kitchen. "I'll get it," I shouted. "And don't touch the roast!"

"Do you want me to stir the gravy?" Mom yelled back.

"No! Touch nothing!"

Skidding to a stop at the front door, I wiped my hands on my jeans. Just a casual meet-the-parents Sunday dinner with Jake, who'd fucked me six ways to Heaven in the last twenty-four hours. I was acting like a giddy girlfriend. Hell, I *felt* like a giddy girlfriend. The fake part of our relationship was getting gray and swampy, and I was up to my hips in the murkiness of it.

I opened the door and wondered if there was anything sexier than Jake Weston, leaning casually against the doorway looking sinfully delicious in jeans and a button-down and that damn leather jacket. He had his motorcycle helmet under one arm and a gift bag dangling from the fingers of his other hand.

"Hey, beautiful."

Yeah, okay. I was swooning inside. So sue me. My body was still on high alert from all those orgasms he'd doled out. It saw Jake and thought of nudity and SpaghettiOs and warm, strong arms wrapped around it. It was biology, plain and simple, that had me slobbering like a dental patient.

"Hey. Hi," I said, playing it supercool. I wasn't fooling him. He crooked his giftbag-holding finger at me until I stepped closer. I knew what he wanted, and I was only too happy to give it to him.

Glancing over my shoulder, I made sure my parents hadn't materialized behind me before I pressed a soft kiss to his hard mouth.

He gave a little growl of approval, and I thought about taking my pants off right there in the foyer.

"Well, look at you two lovebirds," a voice boomed behind me.

"Dietrich, you remember Jake, right?" I said, reluctantly pulling back from the kiss.

Jake put down his helmet, and they performed a manly "good to see you" handshake.

"Marley!" Dad yelped from the kitchen. "The gravy bubbled. Should I add more cornstarch?"

"Don't touch anything!" I shouted.

"You might as well come on back with me," I told Jake. "You and D can grab beers while I finish up."

They followed me into the kitchen.

"Your lady can cook, my friend," Dietrich said.

"Don't I know it, man," Jake agreed.

I felt little wings of happiness at the praise. Cooking had been my way of coping with new places and jobs and so many new starts. Every few years, it was a complete reboot, and I ended up in a new city or a new town knowing no one. I'd spent more birthdays alone than I cared to admit.

Cooking had given me a hobby, an outlet. A way to create something. And I took pleasure in feeding the people who did enter my life.

"Jake's here," I said unnecessarily as I entered the room.

Mom was holding a wineglass and poking at the saucepan of gravy with a fork.

Dad guiltily closed the oven door. They were as fascinated by my prowess in the kitchen as I was baffled by their inexperience.

"Jake! Good to see you," my dad squeaked, offering him his hand.

"Mr. Cicero," Jake said, repeating the dudely handshake.

Mom gave me a very unsubtle wink as if she could smell the hormones that were pumping off me. "That sweater I lent you," she began over the rim of her wineglass.

"Will never be returning to your closet. I have a replacement arriving on Tuesday," I promised.

"Good girl," she said to me before opening her arms for my boyfriend. "Jake, sweetheart. It's so nice to have you here for dinner."

"Jessica," Jake said, miles of charm exploding out of his skin cells. "Thank you for having me. I brought you a little something."

"Oh, you didn't have to do that," Mom said as she ripped the bag open in her haste to get to the gift. Mom and I were like toddlers at Christmas jacked up on cookies and hot chocolate. Turn us loose on a pile of presents and watch us make the living room rain wrapping paper. Zinnia and Dad were much more dignified in their gift receiving.

"Dutch Blitz?" Mom said, pulling the card game out of its massacred bag.

"It's pretty fast-paced. A good way to burn off calories after a big meal," Jake said.

"Fast-paced, eh?" My dad hitched up his Dockers, rising to the challenge. I probably should have warned Jake about the Cicero Competitiveness. It bordered on unhealthy.

"You're too sweet," Mom told Jake. "I can't wait to kick your ass after dinner."

Dietrich snorted. He'd barely survived checkers with my dad two nights ago.

"Care for a beer, Jake? Dietrich?" Dad asked. Their tiny kitchen was overcrowded with bodies.

"Why don't you menfolk go drink your beers in the living room," I suggested. "Dinner will be ready in five."

———

"Blitz! In your face, Jessica!" Jake threw his plow card down with a flourish, just beating my mother's bucket card. He got up and performed a lewd victory dance with lots of thrusting.

"Nooo!" my dad howled, pounding his fist into the coffee table. "I hate this stupid game!"

"Damn you, Jake Weston!" Mom screeched. She reached across the table and shoved Jake's stack of cards onto the carpet.

Dietrich and I were doubled over laughing so hard I worried that the oxygen would never return to my lungs. Tears streamed down my face as my mom and Jake started slapping each other's hands as they waded into the piles of cards on the coffee table.

"I don't care if you blitzed us. There's way more buckets in here than stupid plows!"

"Care to bet on that?" Jake teased.

"Marley, your boyfriend is clearly a cheater," Mom insisted, counting up her cards. "I bet he's been stealing my buckets and hiding them in his sleeves so I don't get credit for them."

"Man! I didn't even get two cards off my blitz pile," Dad whined. He crossed his arms over his skinny chest and pouted.

"Mars, did you even count your cards so I can rub my victory in your face?" Jake asked, sitting back down next to me.

I wiped the tears from my eyes. "I think I'm going to declare the game over at this point before there's any bloodshed."

"I bruised my thumb," Dietrich said, showing us his digit.

"Look at that. You guys injured your guest. This could affect his review."

"Ha! I beat you!" Mom shouted, holding up one last bucket card in Jake's face. "You're a loser! A loooser!" Mom's victory dance didn't involve a lot of gyrating, but it did involve some disco moves.

"I demand a recount!" Jake grabbed Mom's stack of cards and thumbed through them.

"Well?" she asked smugly.

"Shit." Jake threw the cards onto the table and flopped over backward onto the carpet. We were all too old to be sitting on the floor, but the violence of the game made it too hard to play at the dining room table.

I unwound my legs and stretched out beside Jake, still laughing.

"Since I am the queen of Dutch Blitz, I suppose I can cut the coffee cake," Mom said. "Come on, Ned."

"I hate that stupid game," Dad griped as he followed her into the kitchen.

"Well, I'll just, ah…go do something that isn't in this room," Dietrich said, ambling out.

I grinned at Jake.

"I think I overdid it," he said. "I probably shouldn't have 'in your faced' your mom at our official meet-the-parents dinner."

I laughed again and wiped at the corners of my eyes. "I had no idea you would get along so well with them."

"They won't hate me for this?"

"Are you kidding? You're their people, Jake." I rolled to my side and pressed a hard kiss to his cheek. "This was really great."

"You're really great," he said, suddenly serious. He cupped my face in his hand and kissed me long and slow.

My lady parts sent up flares of interest. I opened my mouth for him. This was a real kiss. All of this felt too real. I was in over my head, but I didn't feel interested in saving myself. I was content to drown.

"Cake's cut!" my dad yodeled from the kitchen.

"Come home with me tonight," Jake said roughly.

"Again?" We had work in the morning. I needed my coaching gear and lunch.

"Come on, Mars. Don't send me home alone."

"Aren't we moving a little fast?"

"What other speed is there?"

CHAPTER 52

Marley

I tried to run off my nerves about meeting Jake's mother. Four slow miles later, I still had a bellyful of anxiety, but I could afford all the calories that a birthday dinner entailed. So I considered it a win.

I showered, changed my outfit four times, and did a reasonable job on my hair and makeup thanks to the tutorials my team posted on our message board.

"Meeting the parents is a big deal," Natalee had explained sagely.

They explicitly told me not to half-ass my preparations. I felt obligated to post a picture of the finished product for their approval.

The picture was met with a series of thumbs-up emojis and several "You're going to be late!" messages.

I swung by Jake's house and picked up my two handsome dates for the evening. Jake was sexy as sin in jeans, a tight waffle-weave shirt, and a down vest. I wanted to strip him naked and lick every inch of his spectacular body. But we were running a little late. After a very thorough kiss, he and Homer—wearing a celebratory bow tie—joined me in my car, and we headed across town with Jake directing me to his uncles' house.

We pulled up in front of a classy, two-story brick home with a portico and creative landscaping. I took my time checking my makeup and grabbing my purse.

"You don't have to be nervous," Jake said from the passenger seat where he was watching me with amusement.

"I'm meeting your mom," I insisted. "If I weren't nervous, I'd be considered a sociopath." Andrea had walked me through my nerves yesterday at school, and I wished I had retained more of what she'd told me. Something about me being an adult and a nice one at that. So I should go into the situation expecting to like them and be liked in return.

It made sense at the time. But now that we were here, I wasn't so sure it was a good strategy. I should have brought everyone scratch-off lottery tickets or cash. People liked people who gave them cash, right?

"The sooner you get out of the car, the sooner I can put a beer in your hand," Jake said.

I was out from behind the wheel and on the sidewalk in a flash.

Jake was still laughing when he opened the front door without knocking or ringing the bell. Homer, obviously at home here, ran in the direction of the scent of rich food.

Two toddler-aged kids hurled themselves at Jake, screaming in what I could only assume was delight.

He picked them up like sacks of potatoes and submitted to their sloppy kisses and squeals of joy.

"Someone help! I'm being attacked by rabid children," he called.

Adeline poked her head out of a room and padded toward us barefoot. "You've been vaccinated, right?" she said, pulling the smaller kid off Jake. The foyer filled with people, and I was shuffled through introductions, handed sticky children, and promised alcohol.

"I'm Louisa," Jake's mom said, introducing herself over the din.

"Happy birthday, Louisa. I'm Marley," I shouted back.

His mom was delicate and fine boned. Her wardrobe taste trended toward affordable athleisure, and I felt an instant kinship with her when she shoved a beer into my hand and pointed me in the direction of the appetizers.

There were kids everywhere. The adults congregated in the kitchen near the trendy trays of appetizers.

I'd met Max at poker. He wasn't wearing the Queer T-shirt tonight. Instead he was in a rumpled long-sleeve tee. His hair was still damp from a shower. Lewis introduced himself by pushing a delicate cheese-wonton-like thing into my hand, and I fell madly in love with him. He was the fashionista in the family apparently, dressed in charcoal slacks, a dark purple shirt, and suspenders. My players would adore him, I decided.

The house was a perfect balance between Lewis's style and Max's love of gadgets and order.

Rob, Adeline's husband, refilled drinks and then corralled the kids at a table in the kitchen for gourmet kid-sized grilled cheese sandwiches.

I could have felt awkward, standing in the midst of a chaos the rest of them were so comfortable with. But with a cold beer in my hand and Jake's arm around my waist, I felt anchored. Almost relaxed.

The Weston family was bigger than mine. Slightly less dignified. Zinnia would raise eyebrows over the kids' food fight. And the argument that broke out between Rob and Max over eighties rock ballads. But to me, it made them normal.

We snacked and chatted until the kids were done with their meal. Once they were tucked into the living room in front of an animated movie with singing, we retired to the decked-out dining room.

There were cloth napkins with napkin rings that matched the gold-and-silver tablescape. Candles flickered on the table and buffet.

"This is Uncle Lew trying to class us up," Jake explained, leading me to a chair.

"We keep fighting him on it," Adeline said with a wink.

Lewis heaved a long-suffering sigh from his chair. "You heathens drive me to drink," he insisted, reaching for his champagne glass.

Max reached out and covered his husband's hand, and I saw the flirty little winks they sent each other. We ate and drank and made Louisa open fussy presents. She adored the dog painting from Jake and thanked me profusely for the bottle of wine and fun corkscrew. No one asked me the viability of my reproductive organs or hinted to Jake about engagement rings. They talked politics and current events and argued movies and music.

I observed the give-and-take between the relationships. Max tidied up behind Lewis, who left little plates, crumpled napkins, and reading glasses in his wake. Adeline and Rob bickered constantly. But I noticed the soft looks and gentle touches. And no one could miss the way they both lit up whenever one of the kids barreled into the room to tattle on their siblings or show off what artistic creation they fashioned from pipe cleaners and Legos.

One of their girls, Livvy, took a liking to me and climbed up in my lap. She sucked her thumb and played with my hair while her brothers and sister sang Disney songs at the top of their lungs in the living room.

When no one made any "you're a natural" cracks about me hanging out with a kid, I relaxed.

Together, the Westons had created a unit. A black, white, gay, straight, Irish, loud, confusing, beautiful family unit. I loved it.

Jake was clearly enjoying himself. At least until the "when Jake was a teenager" stories started.

"Tell me more," I insisted after Max finished recounting the time he'd had to pick fifteen-year-old Jake up in the middle of nowhere when he'd tried to jump a hay bale with his mountain bike and ended up with a broken wrist and bike.

"It's your turn," Louisa insisted. "What's your favorite memory of Jake from high school."

I bit my lip and felt my cheeks turn hot.

"Ooooooh," Adeline crooned. "Tell us!"

"We didn't hang out in the same crowds," I said, tentatively glancing in Jake's direction.

He squeezed my hand under the table.

"But he did lure me under the bleachers at a soccer game and gave me a very memorable kiss," I confessed.

The Westons liked that, and I laughed with them, pretending not to remember the fact that he'd unceremoniously proceeded to dump me for my nemesis. *People changed. Didn't they?*

Lewis leaned over when the conversation moved on to the cruise Louisa was taking in January. "You're the only girl Jake's ever brought home," he said in a whisper.

"Really?" I asked quietly.

Lewis nodded. "You must be pretty special," he said with a wink.

Homer chose that moment to wedge his head between my knees demanding my attention and making Livvy laugh.

"We need to decide who's making what for Thanksgiving," Jake announced. "I know none of you want me to be providing any of the main dishes."

"As if you could even find any dishes," Max said with a roll of his eyes.

"Marley's a great cook," Jake said.

"You should bring your family to Jake's for Thanksgiving," Lewis decided. "Do you have a good stuffing recipe?"

"What?"

"Ugh, yeah," Adeline agreed. "That schmancy vegetarian stuffing last year is not invited back."

"I was trying something new," Rob complained.

"Rob was vegetarian for six months," Jake explained to me.

Rob took a big bite of chicken breast and stuffed it in his mouth. "It didn't take."

"I'm signing Marley up for the stuffing," Adeline decided. "You're allowed to make that baked corn stuff again, Jake. That was good, and the kids will eat it."

"Speaking of," Jake said, eyeing Adeline pointedly.

Adeline grinned and leaned into Rob. "Oh, yeah. We have a little announcement."

Max and Lewis sat up straight.

"You guys are going to be gay grandpas again," Rob said grandly.

Lewis stood up so fast his chair fell over backward. Max grabbed Adeline in a half-headlock, half-hug. They both were shouting.

"God, I love it when they get good news," Jake whispered in my ear.

My mother had reacted to the grandparent news the same way. She would love Jake's family. So would my dad. For a minute, I could picture us all crammed around a table at Jake's, eating, playing games, saying inappropriate things while the nieces and nephews destroyed things in another room.

But that wasn't the plan. Jake's life was here. Mine was out there somewhere, waiting for me to find it.

"Our baby's having another baby," Max said. Lewis grabbed Rob for a back-slapping hug.

"The more the merrier," he said, mopping tears from his eyes.

"Speaking of 'the more the merrier,'" Louisa said from the head of the table, "I'm bringing a date to Thanksgiving. His name is Walter, and we've been seeing each other for six months."

The celebrations began again, and I snuck a peek at Jake.

"About damn time, Ma," Jake said.

CHAPTER 53

Marley

It had been a long time since I'd slouched in a classroom desk and listened to a history lecture. And I'd never done so having biblically known the teacher. It certainly made the history part of it more interesting.

"'We hold these truths to be self-evident.' What does that mean?" Jake asked his class.

Hands flew up around the room, and I blinked. That never happened in any of my classes back in the day. Had students changed that much? Or was it just that Jake Weston inspired people to care?

"Jamie," he said, pointing at a girl in the middle of the room who tentatively held her hand at shoulder height.

"It's kind of like they're saying 'Duh. Everybody knows this is true, so let's move on.'"

"Boom. Exactly! Strong opening, don't you think?"

Heads nodded. Shoulders shrugged.

"Because what were our founders trying to do here? They were telling their story and trying to rally allies around the world to recognize their independence."

"Like a PR campaign?" a boy with a headful of dreadlocks and a hunter-safety-orange sweatshirt called out.

"Yes, my friend! Exactly like a PR campaign." Jake tossed the kid a gift card.

"Sweet! iTunes!"

"Thanks to Al here for the lead in, you guys have your assignment. We're going to spend the rest of the week split into groups, and you're going to write your own Declarations of Independence. Except you aren't seceding from British rule. You get to pick what you're leaving behind and what you're forming. Then you're going to decide amongst yourselves how you campaign the rest of the world to recognize you."

There was a buzz in the classroom. The sounds of excited, motivated students were foreign to my ears. No one walked into gym class with that kind of enthusiasm. And the competitive Cicero part of me awakened like a sleeping dragon.

"We're dividing up into four groups of five. You five. You five. You five. And you five," Jake said, gesturing at the clumps of students.

As teenagers dragged desks and chairs into lopsided circles, Jake wandered back to me. Hands in his pockets.

"Having fun, Ms. Cicero?" he asked, playfully perching on the edge of my desk.

My coaching had improved. But teaching was still iffy territory. So here I was in Jake's classroom looking for techniques to steal.

"I am. I didn't know history could be so not incredibly boring," I told him, covertly poking him in the hip.

"The secret is relevance," he lectured. "If you can't make whatever the hell you're teaching relevant to them, you can't really expect them to care."

"Huh." That made sense. What did my students have to look forward to besides being divided into athletic and nonathletic archetypes in activities that were designed to be fun only to the more physically capable?

"That's all you have to say about my prowess in the classroom?" he teased.

"Be quiet. My mind is working."

"You're really sexy when you think," Jake whispered.

I stuck my tongue out at him before glancing around us to make sure none of the horndog teenagers were picking up what we were putting down. But they were all involved in heated discussions about Facebook ads and live streaming declarations of independence.

When the bell rang, sending students scattering, Jake and I headed into the teacher's lounge. We unpacked identical food containers of identical Sunday leftovers. If that didn't say committed couple, I didn't know what did.

"How's it going, Gurgevich?" Jake asked, sliding into the chair next to the English teacher. She was opening a takeout container that held something delectable and red meat-y.

"Is that Kobe beef?" Floyd asked, sniffing the air like a bloodhound.

"It is."

"How do you rate Kobe beef delivery for lunch?" Floyd demanded.

Her shoulders lifted. "I have many admirers." I wanted to be Mrs. Gurgevich when I grew up.

I took the empty seat between Jake and Haruko and dug into my meal. I quelled the reactive grumble when Amie Jo strutted into the lounge. She was wearing a pink wrap dress, nude heels, and a necklace the size of a hubcap.

"Hello, all! I come bearing cookies from fourth period," she said airily.

She dropped a platter of exquisitely decorated sugar cookies on the table in front of Jake.

"Wow, these look like Pinterest," I commented.

"My students take their lessons very seriously," Amie Jo sniffed. I think she thought I was being sarcastic.

"I'm not kidding. They look great."

Amie Jo gave me the side-eye, trying to decide if I was kidding or not. So I reached out and took a heart-shaped cookie with pink drizzled icing.

"Yep. Delicious," I said, taking a bite.

"Well, I just wanted to remind everyone about my Open House this month. You don't need to bring a thing. The caterers have it all covered," she announced.

There was an excited buzz around the room, and Amie left, wiggling her bedazzled fingers in Jake's direction.

"Open House?" I asked Jake.

"Every year, the Hostetters open up their estate to us commoners and throw one helluva party," Floyd supplied. "You do not want to miss it."

I definitely did want to. And planned to. Also, I probably wasn't even invited.

"It's over the top. The food is insane. There's appetizers in one room, a dinner buffet in another." Jake sounded like he was talking about backstage passes to AC/DC.

"And don't forget the indoor and outdoor bars," Haruko chimed in.

"I ate so many crab puffs last year," Bill said, patting his stomach at the fond memory.

"Everyone goes?" I clarified.

"Oh, yeah. You don't want to miss it," Mrs. Gurgevich insisted. "They had a string quartet in the dining room one year and a steel drum band on the patio."

"Remember the year Rich Rothermel got drunk and tackled the swan ice sculpture into the pool?"

"Who was it they found drunk in the master bathtub, fully clothed?"

"That would be Jake, four years ago," Mrs. Gurgevich said, pointing a finger in his direction.

Jake shuddered. "Still can't stand the taste of a Moscow mule."

The teachers continued their reminiscences over the daytime talk show on the TV playing in the corner.

"Trust me, Mars. You want to go to this shindig," Jake whispered in my ear.

I *did* kind of want to see the inside of the house. I mean, the Greek columns on the outside couldn't be the only ridiculous display of wealth, right? "Am I even invited?"

"Everyone is invited. Part of the fun is all the feuds and arguments that break out."

"Fun," I quipped. I turned my attention back to my pot roast.

"So, Cicero, you ready for some rainy fall v-ball?" Floyd asked.

The morning classes had been able to go outside for another sweaty mess of field hockey and flag football. But the skies had opened up and were currently dumping buckets of cold rain.

"About that. How much say do we have over the curricula?" I asked.

"You guys are lucky," Haruko piped up. "While the rest of us schmucks have to worry our butts off about standardized testing, you guys can do pretty much whatever the hell you want."

"Is that true?" I asked Floyd.

He shrugged his burly lumberjack shoulders. "There's always the presidential fitness bullshit. But other than that, we're really only limited by the equipment required. You got something in mind?"

I looked at Jake and found him watching me with a mix of interest and affection. It made me feel like I'd just drunk a mug full of hot chocolate with marshmallows and whipped cream.

"I might have an idea. Do we have any Ping-Pong tables?"

"We can check. They might be buried in the back of the supply room," Floyd mused.

CHAPTER 54

Marley

The kids looked at me like I was speaking Pennsylvania Dutch to them.

"So we're *not* playing volleyball?" a curly-haired senior with an overbite asked.

"No volleyball."

"And no Ping-Pong either?" a freckle-faced sophomore clarified.

"No Ping-Pong," I confirmed. "Instead, we're going to break into teams to design and perform Ping-Pong ball trick shots."

They blinked at me, trying to figure out if this was some kind of elaborate gym teacher trap. At any second, they expected me to blow my whistle and force them all to start pumping out push-ups.

"We brought you some visual inspiration," Floyd said, whipping out his iPad cued up to a YouTube video.

"That's *Dude, Nice Shot*," one of the kids said as they all crowded in closer.

The class watched as four grown adults set up what was essentially a beer pong shot from an upper-level running track down onto a Ping-Pong table at center court.

A collective "whoa" arose when they successfully made the shot.

"You guys will be evaluated on the difficulty of the shot, teamwork, and your victory dance. Extra credit for a successful shot," I explained.

"I call Milton for my team," one of the boys' soccer team stars shouted.

"Nice try, Danny. Mr. Wilson and I have already divided you all up into teams." Diverse teams from all social backgrounds. *Take that, punks.*

We split the kids up and sent them off to their respective tables. We'd found five in the bowels of the storage room and had done our best to dust them off. The kids were already deep in conversation over strategy.

Damn if I wasn't getting excited just seeing them get excited. Jake was on to something when it came to relevancy and involvement. The beauty of *Dude, Nice Shot* was no one needed to be an athlete. In fact, it was better to be smart than physically strong. Everyone could participate.

"Cicero, this is fucking genius," Floyd said as we watched the teams launch into a thorough examination of the props we'd provided, including red Solo cups procured from Mrs. Gurgevich's desk drawer.

"You know," I said, nudging him with my elbow. "There's one Ping-Pong table left."

"Oh, I'm picking up what you're putting down."

———

I wasn't going to lie. Watching several of Culpepper's high school star athletes and general popular population lift the scrawny Marvin Holtzapple on their shoulders to celebrate the physic geek's Rube Goldberg–style trick shot got me a little verklempt.

"That was fucking beautiful, Cicero," Floyd said, mopping at the corners of his eyes with his sweatshirt sleeve when the kids cleared the gym.

"Yeah, it wasn't bad," I sniffled. For a brief, shining moment, an idea I had lifted the misery of unpopularity for a student who probably dreaded school as much as I had back in the day. I felt like a goddamn hero.

"We need to do more of this," Floyd decided. "Gym class should be inclusive. Even the pregnant girls can participate in shit like this."

"You'd be open to something besides volleyball?" I teased. Floyd's hatred of spending five months of the school year watching bored kids play boring v-ball badly was legendary. The Pennsylvania winters were long and annoying, but budgets didn't exactly allow for a ton of athletic equipment. So our options for the cold weather months were limited.

"This was the most fun I've had in a class since Lindsay P. pegged one of the Hostetter twins in the nuts with a lacrosse ball."

I laughed and headed into the locker room, a few ideas rippling beneath the surface.

The high of doing something good and being actually *liked* within the walls of a high school stayed with me into lunch.

"Gimme gimme!" Andrea wiggled her fingers when I poked my head into the guidance office. "I'm starving," she exclaimed.

"I hope you like horseradish," I said, unpacking the two roast beef melts I'd packed this morning.

"As long as it's not made out of actual horse, I'm sure I'll love it," she insisted. Her red mermaidlike hair was draped over her shoulder in a long braid. Curls exploded out of it in all directions.

I dropped into my usual chair and popped the top on the sole soda I allowed myself a day. I'd discovered that cutting back on the sugar combined with running was having quite the positive impact on my waistline—as in, I had one now. If I'd known returning home humiliated and getting myself a hot, fake boyfriend was this good for me, I would have tried it years ago.

"How's your day so far?" I asked, taking a bite of sourdough bread, Swiss cheese, tomato, and roast beef.

"Mmm. Mmm." Andrea rolled her eyes as she chewed quickly. "Not bad. No aggressive parent phone calls or sobbing teenage girls yet today. I heard *your* day is going well."

I cocked my head to one side, silently questioning while I chewed.

"Kids are loving the Ping-Pong trick-shot thing," she said.

"Really?" I felt as victorious as I had in third grade when my teacher had given me a literal gold star for memorizing my multiplication tables.

"It's creative and fun and includes students of all abilities. Essentially, you just removed the misery of gym class for the fifty percent of the school population that isn't athletic," Andrea said.

"I was just looking for something fun for them to do," I said, brushing off the praise.

"But I can tell it made you happy," she said, pointing her sandwich at me.

I shrugged, blushing on the inside. "It was fun."

"I'll tell you what it looks like to me," she said, opening a lunch bag and unpacking two baggies of baby carrots. She passed one to me. "It looks like you're finding your place. Hitting your stride. You're identifying problems like boring, socially painful gym classes, and you're offering up creative solutions."

"What are you getting at?" I asked, biting into a baby carrot.

"You look happy. In just a few short weeks, you've gone from displaced and feeling alone to making a place for yourself here. That's no small feat, especially in high school."

"I'm an adult in a high school," I clarified. This wasn't exactly my shot at a redo.

"Trust me, the same popularity power plays exist at the

adult level," she said. "You look like you're thriving. Your team is playing well together. You've landed the George Clooney of Culpepper. And if I'm not mistaken, you're looking leaner than when you first started, you bitch."

I let out a strangled laugh.

"Now, your students are starting to enjoy the effort you're putting forth. You've really turned things around. Imagine where you'll be at the end of the semester."

I chewed and imagined. I wouldn't be here anymore. At least, I shouldn't be. I hadn't given much thought to "after Christmas" or "after the semester." I'd been distracted by a certain tall, sexy, tattooed, naked cross-country coach. And his derpy dog. And reacquainting myself with my childhood best friend. And spending quality time with my parents.

None of those things were *bad*. But I needed to refocus on what was important: The Future. My wounds were healing here in Culpepper. But I wanted more than this dusty little town had to offer. I wanted a corner office and stock options and people who said things like "Thank God you're here" when I walked in the door. I wanted to wear heels every day and buy a round of drinks for my team to celebrate a victory.

"You look like I just punched a puppy in the face," Andrea observed.

"Do you help students with their résumé?" I asked, changing the subject.

She nodded and inhaled another bite of sandwich. "Yeah. Sure."

"Think you could help me polish mine?" I asked.

"If you're sure that's what you want," she said in that way adults speak to kids who are being dumbasses.

I rolled my eyes. "Stop trying to guide me. Spit it out."

"I'm just wondering why staying here and continuing what you're doing aren't on the table?"

"I spent my entire life trying to get out of this town. I'm not going to let a stopover suck me back in," I said lightly.

She wiped her mouth delicately with a paper napkin. "All right. But I think you're making a mistake not considering it as a possibility. Especially since that possibility involves seeing Jake Weston naked all the time."

"Yeah, well. This is fun for now. But it's not what I want long-term." I wanted Zinnia's life. A sense of importance to what I was doing. I wanted to matter. To be irreplaceable. I wanted a husband or sexy life partner type to share a glass of crazy-expensive wine or liquor and chortle over something supersmart in front of the fire.

Jake wouldn't leave Culpepper for me. And I wouldn't stay here for him. That was the bottom line. The only thing that had remained constant in my life was The Plan. I couldn't veer off course now.

"Then I'd be happy to take a look at your résumé," she said.

"It's kind of a mess," I warned.

"I love a challenge. Also this sandwich. I love this sandwich."

Her desk phone rang. "This is Andrea," she said perkily into the receiver. Her gaze slid to my face, and she pursed her lips together. "Sure. I'll send her right over."

She hung up. "Principle Eccles would like a moment of your time. It seems a certain home ec teacher was very upset about her poor, delicate sons being taught to play beer pong on school grounds."

"Oh, for fuck's sake."

CHAPTER 55

Marley

"Heard you got called to the principal's office," Vicky said, cranking Bon Jovi on her minivan radio. The windows were up in deference to the cold rain that pattered outside. I adjusted my air vent. There was an unidentifiable, disgusting smell permeating the interior of the vehicle that I couldn't put my finger on.

"For the love of…is the school bugged?" I demanded.

"No. It's just full of a few hundred loudmouths with ears and Wi-Fi."

"Amie Jo called the principal to complain about the gym class Floyd and I taught."

"I heard you taught the kids how to make bongs out of fruit," she said chipperly. She chewed her gum as if it were in danger of escaping her mouth.

"Ha. Actually I taught them how to pass a field sobriety test."

"Life skills, my friend. Life skills," she said, steering us out of Culpepper.

"Amie Jo told her I was teaching the kids to play beer pong. Principal Eccles didn't take the complaint seriously."

"But she had to appease the beast by making a show of disciplining you," she said.

"Exactly. Annoying but not life-threatening." I realized

that that's how I felt about Amie Jo now. She was annoying. Irksome. A buzzy little gnat. But she and her feelings about me had no actual bearing on my life. I sat a little straighter in the seat. I, Marley Jean Cicero, was finally growing up.

"That Libby was one hell of a find," Vicky said, changing the subject. "That girl's footwork is National Team level."

"Tell me about it," I said smugly. "She seems to be fitting in with the rest of the team, too."

Practice had gone well tonight. The girls were in good moods, a rare feat. And everyone enjoyed getting a little muddy running drills. There was something about being coated in dirt and mud that made us all feel like serious athletes.

When the rain had picked up, we'd called it an early night. Vicky and I had declared it to be a two-margarita evening. I finally had a little money in the bank and was ready to treat my lifelong friend and assistant coach to some bottom-shelf tequila. Afterward, Faith, Mariah, and Andrea were meeting us for dinner.

We sang along to the radio, a nostalgic nineties station, and I tried not to think too hard about the smell that was seeping into my clothing.

The restaurant was a cute little Mexican place in a mostly okay portion of Lancaster. A real estate agent would call it "up and coming." I'd call it pretty shabby. But the fajitas were to die for, and they'd come really close to passing their last health inspection on the first try.

"So, how's life?" I asked Vicky after we ordered our margaritas—mango for her, traditional on the rocks for me.

"You know, it's pretty damn good," she said, diving into the bowl of tortilla chips between us.

I raised my eyebrows. "You have three kids—one of whom is an angry teenager—and a husband who's on the road doing whatever he does for a living fifty percent of the time."

She pointed her chip at me before biting into it. "Don't

forget a mother-in-law who lives with me and demands that I wash and fold her delicates in a very particular way."

I gasped. "When did Rich's mom move in with you?"

Vicky scrunched up her nose and thought. "Three years ago? Yeah. Right after Rich's dad died."

The margaritas arrived, and I took a guilty sip. I'd had no idea Vicky's father-in-law had died or that her mother-in-law had moved in with them. Granted, we'd drifted apart. But given the fact that she'd willingly jumped in to keep me from drowning with the soccer team, well, I felt I owed her a whole lot of back interest.

"I'm so sorry, V."

She waved it away. "It's fine. We make it work. And honestly, it's nice having a third generation in the house. She doesn't take any shit from Blaire and helps me out with the littles. I'm never going to be good enough for her son, but that goes with the territory."

I sampled the salsa with a still-warm chip.

"Did you guys always plan on three kids?" I asked, feeling like I was making awkward small talk with a stranger. I'd been absent from Vicky's life for so long, I forgot that she wasn't still a seventeen-year-old wild child.

She sucked down some mango margarita and nodded. "Yeah. Three was always the magic number. Of course Blaire was a bit of a surprise right out of college. But by the time we got around to the other two, she was a built-in mini nanny."

"You seem really happy," I observed.

She shot me a grin. "I am. I mean, I'm unemployed and driven insane daily by my family. But honestly, it's a great freaking life. I'm surrounded by people I love every day. I'm watching these little weirdos that I created turn into people. My parents are minutes away. And Mama Rothermel is teaching me all about the kind of mother-in-law I don't want to be."

"It sounds pretty great," I admitted.

"Yeah, well, I'm no Zinnia," she said with a wink. "But I'm really, bone-deep happy. You know?"

No. I didn't know. Nothing I'd ever done in life had given me that feeling. I'd been chasing it since forever. And the harder I ran, the farther away it seemed to get.

"Is this where you thought you'd be at thirty-eight?" I asked her.

"God no," she snorted. "I was going to be a Broadway choreographer. Or a record label something or other. Oh! Or—"

"An MTV reality TV star!" We said it together, remembering our teenage obsession.

"What about you, Marley?" she asked. "How's life these days? And by how's life, I mean what does Jake look like naked?"

I choked on the salsa and washed it down with margarita.

"Life is good," I said lightly. "And what makes you think I've seen him naked? We're faking the relationship, remember?"

"Girl, you go from 'woe-is-me' wounded woman to strutting, smiling badass. You may be faking the relationship, but you're not faking the orgasms."

"I didn't intend to sleep with him."

"But?" Vicky rested her chin in her hands and sucked on the margarita straw.

"But have you seen him? He's a sweaty sex god! And worse, he's *nice*. He's still got a little bit of that bad boy rebel going. But deep down, he's this present-buying, dog-loving guy who just wants the best for everybody."

"Oh, boy. You've got it bad."

"I can't help it. The man's pheromones should be considered narcotics."

"Then I've got to ask. Why, when you have Jake Weston's presumably spectacular penis inside you and a job you're starting to enjoy, would you just pack up and leave?"

I stumbled over the question and stuffed a chip in my

mouth to buy myself some time. "Things with Jake and me are just temporary. He's trying the whole relationship thing out to see if it's something he's really ready for. And I'm killing time before I can regroup and move on to something…bigger." What was it with everyone questioning my decisions? I wasn't about to stop chasing down the dreams I'd always had just because I got a little derailed.

"Bigger than Jake's penis?" Vicky clarified.

"Bigger than Culpepper. I wouldn't be happy here. Not long-term." I hadn't been happy here growing up. Why would I be happy here now? "By the way, Jake looks even better without clothes than he does in them." I threw my naked fake boyfriend up as a distraction.

"Damn it! I knew it! Where does he fall on the orgasm Richter scale?"

"What's the upper limit again?" I asked slyly.

"Oh, I hate you."

"He's really great," I told her seriously. "He's going to make some woman very, very lucky someday."

"It sounds like you've forgiven him for his senior year transgressions," she mused.

"Should we really hold anyone responsible for the hurt they dole out at eighteen? I mean, maybe I misread the signs?"

"He dragged you under the bleachers, kissed the crap out of you, and then told you you were with the wrong guy. And then he asked you to Homecoming and—"

"I am well aware of what happened," I interrupted her. Some humiliations were better left locked in the dark, hidden away for all eternity.

"I'm just pointing out that we all made mistakes, and we all survived them. And just because you're bearing some adolescent scars doesn't mean that you have to avoid Culpepper forever. I've missed you."

I sighed. "I've missed you, too, V."

"So, let's make a pact that no matter where you end up, we do this margarita thing at least once a year."

"It's a deal. So, how's old, married sex with Rich?"

CHAPTER 56

Marley

800 years ago. The Fallout.

I broke up with Travis the night Jake kissed me.
Unceremoniously.

Two weeks before Homecoming. The dress my mom and I got for the dance hung from my closet door taunting me.

I didn't know what Amie Jo had seen, but I wasn't about to give her the pleasure of destroying my relationship. No, I had to do it myself.

It was hard. Travis was hurt, even though I'd left out the part about kissing another guy. There was no need to dent his self-esteem that way. I felt like a bad person. But the relief I felt at not being tied down to a guy I didn't love was swift. Despite the guilt, despite the instantaneous plummet out of the in crowd back into the teeming mass of obscurity, I knew I'd made the right decision.

The cheerleaders and field hockey players no longer had to pretend to be nice to me. I even found something oddly comforting about Amie Jo's snide comments between classes.

Things were back to normal.

Until I found THE NOTE.

Marley,

*You and me. Homecoming. Don't tell anyone. We need to
play it cool since you just broke up with Travis. See you
at the dance.*

Jake

*I'd tried not to have any expectations about Jake. He was the
bad boy, the rebel. Rumor had it he'd been caught kissing a substitute teacher last year. And I was well aware of who and what I was.
A mousy, socially awkward introvert. I was not the kind of girl who
made a guy turn in his "playing the field" card.*

*We hadn't talked more than a few flirty sentences since that
night. Sure, we'd shared a few steamy glances across crowded cafete-
rias or hallways. And maybe I'd had a few fantasies about dancing
in my pretty dress with Jake at Homecoming.*

But I hadn't actually believed that he'd ask me.

*After I'd stopped jumping up and down and squealing, Vicky
and I spent approximately seventeen hours dissecting the note word
by word. Play it cool? Did that mean I didn't approach him about
the note? You and me. Homecoming? Was he asking me or just
stating that we would both be in attendance?*

*Vicky and I had decided to pretend like nothing had happened
and let Jake approach me. The day after I found the note in my
locker, he'd sent me a sexy head tilt and a wink in the cafeteria.*

It was proof enough for Vicky and me.

*I'd been "playing it cool" now for three days. Jake was clearly
playing it cool too, seeing as how he hadn't even looked in my direction for days. But that was okay. In just over a week, I'd be dancing
with the bad boy in front of our senior class. I couldn't freaking wait.*

*I slammed my locker door shut and jumped a mile when I
realized Vicky was on the other side of it.*

"What?" I asked, taking one look at her horror-stricken face. "Cafeteria run out of French bread pizza again?"

"Worse. Much worse," she said and winced.

This was serious.

I stuffed my history textbook into my backpack. "Lay it on me."

"You know how Amie Jo's dad is a gynecologist?"

"Yeah. I guess."

"She's telling everyone..." Vicky trailed off and looked over her shoulder to make sure no one was eavesdropping.

"Telling everyone what?" I demanded impatiently.

Vicky dropped her voice to a whisper. "That you're pregnant."

"I'm pregnant?" I didn't mean to shout it, but judging from the looks I got from my fellow hall dwellers, I hadn't whispered.

Vicky nodded. "Amie Jo is telling everyone that you went to her dad for the blood test and that you don't know who the father is."

I rolled my eyes. "That's ridiculous and unimaginative." Pregnancy rumors were the go-to mean girl prank from the unimaginative. "Who's even going to believe her?"

———

Everyone, it turns out. Well, except my close friends and hopefully Jake.

In less than two days, Amie Jo Armburger had succeeded in spreading the rumor far and wide.

So far, I'd been impregnated by a high school dropout who worked at Dollar Tree. Or maybe it was the sweaty eighth grader I'd seduced after school in my car.

I ignored it when someone taped diapers to my locker. I paid no attention to the crying baby doll some joker shoved into my backpack in the cafeteria.

But I started to worry when Coach Norman took me aside before our away game and told me he didn't feel comfortable playing me without a doctor's note about my "condition." Vicky told him he was being a dumbass for believing a stupid rumor, but it didn't do any good.

I sat on the bench and stewed. My senior year was supposed to be the best yet. Steffi Lynn was long gone, having graduated and moved on to—and failed out of—cosmetology school.

Yet here I was riding the bench until I was able to corroborate my non-pregnant condition to the coaching staff. All thanks to another Armburger Asshole. It couldn't possibly get any worse.

And then my parents sat me down for dinner.

"So, snack cake," my dad said, sounding as if he were being strangled. "Anything you want to tell us? Any news you have that won't make us love you any less because we love you very much no matter what?"

I suddenly wished Zinnia wasn't off enjoying her freshman year at Dartmouth. I could use a big sister right about now.

My mom, with tear-filled eyes, covered my hand with hers. "I'm happy to make you a doctor's appointment if you want me to."

I decided that I would die of humiliation on this spot, in my kitchen, never having lived a full life.

"Mom!" I stood up so abruptly, my chair tipped over behind me. I felt the need to stand for this proclamation. "I'm not pregnant! I swear!"

My parents sagged back into their chairs and blew out sighs of relief. "Oh, thank God. I'm too young to be a Pop-Pop," my dad squeaked.

"I'm too young to be some poor kid's mother," I complained.

"Sweetie, I hate to do this," my mom said with a wince. "But I feel like we need to have the c-o-n-d-o-m talk again. Just to put my mind at rest."

"Mother! I understand and have practiced safe sex. I am currently single and have no plans to start having sex with random strangers."

"Ned, do we have any bananas?"

Marley,

I decided to take Amie Jo to Homecoming instead. She's obviously more my type. Good luck with everything.

Jake

In school the next day, I marched past my locker—today they'd covered it in cutouts of unfortunate-looking babies with unibrows and giant adult-sized noses. I yanked off the ugliest baby and steamed down the hall.

Amie Jo was going to hell. Or at least she was damning herself to have terribly unattractive children when the time came for the gates of hell to open and allow a demon spawn to be created.

She'd cost me a game and a date with the boy I really, really liked. I'd underestimated her deviousness.

I found her, blond and perky and evil, hanging out in a circle of minions checking their mascara in compacts and probably plotting how to destroy other classmates' lives.

"Amie Jo." I slapped the ugly baby picture against her shoulder. "This needs to stop."

"Well, bless your heart. You probably shouldn't upset yourself. It's not good for the baby," she said in a stage whisper. She fluttered her thick, dark eyelashes. Her foundation cracked a little under her eyes.

"I'm not pregnant, and you know it."

"But it's what everyone else believes that counts," she reminded me brightly. "As far as Culpepper is concerned, you're a pregnant whore."

I wished I had no concern about consequences. That I could just break her stupid little perfect nose and make her feel an ounce of the pain she doled out for others on a daily basis.

But I had a healthy fear of authority. And my parents couldn't afford to buy me out of trouble.

"Why are you even doing this? What have I ever done to you?" I demanded.

She took a step into my space, her pretty face twisting into an ugly mask of hate. "You exist. You think that you deserve to date someone like Travis? You think that someone like Jake would be into you? You need to stay where you belong. At the bottom of the food chain with the rest of the losers in this town."

Her cronies giggled nervously behind her.

"Why?" I insisted again. I told myself the answer just might set me free. That kicking her in the shins and unleashing a gallon of sardines in her cute little convertible wouldn't solve anything.

"Because you're nothing. You'll never be anything. Just like the rest of these pathetic losers in this school. They at least know their place. You need to remember yours."

"If you don't stop torturing me, I'm going to tell someone."

She let out a peal of laughter. "Who? That garden gnome, Mr. Fester? My dad basically owns him."

"Your dad is a gynecologist. He doesn't own people." The Armburgers had money. More money than the Ciceros and most other people in town. They had 'get whatever you want at the Gap and not just for back-to-school' money. But not 'own people' money.

"Why don't you do us all a favor and just stop existing. No one likes you. No one wants you around. You're a waste of DNA."

I flicked her off and, with a snarl, turned around and marched away, reminding myself of how much I didn't want to get suspended my senior year. Dear God, I wasn't so sure that I'd survive the rest of the school year. Not without a meltdown.

But this time, I wasn't going down without a fight.

Victoriously, I pulled out Vicky's little pocket voice recorder and hit Stop. Her parents got it for her when she started working on the school newspaper. And I was going to use it to bring down the high school nobility.

"Did you get it?" Vicky hissed, appearing in the hall next to me. She danced from foot to foot while I tore the rest of the sad babies off my locker.

"Oh, I got it. Now I just need to figure out what to do with it."

"Make it diabolical," Vicky encouraged.

CHAPTER 57

Marley

October

Yeou want me to ride what?" I squeaked.

Bill Beerman batted his blond lashes at me. "A donkey."

"You want me to ride a donkey?" I knew things had been going too well. We were into October. The leaves were changing, the air was crisp, my team had won more games than they'd lost, and I'd lost count of the orgasms Jake had so generously bestowed upon me.

"It's a tradition." Bill warmed up to make his case for why I should consider sitting astride a beast of burden in the high school gymnasium where I had finally become a respected member of the faculty.

Respected members of the faculty did *not* participate in the Donkey Basketball game. At the very most, they wore matching T-shirts and collected donations from the crowd during the annual Donkey Basketball game.

I remembered well, laughing my ass off at our young chemistry teacher when she had to shovel up the steaming heap of donkey shit her ride gifted to her.

"I don't think my insurance covers donkey-related injuries."

"You wear helmets," he said as if that made it better instead of significantly worse. "Jake's doing it, and we thought it would be really funny to put you on opposite teams."

"Hilarious," I scoffed. "There is absolutely *no way* I'm riding a donkey."

Donkey Ote—a clever take on everyone's favorite windmill-slaying Man of La Mancha—had a bristly coat that made my skin itch. What we lacked in common with body hair we made up for in sheer reluctance.

"I don't want to do this any more than you do," I promised him. He shoved his nose into the hood of my sweatshirt and snorted.

Oh, shit. Did donkeys bite?

A grating peal of laughter stabbed into my eardrums.

Amie Jo, in white stilettos and bubble-gum-pink skinny pants, pointed and giggled at me and my donkey.

"Don't listen to her, Ote," I whispered, ruffling the coarse tuft of hair between his ears. "She's just jealous she doesn't get to play."

"You look *positively ridiculous*," she said as if I were unaware of this fact.

"Yeah, well. It's for a good cause," I said.

Every year, the Donkey Basketball game raised funds for the local food bank. Ninety percent of the funds that fed families for Thanksgiving came from this damn game. And one of those families on the list was Libby's foster family. Thank you very much, Jake, for finding that tidbit of information and emotionally blackmailing me into participating.

I might not have cash to donate to the cause. But my dignity? That I was willing to part with.

"That's a sizable *ass* you've got there, Marley," Amie Jo said, batting her long purple-tinted lashes. She cracked herself up and doubled over again.

"You ready to be defeated, Mars?" Jake asked, smugly escorting his significantly larger steed up next to mine in the hallway. He ignored Amie Jo's giggle fit and gave me a kiss.

His donkey leaned in and grabbed the hood of my sweatshirt.

"Gah!" I choked.

"Knock it off, Bertha!" Jake wrestled his mutant donkey away. Bertha took part of my hood with her.

Donkey Ote eyed me.

"Oh, *I'm* the dumbass?" I asked. The donkey tossed his head in an emphatic "yes."

"Look at you two bonding," Bill said, appearing cheerfully with a helmet and a clipboard. He reached out to pet Donkey Ote, but my donkey did this weird thing where his jaw opened, sending his upper teeth in one direction and his lower teeth in another. The noise was like a banshee scream.

Amie Jo was in hysterics again. At least until Bertha lunged in her direction, big yellow teeth snapping.

She shrieked and threw herself at Jake. "Save me!" Jake wrestled woman and donkey until there was a loud, flatulent *fermp* followed by a louder *splat splat splat*.

"Oh, shit."

It was my turn to laugh as Bertha let loose a half ton of donkey shit on the linoleum floor.

Amie Jo lost her grip on Jake. Her arms fluttered helplessly, and I watched in horror as her heels lost their traction on the edge of the shit pile. She slipped and skated, her pale blue eyes wider than dinner plates.

I reached for her from Donkey Ote's back, trying to catch a fluttering hand, but gravity and karma were faster.

Amie Jo's feet slipped out from under her, and we watched as she landed in slow motion with another resounding splat. Right on her ass. In the middle of the steaming pile of donkey shit.

Jake had tears of laughter streaming down his face as he offered her a hand. He couldn't talk, could only shudder in silent hysterics.

Bill fluttered around apologizing and offering to get paper towels. I doubted that there were enough paper towels in all of Culpepper to clean up this disaster.

And in the middle of it all, Amie Jo screamed bloody murder.

The screams and the laughter started to draw a crowd. Which led to more laughter and more screaming. Amie Jo's cheeks burned hot with humiliation. I handed Donkey Ote's bridle off to the woodshop teacher and hauled Amie Jo to her feet. Something Jake was incapable of, since he was currently trying not to piss his pants.

Bill had scampered off in search of one of the shit shovels.

"Come on," I said, herding her down the hall, careful not to touch her. "Let's go to the locker room."

"I wanna go home!" Amie Jo wailed.

"You can't get in your car like this," I told her, guiding her into the locker room. She drove an Escalade worth more than my sister's husband's medical school student loans. Donkey shit would probably total the car.

Fat tears trickled down her cheeks, sluicing through her thick makeup.

I turned on the water in one of the individual shower stalls and pushed her toward it. "Go, shower. I'll bring you a bag for your clothes and something to change into."

Amie Jo was still sucking in angry, shaky breaths but didn't argue. She simply snapped the curtain closed.

I dug out a plastic grocery bag from my office and delved into my emergency clothes. Yoga pants and an oversized hoodie.

I found a left Puma sneaker and a right flip-flop in the lost-and-found box and a couple of scratchy sweat towels. Returning with my arms full, I dumped everything in the dressing area of the shower stall.

Ducking my head back out in the hall, I saw that cleanup was beginning on the Shit Heard Round the World. The shop teacher was patting Donkey Ote's nose with his good five-fingered hand. It looked like it was all under control. I turned to head back into the locker room when someone calling my name stopped me.

Travis. I wondered when I'd stop reacting to him with visceral guilt.

"Hey," he said.

"Hey." He really was pretty. I wondered what a nice guy like him was doing with a hell beast like Amie Jo.

"Uh, is Amie Jo okay?" he asked.

"Oh, yeah. She's in the shower. But I think she's going to need new shoes."

"She's got her driving Uggs in the car. I'll grab them," he volunteered.

"Cool," I nodded. *Driving Uggs. Eye roll.*

"Yeah," he said, running a hand through his thick hair. "Hey, it's nice to have you back in town."

I bobbed my head in what I hoped was an appropriate response. "It's nice to be back."

"Well, I guess I'll…" He pointed his thumb over his shoulder toward the parking lot.

"Yeah."

He walked away, and I watched him go. His butt was nice. Not as muscley and firm as Jake's but still appreciable. I'd rather stare at his butt than have another conversation with him though. My guilt over the breakup and ensuing broken leg still weighed on me.

Travis and I hadn't spoken much after I broke up with him. Really only to confirm that he was not the fake father to my fake baby. After Homecoming, well, he'd understandably avoided me. By January he'd been dating Amie Jo. We moved in different circles, and I'd hurt him. Mentally and physically. I didn't know if he hated me or if he was grateful that I'd ended things when I did so he hadn't been saddled with me. There were a lot of things I didn't know. But one thing I did know was that between the teenage and adult versions of Travis and Jake, only one of them consistently tied me up in knots.

And I'd be walking away from him in a few short weeks.

"Mars?"

I jumped, turning away from Travis's retreating butt. Jake was eyeing me, his hand firmly grasping Bertha's bridle.

"Everything all right?" he asked. Bertha crossed her eyes at me.

I nodded. "Yep. Great. I, uh, gotta check on She Who Shall Not Be Named."

Amie Jo was out of the shower and done crying when I returned.

I was annoyed by how cute and approachable she looked with wet hair and my clothes. Why couldn't mean people be ugly on the outside, too?

She handed me the plastic bag full of shitty clothes as if it were my job to dispose of them.

"They all laughed at me," Amie Jo said flatly.

"Well, you did do the backstroke in a half ton of donkey shit," I pointed out. "Imagine if it had been me. You would have laughed."

She looked at me, eyes narrowing. "But you didn't laugh. Everyone else did."

"I know what it's like to be laughed at." It was as simple as that.

"Oh," she said.

"Travis is getting you your driving Uggs," I said, pointing at the mismatched shoes on her feet.

"Why? I want to go home!"

"Look, Amie Jo. Take it from me. If you go home in shame, this will follow you. However, if you march out there in your driving Uggs and your borrowed clothes and collect donations and at least pretend to laugh it off, it'll slide right off of you, and you'll be back to your reign of terror in no time."

There was a knock on the locker room door. "Amie Jo? Honey? I've got your Uggs and your emergency perfume," Travis called.

Nostrils flaring, Amie Jo straightened her shoulders and marched around me to the door.

CHAPTER 58

Jake

"Everything go okay in there, or do you need a mop for the bloodshed?" I asked Marley when she came back out of the locker room.

She took her donkey's bridle and scratched his nose with a small smile. Dressed in a hoodie and jeans, her hair in a messy knot, she looked edible to me.

"Everything's fine," she said.

"That was really nice of you, by the way," I told her. "You didn't have to help her after all the shit—ha—she's pulled with you." Something about the fact that this woman had just gone out of her way to show kindness to a mortal enemy made her even more attractive to me. What the hell was happening to me? I fall in love and instantly turn into a teddy bear of mush? Love made men pathetic, I decided.

She tried to shrug off the compliment, but I pulled her into me and wrapped her in a one-armed hug. I used my other arm to elbow Bertha away from Marley's already mangled hood.

"I'm serious, pretty girl. You're a good person."

"I'm probably going to laugh really hard about it later tonight," she confessed.

"You wouldn't be human if you didn't. It was fucking

hilarious. Now, are you prepared to have your ass—man, I'm hilarious tonight—handed to you?"

She laughed appreciatively. Another point in her favor. The woman had the good taste to find me amusing. I loved her. Completely and without question, and I had no fucking clue what to do about it.

"On a scale of one to Peeing Your Pants in School, how humiliating is this going to be?" she asked, wincing as the crowd in the gymnasium broke into enthusiastic applause.

"Baby, you didn't just fall ass-first into donkey shit. You'll be just fine. Have fun with it."

"Where's your helmet?" she asked, eyeing my bare head.

I grinned and picked up my motorcycle helmet from the floor.

She rolled her eyes. "Always a rebel."

I gave her a quick kiss for luck on the cheek and went off to huddle with my team. The rules were simple. There were five to a team. Four players from each team took to the court at a time. You could run alongside your donkey leading it down the court, but in order to shoot the ball, you had to be astride.

Our donkeys were fat, happy pets from several local farms that rented out their specially trained herds for one fundraiser a year and Nativity plays at Christmas. They arrived in a train of Cadillaclike trailers and received pets, hugs, and treats from VIP donors prior to the game. Bertha here lived in an actual house. Ezekiel, the short brownish donkey, was a certified therapy animal allowed to visit the senior citizens at the nursing home.

Riders were given a crash course in donkey handling that boiled down to *"Don't make your donkey do anything it doesn't want to do."* That added to the hilarity of the event. Last year, I'd been saddled—ha—with a donkey that felt like walking off the court and into the hallway every five minutes.

I hoped Marley ended up with a lazy ass. I mean, I loved

the girl and all, but I was competitive. I wanted to win. Besides, learning to laugh at herself would be good for her.

We took to the court, awkwardly leading our four-legged partners to the center where the Media Club announced the riders and steeds. I waved like a star athlete when it was my turn and scanned the stands. My uncles were in attendance somewhere. I spotted the Ciceros holding a calligraphy *Marley Cicero Is Our Daughter* sign in the front row looking excited. They waved to me, and I waved back. For in-laws, a guy could do a lot worse.

Holy fucking shit. Where the hell had that come from?

"Yo, Weston," Haruko called. "Let's huddle up."

I would freak out later, I decided.

"Okay, Team Ass-tonishing All-Stars," the official donkey handler said. "Remember, our primary goal is gentle donkey management. Don't pull. Don't push. Don't kick. The donkeys are the stars, and you are their personal assistants. If poop happens, there are buckets and shovels at the end of each court. You are responsible for your donkey's poop."

Heh, Bertha had already unleashed her bowels, so I was covered for the duration of the game.

"We'll be breaking for water, treats, and rest halfway through."

The game lasted thirty minutes, which was about as long as the crowd could laugh without pissing their pants. And it kept the donkeys within their allotted cardio conditioning for the day.

We stood for the national anthem, and then it was game time. I gave Marley a sassy wink.

Marley was a surprisingly good donkey rider. Or her damn donkey had a crush on her. While Bill Beerman proceeded to fall off for the third time—the guy had zero balance—and Floyd chased after his escaped donkey, Marley trotted down the court clutching the ball. She missed the basket. But Principal Eccles rebounded it and swished it for two points. The two women high-fived from the backs of their respective donkeys as the crowd cheered.

Bertha was a heat-seeking missile on course to return to half-court when she got distracted by something. The entire girls' soccer team. They were lined up on the first bleacher unbagging apple slices and carrot sticks.

I heard Marley's laugh and flipped up the visor of my helmet to give her a stern glare. Of course she'd cheat. I was mad I hadn't thought of it myself.

Three of my team's four donkeys trotted over to graze happily out of the girls' hands while Haruko faced the Ass-tute Achievers alone. The crowd was eating it up. I waved the ref over and demanded he call a foul. Marley rode over, and we went toe-to-hoof in a good-natured shouting match.

"She's cheating, ref!"

"He's just jealous he didn't think of it first!"

The crowd was on its feet, and there was nothing even happening on the court. I could see the can collectors accepting fistfuls of cash and winked at Marley.

She grinned and then covered it with a fierce glare.

Bertha lunged at Marley's hood and got another good bite.

"Ahhh! Control your noble steed, you jackass," Marley screeched at me as Bertha accidentally choked her with her death bite on the hood.

"Yellow card for trying to asphyxiate a member of the opposing team," the ref said, shoving a yellow card in my face.

"Now you're just making shit up," I complained, wrestling Marley's hood away from my hungry donkey. "Bertha, you're making me look bad." I swear to God she winked at me.

Marley skipped off with Donkey Ote and gave her team the thumbs-up. Karma was swift and judicious. When Marley tried to climb onto her donkey's back, he turned in a tight circle, and she slid right over his back onto the gym floor. Her soccer team was hysterical. I jogged over and sidestepped Donkey Ote.

"Are you okay?"

She rolled over, tears streaming down her face.

"Oh, shit. Are you hurt?"

Marley shook her head and sucked in a breath. Her bun was crooked under her helmet, her cheeks were flushed, and her shoulders were shaking with silent laughter.

"I. Can't. Breathe," she squeaked out, wiping away the tears. "I fell off a donkey." She covered her mouth with her hand, brown eyes twinkling, and I realized I'd never seen anyone more beautiful in my entire life. I was going to marry this woman. And I was going to mention this exact moment in our vows.

Donkey Ote got tired of not eating snacks and nudged me in the back hard enough to shove me into Marley. It started her laughing all over again. We were a tangle of limbs and donkey leads, and neither one of us could stop laughing long enough to help the other one up. Around us, the game continued in fits and spurts. But I was too busy falling deeper in love to do anything about it.

We sat up and did our best to untie the donkey halters.

"Yo, Cicero!" Floyd called from down the court just as we got untangled.

He heaved a Hail Mary in our direction. In slow motion, I watched as Marley shoved me back onto the floor and caught the ball to her chest. She stuck her tongue out at me and slid onto Donkey Ote's back. I lay there slack-jawed as her ass jogged down the court and Marley executed the perfect donkey-assisted layup.

It was pure pandemonium in the gym.

CHAPTER 59

Marley

W e won. Get over it," I told Jake smugly as we walked up the driveway.

"You cheated," he argued.

"Listen, I don't know how my team all ended up with cans of Silly String. I'm completely innocent," I lied. My team had squeaked by with a victory after we'd unleashed a silly string assault on the other team's riders with a minute left in the game.

"You're a Cicero. I should have known you'd take winning too seriously," he teased. "I think my wrist is still sprained from Dutch Blitz."

"It's your own fault for assuming my family is normal. And you should see Zinnia play chess. She's got a victory dance for a checkmate that is not safe for work."

We stepped up onto the front porch, and I glanced around at the columns. Even the front of Amie Jo's house was decked out for the party. There were balloons in Culpepper blue and white, hurricane vases with candles, and what looked like several large Barn Owl piñatas hanging from the rafters.

Living next door had given me a front-row seat to witness Amie Jo's party preparations. The swan had been corralled in a white picket pen in the front yard where it squawked at the steady line of caterers and party planners and other strangers in uniform carrying mysterious boxes and bins. Vans and trucks drove onto the grounds in a steady stream starting at 10 a.m.

I couldn't wait to see what was behind the large double front doors. On the other hand, I also couldn't wait to go the hell back to Jake's house. I was willingly going to a social event in Culpepper. At my sworn enemy's house. Sure, I was interested in what was behind door number one, but I'd rather be getting naked with my boyfriend.

"Are you ready for this?" he asked, tugging at his sports coat.

"Amie Jo hasn't reported me to Principal Eccles in a few days," I told him. It was a Culpepper miracle. Seemingly, her slide through warm donkey shit had, at least temporarily, dulled the woman's hatred of me. I'd expected another conference with the principal when Floyd and I worked out a deal with a local barre studio to borrow their freestanding barres. We were in the midst of two weeks of clunky ballet moves and quivering thighs as we all held unnatural positions. The kids freaking loved it.

"Maybe she's finally decided to grow up," Jake said optimistically. He reached around me and pressed the doorbell I'd been working up the nerve to poke. "Relax, Mars. You look great, and I guarantee you're going to have a damn good time."

"I'm walking into the lion's den, and you act like we're going to an ice cream social," I complained.

"Trust me. There ain't nothing ice cream social about this party," he promised cryptically.

The front door opened, and I could only blink at the camouflage tuxedoed man before us. "Welcome to the Hostetter Estate," he said in a British accent. "May I please have your names?"

"Jake Weston and Marley Cicero," Jake said with a straight face when I appeared to be incapable of speech. *Where did one even find a camo tux?*

Jeeves looked down his nose at the clipboard in his gloved hands. "Yes, of course. Welcome, Mr. Weston, Ms. Cicero."

Jake pushed me inside, and my heels clicked on the marble floors. We were in a two-story foyerlike room. Jeeves was pointing out the coat check closet, an actual walk-in closet just off the front door with an actual attendant standing behind an actual Dutch door. I turned to roll my eyes at Jake and gasped when I realized the entire wall above the front door was decked out with dead animals. I'd forgotten Travis was a hunter. I wondered if there were any animals left in the Pennsylvania forests.

A server in a camo vest and black pants paused to offer us wine from his tray. "Boone's Farm. There's a fountain in the conservatory."

I took a plastic glass and stared at Jake. "Did he just say there's a Boone's Farm fountain in the conservatory?"

"Yes. Yes, he did. But Mars, you're missing the best part."

He took me by the shoulders and turned me around.

Looming above us was the largest family portrait I'd ever seen. Amie Jo, Travis, and the boys—all dressed in white, Amie Jo wearing a tiara—were immortalized in oil paints and accented by the largest gilt frame in the world. It had to be at least twelve feet high.

"Holy shit," I murmured.

He clunked his plastic glass to mine. "Oh, baby, you ain't seen nothing yet."

We checked our coats with the perky attendant, and I let Jake lead me further into the house, past the gold leaf, curved staircase. There was a formal living room with white leather furniture and more gold leaf. The walls were painted a fishy salmon. The art was a collection of pink and blue abstracts. There were more floating Greek columns and thick draperies over the windows. It was like 1980s wealthy Miami had thrown up in here.

There were a handful of guests here dressed to the nines, laughing and drinking.

"Just think. This could have been your life," Jake teased.

I shuddered. Sure, money would be nice. But I couldn't imagine myself relaxing on the weekends in a place like this. Not with that many dead animals on the wall. The formal dining room was across the hall. It was crowded with party guests who were vying for the wedding reception-worthy spread on the glossy table long enough to seat at least twenty guests. There was a large stuffed boar in the corner poised to charge.

Mrs. Gurgevich, looking fancy in a black sequined kimono, was loading her plate with deviled eggs and sushi. Floyd was behind her, juggling two plates overflowing with food and a beer. "Yo! Cicero! Weston!"

I held up my wine in a toast to him.

Floyd bobbled a meatball, and it rolled off the plate onto the thick white rug under the table.

"Ooooooh!" the crowd crowed. Out of nowhere a very tiny *thing* with perky ears and perfectly trimmed white facial fur bounded into the room.

"What the hell is that?" I asked.

"That's Burberry," Jake said.

Burberry pounced on the meatball.

"He's a designer dog," Lois, the school secretary, said. "I heard Amie Jo bought him from a breeder for seven thousand dollars."

"He doesn't bark," Belinda Carlisle added. "It's bred out of him."

Burberry licked his neatly trimmed chops with a tiny pink tongue before happily trotting out of the room.

"That was a *dog*? I've seen dust bunnies bigger than that," I commented.

Jake squeezed my shoulder.

I liked how he delivered casual physical contact reliably. He didn't make a show of keeping his sexy hands to himself. And being "handled" by him made me feel like he was constantly reminding me that he was here.

"Let's get in line for the food, then we'll find the bar and the DJ."

"There's a DJ?" I asked.

He held up a finger, and I listened. Over the buzz of excited party people, I could hear the steady thump of music.

We loaded up plates with pasta, cheese, sushi, and delectable skewers of meat that the server promised no one we knew had killed and went in search of the bar. If I was going to spend an evening in the Hostetter "estate," I required liquor. And lots of it.

Jake led the way down into the hallway and past the massive kitchen teeming with catering staff.

We found the bar in a room that had a baby grand piano and a wall of bookcases. Amie Jo never struck me as a reader, and I got the feeling that the books—all spines facing in—were just decoration.

Unfortunately, we also found our hosts.

Amie Jo was dressed in a gold cocktail dress with a neckline that showed her belly button. There was *no way* those gravity-defying boobs were real. No friggin' way.

She had a gold star stuck to the skin at the corner of her eye, and her extensions were waist-length now. Travis was dutifully handsome in slacks and a button-down. I felt like I was staring at Small-Town Party Barbie and Ken. They were blindingly attractive together. It looked as though Amie Jo had survived her slide through shit and come out smelling like a rich rose.

"You ready to greet our hosts?" Jake asked.

"Would it be rude if I waited until I had more than Boone's Farm swimming through my system first?"

His eyes lit up with a devilish light that I'd come to recognize as a promise of trouble.

"Then I'll just have to take you over into this dark corner and kiss you until they're gone," he said wickedly.

I put a hand on his chest when he started to move in like a shark. "Wait. You're not just doing this to put on a show for Amie Jo, are you?"

Jake gave me a very slow, very thorough once-over. "Baby, I'm doing this because you look so good in that dress, I know I won't be able to keep my hands to myself all night."

"Good enough for me." I grabbed him by the lapel and kissed him until I forgot all about Amie Jo and her gold-dipped house and dust bunny dog.

CHAPTER 60

Marley

After kissing the hell out of Jake, I was separated from him by partygoers.

Vicky, in a dirt brown dress with huge bell sleeves, dragged me to the bar for Fireball shots with the language arts teachers and their spouses.

Jake was invited to an impromptu poker game in Travis's man cave.

"It's crazy, right?" Vicky screamed over the music. The DJ was playing this party like she was in a club in L.A. and it was 3 a.m. Only the tunes were more "we peaked in the nineties" than "we're drunk and grinding to electronic dance music." The audience reacted like underage starlets misled by bad friends and predatory management. Everyone under the age of forty-five in Culpepper was in this house, shedding inhibitions with Coors Light and Fireball.

"I can't believe this kind of party exists in Culpepper," I shouted back. I'd seen a couple who'd been married immediately after graduation making out up against the baby grand piano *Pretty Woman*–style.

"See what you've been missing?" Vicky hollered.

Someone bumped me hard, making me spill beer down my arm.

"Oops. Didn't see you there," a mean, drunk Coach Vince sneered at me. I'd forgotten how sweaty and hairy he was.

He burped right in my face, and the fumes of it singed my hair. I was going to need to do a deep conditioning treatment stat.

"Lovely as always to see your hulking, beastly frame," I said sweetly.

He pointed a thick, fungal-nailed finger in my face. "You think you're hot shit. Doncha?"

"Well, at least body temperature shit."

Vicky snort-laughed so hard she choked.

That grated cheese finger poked me in the shoulder. Hard. "You think because you win a few games that makes you a coach?"

"No, I'm pretty sure you can still be a coach and lose."

"You're a smartass," he slurred, dipping his receding hairline into my personal space.

"Better than a dumbass."

"Whatdu call me?"

Vicky sidled in closer. "A dumbass. *SHE CALLED YOU A DUMBASS*," she yelled over the throbbing beat of R.E.M.

"Would a dumbass have the Homecoming game every year?" he scoffed.

"Do you always get the Homecoming game?" I asked him, already knowing the answer. Culpepper Homecoming always fell on a boys' soccer game night. The Homecoming Court parade took place in the afternoon with borrowed convertibles from Buchanan Ford & Tractors escorting the Homecoming princes and princesses. The always out-of-tune marching band followed, usually playing a Beach Boys song. Then there was the game and the crowning of the queen at halftime, followed by the dance.

"Hell *yeah*, I get the Homecoming game. Under the lights,

the stands packed with feering chans. It's the single biggest athletic event all year."

If he kept poking me with that finger, I was going to have to break it off and feed it to him like the gourmet cocktail weenies in the music room.

"Then I guess it's true," I said.

"What's true?"

Too much time had passed since the original dumbass insult. It wasn't worth my effort trying for a callback.

"Never mind, Vince."

Drunk Coach Vince sneered in my face. "You think you're—"

"Hot shit," I filled in. "Yeah. You already said that. Got anything new you'd like to add?"

"Pfft." The smell of cheap beer and unbrushed teeth assailed my nostrils. "You're a loser, Sickero. A loooser."

In the past, when someone other than me identified my loser status, I'd felt shame. It was an open wound I dealt with secretly, never being good enough. However, hairy-backed Vince breathing gum disease in my face while calling me a loser was not upping my shame factor.

Huh. Weird.

"Well, Vince. It was great talking to you, as always. You should probably head back upstairs to that Boone's Farm fountain," I said, turning him around and giving him a gentle shove in the direction of the basement stairs.

Either I misjudged my own strength or his grip on sobriety. He tripped over a pink fur ottoman and landed chest- and face-first in the salsa and guacamole spread next to the bar.

"Uh, we should probably go upstairs immediately," Vicky said, grabbing my hand and towing me toward the stairs.

"Sickero!" Vince roared. His face was a green mask of wounded rage. I choked down a laugh and ran for my life.

We escaped to the first floor of the house before we lost our shit.

"This definitely makes the Top Five Favorite Memories from the Hostetter House Party." Vicky gasped for breath.

"There are memories that beat *this*?" I asked, jerking a thumb in the direction of the wounded wildebeest who couldn't get his size 15 shoes to carry him up the stairs.

"Rich and I had sex in Amie Jo's whirlpool tub about eight years ago."

I gaped at her.

"What?" Vicky asked innocently. "Married people can't fornicate drunkenly at parties?"

"You are so much cooler than I give you credit for."

"There's my girl!" Jake hustled toward me, goofy grin on his face and a distinct lean to his gait. My cute, sexy boyfriend was drunk.

He picked me up and twirled me around while listing dangerously to the left. I bumped my head on a low-hanging hallway chandelier with—what else?—gold freaking swan necks and heads.

"Hey, you," I said, patting him on the head. "How about you put me down?"

Jake pondered this suggestion while still holding me aloft.

"I beat your old boyfriend at poker," he said.

"Let's talk about it with my feet on the floor."

He put me down. But before I could compliment him on his listening skills, he bent at the waist and tossed me over his shoulder.

A long-forgotten teenage girl survival mode kicked in. I knew exactly what Drunk Jake was planning to do.

He cheerfully slapped my ass and took off toward the back of the house at a labored jog.

"Vicky, stop recording," I yelled at my friend who was chasing after us with her phone out.

"You might want to stop flicking me off and hang on for dear life," she suggested.

"Carry on," Jake said, saluting the catering staff in the kitchen before wrestling the back door open.

"Someone throw me a meat cleaver," I begged.

But they ignored my pleas. We were drawing quite the crowd. I stopped wriggling when I felt cold night air on my ass. Great. I was mooning half of Culpepper.

"Jake, don't you dare—"

My threat was cut off when he simply walked off the patio and into the deep end of the pool.

I screamed underwater and tried to strangle him, but he was slippery, and the cold made my finger joints useless. We surfaced together. Me gasping and choking. Him laughing his fine ass off.

"You son of a bitch!" I launched myself at him and dunked him.

He went under, and I felt his hands sliding up my bare legs under water.

It was then that I realized the skirt of my dress was floating up around my neck leaving my entire body, clad only in a bra and underwear, exposed to the view of the rest of the party.

There was cheering and applause coming from the patio. My teeth were chattering. The pool heater could only take the edge off of the October chill.

Jake was grinning as if he'd just told the greatest joke in the history of the world. I splashed him in his stupid handsome face and mustered as much dignity as I could to climb the ladder.

"C'mon, pretty girl," he called after me. "Don't be like that."

Everyone was laughing. And then I realized I was too. I didn't freak out over being called a loser. And now my entire hometown had seen my pink underwear and was laughing at me. Yet I wasn't curled in the fetal position, humiliated and wounded.

Was I too drunk to care? I blinked the salt water out of my eyes a few times. Nope. I wasn't seeing double or tequila triple. Was this growing up? Had my skin magically thickened?

I turned around to face the pool. Jake was floating on his back, staring up at the night sky, spitting water out of his mouth like a fountain.

I felt something warm break free in my chest. Probably the Fireball. Instead of shivering my way back into the house, I found myself running at full speed back to the pool.

"Cannonball!" I yelled, vaulting into the air. I tucked my knees and had the pleasure of watching Jake's eyes fly open as I hurtled toward him.

I landed on his chest, and we both went under. The cheer of the drunken crowd was muffled by the blue water. We grappled, hands sliding over each other. And when we surfaced together, we were both laughing.

"You're a hell of a girl, Marley Cicero," Jake said, hooking his hand around the back of my neck. The kiss was wet and cool and one of the most joyful experiences my lips had ever had. It ranked up there with chocolate chip cookie dough ice cream on a hot summer night.

"Everybody in the pool!"

We were drowned in the splashes of drunk bodies hitting the water.

CHAPTER 61

Marley

I sloshed into Amie Jo's house and decided I might as well sneak next door to my parents' to grab dry clothes. Jake, a science teacher, and the minister from the Culpepper Methodist Church were competing for a diving competition title. Winner takes the terra-cotta yard gnome. The judges were lined up in lawn chairs with hand-drawn scorecards.

My hair hung in clumps around my face, and I was half frozen.

"Here's a warm-up for you," Vicky said, shoving a glass into my hand.

I drained it and shuddered. "What the hell was that?" I gasped.

"Brandy? Whiskey? Maple syrup?" Vicky guessed. She was staring at me with one eye closed. This was Drunk Vicky. My very favorite person on Earth.

"Drunk Vicky!" I slapped her on the back a little harder than I intended. My hand-eye coordination and depth perception were a little iffy. "How the hell are you?"

"Fucking fantastic," she said enthusiastically.

"Ladies."

"Uh-oh," Vicky stage-whispered.

Amie Jo stood in the doorway, arms crossed. She tapped her disco ball nails in a staccato rhythm on her biceps.

"Sorry about the dripping," I said, looking down at my bare feet and wondering where the hell my shoes had gotten to.

"A word, Marley?" she said.

"Sure."

"You're in trouble," Vicky sang as I followed Amie Jo to the back staircase.

"Upstairs, please," Amie Jo said without looking back to see if I was following her.

"Don't let her murder you and roll you up in a rug," Vicky called after us.

I trudged up the carpeted stairs, trying not to rain pool water over everything. I wondered if Amie Jo was leading me up here to lock me in a wrapping paper closet/dungeon. Wait. Scratch that. She probably had a wrapping paper *room,* and with Christmas just around the corner, she wouldn't want to have to clean up the blood spatter.

Amie Jo paused in front of French doors and opened them with a flourish. I followed her inside and found myself in the mastery-est master suite in the history of the designation. The white carpet was so thick I sank in up to my ankles. The walls were wallpapered silver with delicate threads of gold woven into the silky texture. There was a sitting area with snow-white armchairs and a modern glass side table. The bed…

Holy mother of God. The bed.

It was NBA-player-orgy sized.

White upholstered headboard. Silver duvet. Approximately three hundred throw pillows in silvers, grays, and golds. I wanted to jump on it and see how many times I could roll before I got from one side to the other. I guessed at least nine.

"Wow."

I must have said it out loud because Amie Jo popped her head out of the door on the far side of the room.

"Here," she said, holding out a plastic bag to me and crossing the fifty yards of polar bear carpet.

I accepted the bag. My first guess was rattlesnake. My second guess was vibrator. I wasn't sure why Amie Jo would give me a used vibrator in a plastic bag. But I was a little drunk, so I wasn't too hard on myself.

Peeking inside, I discovered I was wrong on both counts. "My clothes," I said, pulling out the yoga pants and sweatshirt I'd lent her after the Donkey Shit Incident.

"Thank you for letting me borrow them. I had them dry-cleaned for you," she said, interlacing her fingers in front of her. She looked uncomfortable, like being nice to me was so foreign she didn't know how to do it.

I wondered if old, overwashed clothes like these yoga pants could disintegrate from dry cleaning.

"Thank you."

"You can change in here so you don't destroy my house with pool water," Amie Jo sniffed. We had officially moved past the polite part of the evening.

"Okay," I said lamely.

She started for the door.

"Thanks, Amie Jo," I called after her.

"You're welcome. Try not to touch anything." She closed the door, and I was left alone in the Arctic beauty of her master suite. The temptation to touch something was strong. But I was an adult. An inebriated one. But still. I could control myself.

My leg brushed against the white fur throw at the bottom of the bed. I wondered if it was polar bear and if Amie Jo had killed it herself.

I ducked into the closet to change and got distracted by the fifty-two pairs of stilettos neatly organized, one shoe facing forward, one shoe facing back. Travis's belt rack held over a dozen brown and black belts. The closet, which was larger than my childhood bedroom, was organized with a militant precision. Cashmere in every color of the rainbow was neatly stacked on shelves. Jeans, an entire corner of them, hung so straight they had to be starched.

Raucous laughter wafted up from the first floor through the ventilation system, reminding me there was a party going on. I changed quickly, losing my balance as I wiggled into my yoga pants and tipping over into Travis's dress shirt museum.

"Damn it!" I took half a dozen perfectly pressed oxfords with me as I crashed to the thick carpet.

"Everything all right in there?"

I froze in my puddle of monogrammed shirt sleeves. Travis Hostetter stood in the closet doorway looking pretty and preppy.

"I was just changing. Into my own clothes. Not yours," I said quickly, trying to stand back up and only succeeding in ripping two more shirts from their hangers.

Travis entered the closet and helped me to my feet.

"Don't worry about it," he said when I bent to collect the massacred wardrobe.

"I can hang it all back up," I insisted.

"Marley, relax. They're just shirts."

I was more nervous around Travis than I was Amie Jo. His wife was predictable with her aggressive meanness. Travis, on the other hand, a boy I'd wounded deeply in high school, was an unknown.

It might have been the Fireball swimming through my veins, but I was hit with a sudden clarity. I owed this man an apology. Even if he didn't need to hear it, I needed to say it.

I plucked my dripping dress off of the carpet and stood in front of the sodden puddle and cleared my throat. "Travis, I owe you an apology. Several actually. It's always bothered me how I ended things with you. I want you to know that I'm

sorry for hurting you, and I hope you'll consider forgiving me."
Booze brave, I blurted out the words.

It was true.

Hurting Travis, who'd never been anything but nice to me, had haunted me. Breaking up with him had been the right thing to do. But I'd been clumsy and artless about it. I'd caused unnecessary pain.

"Marley—" he began. But I plowed on ahead.

"I'd also like to apologize for breaking your leg and ruining your chance at a soccer career in college in a mean-spirited bid for vengeance."

"Okay—" he began again.

"Against Amie Jo, not you," I added quickly. "I wasn't trying to get revenge on you. You were nice." This was going to go down in the history of worst apologies ever.

He waited a beat, probably to make sure I was done talking.

"I haven't been holding a grudge. If that's what you mean," he said finally.

I breathed a sigh of relief. "Are you sure?"

"I'm sure." He grinned.

"But you ended up back here with *Amie Jo*." I probably shouldn't have said that. I'd just apologized to him and in the next breath insulted his wife.

Travis laughed and waved me out of the closet. "What makes you think that's not what I wanted? Culpepper is home. Everyone I love—including my very high-maintenance wife—is here. She's different with me and the boys than she is to—"

"Everyone else in the universe?"

"Yeah. I'm happy. I adore her, and I love our life."

"You have a swan in your yard," I pointed out. "And a twenty-foot-tall family portrait in your foyer."

"Making Amie Jo happy makes me happy," he said simply.

Maybe it was as easy as that. Or maybe Amie Jo was a circus acrobat in bed.

I'd hurt Travis, but he'd ended up happier than I could have made him.

"You're not mad about Homecoming?" I pressed.

"It was an accident," he assured me.

"Well, the thing with you was. I kinda planned all the rest of it," I admitted.

He laughed.

"So we're good?" I asked with suspicion. This guy didn't hold on to grudges like I did.

"We're good," Travis promised.

"There you are!" an adorably drunk Jake bellowed from the door. He frowned, looking first at me and then Travis. "You two are alone in a bedroom?"

"I was changing out of my pool clothes," I explained. "And then I destroyed their closet. And then I apologized to Travis for high school."

"All of high school?" Jake asked, confused.

"No, just the parts that I messed up for him."

"And I told Marley that there's no hard feelings. It's all good." Travis slapped Jake on the shoulder. "So when are you bringing that piece-of-shit SUV in and trading it for an Escalade?"

"Pfft," Jake snorted. "When you start offering fifty percent off for high school classmates. So, Mars. I hunted you down because Vicky says it's time for your Spice Girls routine."

I perked up. Vicky and I had spent part of junior high coordinating a spectacular dance routine to most of the Spice Girls' catalog.

"If you gentlemen will excuse me, there's an ass I need to shake. Spoiler alert: It's mine."

CHAPTER 62

Jake

A rhythmic sawing noise woke me, and I wondered who the fuck let the lumberjack in the house. I opened one bleary eye and immediately slammed it shut against the abrasive light of day.

I had a Hostetter Hangover. Something I'd avoided for the past four years since the "drunk in the whirlpool tub" incident.

My headache had a pulse. It was a living, breathing thing, and I wanted to kill it.

A desert. The motherfucking Sahara Desert. That's what was inside my mouth. There were cacti growing on my tongue.

Someone else moaned, and I realized my body was contorted around Marley. I could tell by the smell of her shampoo, the shape of the ass pressed against my crotch. Wait. What was happening with my crotch? It felt like it was being hugged.

I cracked my other eye open and looked down.

"How the hell did I get in bicycle shorts?"

"Huh?" Marley groaned into a Harry Potter pillow.

I didn't have a Harry Potter pillow. Or bike shorts.

The horror was just sinking in when there was a cheery knock at the door. And then I was making eye contact with Ned Cicero.

"Marl—holy shit," he squeaked.

I tried to wrestle the bedspread up and over my body.

"Are those my bike shorts?" Ned asked.

"Dad?" Marley finally roused herself from the depths of her hangover to join me in this misery. "Jake?"

"Apparently we decided to crash here last night?" I guessed.

It was coming back to me in bits and pieces. Whiskey and beer. Jell-O shots. Boone's Farm Pong. It was easier to just stumble next door than call for a ride.

"I'll just leave you to it," Ned said, his voice two octaves higher than usual.

It. He was going to leave us to *it*.

He slammed the door, and I could hear the pitter-patter of his size 8s as he ran down the stairs to get as far away from this nightmare as possible.

"Marley." I shook her.

"Let me die in peace," she groaned.

"Your dad just walked in on us in bed together, and I'm wearing his bike shorts."

She rolled toward me, wincing at the motion. "Why are you in his bike shorts?"

"How the hell should I know? Also, I might be new at this relationship thing, but even I know it's bad form to be caught in your girlfriend's bed in her parents' house."

"We're thirty-eight years old, Jake," she rasped, exploring her own cotton mouth.

"It doesn't matter if we're eighty. It's disrespectful! And now I've got my junk all over his bike shorts. What kind of message does that send?"

She yanked the blanket off me and wrapped it around her head. "Can we discuss this next week when I'm not actively dying?"

The door opened again. But this time, instead of a bewildered Cicero, it was a short stranger in a blue bathrobe. "This isn't the bathroom," he observed, backing out of the room. His gaze lingered on my bike shorts.

"Across the hall," Marley croaked.

"Yep. Cool. Sorry." He shut the door.

"Who the fuck is making all that racket? If it's one of my kids, I'm selling them to the gypsies when they come through town again."

Marley and I stared wide-eyed at each other before peering over the side of the bed. Vicky had made a nest in clean laundry and had one of Marley's bras wrapped around her head to block the light.

"Are your kids here?" Marley demanded.

"That depends," Vicky said, pulling a pair of sweatpants over her shoulders. "Where is here?"

"My parents' house."

"Oh, good. Then they're probably not here."

"Shit." I reached for my phone and realized I had no idea where it was. It was probably in my pants, which were also missing.

"What's wrong besides the obvious?" Marley asked.

"Homer. He needs breakfast and to be let out. What time is it?" I was the worst dog parent in the history of dog parents. I imagined my poor canine pal pinching his back legs together to keep from pissing all over the kitchen floor and staring mournfully at his empty food dish.

"Here," Marley pressed her phone into my hand. "Call your uncles."

I dialed and lay back down to stop the room from spinning.

Uncle Max answered with his trademark "Good morning!"

"Uncle Max," I croaked.

"Well if it isn't our little Frankie Valli."

"It's Jake," I corrected him.

"You don't remember a damn thing about last night, do you?" Max laughed.

369

"If you could be more specific, I'd appreciate it. I just woke up in my girlfriend's bed in her dad's bike shorts."

Max's laugh was loud and long. "Hang on. I can't breathe. Wooo!"

"Uncle Max, I need you to go check on Homer for me—"

"You mean the furry beast who just conned me out of my last doughnut hole?"

"He's with you?" I sat up in bed and immediately regretted it.

"You don't remember calling last night and leaving a voice mail singing about how much you love your Homie? Marley sang backup."

"I do not."

"Don't worry, I forwarded it to Lewis and your mom. Also your cousin. You did an enthusiastic version of Frankie Valli's 'Sherry,' and you creatively changed Sherry to Homie."

That explained the sore balls and throat.

"I'm never going to that party again," I groaned.

"Well, take your time apologizing to the Ciceros for being an inconsiderate drunkard. Homer is farting all over Lewis's armchair."

"Did you walk him?"

"To the park, where he flirted with some Maltipoo one-quarter his size."

"Feed him?"

"Do doughnuts count?"

"No, they do not."

"Relax. He had his ration of kibble before his doughnut."

"Thanks, Uncle Max."

"Thank you for the entertainment. I'll forward you the voice mail," he promised.

I said goodbye and hung up.

"Homer okay?" Marley asked over Vicky's snoring.

"He's farting up my uncles' house."

"I guess I should go explain this tableau to my parents," she yawned.

"Marley, I'm not exaggerating when I say I would marry you for a Gatorade right now."

She snorted, unimpressed with my profession of love. "I'll see what I can do."

I'd never done the walk of shame to the breakfast table in a woman's parents' house before. Then again, I'd never gotten caught in a girl's room before.

Marley found sweats for me, so I didn't have to make my appearance in Ned's bike shorts. Unfortunately, her clothes weren't much better. The sweatpants accentuated my junk in a creepy porn movie sort of way. The sweatshirt was so tight I worried I'd bust the seams if I coughed too hard.

"Good morning," Jessica said chipperly. She made a valiant effort to ignore the inappropriate bulge in my pants.

"Morning, Mom," Marley whispered, her voice gravelly. "Sorry for the unannounced guests."

"It's no problem," Jessica said, attention stolen by Vicky stumbling into the kitchen.

"Please tell me there's grease and coffee," Vicky begged. She was clutching a pillow over her head and ears.

"Mom, if I give you directions on how to make a hangover breakfast, do you think you could make it for us?" Marley asked, slumping into a chair at the table.

"Sure thing, sweetie."

While Jessica flipped bacon and Marley made a second pot of coffee, Vicky and I divvied up ibuprofen.

"And this is the kitchen," Ned said, waving the stranger from earlier into the room. "As you can see, we have a few extra guests this morning."

The guy, now fully dressed in jeans and a sweater, offered a shy wave.

"Come on in, Vicente," Jessica said, pointing him in the direction of the coffee.

I cleared my throat. "Mr. Cicero, about your shorts."

"Keep them," he said. "And let's never speak of this again."

CHAPTER 63

Marley

O ver my dead body!" Coach Vince loomed over Principal Eccles's desk in his best impression of a sweaty vulture.

"I understand that you're disappointed," Principal Eccles said blandly.

I wondered if she kept pepper spray or a Taser in her desk drawer in case students, staff, or parents got too aggressive. I hoped she at least had a bottle of booze in there somewhere.

"The Homecoming game is *mine*," Vince shrieked like a wounded zombie. Spittle flew from his thin lips and dotted the desk.

Principal Eccles jerked her thumb toward the window. "You want to play in this? You think anyone is going to turn out for a parade *in this*?"

The remains of Hurricane Patricia were bathing Culpepper in a torrential downpour of biblical proportions. Now a tropical storm, Patricia had lumbered her lard-ass up the East Coast, turning the Outer Banks and most of Virginia into a dumping ground of floodwaters. Pennsylvania was enjoying her wrath now.

The stadium field was under four inches of water, and we were ten minutes away from an early dismissal before all the local creeks barfed up storm water and closed roads. I was packed and ready to go spend an unexpected free afternoon naked at Jake's.

At least, I had been before receiving the summons to the principal's office.

"Then we'll reschedule," Vince said stubbornly.

"We *have* rescheduled. Homecoming will be next Friday."

It was becoming clear why I was invited to a front-row seat of Coach Vince's rage. I swallowed hard.

"We have a home game Friday," I said. Not just any home game. We were playing Culpepper's rivals the New Holland Buglers. Buglers sounded friendly and peppy. Unfortunately, the New Holland Buglers were aggressive, eyeball-gouging Amazonians who could put the ball in the back of the net better than any other team in our league.

I remembered losing to them spectacularly my junior year. One girl hit me so hard going for the ball that I lay there staring up at the lights wondering if I should head toward them or not.

"Ms. Cicero, your game is now the Homecoming game," Principal Eccles announced.

Shit. Shitty shitty shit shit. Homecoming games were meant to be *won*. No one wanted to get slaughtered on the field in front of the entire town and then go to a dance where your classmates made fun of you.

"This is bullshit, Eccles," Vince raged. I wondered if I could talk him into the nurse's office next door for a blood pressure check. I didn't like his color. "I demand that you reschedule. We have a game that Saturday."

"Your Saturday game is an hour away," she pointed out, not particularly disturbed by the hulking primate throwing a hissy fit inches from her face. "And now, if you'll excuse me, I demand that you get out of my office so I can send everyone home before the buses float away."

I stood up and followed Principal Eccles out of the office

in a fog while Coach Vince snarled his disappointment behind me.

"Uh, Principal Eccles. I don't know if you're aware, but I was kind of banned for life from Culpepper Homecomings," I explained, jogging after her.

"That was just a rumor started by a disgruntled student. I checked," she said, ducking outside to check the bus line.

"A rumor?" *Amie Jo.* Oh, for fuck's sake. I'd adhered to a punishment that hadn't even been real.

Coach Vince elbowed his way past us. He kicked at a fire hydrant and then howled in pain.

There was a hard glint in her eye. "I'm going to admit that it gives me a small sliver of pleasure to take something away from that gigantic ass."

"I can't imagine why," I said dryly.

"Just do me a favor and don't screw it up," Principal Eccles said.

I nodded and swallowed hard.

She paused. "Oh, by the way, thank you for volunteering to chaperone the dance."

"I did what now?"

She gave me a knowing smile. "Ask Jake. He volunteered the two of you to chaperone the Homecoming dance."

I had several more important questions for her, but the dismissal bell rang, and hundreds of excited students came flooding toward us. We'd made it past lunch. The school day counted and wouldn't have to be made up. I'd initially felt the residual excitement of the students at an unexpected surprise afternoon off. But the damn New Holland Buglers had stolen that excitement from me.

It would take a miracle to beat them. And we had a week to figure out exactly what that miracle would look like. And a week to find a stupid Homecoming dress.

Coach Cicero: Okay, gang. Breaking news. Our home game Friday is the new Culpepper Homecoming.

Phoebe: Awesome!

Morgan E.: I'm wearing my tux to play!

Ruby: Wait a second. Friday? We're playing the Bulging Buglers. They'll murder us and paint their faces with our blood while everyone else is too depressed to go to the dance.

Angela: Crap.

Natalee: I think I'm coming down with something. *Cough cough cough*

Ashlynn: Guys, we've been winning this season. There's no reason we can't beat the Bugling Bastards.

Sophie S.: Are you drunk right now, Ashlynn? We've never beat New Holland. Not in the entire history of girls' soccer in Culpepper.

Libby: First time for everything.

Coach Cicero: That's the spirit.

Morgan W.: Coach is drunk.

Natalee: Coach and Ashlynn are drunk!

Coach Cicero: Excuse me. This is how people get fired, jerks. I AM NOT DRUNK. NOR AM I FURNISHING ALCOHOL TO MINORS.

Sophie P.: Who is Coach yelling at?

Libby: Big brother.

Ruby: Coach has a big brother?

Libby: No, whoever supervises this message board to make sure no one does anything inappropriate or illegal.

Sophie S.: We're being watched??? *Deletes entire collection of duck-lip selfies*

Phoebe: Why is it furnishing alcohol? Like, here's a Zima and an ottoman?

Coach Cicero: Oh my God. Are Zimas still a thing?

Coach Cicero: NEVER MIND! I'M NOT TALKING ABOUT ALCOHOL TO A BUNCH OF MINORS! STOP TRYING TO GET ME FIRED!

———

"Ladies," Jake said as he clapped his hands and shouted over the din of thirty-some girls, ages fourteen to eighteen, crammed into his living room. Girls were stacked on the couch, sharing the arm chairs, sprawled out on the floor. There were a handful of parent chaperones, mostly hanging out in the kitchen with bottles of wine and frozen eggroll appetizers. After hearing my predicament—impending public humiliation—Jake insisted on getting involved.

Also, he had the biggest TV of anyone I knew.

I climbed up on the coffee table and blew my fancy whistle. "Yo, Barn Owls." That shut them up.

Vicky started distributing the pizza my very generous boyfriend had ordered for my bottomless pit of a team. Her two-year-old, Tyler, was on a leash that she kept double wrapped around her wrist.

"Since our practice field is a mud pit from the rain, we're here to watch tapes of the Buglers games so we can anticipate their moves on the field," I announced.

"Can't we watch *The Great British Bake Off* instead?" Morgan E. asked.

"No GBBO! We are watching game tape and making thoughtful observations that will help us win Friday," I said.

"Maybe we should set our expectations a little lower," Natalee suggested. Tyler lunged for her pizza, and she held it aloft out of his reach while Vicky reeled him in like a fish.

"Yeah, like instead of winning, we should focus on not humiliating ourselves," Angela grumbled.

"Shut up and eat your pizza," I snapped.

"Coach Cicero, if I may," Jake said.

I stepped off my coffee table pulpit. "By all means."

"Ladies, what's the point in aiming low with your expectations? You know what low expectations get you in real life?"

They stared at him, enthralled.

"Low expectations get you lousy boyfriends—or girlfriends," he said, nodding at Morgan E. She pressed her palms together and gave him a little bow of thanks. "Low expectations get you crappy jobs that never pay you what you're worth. They get you friends and coworkers who walk all over you. Is that what you want?"

They were shaking their heads, pizza forgotten in their laps. Jake Weston, gorgeous hunk of man, was talking.

"There's no point in aiming low. You think you're protecting yourself from disappointment, but what you're really doing is setting yourself up to never have the best."

I sat down next to Rachel on the floor and listened raptly.

"He should totally be, like, a life coach," Rachel whispered.

"Totally," I agreed.

"What if we don't win?" Ruby asked, still not sold.

"What if you do everything in your power to win and you still lose?" Jake asked. "What if you try and fail?" He scanned the crowd that filled the room to capacity. "What if you put it all out there and have nothing to regret because you did your very best?"

I had goosebumps. The man was wasted on teaching history. He should be inspiring high-school-age girls everywhere. And thirty-eight-year-old temporary soccer coaches too.

"We already practice all the time," one of the JV girls said from the corner by the fireplace.

"Practice is one thing. You're preparing for battle!"

The girls eyed each other. A few looked skeptical, but the vast majority were ready to stare down the enemy.

"Okay. How do we prepare for battle?" Ashlynn asked.

CHAPTER 64

Marley

We ran like we'd never run before. Drilled like we'd never drilled. Whined like we'd never whined before. The Barn Owls were a machine of determination. Every day, as soon as the last school bell rang, we gathered together and did whatever the hell we could that might help us win.

Saturday, we watched game tape.

Jake lent us a couple of his top distance runners and sprinters, and my team spent Sunday huffing and puffing their way through running drills and breathing exercises. Ruby nearly tore a hamstring chasing after the cute Ricky. I noticed him slow down a little bit, allowing her to catch up to him.

Monday, Floyd got into the spirit and dressed up like a New Holland Bugler, and the girls spent two hours working on footwork drills around him.

Tuesday, we refreshed our plays for restarting play. It was go big or go home, so we let our creativity run wild with corner kick plays and a few fancy throw-in maneuvers. Rachel surprised us all with a front flip throw-in that lofted the ball across the goal. Since Lisabeth was no longer a part of the team, I'd bumped the small sophomore up to varsity, and she was thriving with Libby and Ruby on offense.

I assigned each girl a player on the Buglers to shadow. I

meant for them to memorize their moves on the field. However, by Wednesday, my girls were turning in dossiers on the Bugler players and their boyfriends, grades, and after-school jobs.

I shuddered to think how much personal information was available online.

Thursday, I gave everyone the day off with strict instructions not to do anything that could get them hurt or grounded. I remembered my coaches running us into the ground the day before big games. We stepped onto the field already tired.

"You're gripping the wheel like you're going to strangle it," Libby observed over my shoulder.

Jake and I were heading out to an early dinner, and Libby had bummed a ride home after school.

"I am not," I said, loosening my grip and feeling the blood slowly trickle back into my digits.

"You guys are going to do great tomorrow," Jake said. "I haven't seen a girls' soccer team this in sync ever."

"Do you think so?" I asked, desperate for reassurance. I had a lot to prove tomorrow. I would do anything in my power not to ruin a second Culpepper Homecoming.

Libby patted my shoulder. "We won't let you down, Coach."

"I'm more worried about letting you guys down," I confessed. I was the head coach, for Pete's sake. Shouldn't I know what I was doing? Shouldn't I be leading my team with confidence? Instead, I was going to have to stash a barf bucket behind the bench so I could puke up my nerves.

"Everyone has to learn how to win and lose," Libby said philosophically.

"I'd really like to learn how to win."

Libby and Jake snickered.

"So, Libs, how's Culpepper working out for you so far?" Jake asked, changing the subject.

She gave a teenagery shrug. "It's not awful."

"She means she adores it here and thinks I'm the role model she's been looking for her entire life," I interpreted for Jake.

"Naturally, that's what I assumed."

"How are things at home?" I asked her. I'd yet to meet Libby's foster mom. We'd spoken on the phone and over text. But she was an RN working double shifts. I had the feeling there wasn't a lot of adult supervision in Libby's house.

"Fine," she said.

I turned onto her road, not buying the fib. I had been a fibbing teenager myself...twenty years ago. I almost swerved off the road doing the math.

"Why don't you come out to dinner with us?" Jake suggested as I pulled into her driveway.

Was there anything more attractive in this world than a good man? With tattoos. Who looked sinful in sweatpants. And had a doofy dog. And could bring me to orgasm with the bat of his manly eyelashes.

All the lights in Libby's house were on, and there were two kids with their faces smooshed up against the big window overlooking the front yard. They waved excitedly at us. The driveway was empty, but the front door was cracked open.

Libby sighed. "Can't. It's my night to babysit the littles."

"We could bring dinner back," Jake offered.

She opened the back door and dragged her backpack out. "Thanks, but I got it covered. Hot dogs and mac and cheese. Yay."

Jake pointed at her. "The dinner of champions."

She waved, and I waited until she got inside and secured the front door before putting my car in reverse.

"She's a great kid," he observed.

"Yeah. I wish she could get a little more attention," I sighed, backing down the driveway. "I think she spends too much time either alone or being responsible for a bunch of kids."

"What you're doing for her is a good thing," he said, putting his hand on my leg. "I remember what it was like to be an unsupervised teenager. My uncles were the best thing that could have happened to me then."

"Do you want to have kids?" I asked. I don't know what made me blurt it out.

He choked on his own spit and hacked and coughed from the passenger seat.

I shoved my water bottle at him. "You okay?"

He guzzled it down and took his time recovering.

"Was that too personal?" I asked.

"Not when we're dating. You just…took me by surprise," he admitted.

"You've never thought about it?"

Jake scraped a hand over his jaw. "Not really. I don't *not* like kids. But I also never pictured myself to be building a dollhouse at 2 a.m. on Christmas morning only to drag my ass out of bed two hours later when someone wants to see if freakin' Santa Claus came. No, kid! There is no Santa! It was all me, and I want some credit!"

I laughed and envied the maleness of his answer. A thirty-eight-year-old man could afford to have never considered starting a family up to this point. A thirty-eight-year-old woman had to have the conversation much, much earlier.

"What about you?" he asked.

"Eh. I like my nieces and nephew. But I've never felt that overwhelming urge to create a mini me. I'd like to save the next generation from the genetic torture that was high school and rock-bottom self-confidence. Besides, my eggs have got to be scrambled by now. Too much Coke and sushi over the years. Not enough sleep."

I'd always been ambivalent about the idea of babies. I admired women who threw themselves into pregnancy and parenting. But I'd had no real biological urge to make my own human being.

"That's cool," Jake said.

His acceptance released the tension that reflexively lodged in my shoulders. "You know what most people say when I tell them that?"

"What?"

"'You'll regret it,' or 'Being a mom is the most important thing I've done in my lifetime,' or 'Don't worry. You'll change your mind.'"

He winced. "You know what people say about me not wanting to make a million babies?"

"What?"

"Not a damn thing."

I sighed. "It must be nice to have a penis."

"Guilt-free biological choices," Jake teased. "But seriously. Not everyone needs to have a baby. What's right for someone else doesn't make it right for you. You know that, right? You don't have to feel guilty for not doing what everyone else is doing."

What's right for someone else doesn't make it right for you. It sounded true. It had that Oprah aha moment ring to it. But it was easier for Jake, I reminded myself. He hadn't spent the years since high school failing. He didn't have a perfect older sister who set the example for success. He didn't have to think about whether or not he *should* start a family. He didn't have an empty savings account and no place to live. Jake Weston was right where he belonged, doing what he was meant to be doing.

"Okay, so tell me about a Christmas without kids," I asked. "You're not building dollhouses or moving elves on shelves. What are you doing?"

"So here's how I see it. We sleep late. Wake up naked. Christmas morning sex." He shot me a naughty grin.

We. "Of course. And after Christmas morning sex?"

"Christmas morning coffee, brunch—you cook—and presents."

"No kids but still presents?"

He looked horrified. "*Of course* there are presents. What kind of Grinch are you? Kids aren't the only ones who deserve gifts. And I'll have you know, I could give a master class on gift giving."

"Sex. Brunch. Presents. Got it."

"Then we'd head to your parents' or to my uncles' place for a big Christmas dinner. Lots of wine. More gifts. Maybe some games. Or maybe if our families get along, we host. We've got the room. You're a hell of a cook, and I could probably be trained as a sous-chef," he mused.

We meant *me*. Jake was talking about Christmas with *me*. Marley Jean Cicero, eternal screwup.

And for one shiny, holiday-scented second, I could see it. Homer in his elf hat. Jake pouring me a glass of wine. My parents laughing with his uncles. My throat felt a little tight, so I cleared it.

"What if you end up with a woman who wants a family?" I asked suddenly. The need for reality, a reminder that all of this was temporary, rose fiercely.

He was quiet for a long beat, and then he squeezed my knee. "I'm with you, Mars. So that's not a problem."

CHAPTER 65

Marley

Another lifetime ago. The Homecoming Incident.

I spent every waking minute before Homecoming plotting my revenge. *In general, I was an easygoing kinda gal. I had a high tolerance for stupidity. I was patient for my real life to begin after the torturous high school years.*

But Amie Jo had pushed me too far. I was done being a silent victim. And it was time for her to pay.

I kept Vicky out of it. Not only did I want to save her from any collusion accusations, I also wanted full credit for this one.

Homecoming was the obvious choice. Of course she was on the court. She was a shoo-in for Queen. Or at least, she would have been.

Step One was already complete. Instead of the Homecoming 1998 banner hung from the back of Amie Jo's borrowed convertible, I'd swapped it out with a cheery sign that said I gave hand jobs to half the boys' soccer team.

The best part? She made it half a mile through the parade before someone took pity on her and ripped the sign from the car. The other best part? Amie Jo's supposed BFF, Shonda, was also on the court and in the convertible behind her and never said a word.

That was just an appetizer. The main course was arriving at any moment now.

I was ready, standing on the sidelines at halftime. The photographer to Vicky's school newspaper reporter. I wasn't going to miss a second of this.

And then it began.

The marching band lined up on the far end of the field for their half-time show to present the Homecoming Court. There was a tension in the air that only I could feel. Things were about to go off the rails.

The color guard marched forward, a rolled-up paper banner clutched in junior Gwen's hands. I hadn't even had to bribe her. Amie Jo called Gwen's little sister "Fatty Too Ugly" in gym class last week. Gwen found her sister crying and doing endless sit-ups in her bedroom.

I trained the school's camera on them and held my breath. This was for all of us.

"Are you getting this?" Vicky asked, chomping on her gum.

"Oh, yeah," I said.

At that moment, one of the drummers tapped off a jazzy three-count.

Just as the music started, Gwen and her color guard compatriot unfurled the long paper banner.

It was supposed to say Culpepper 1998 Homecoming.

Instead, it read Amie Jo hates Jesus.

I was going for the jugular. People in Central Pennsylvania were not allowed to hate Jesus. It just wasn't done. Amie Jo's gynecologist father was a church deacon in the Culpepper Emmanuel Lutheran Church.

The crowd went from cheering to gasping in horror as the band innocently advanced onto the field. They made it all the way to center field, giving everyone a good, long look at the message, before a vice principal jogged out and physically ran through the banner, tearing it in half.

"Was that you?" Vicky asked out of the corner of her mouth.

"Oh, yeah," I smirked.

"Genius," she said proudly.

I turned the camera to its video setting and waited for Step Two to commence.

"Well, that was an interesting start," the announcer in the booth chuckled nervously. "Let's get on with the good old-fashioned Homecoming fun. It's my great pleasure to introduce you to Culpepper Junior/Senior High's 1998 Homecoming Court."

I pressed Record.

I could hear the click and whirr of the tape the announcer slipped into the stereo and smiled. I hoped my timing was close.

Stately, classical music crackled over the loudspeakers, and the announcer introduced the first couple. A blond in a tweed blazer and pencil skirt and a tall, gangly guy in a suit. The next couple sauntered out after them. Another blond. Another blazer. This one's escort was a soccer player still in his uniform.

I held my breath.

"Our next court couple is Amie Jo Armhurger and Travis Hostetter."

Travis? What the hell?

Was she really that greedy that she had Travis for her escort and Jake for her Homecoming date?

Amie Jo's smile looked tense and faker than usual. Someone must have told her about the banner. Good.

As she waved at the very quiet crowd, the music stopped and was replaced with voices.

"I'm not pregnant, and you know it."

"But it's what everyone else believes that counts," she reminded me brightly. "As far as Culpepper is concerned, you're a pregnant whore."

A gasp stirred up in the crowd.

"Oh my God. You didn't!" Vicky squealed.

"Oh, I did."

The tape continued. "You're nothing. You'll never be anything. Just like the rest of these pathetic losers in this school."

Someone in the crowd started to boo, but it wasn't loud enough to drown out the earful of the real Amie Jo from the loudspeaker.

"Of course I cheated on Ricky with Phil," tape Amie Jo confessed. She'd forgotten that the losers of Culpepper had ears too. In less than a week, I'd been able to collect forty minutes of voice recordings of her being an ass. I had a hard time paring it down to just the highlights. Thankfully the AV Club had been helpful with the editing.

"Ugh. I don't know why Becky thinks she's so pretty and popular. If it weren't for me befriending her, she'd still be the fat, ugly loser she always was."

One of the blond girls on the court turned scarlet. Amie Jo shook her head vehemently. "I never said that," she lied.

"Shonda is so into her stupid boyfriend, she thinks she can blow me off on a Saturday? We'll see who blows who off when I tell everyone he gave her herpes!"

"That garden gnome Mr. Fester? My daddy owns him."

"Get off the field," someone yelled from the stands.

Someone else started chanting, "Asshole." It caught on quickly.

But the tape continued. I grinned as my mix tape of Amie Jo's greatest hits—gossiping about her best friends, discussing sexual encounters, and exuding bitchiness—echoed through the stadium.

Travis looked pale next to Amie Jo's full fury.

"You!" I couldn't hear her over the crowd's displeasure. She looked at me and pointed like a witch casting a spell.

I gave her the sassiest shrug I could muster. The villain was finally unveiled.

Looking back, it was probably the wrong move. I probably should have at least feigned innocence.

But I didn't. And then Amie Jo was charging at me, closing the distance between us as fast as her heels would let her.

"Oh, shit," Vicky whispered. "Don't get suspended!"

But it was too late for that. Amie Jo stormed up to me and slapped me across the face.

It was a blur from there on out. I didn't exactly remember tackling her to the ground. But that's what Vicky swears I did. As we rolled on the grass, shouting insults and throwing elbows, I wasn't worried about my punishment. I wanted to teach her a lesson. That there were consequences to treating people like garbage. Tonight, I was Amie Jo's karma.

Her nicely painted talons dug into my neck as she went for my jugular. I threw her off me and rolled to reclaim my dominance. We were a tangle of teeth and profanity and pure hatred. I was dimly aware of the crowd as it reacted to my spectacle.

I wished I had taken a self-defense class. Or a How to Kick a Bully's Ass class. I didn't want this to devolve into some embarrassing slap fight. I wanted to physically damage her horrible, nasty, cruel exterior.

Suddenly, there was an extra set of hands in the mix, and someone was trying to pull us apart. But hell hath no fury like two high school seniors locked in a battle for supremacy. We rolled again, and I swore it was Amie Jo who got her legs tangled up with the good Samaritan's. I didn't realize we were this close to the player's bench.

There was a scuffle, a tumble, and an audible pop. And an "Ooooooh" from the crowd. The howl of pain that followed had me shoving Amie Jo off me and prying her hands out of my hair.

It was Travis on the ground hugging his knee to his chest.

"Oh God. Travis, are you okay?" I asked.

"Leave him alone, you skank," Amie Jo shrieked. She pushed my face into the dirt and crawled her way to him. "Travis, honey, are you okay?"

He wasn't. And neither was his ACL.

A lot of things happened very quickly.

The two team mascots got into a shoving match that escalated into a brawl on the field. Referees and coaches and parents waded in.

Amie Jo and I were collared by Principal Fester and dragged off the field while Travis was carried off on a gurney.

"I am horrified at your behavior, ladies," Mr. Fester hissed. "This is beyond intolerable."

"I had nothing to do with this, Mr. Fester," Amie Jo began.

"That was your voice on the loudspeaker, wasn't it? Calling me a garden gnome?"

Amie Jo was prepared to lie, but Mr. Fester wasn't having any of it.

"You're both suspended for a week starting tonight."

"But Homecoming! I'm going to be Queen," she shrieked.

Her parents pushed through the crowd that was gathering around us. They were followed by Steffi Lynn.

"One week. You both will leave school grounds immediately," Mr. Fester said, his face turning a shade of purple that I didn't think was healthy.

"I want my crown," Amie Jo screeched.

Her mother slipped an arm around her shoulders. "We'll get you your crown, sweetheart," she crooned.

"Mr. Fester, clearly there's been some sort of misunderstanding here," Dr. Armburger said. "My daughter is a victim here."

Was the man deaf? Had he not heard his daughter talk about stealing his wife's bottle of Vicodin over the loudspeaker?

"Dr. Armburger, your daughter is no victim. My decision stands. One-week suspensions starting now."

Steffi Lynn glowered at me as her parents guided a sobbing Amie Jo toward the stadium entrance. "I'm not in school anymore, so I can't get in trouble for this," she said, before shoving me to the ground.

The gravel bit into my palms.

"I heard you flunked out of cosmetology school," I said. She probably would have kicked me there on the ground had it not been for an incoming hero.

"Hey! You bloated ox!" Vicky's voice rang out as she hustled forward, getting into Steffi Lynn's face.

I jumped up, inserting myself between them. I didn't need Vicky joining me in my suspension.

"I'm already suspended," I told her. "Let me handle this."

Vicky let out something close to a growl and bared her teeth at Steffi Lynn.

"You're right," I said to Steffi Lynn. "You're not in school anymore. You're not on my team anymore either. Which means I can tell you that you are a miserable, abusive, dead-on-the-inside asshole who will spend the rest of her life ruining other people's lives. You're not special. You're not better than everyone else. In fact, deep down, you know that you're not good enough. So you can take your shitty attitude, and you can go back to Mommy and Daddy's house where you'll be living between divorces for the rest of your life!"

I was still standing there shaking when half of the sheriff's department showed up and jogged onto the field to break up the melee.

CHAPTER 66

Marley

I f the JV Homecoming game was any indicator of what the varsity match would be like, I was going to drive home between games, pack my suitcase, and leave town in shame. The Buglers were turning my girls into ground beef on the field.

It was hard to watch.

I flinched over a particularly violent exchange between one of my midfielders and two Bugler girls who were six inches taller. "Way to stick, Matilda," I called.

My team wasn't sucking. They just didn't have much experience yet, and I hoped to God this particular beatdown wouldn't turn them off of soccer forever.

"Lozenge?" Vicky shoved a bag of cough drops at me. "Homemade whiskey and honey. Heavy on the whiskey."

"I'm afraid I'll choke," I said, pushing the bag back at her.

"Just make sure you save some voice for the next game," she cautioned me.

"How can you be so calm?"

My friend shrugged under her oversized coach jacket. "Last year, the score would have been 8–0." She gestured at the scoreboard. "It's 3–1 with ten minutes left. That's a huge improvement already. These girls are going to be even better next year."

Next year, I wouldn't be here. Next year, someone else

would be coaching them. Probably someone else who knew what they were doing.

The field lights clunked on above my head, and I felt the heat of them as if I were in a spotlight.

———

We lost the JV match. It wasn't a surprise. But it didn't do anything to calm my nerves. Between games, I stole five minutes and sought solace in my car. Deep cleansing breaths fogged the windows and did nothing to calm my racing heart. I was going to have a heart attack on the sidelines. Just like their last coach. I'd traumatize my team, ruin Homecoming for the crowd. They'd probably still have the dance later tonight, I rationalized. I wasn't that much a part of the school and town.

Maybe the DJ would offer a moment of silence before they introduced the King and Queen.

A fist connected briskly with my window and scared the bejesus out of me.

I opened the door and found Jake grinning down at me.

"I've come to save you from yourself," he announced, pulling me from the safety of my car.

"Oh my God. Look at all those people," I breathed. The entire town of Culpepper was braving the chilly October night to watch my girls play… Well, mostly they were here to see who was crowned Homecoming Queen at halftime.

"Listen to me, Mars. You have a captive audience in those stands. You and those girls have worked your asses off. Show them."

"What if we lose?" I hated the desperation I heard in my voice.

"Losing is never the end of the world. Losing is where the learning starts."

"I've learned enough. I don't need to learn anymore."

He squished my cheeks in his hands, fish-facing my lips. "You put in the work. Your players put in the work. All you have to do is go out there and do your best. Leave it all on the field. It's okay to care. It's okay to want to win. It's not okay to tie your worth as a human being around something like a win or a loss. Got it?"

"Gosh it," I mumbled through my duck lips.

"Good girl. Now, do you want your present?"

"Yesh pwease."

He released my face and handed me a small, neatly wrapped box. I took one second to admire the silver wrapping paper before destroying it.

"A fitness watch?" A very expensive fitness watch.

"For your running. Or when you're walking Homer," he said, popping it out of the box and fastening it to my wrist. "You can track miles, heart rate, calories. And it's got Bluetooth. So if I text you some encouragement during the game, you can just look at your wrist instead of digging your phone out and looking like you're scrolling through Snapchat instead of watching the game."

I stared down at the glowing watch face. "This is really thoughtful, Jake," I said. "By encouragement, you don't mean dick pics, do you?"

He pulled out his phone. "Hang on."

The watch vibrated on my wrist.

Jake: I'm proud of you, Mars. <3

"Oh." It was the best I could do. What I wanted was to climb into his arms and smash my face against his chest. But even Jake Weston couldn't protect me from my fears tonight. I had to face them myself. At least I'd do it with him on my wrist.

He nudged my chin up. "I'm proud of you already. You

better be too. Now, go give your girls a movie-worthy pep talk and have some fun tonight."

"Okay. And thank you for this." I held up the watch. "And everything else. You've been a really great friend." My voice cracked.

"Don't you dare start that, Mars," he said, his voice thick with emotion. "You might not know this about me, but I'm an empathetic crier. So pull yourself together, woman, or we'll both go in there bawling."

I straightened my shoulders and ran a finger over the watch face.

Jake slapped me on the ass and pushed me in the direction of the stadium entrance.

"Can you text me encouragement, like, every five minutes or so?" I asked.

"Hell yeah, I can."

———

The Culpepper Barn Owls looked as sick and scared as I felt. We were crammed into the same utility room under the announcer's booth that I'd broken into just a few weeks ago. The sprinkler system panel was now under lock and key. However, I was confident I could easily pick the lock should the need arise. For instance, in case of a 13–0 Homecoming shutout.

"Ladies." I took a deep breath. "It's a big game tonight. But you've prepared. I know it feels like there's a lot riding on this game. There are a lot of people in those stands who don't think we can win. But they have nothing to do with this. Their expectations have nothing to do with us. We are underestimated. And, let's face it, this isn't the first or last time someone is going to underestimate us."

There were nods around the ragtag circle.

"We can't control their expectations. But we can control

our effort. You've put in the work. You've put forth the effort. There's just one thing left to do."

"Win!" Vicky shouted, jumping on a dusty bench, fist held high.

The team stared at her.

"While a win would be *nice*," I said, pulling Vicky off the bench, "I'd rather see you go out there and make yourselves proud. You've already done the hard part. All I want you to do is go out under those lights and play as a team of fierce women."

"Fierce!" Vicky howled.

"What if we lose?" Angela asked, gnawing on her thumbnail.

"Then we do it with mud on our knees and smiles on our faces," Libby said. "We've got this, guys. We're good enough to put on a hell of a show. We're good enough to win. And we're good enough to survive if we lose. Even though we're not going to."

"What she said!" Vicky screeched, pointing both index fingers at Libby.

I saw smiles appearing around our little circle.

We huddled up, arms around each other, closing the gap. "The hard part is over," I told them. "All the practices, the drills, the running. This is the fun part. Go play under the lights. And have a damn good time doing it. Win, lose, or forfeit for brawling, I am so proud of you guys."

"Barn Owls on three," Ruby barked.

"One, two, three. Barn Owls!" the team shouted. They broke the circle and headed out the door like warriors preparing for battle.

"Listen," Vicky said, slapping me on the shoulder. "I stuffed a couple of plastic bags in my gym bag in case we need to barf."

"Got any more of those whiskey lozenges?" I asked.

"I kinda ate them all," she confessed with alcohol-scented breath. "But I do have a spare bourbon in my fanny pack."

"Hang on to it in case we need it at halftime."

The national anthem choked me up as it always did, but I refrained from wiping at my eyes so the crowd didn't think I was already a sobbing mess. Besides, if Jake really was an empathetic crier, I didn't want him to burst into tears in the stands. The Buglers won the coin toss. I wondered if it was the hormones in New Holland milk that had their team captains towering over my own. And was that a gold tooth on the broad-shouldered number 24?

Vicky and I walked off the field as the starters lined up, and I spared a glance at the crowd. Jake and his uncles were sitting with my parents. Dad held a *Coach Cicero Is Our Homecoming Queen* sign without a hint of irony. My mom was clutching the insulated travel mug Jake had given her "to keep her warm." I had a feeling it wasn't coffee inside. The JV team was snuggled up together with boyfriends and friends right behind the team bench.

I high-fived the cheerleaders' head coach.

"We've got a hell of a show planned for you," she promised me.

"Good luck tonight," I told her.

Andrea, Bill Beerman, Haruko, and Floyd whistled for my attention, and I cracked my first real smile of the night. They'd painted their faces Barn Owl blue and had foam beaks affixed to their noses. They looked like idiots, and I loved them for it.

"Let's go, Cicero," Floyd barked from the stands.

To my eternal humiliation, half the Culpepper student body echoed the cheer, clapping and stomping on the metal bleachers.

"You ever think you'd be on this field again with people cheering your name?" Vicky mused next to me.

"Nope. Hopefully there won't be any police involvement this time around."

"Ah, memories," she sighed fondly.

CHAPTER 67

Jake

Everyone around me on the cold-ass bleachers was watching the game. Well, in between planning who was bringing what to Thanksgiving. As predicted, Marley's parents and my uncles had hit it off big-time.

I was too busy watching my girl to participate in the great pie debate. Marley stood on the sidelines, a deceptively relaxed stance. Her hands were in the pockets of her jacket. Her feet braced apart, and she nodded to herself as she followed the action on the field. Vicky bounced and vibrated next to her, her frizzy red curls seeming determined to escape the ear warmers clamped over her head.

"I can't watch," Ned wailed next to me. He peeked through gloved fingers as the Bugler's offense drove down into Barn Owl territory.

"It's gonna be fine. We've got this," I promised.

The Bugler forward, the one who had to be close to seven feet tall, booted the ball with a thunder foot. I held my breath with the rest of the stadium as it sailed over the heads of our defense and through Ashlyn's competent hands into the back of the net.

"Fuck. I mean—" I scrambled to cover my *Sunday Night Football* beer-and-bean-dip reaction. I saw Marley's shoulders slump and wanted to climb over the people and short fence between us.

"Ha! Loooser!" Coach Vince, in a Barn Owls parka and knit hat that hid his massive bald spot, cupped his hands and howled from a few rows down.

There was no way I was going to get through life without punching that asshole in the face. I made a mental note to figure out what the legal repercussions would be. Maybe I could enlist Marley's help for another prank. The woman had a gift.

"I hate that fucking guy," I muttered under my breath.

"My sentiments exactly," Jessica growled next to me. She picked up her not-quite-empty chicken soup bowl and chucked it.

I watched in horror and delight as it flew gracefully through the air and landed in upside-down perfection on top of Coach Vince's head.

He howled, whirling around and sending pieces of corn flying. Broth seeped through his hat. Every person in the section suddenly became engrossed in watching the Buglers celebrate their goals. Not a single spectator pointed in our direction. Jessica Cicero was a beloved part of the entire last generation's elementary school years. No one was going to rat her out to an overgrown jackass.

"Who did it?" Coach Vince screeched.

"You wanna sit down so we can see?" someone suggested, trying to peer around Vince's girth.

While the Buglers celebrated the goal, the home team jogged back to take their positions for kickoff.

I whipped out my phone, my thumbs flying across the screen.

Me: It's a psychological move, not an indicator of the outcome of the game. Also, your mom just beaned Coach Vince with chicken corn soup.

I looked up, saw Marley glance down at her watch and then whirl around to look into the stands.

Vince was still on his feet threatening everyone within earshot that he was going to either sue them or kick their asses.

Marley's eyes met mine, and I flashed her a thumbs-up. She grinned and turned back to the game.

"Coach Vince, a word?" Principal Eccles managed to look stern in a blue puffy jacket and blue painted face.

"Ooooooh," the crowd crooned as Coach Vince marched off for some much-needed disciplinary action.

I fist-bumped Jessica and turned my attention back to the field.

The Barn Owls didn't appear to be too rattled by the early goal, and to Marley's credit, neither did she. In fact, she seemed even calmer now. The team lined up for the kickoff, and I noticed the front line was looking at Marley.

She held up two fingers, and the girls nodded.

"That's my girl," I said under my breath.

Natalee tapped the ball with the outside of her foot to Libby and took off running down the field. Libby turned around and passed the ball to the midfielder behind her and followed Natalee down the field in a dead sprint. The midfielder, facing down the Bugler front line, crossed the ball to a defender on the far side of the field. Our entire front line was running into enemy territory while the Buglers' offense chased the ball. Angela dribbled the ball out in front of her, gazed down the field, and booted it.

I was on my feet with the rest of the crowd, watching the perfect arc of the ball as it crossed midfield and sailed toward the Buglers' penalty area. Libby was waiting for it. With her back to the defender, she trapped the ball and neatly crossed it to Natalee.

"SHOOT IT!" Jessica and I screamed together. We were joined by the rest of Culpepper screaming similar sentiments.

Natalee didn't even trap the ball. She swung her leg like a baseball bat. The ball hit the crossbar with a resounding clang and then bounced off a defender out of bounds.

The crowd groaned its disappointment, but Natalee and Libby high-fived, their grins a mile wide. They were having fun.

"Nice try, ladies," Vicky bellowed from her perch on the team bench.

Marley was grinning.

I pulled my phone out.

Me: You are fucking fantastic.

They hadn't scored, but in one play, Marley had invested the crowd in the game, in her girls. And she'd ratcheted up the team's confidence. They had a shot. A real one, and every person in the stadium knew it now.

Ruby scored the Barn Owls' first goal on a fast breakaway, tying the game up at 1–1. The crowd was hooting and hollering like they'd spent the afternoon drinking two-for-ones at Smitty's. Even the guys' team, sans Coach Dipshit, who had been escorted out of the stadium by security, was watching raptly.

The cheerleaders in full winter gear sashayed over to the fence dividing the stands from the sidelines. and Jessie J's "Bang Bang" blasted over the speakers.

"I love this song," Ned screeched on Jessica's right. He bounced his nonexistent ass on the cold bleacher.

The squad broke into a dance number that made me think they'd watched *Bring It On* a few times. Shocked, the crowd watched as two girls backflipped their way down the sidelines. The two lone guys on the team tossed their ladies in the air, caught them, and then dropped into clapping push-ups while three cheerleaders frontflipped over them.

"What the hell is happening?" the guy in the flannel jacket on my right asked in amazement.

The male and female cheerleaders had switched positions with the girls doing the clapping push-ups—could I even do one?—and the guys backflipping over them.

"Awesome," I told him. "Awesome is happening."

"This is so exciting," Jessica said, linking her arms through mine and Ned's. "I feel like women's lib finally made it to Culpepper! I want to set my bra on fire!"

The boys' team sat slack-jawed while the rest of the crowd exploded. Marley high-fived the cheer coach. It was pandemonium in the stands, and goddammit, I was a little bit teary-eyed. That was my *girl* down there, and she was awesome. She had no idea the effect she was having on the entire community. I'd been going to sporting events in this town for more than twenty years, and I'd never once seen the cheer squad get a reception like that. Hell, the guys' soccer team had a bounty for who could hit the squad with the most number of tortilla chips from the stands.

It was Marley. She inspired people to be better. Myself—who was really already as close to perfect as you could get—included.

I was going to marry her. Really, I had no choice. Marley Cicero was meant to be mine, and I was meant to be hers. We would hash out the details later.

The action on the field started again, and I, along with the rest of the town, watched as the two teams battled it out on the green grass under the lights.

Every breakaway, every tangle resulted in groans and cheers from the stands. And when the Buglers managed to put another ball past Ashlynn in the Barn Owls' goal, I felt the devastation of the crowd as acutely as if we were all connected. The time ticked down in the first half, and with each passing minute, the Buglers seemed to grow bigger and stronger, forcing our defense to fight hard.

"This is bad. This is real bad," Ned moaned.

"It's going to be fine," Jessica promised him, squeezing his mittened hand with her gloved one. "Marley can turn it around with the half-time speech."

CHAPTER 68

Marley

I blew it with my half-time speech. I was so amped up from the first half that I stumbled my way through "awesome jobs" and "way to gos" until Vicky elbowed me out of the way and danced and howled her way around the circle shouting things like "victory" and "ass-kicking."

The girls were more bewildered than amped up. But pride strangled any real coachy motivation from my throat.

They were playing at the Bugler's level. Sure, the opposing team had gotten lucky twice now. But that didn't mean we weren't going to return the favor. Down 2–1 at halftime was better than anything I could have imagined at the beginning of the season.

I turned the team loose so we could watch the Homecoming Court take their place at midfield. Surprising us all, Ruby had been nominated to the court. The girls pulled Ruby's long braids out of their thick ponytail and draped them over one shoulder. Natalee had touched up her makeup during my woefully inept speech.

The other girls on the field were preptastic in plaid blazers and pencil skirts. Ruby stood out like a tall, gorgeous sore thumb in her grass-stained uniform. Tall and proud.

"Is that…?" I squinted at the field.

"Yep. Ricky the cross-country kid. She asked him after he ran with us Sunday."

"Nice going, Ruby."

I noticed Milton and Ascher were both dates for blond, skinny, field-hockey-playing queen nominees. I imagined Amie Jo was in the stands with a professional photographer and a telephoto lens capturing the moment for their Christmas card.

At least she and I weren't wrestling on the field humiliating ourselves in front of a few thousand witnesses.

Bill Beerman took to the field with a wireless mic, and Vicky gripped my arm. "Here we go!"

Bill launched into an adorably awkward speech about the history of student democracy while everyone shuffled nervously.

My watch vibrated, and I peeked down at it.

Jake: Have time for an under-the-bleachers make-out sesh for old times' sake?

I grinned. It was nice sharing a history with someone. Not just a coworker who I'd met and befriended six months ago.

Things had changed. I wasn't the terrified teenager with zero self-confidence anymore. I was an adult. An adult who could run four miles and handle a gym class full of twenty-five teenagers who would rather be texting. An adult who'd landed herself an incredible fake boyfriend. An adult who'd shed eight pounds since August and was coaching the Homecoming game instead of plotting how to ruin a classmate's life. I never thought I'd be standing here in the middle of most of my hometown feeling good about myself.

Yet here I was. Wonders never ceased.

"And with that," Bill said, "I'm proud to announce this year's Culpepper High Homecoming Queen. Ruby King."

"She won! She won!" Vicky was clawing her way through

the sleeve of my jacket. But I was too busy jumping up and down and screaming to notice. My girls, God love them, exploded. They rushed the field and tackled our beautiful Homecoming Queen before last year's queen could put the crown on her head.

I hugged Vicky hard and felt like tonight was the beginning of healing a whole lot of old wounds. It was a new beginning, a fresh start, and a redo all in one.

———

Ruby's royal win gave us the boost of confidence we were looking for. We took to the field with swagger, and the crowd, as if sensing the shift, was electrified. On the opening drive down the field, a defender fouled Natalee in the penalty area. And that sassy fashionista drilled the ball in the lower left corner so hard I bet they were going to have to restring the net.

We were tied up 2–2, and I felt *good*. I felt fucking wonderful.

We dominated, our offense crowding the Buglers' defense on their half of the field. The Buglers managed a breakaway, and Angela thwarted it with one of her patented sliding tackles that had the crowd on its feet.

It was magic happening on that field, and I had goose bumps that had nothing to do with the cold…or Jake's mouth for once.

Ashlynn made a terrific diving save. My midfielders ran their asses off, showing no signs of exhaustion. We were riding high on a magic wave of energy as the minutes in the second half ticked down. The Buglers' defense was strong but showing cracks.

"We're gonna win this," I said, feeling it in my bones. Confidence. Belief. My girls were going to take home a Homecoming victory and walk into that dance as heroes. And I was going to slow clap for them until my hands bled.

We were down to the last two minutes of the game. The clock was ticking down steadily. Each passing second taking us closer to the end of regulation play. I wasn't nervous. I had a team full of women who needed to shower, change, and do full makeup for the dance. We were *not* going into overtime.

"Barn Owls," I shouted from the sideline, waving both arms toward the Buglers' goal. It was our swing-away signal. Full-court press. All offense, all the time.

And just like that, the tempo of the game changed.

Rachel took off with the ball down the sideline while the rest of my forwards headed toward the goal. A tangle between two defenders sent the ball out of bounds on the sideline.

"Throw-in," Vicky said. "Are you going to let her do it?"

Rachel was looking at me. "Oh, hell yeah." I grinned and nodded, rolling my hands in a circle. "Heads and tails," I called.

My front line backed off the goal and lined up. One of the midfielders jogged up to play decoy to Rachel's throw-in.

"This could be the greatest moment in Culpepper sports history," Vicky breathed.

This could be the greatest moment in *my* history.

We clung to each other on the sideline. The players on the bench stood and joined us, arms wrapped tight around each other. I could feel the confusion from the crowd behind us. They knew something was about to happen.

Rachel backed up off the sideline several paces. The ref blew the whistle, and she started running toward the line. Six feet out, she bent, planted the ball on the grass, and flipped.

The crowd gasped.

The momentum from the flip sent the ball in a high arch toward the Buglers' goal. Vicky clung to me, her arm around my neck like a hungry boa constrictor.

My front line started running. The defense was left flat-footed and confused. And my girl Libby left the ground like an

NBA dunker. With a deft flick, Libby headed the ball, changing its direction.

The goalie leaped into the air.

The entire stadium held its breath.

And then erupted when the ball found the net.

"Oh my God!" Vicky shrieked over the final buzzer. She shook me like a rag doll until my teeth chattered.

Game over. Victory Barn Owls. We did it. We fucking did it.

The field was pandemonium as players tackled Libby and Rachel at half field. Fans poured forth from the bleachers, jumping the low fence and joining in the celebration.

It was a mob scene, and I stood all alone in the middle of it, soaking it in.

Then there were hands on my waist, and Jake was lifting me in the air, spinning me around under the field lights.

"You fucking did it, Mars!" My parents were behind him, his uncles behind them. My faculty friends. The team parents. Rachel and Libby and Ruby were lifted on shoulders as the boys' soccer team joined the party.

And when Jake slowly lowered me to the ground, when his mouth found mine, when he kissed me twenty years after that first kiss, I felt like I was the winner.

Until they upended the cooler of ice water over me.

CHAPTER 69

Marley

After the Homecoming That Shall Not Be Mentioned

I was simultaneously a hero and a pariah. My parents were baffled with my revenge plot and suspension. Rather than punishing me—a parental responsibility with which they were entirely unfamiliar—they took a "wait and see if she does it again" attitude.

With people Amie Jo had emotionally tortured and personally victimized—students, teachers, and the entire register staff at Weis Markets—my Homecoming stunt and subsequent suspension gave me mythical popularity.

Unfortunately, there were just as many Team Amie Jo members who felt that "poor, sweet, Jesus-loving Amie Jo" had been unfairly targeted because of her God-given popularity. Their party line was that I attacked her because I was jealous of her hair, her car, and her breasts. In that order.

Team Amie Jo numbers were growing thanks to her post-suspension goodwill tour. She joined the Culpepper Emmanuel Lutheran Church's choir and handwrote apology notes with the i's dotted with hearts. The pièce de résistance was a spa sleepover at the Hotel Hershey scheduled for this weekend. She invited every girl in our class.

Except me.

I suspected Dr. and Mrs. Armburger had hired a publicist to spiff up their daughter's image. And as my edge of self-righteous victimhood dulled, I was left with a low-level guilt. Revenge hadn't been sweet. It had been a little icky. Okay. A lot icky.

Essentially, I'd stooped to Amie Jo's level and now I was covered in mean girl cooties. Really, the only upside to the whole mess was that Amie Jo now gave me a wide berth at school. I'd bitten back, and she had to inflict her damage from a safer distance now.

I headed in the direction of my locker, accepting a high-five from Marcus Smith, whose reputation as a booger eater originated from second-grade Amie Jo after he took the swing she wanted during recess. I ignored the pointed giggles from Mindy Leigh and Leah, starters on the field hockey team and Homecoming Princesses.

Today, my locker was covered in prayer requests from the Culpepper Emmanuel Lutheran Church's youth group asking that I recognize the wrongness of my ways. And that I start practicing abstinence.

I sighed.

"At least they stopped with the diapers," Vicky observed, tearing off one of the requests.

"I wish I was done with this place. No one is ever going to see me as me. I'm either going to be the biblically smited pregnant whore or the vindictive, unhinged badass."

"I feel like you're probably somewhere in the middle," she mused.

"New game plan," I decided. "I'm just going to fade into the background. Become a wallflower. I'll become a Zen master and I won't respond to Amie Jo's provocation."

Vicky's eyebrows winged up skeptically. "Can you put the monster back in the closet after you've let it out?"

"Nothing is going to get to me," I promised.

"Huh. Looks like nothing is coming this way."

I glanced over my shoulder in the direction Vicky was staring, and there he was.

Jake Freaking Weston.

His leather jacket slung over one shoulder, jeans worn through at the knee. Scarred motorcycle boots.

His walk was more of a strut.

I hadn't seen him since right before Homecoming. Hadn't talked to him since he'd stuffed that stupid note in my locker. Hadn't had the opportunity to tell him what a shithead he was. And now that I was a Zen master, I'd never have that chance.

I was cool. Cucumber cool. Ice cube cool. Vinyl seat in February cool.

"Hey, Mars," he said with a jut of his chin.

I hated how my heart got louder in my ears. The guy kissed me, didn't ask me to Homecoming, and then told me he wasn't "into pregnant chicks." What more did the dumbass have to do to prove he wasn't worthy of my medium amount of awesomeness? Flip off a horse and buggy?

I felt stupid for expecting more from him.

"Hey, Vic," Jake said.

"Well, would you look at the time? I need to go stand across the hall," Vicky said, pointing at the lockers on the opposite wall. She pointed at her own eyes and then at Jake. "I'll be watching," she hissed.

He seemed more amused than perturbed by the vague threat.

He waited until Vicky crossed the hall before turning back to me.

"Heard you were pretty badass at Homecoming," he said.

I grunted, not willing to waste words on him.

"Got any plans Saturday?"

"You're kidding, right?" Okay, I could waste a few words on the jerk.

His eyebrows winged up. "Pretty sure I'm serious. Why? You already have a date?"

My cool thawed. Then boiled.

"You listen to me, Jake Weston." I jabbed him in the chest with my finger. "I'm not some girl who likes being walked on. You don't get to make out with me and then be an ass. You had your chance with me and blew it. So just strut your ass out of my way."

"It's more of an amble."

I narrowed my eyes at him. "You think you're so cute and so charming. That doesn't make up for how you treat girls."

He blinked. "I think I'm missing something."

I cut him off with a slash of my hand. "Don't talk to me ever again."

"Our class has 102 people in it. Odds are our paths will cross again. Like, seven times a day," he pointed out.

But I was immune to his funny guy, bad boy charm.

"From now on, we're complete strangers. I hope you and Amie Jo will be very happy together."

"I feel like I need a translator," he confessed.

With a snarl, I slammed my locker shut and stormed down the hall.

Graduation couldn't come soon enough.

CHAPTER 70

Marley

Riding high on our victory, the Barn Owls descended on the girls' locker room. Garment bags with Homecoming dresses hung from lockers, and steam billowed from the showers. Laughter and excited chatter filled the room, bouncing off concrete block and metal.

I showered as quickly as humanly possible, grateful that I'd thought ahead and shaved all of the body parts that required shaving this morning. I pulled on my navy halter dress in the privacy of a bathroom stall. As close as we all were now, I still didn't need a bunch of perky teenage girls seeing my mostly naked body.

Back in my office, I dumped my cosmetics out on my desk.

"I'm here to do your hair," Morgan E. said, reporting for duty.

She was already dressed in a suit with a sparkly blue bow tie and was wielding dry shampoo and hair spray.

"Have at it," I said pointing, at my head. I sat in my desk chair and faced the locker room while she tugged and twirled my hair into who knows what kind of a style.

Through my creeper window, I spotted Libby bebopping toward her locker and held my breath.

She'd said she wasn't going to the dance. No date. No dress.

What she hadn't said was "No money for the ticket or everything else a dance required." Ashlynn's parents were hosting a teamwide sleepover after the dance in their finished basement. Libby planned to go home with Ashlynn's parents and wait for the rest of the team. To me, that was unacceptable.

She frowned at the garment bag hanging from her door. Fingered the dance ticket stapled to the bag. With careful movements, she unzipped the bag, and part of the full black skirt spilled forth.

I bit my lip and hoped.

She glanced around and then pulled the dress out. It was edgy and fun, just like her. I'd found it on a rack in a department store when I'd been scouring the "you're an adult and should dress like one" section for my own dress. Hers had a high neck and a full skirt. Pleather edged the skirt and waist and wrapped up around the neck. It was superhero meets skater girl. And it was exactly Libby. It cost twice as much as mine, and I cried when I bought it because it was so perfect.

Holding it, she turned and met my gaze. She held the look for a long beat and then mouthed "Thank you" through the glass.

I held up my hands, fingers in the shape of a heart as my throat constricted. It was the best thing I'd done in a long-ass time.

"That was damn nice, Coach," Morgan E. said through a mouthful of bobby pins.

"I don't know what you're talking about," I sniffled.

She snorted. "Okay. You're all set. Slap on some makeup and get ready to party."

"Thanks, Morgan," I told her, feeling around on my head and finding my hair in a low, fluffy bun.

"Thank you, Coach," she said seriously. "For everything."

"Get out of here," I said, affectionately pushing her toward the door.

Morgan grinned. "See you on the dance floor."

I waited until all the girls were dressed and on their way to the cafeteria before locking the locker room door. This was too good of a place to sneak away and make out in.

I stuffed the keys in my clutch and cut through the auditorium and headed toward the dance I'd missed all those years ago. Toward the man I'd fallen hard for twice now.

I pushed through the heavy doors of the senior hallway and stepped into the cafeteria. We'd eaten French bread pizza and green beans here earlier today. But since then, it had been transformed into a blue-and-silver crepe paper wonderland. There was a DJ, the same old-ass throne that they'd used for Homecoming back in the day, and dozens and dozens of students awkwardly masquerading as confident people in nicer clothing.

I spotted Jake near the refreshments laughing at something Amie Jo said to him.

Past experience had my stomach tying itself in knots. She was wearing a pink cocktail dress six shades too fancy for a simple chaperoning gig. It said, "I don't want the students to get all the attention."

I hated myself for looking at them and remembering twenty years ago. We were all different. We'd all grown and changed, I reminded myself. Well, maybe not Amie Jo. But Jake and I were different. He wasn't passing me over for Amie Jo a second time.

I swallowed hard and slapped a smile on my face.

He'd run home to shower and change after getting caught in the celebratory ice water deluge on the field. He was sexy as hell in a dark pair of trousers and a dark gray jacket. His shirt was unbuttoned at the neck, and I wanted to taste him there.

I walked in, surprised and embarrassed by the spontaneous applause from the students. I knew what to do with failure and losses. But recognitions for victory were new to me and made me feel vaguely uncomfortable. I thought I'd be able to bask in the glow of admiration. But I felt more comfortable in the shadows.

Jake stopped in what looked like mid-sentence with Amie Jo and crossed to me, rescuing me from the spotlight. I breathed a small sigh of relief. He was always showing up for me.

"You look incredible," he said, a wolfish glint in his eyes.

"Thank you," I said. "The girls helped with my hair."

"I really want to mess up your hair and makeup and find out what you're wearing under that dress," he confessed.

"You're the worst chaperone in the history of chaperones," I teased.

"I feel like celebrating tonight. What do you say we pop a bottle of bubbly when we get home, and I'll pour it on you and lick it off?"

"If you get a hard-on in those pants, every student will be talking about it for the rest of the school year," I warned him.

"Nice game, Coach," one of my students said as he shimmied past me with a pretty junior on his arm.

"Thanks, Calvin."

"Look at you knowing their names," Jake said. He took my hand and spun me away from him before pulling me back in.

I did know their names. And who was unhealthily attached to their phone. Whose parents were going through a divorce. Who was going to whine about being forced to do yoga for forty-five minutes instead of an endless winter of volleyball. I'd learned as much as I'd taught. If not more.

"I'm beyond proud of you, Mars," Jake said, his voice low.

I was proud of myself.

I put my hands on his shoulders and swayed to the beat. It wasn't a slow song, but I didn't feel too weird slow dancing in the shadows with him. I'd been waiting for this moment for a very long time.

My cheeks flushed. "Thank you. Now can we please talk about something else?"

"I want to make sure you savor this moment. Think back to August. And look at yourself now. Look at your players now. Hell, look at your students now."

He jerked his chin toward the dance floor. Milton Hostetter called out to the skinny, gawky Marvin Holtzapple and high-fived him.

"That never would have happened without your beer pong lessons."

"Trick shot lessons," I corrected him with a laugh.

"You've done a lot of good for a lot of people, Marley. Feel good about it."

"I can't believe you asked me to Homecoming again and we're finally here," I sighed.

"Again?" he asked.

Our conversation was cut short by the festive entrance of the Homecoming Queen. Ruby gave me a regal wink as she settled onto her throne in her purple, sparkly dress. We laughed as my team requested "We Are the Champions" and then sang and danced to it in front of everyone.

Duty called. Jake and I divided and conquered, rustling horny teenagers out of dark corners and quelling minor heartbreaks on the dance floor.

But I felt him watching me. Even when we were apart. Jake was watching me. Jake was with *me*.

Maybe this crash landing in Culpepper was going to be the best thing that ever happened to me. And just maybe I would finally find my path forward from here.

CHAPTER 71

Marley

"A ren't we supposed to be chaperoning this thing?" I asked as Jake dragged me down the hallway away from the cafeteria. Away from the thumping bass of Macklemore and squealing teenagers. The hallway was dark and quiet.

"I paid Bill fifty dollars to cover for us for fifteen minutes," he said, not the least bit embarrassed.

"He's going to think we're—"

"We are," he said devilishly, coming to a stop in front of the girls' locker room. "Now, unlock this door right now, Mars, or I swear to God I'm going to find out if you're wearing a bra right here in the hallway where anyone can come along."

With shaking hands, I yanked my keys out of my clutch and pushed them at him.

Smugly, he unlocked the door and pushed me inside. The deadbolt clicked into place behind us, and I suddenly felt like a tiny field mouse in the presence of a very hungry hawk.

And then Jake's hands were on me. They locked on to my breasts like heat-seeking missiles, pushing the straps down my shoulders.

"I fucking knew it," he said with reverence. "You're a bad girl, Mars. Coming to a high school dance with no bra."

"I didn't think anyone would be doing a thorough exam," I

shot back, gripping his hard-on through his pants. I could feel the pulse thumping in his flesh, and it added to my excitement.

He maneuvered me into my office and propped me against my desk. Jake leaned in and down, holding eye contact while his tongue darted out to stroke over one nipple.

He did it again, and I sucked in a sharp breath. Goose bumps broke out on my skin and made my nipples pebble.

"God, baby. You are a fantasy come to life."

He shifted to my other breast and repeated the process. Within seconds, my nipples were damp and painfully erect.

"Fifteen minutes," I reminded him, not willing to let him spend all of those minutes on just my breasts.

"I'll be back later, ladies," he promised my boobs.

They missed his attention, but when he dropped to his knees in front of me, other parts started to get excited.

He pushed the skirt of my dress up to my waist. "Hold it here," he said, hooking a finger under the black thong I wore. His knuckle rubbed against my folds, and I shivered at his touch. "Hold that dress up, baby," he reminded me when I let the skirt fall.

I collected the hem and held it high while he pulled my thong down to my knees. He looked up at me, a devilish, dirty smile on his face.

"I want a picture of you like this," he said. "Tits out, skirt up. You're a fucking sight to see, Mars."

"Maybe some other time when we have more than eleven minutes."

I could feel his breath on my thighs and clamped them together trying to do something, anything to relieve the pressure that was building between them.

"Open up for me, pretty girl," he said, nudging my knees apart.

I did as I was told and watched in fascination as he leaned

in and pressed his mouth to my slit. A soft, closed-mouth kiss that ignited my desire like a wildfire.

"Oh God."

"Wider, baby," he insisted, and I obliged, my thong digging into my knees as I stepped my feet as wide as I dared. The cold metal of the desk dug into my bare ass, but Jake's warm mouth made up for the discomfort.

We had minutes. And I didn't want to walk out of here without an orgasm.

Reading my mind, he thrust a finger into me and then a second one. He gave me a cocky grin when I smothered my scream. And then he was tonguing into my slit, dancing the tip over my clitoris and skating it back through my folds to where his fingers pleasured me.

I was on a hair trigger already. Another few licks and I'd be a puddle of orgasm all over him.

"I want you inside me," I breathed.

He paused, his fingers buried in me. "I don't have a condom on me, baby."

"I'm on birth control. I want to feel you, Jake. I want to come on your cock and feel you let loose inside me. Give me that."

He was on his feet, yanking his cock out of his pants. "Are you sure, Mars? I need you to be sure."

In answer, I slid up on the desk and spread my legs in welcome.

"I fucking love you, Marley."

His words didn't register right away because he was driving his raging erection into me, and I was busy clinging to his shirt and muffling my screams with his jacket.

It felt like fucking Heaven. Nothing between us. Nothing separating us. I felt every ridge and vein of his shaft. And he felt *me*.

I probably misheard him, I decided. Or if he had said it, he didn't mean it *that* way. My boobs were out. He'd been known to blurt out stupid, inappropriate things in their presence.

His thrusts were wild, out of control. All I could do was hang on and take it.

"Marley, baby."

He dipped his head down to suck at my nipple, and I dug the heels of my shoes into his bare ass.

I would never look at this desk the same way again. Never sit behind it and not think of how it felt to be filled by Jake, touched by Jake, loved by—

"Are you with me, baby?" he grunted. "I need you with me."

I was so fucking close the entire school board could have walked in, and I still would have orgasmed.

"Now, Jake. Now," I chanted.

And then he was coming. I felt him. I felt the throb inside me and the wave of heat. Felt his body tense as his orgasm wrenched itself free from the depths of him into the depths of me. I came, closing around him even tighter, sobbing as I felt another hot rope of his release loose inside me. This. This. This was everything.

I came, trembling and shaking, laughing and crying, as Jake thrust and held inside me. As close to one as we could be. And even as my orgasm subsided, I ached for more.

CHAPTER 72

Marley

November

The Homecoming win was just the beginning. Not only did the wins continue, but the crowds in the stands grew, the cheer squad's half-time show went viral, and Floyd and I were leading our gym classes in four weeks of yoga classes. Jake and I spent our free time between the sheets when we weren't running, attending family dinners, and enjoying quiet nights snuggled up with Homer.

To top it off, my team made it to districts. The first Culpepper High girls' soccer team to do so in seven years. Take that, Steffi Lynn. I celebrated by chiseling off part of my paycheck and treating my mom and myself to pedicures.

Best of all, I felt like I'd finally given Culpepper something new to remember about me. I'd replaced Homecoming 1998 with a fresh, bright, happy memory. And an old wound in me healed.

With good things finally flowing my way, I funneled my energy into that damned résumé. I was embarrassed that I hadn't touched it since I showed up on Mom and Dad's doorstep this summer. My future would not plan itself. I needed a fresh résumé and some new job prospects.

"Don't you think it's weird to lead with a temporary position?" I asked Zinnia over the phone, admiring my cranberry-sparkle toes.

"I think a temporary position that shows leadership capabilities and the ability to make an impact is more interesting than a four-month hole," my sister said, crunching down on a carrot stick, part of the macrobiotic cleanse she was doing leading up to Thanksgiving.

"Good point. Okay. Gym teacher and soccer coach," I said as I typed.

"Physical education instructor," Zinnia corrected.

I deleted, retyped.

"Have any job listings caught your eye?" she asked me.

I hated to admit it, but I hadn't even looked. Between Jake and soccer, my free time had dwindled down to nonexistent. I was either cooking in Jake's kitchen, naked in Jake's bed, jogging after Jake's sweaty ass, brushing up on new coaching and gym class ideas, or spending time with my parents and Vicky.

"Nothing yet," I fibbed. "But I'm casting a pretty wide net, so I'm sure I'll find something appealing." Whether that "something" would even consider me as a candidate was another story.

"Mmm," Zinnia said, crunching another carrot stick. "So listen, I'll be home for Thanksgiving."

I perked up. "You will?" With jobs as important as hers and Ralph's, we usually only got a weekend-after-Christmas visit from them. And then they were so exhausted from work, their 10,000 child activities, and their holiday social obligations, they weren't much fun.

"Yeah. I'm taking some time off."

I narrowed my eyes. The only time my sister took time off was for their annual ten-day family trip to Disney and her weeklong, kid-free European shopping spree or butlered all-inclusive Caribbean vacay. She did *not* take time off for the holidays.

"Is everything okay?" I asked.

"Yes. Everything is fine. I just thought it would be nice for the whole family to be together. I haven't told Mom yet," she said. "I wanted to figure out the arrangements first so she wouldn't try to set up air mattresses in the hallway again. I'll look at hotels tomorrow while the kids are with their music tutors."

"You don't need a hotel." My parents would be horrified if one of their children came home and stayed in a hotel.

"Marley," Zinnia sighed. "I'm not sleeping on a couch. I have a bad back from summiting Mount Rainier last year. And I'm not asking you to do it either. We're too old for that."

I clicked into the Airbnb calendar. "Look. I just checked the calendar. No one is renting the room over Thanksgiving. You and Ralph can have your old room, the kids can stay in mine, and I can stay with Jake." I was there most nights anyway. It wouldn't be a big deal.

"Wow. Things are really getting serious with you two, aren't they?" she asked.

"Uh. No. We just like hanging out. Having fun." I was majorly crushing on the man. "I've got some stuff already there," I continued. Like all of my laundry and half of my cosmetics.

That didn't define serious. Sure, we were somewhere gray and fuzzy between fake relationship and long-term fling. I was having fun and didn't really feel up to defining it. We both knew the score though. I would be leaving after Christmas. We would part as friends. I would flit off to a new, important job somewhere exciting. And Jake would find the woman of his dreams.

I suddenly felt queasy. Like "old tuna salad left out in the sun" queasy.

"If you don't mind and Jake doesn't mind, that would simplify things greatly for me."

"It's not a problem. I'm excited to see you."

"Me too. I could use some family time," she said. Again there was a tightness in her voice, and I knew there was something she wasn't telling me.

"Are you sure everything is okay?" I pressed.

"Of course. Don't be silly," she said brightly. "I've got to go. I have three meetings and an employee review standing between myself and two very nice glasses of chardonnay. Send me your résumé when you've drafted it, and I'll doctor it up."

"Thanks, Zin," I said.

"Don't mention it. Talk soon."

I hung up and stared at the résumé on my laptop. Physical education instructor. It was a far cry from Director of Internet Sales and Social Media Management.

My phone rang again on the kitchen counter. I saw the name on the screen and debated whether or not to answer it. It couldn't be good news. And to be fair, I had no obligation to answer the call.

"Hello?" I said, a masochistic martyr to the end.

"Marley! Great to hear your voice again," my old boss Brad sang into the phone. Brad never said anything without a great deal of enthusiasm. It had been annoying in normal workday conversation and had nearly caused me to commit homicide when he'd cheerfully told me the company was folding and I was out of a job and my life savings.

"Brad. What do you want?"

He laughed. Or was that a chortle? "Always straight to the point! One of my favorite things about you! Anyway, I'm calling with good news. We were able to sell the office space and some of the equipment and furniture. I'm sending you a check."

"A check?"

"I know you invested some of your savings with us," Brad continued.

Some? How about every dime?

"Anyway, it's not everything you invested, but it's something."

"How much something?" I asked, closing my eyes and sending up a prayer to the goddesses of financial security.

"Just a touch over ten grand," he said perkily.

"Ten grand," I breathed. Ten thousand dollars would give me start-over money. I could afford a security deposit on an apartment. Maybe a bed and a couch. Pay off another piece of those loans.

A weight that had taken up residence on my chest lifted, and I took a sweet, easy breath.

"I'm sorry it can't be more," Brad said. "But I'm glad we were able to give something back to you."

"Thanks, Brad. Really," I said. And I meant it. At this point in my life, ten grand had the power to change everything.

"I'm happy it'll help," he said.

I gave him my mailing address and rested my forehead on the cool laminate of the countertop when we hung up.

"Ten thousand dollars," I repeated.

It would go a lot farther here in Culpepper than Philadelphia or Baltimore or Charleston. I chewed on my lip and just for fun let myself imagine what it would be like if I decided to stay here. If I made Culpepper home again.

Would the district give me the job permanently? Was that something I'd want? Gym teacher and soccer coach. Those were not the titles I'd envisioned for myself. I'd always wanted something that started with "vice president of" or "director of." Something that meant importance. Well-compensated importance. I wanted an office and an assistant. And weird benefits like in-office acupuncture or Sushi Tuesdays.

Didn't I?

Jake was here. Jake was a benefit that no other job or city could match. But we weren't serious. *He* wasn't serious. He'd told me he loved me in the throes of sex and never said it again. If he meant it, he would have repeated it. It was best to stick with the plan. If I fell for the man and he moved on again…it would be the worst loss I'd ever faced. I couldn't survive that. Could I?

My parents tumbled through the door that led to the garage, laughing and carting shopping bags. Their faces lit up when they saw me, and I remembered how happy they'd been to have me home.

Would they understand when I moved on?

Would I miss them more this time?

"Guess who's coming for Thanksgiving," Mom said, setting down her bags and wrapping me in a hug. "Zinnia and her whole family are coming. I get both my girls here for the holiday!"

"This is going to be the best Thanksgiving ever," Dad chirped.

"Let's have takeout pizza and wine for dinner tonight to celebrate," Mom said. "Call Jake and have him bring Homer."

I swallowed hard and nodded. "Sounds good." And it did. A lazy night in with my parents and my boyfriend? It sounded great. But so did a corner office and my name on a business card.

I needed a sign. A big, bright neon sign telling me what to do.

427

CHAPTER 73

Marley

Zinnia arrived in a cloud of Chanel N°5, a smart pencil skirt, and a black cashmere turtleneck carting matching luggage. Her luxury SUV ate up my parents' entire driveway. And her three kids bolted from it as if it were on fire. They were still in their school uniforms. Even her youngest, Rose, who was four, went to a fancy private day care that taught its charges how to count in Spanish, French, and German.

At eight, Edith was the oldest. She was the violin maestro. Maestra? Chandler was the middle child and only boy. From what I could gather, he was much more interested in being a normal kid with video games and junk food than a future Ivy Leaguer.

My parents charged forward, wrapping their grandchildren in too-tight hugs, planting too many kisses on their faces.

I bypassed the fray and hugged Zinnia, who was unloading the kids' Louis Vuitton from the hatch.

"Where's Ralph?" I asked, peering in the SUV expecting to see Zinnia's husband on a conference call in the passenger seat. He spent a lot of time excusing himself from our family to take important calls.

Zinnia dropped a child-sized backpack on the ground. "He couldn't get away," she said, busying herself by arranging the kids' fancy, healthy snacks in the insulated picnic basket she carted everywhere.

Have hummus, will travel.

She paused and gave me the once-over. I knew it was stupid and childish. But I'd made an extra effort with my appearance tonight. I didn't want to feel like a wallflower next to my gorgeous, educated sister. I didn't want to just fade into the background.

I'd styled my hair in loose waves around my face and watched four YouTube makeup tutorials before I attempted my first smoky eye. I didn't want her to know that I was trying. So I'd gone with nicely fitted jeans and a boatneck evergreen sweater.

"You look great," she said finally.

I squealed internally at the compliment. It didn't sound like it came from a place of pity.

"Thanks. Will he be here for Thanksgiving?" I asked, hefting two kid-sized suitcases.

She reached up and pressed the button to close the hatch. "I'm not sure. He's really very busy." I knew that tone. The professional, apologetic sound of it. I dropped the subject.

"Mom! Grandma said we can have spaghetti for dinner," Chandler yelled from the front yard.

"Isn't that lovely?" Zinnia said in the same tone. I could practically hear her rearranging her children's macros to account for the extra carbs. "Then maybe I can make our famous zucchini noodles," she said with forced cheer.

I watched my parents hug Zinnia and welcome her into the house. No matter how old we were or how successful or important we were, Mom and Dad welcomed us home like we were queens. It was something I could always count on.

———

"Zinnia, I'm so excited you came early," Mom said, pouring another glass of wine while my sister spiralized the crap out of an organic zucchini.

I gave the sauce another stir and sipped from my own glass.

"You can go to Marley's game tomorrow," Dad chirped.

Zinnia looked a little shell-shocked.

"Oh, uh. You don't have to go to the game. It's cold. And pretty far away."

I was far more confident than I'd been this summer. However, that didn't mean I was ready for Zinnia to examine my meager successes that paled in comparison to her own. I was always afraid that she would dole out pity congratulations. It would ruin what tenuous sisterly bond we shared.

Ten minutes in her presence, and I could already feel my self-esteem chipping away.

"I'd love to go," Zinnia said, smiling over her perfect vegetable noodles. I had a pot of boiling water ready to go for actual pasta just in case zucchini noodles tasted like garbage.

"I'll see if Mrs. Lauver can stay with the kids. You can ride with Dad and me," Mom said, clapping her hands together.

It was our second game in districts. We'd made it through the first round with a nail-biting yet satisfying win over the Huntersburg Bees, who had murdered us earlier in the season. The quarter-final game was tomorrow. I'd already been nervous. But knowing the perfect Zinnia would be watching from the stands was more terrifying than if my entire fan section were made up of Coach Vince, Amie Jo, and Lisabeth with throwing knives.

The doorbell rang, and I dropped my spoon on the counter with a clatter. Jake. What had possessed me to invite him for dinner?

"I'll get it," my dad screeched.

A second later, Homer romped into the kitchen and made a beeline for me. He shoved his nose in my crotch and

430

wriggled with delight when I dislodged him and gave him a good scruffing.

"Doggy!" Children appeared from all doorways staring gleefully at Homer, who was busy telling me about his day in a series of grunts and groans.

"A dog *and* presents!" Jake announced from the doorway.

He held up gift bags, and I shook my head. He'd dragged me into a toy store last weekend with the plan to buy the affection of my nieces and nephew.

It appeared to be working. The kids couldn't decide whether they were more excited over Homer or the mystery gift bags. Jake swooped in and gave me a steamy, hard kiss on the mouth. "Hey, beautiful. I missed you."

This sexy son of a bitch was going to make some woman feel like the most important thing in the world someday.

Zinnia's eyes widened as she watched us.

"Nice to see you again, Zinnia," he said charmingly when he was done kissing the crap out of me.

They shook hands politely, and then Jake plopped down on the kitchen floor, calling Homer over and distributing the gift bags to the kids.

"Whoa! Glow-in-the-dark slime!" Edith was delighted. Zinnia was vaguely horrified. Score one for Jake. I'd told him the kids only got educational toys. He called bullshit and scoured the shop for the perfect gifts.

"Sticky bugs," Rose yelled at playground volume. She held up giant blister-wrapped insects.

"Zombies that shoot darts!" Chandler triumphantly held up his prize action figures.

"So my thought is, after dinner we have a sticky bug vs. zombie war, and they throw darts and slime at each other," Jake said.

The three kids looked up at him like he was Santa in a

candy store offering them ponies and unlimited bouncy house time.

"Aunt Marley, will you play with us?" Edith asked as if daring to hope.

"Only if you let me throw slime at Jake," I told her.

They all squealed. My sister closed her eyes and took a long drink of her wine.

Poor Zinnia. She and Ralph worked so hard to make sure their children were well-mannered little geniuses. All Jake had to do was roll in with disgusting toys, and all their hard work and private schooling went out the window.

My phone buzzed on the counter, and I glanced at the screen.

It was an unfamiliar number, but...

I snuck into the foyer and answered with a professional, "This is Marley."

"Ms. Cicero, this is Thad from Outreach in Pittsburgh. I received your résumé for our data mining team and wanted to schedule an interview with you."

My heart rolled over in my chest. The knee-jerk urge to say "No thanks" and hang up was overwhelming. I wanted to stay in Culpepper. With Jake and my parents and my team. I wanted the life I'd somehow stumbled into.

I was so surprised by the visceral certainty of it, I went into an immediate backpedal. I "uh-huhed" and "sure thinged" my way into scheduling an interview for the day before Thanksgiving.

I didn't have to keep it. I could change my mind. Or I could go. I could interview. I could try to envision a life in a busy office in a busy city four hours away from my old life.

When Thad hung up, I covered my face with my hands and took a deep, shaky breath. The fork in the road was rapidly approaching, and I had to make a decision soon.

CHAPTER 74

Marley

It was cold, wet. The rain turned to sleet that sliced its way through my warm layers and chilled me to the bone.

The seconds ticked down on the game clock, and as every moment passed, I could feel the hope drain from my body.

We were down by two. Our offense couldn't make a dent in the Bees' defense.

I felt it in the pit of my stomach. I knew what a win felt like, and this wasn't going to be one.

Twenty. Nineteen. Eighteen. The game clock plodded on, determined to deliver the loss.

Jake, his uncles, my parents, and Zinnia were in the stands. They were here to cheer me on. Instead, they were witnessing my failure.

I had wanted so badly for Zinnia to see me win. To finally prove to her that I wasn't the eternal screwup she knew me to be. I knew it was stupid. Pathetic. And I wondered if somehow my neediness had karmically ruined it for all of us.

The girls on the bench were standing up, shoulders slumped. I felt their disappointment like a wet blanket that was smothering me. It had been a long, cold, dirty game. And nothing we'd done had been enough to come out on top. It was a terrible end to the season.

Ten. Nine. Eight.

I'd let them down. I hadn't been a good enough coach to get them farther. The guys' team won their game yesterday and were headed to the semifinals. There was a pep rally scheduled for Monday.

I kept imagining Coach Vince's smugness.

Those field lights felt like a spotlight of shame.

Three. Two. One.

The final buzzer sounded, and the Bees' fans and bench erupted. The victors celebrated on the field while my girls hung their heads.

Libby and Ruby, arms around each other, limped off the field, wiping tears away, and I felt the guilt like a fist to the chest. I'd let them down. I'd set them up to fail.

I stared up at the scoreboard. 4–2 Bees. My watch vibrated, and I didn't bother looking at it. I didn't need a pity text or a pep talk. I wanted to wallow, to embrace the familiar darkness of failure.

"Well. It's over," Vicky sighed, standing shoulder to shoulder with me.

No more games. No more practices. No more bus rides and makeup tutorials. No more wins. My tenure as coach was officially over, and it had ended on a loss.

That scoreboard was my bright, glowing sign from the universe. The tears of my team were another.

Once again, I'd lost. Once again, my sister was there to witness it. And this time, I'd disappointed thirty-some teenagers.

"Let's go shake hands, ladies," Vicky said, taking charge when it was clear I was too busy wallowing. "Come on, Coach."

Blindly, I slapped hands with the victors. Shook hands with the coaching staff and congratulated them on their victory. Their win was my loss. Their joy, my misery. I'd let so many people down. And proven so many people right. I was a loser. I'd always been one.

I was sinking into the shame of it, and I couldn't pull myself out of it. It was all so familiar. Just like every layoff. Every breakup. I was always destined to get knocked down again.

Numbly, I greeted Jake and our families. Zinnia gave me a sad, frozen smile. Just like she'd always done when I screwed up. She never threw it in my face. Never brought attention to my failures.

Jake wrapped me up in his arms, and I wanted to just melt into his warmth. I wanted to give him my shame, my disappointment, and let him take it away from me.

"I'm so fucking proud of you, Mars," he whispered in my ear.

But I didn't believe him. I hadn't done anything to be proud of. I'd disappointed my team.

The bus ride home was quiet except for the occasional sniffle and nose blowing. I wished that I had the words to make them feel better. *They* hadn't failed. I'd failed *them*.

When we got back to the high school parking lot, I lamely congratulated each girl as she got off the bus. "Great season." "Good job." "Way to play."

But they could see right through me.

I waited until they'd all gotten in their cars and driven off. Waited for the bus to leave. Waited for Vicky to head home to her family. Then, and only then, I sat in my car in the dark and cried myself sick.

The knock at my window while I was blowing my nose into a fast food napkin scared the shit out of me. I recognized the crotch outside my window. I wasn't ready to talk to that crotch or the man it was attached to.

Jake knocked against the glass again.

He was going to make me talk to him. And if I tried to drive away, he'd just chase me down.

I opened the door and stepped out.

"You okay?"

I shrugged, not trusting my voice.

"Aw, baby." He gathered me close. "It crushes me to see you crushed."

"I let everyone down," I whispered.

"Mars, you lost a game. Not a war. Where's the perspective?" he teased.

But I wasn't in the mood.

"I was looking for a sign, and I guess I got it."

"A sign for what?" He rubbed his hands up and down my arms. I didn't deserve to be comforted by him.

"I thought I was finally getting my act together, you know? I thought things were going well. That maybe I was supposed to stay here."

"Of course you're supposed to stay here, Mars. What the hell are you talking about?"

"All I do is screw things up, Jake."

"You're speaking a foreign language right now. Come on. Get your stuff. I'll drive you home."

I shook my head. It was clear now. What I had to do. My team deserved better. My students. Jake deserved better.

The sleet had changed over again. Now fat flakes were floating down from the dark sky, landing in slush. Trying to whitewash the mess.

I didn't belong here now any more than I did when I was a teenager.

"Marley, get in my car," he said sternly.

When I didn't move, he physically dragged me to his vehicle and tucked me inside. He closed the door, and the dome light went off. I sat there in the dark, in the silence.

Jake returned with my gym bag and water bottle. He tossed my things in the back seat and without a word drove us home.

CHAPTER 75

Marley

I didn't want to go inside. Jake pulled into his driveway, and I sat staring at the house that I'd fallen in love with. I'd fallen in love with the man too.

The man who was carting my things out of the back seat and telling me if I didn't get out of his car, he was going to drag me inside caveman style.

Numbly, I followed him to the front door.

When Homer charged me, demanding all the love I had in my body, I sank to my knees and pressed my face into his fur. At least he still loved me. It didn't matter to Homer if I won or lost. As long as I loved him and fed him and scratched his belly.

I'd failed before. But this time I'd taken a lot of people down with me. I'd disappointed them all, let them all down. And that was what hurt. I kept seeing the tear-stained faces of each girl as she exited the bus. All that hard work for nothing. For a lousy loss under sleeting skies.

Jake dumped my things on the floor and pulled me up.

He looked at me long and hard, and then he spoke.

"I'm asking you to stay, Mars. Stay here. Be mine. Let me be yours. Live in this haunted house with me and Homer. Work with me. Run with me. Make me lunches. Let me hold you while you fall asleep on the porch."

"Jake." I was desperate for him to stop painting this picture.

"Grow old and obnoxious with me, Marley Jean Cicero. I want to be raising a ruckus at bingo with you when we're eighty and don't give a fuck."

"Jake," I said again, feeling hot tears course down my cheeks.

Panic clawed at my chest. I could *see* it. See a life here with him. But it wasn't what I'd planned. What I'd been pursuing my entire life.

"I have an interview Wednesday," I told him, desperate to remind us both of the plan. "This was only temporary. You can't change the deal on me. I was always going to leave in the end." It was the only thing that made sense.

"Tough shit, Mars. I didn't mean to fall in love with you, but I did, and here we are."

"What?"

"Oh, like you're surprised?" he scoffed.

I was fucking shocked. Like electrical-current-to-the-heart dead shocked. He'd actually meant what he'd told my boobs? He was in love with me? "Why did you go and do a dumbass thing like that?" I demanded. This added Jake to the top of the list of people I'd let down.

"I don't fucking know! It wasn't exactly a choice."

I turned around, shoved my hands in my wet hair.

"But now you're asking me to make one. Why are you making me do this, Jake? You knew the deal. You knew I wasn't staying." He'd known from the beginning, and now he was forcing me to hurt him.

Jake shucked out of his wet coat and let it fall to the floor with a splat. He was doing it on purpose. There was a coatrack next to the door. And we'd spent four hours on a Sunday cleaning out his coat closet under the stairs. "So you expect me to fall in love with you and just let you walk away?"

I stared at his wet coat as the water dripped and pooled onto the hardwood.

Homer barked.

"Shut up, Homie," we both said together.

"I expect you to hold up your end of the bargain," I told him. I turned around again, but I couldn't bear to look at him. Couldn't stand to see the disappointment on his face.

"You would rather I kept my lips zipped and waved you off at the end of December without a word?"

"Yes! That is exactly what I would have wanted you to do."

"Why in the hell should I make this easier on you when you aren't doing a damn thing to soften the blow for me? I'm in love with you, jackass!"

"How do you know?" I demanded stubbornly. "You've never even been in a relationship before."

"I'm smart enough to know what love is. And I'm not a chickenshit about it. I love you, Mars, and you fucking love me back."

I was speechless. I wanted to deny it. To lie to his face and tell him that I didn't have those feelings. But the truth was, I'd loved him for months. Maybe even since the first time he'd yelled at me. He cared enough to try. But he could do better. He deserved better. So did my girls. My students. They deserved someone better.

"Look. We don't have to get married right away if you don't want to," Jake said, running a hand through his damp hair.

"*Married*? Are you thinking about *marriage*?" I couldn't breathe. I couldn't breathe, *and* I wanted to throw up. None of this was part of the plan. Why was he making me hurt him like this?

"The thought had crossed my mind a couple of times before I heard your blood-curdling scream at the idea a second ago."

"Jake, I'm not supposed to be here! Do you see the damage

I inflict? Those girls gave me their all. They did everything I asked of them. And I ruined it for them. This time, it wasn't just my own life I was ruining. I got those girls' hopes up. I told them they could do anything they set their minds to, and then I sent them out on that field to get crushed. *I* crushed them. They were devastated tonight."

"I don't even know where to start with that idiotic statement. First of all, it's a sport, and someone has to lose. Losing doesn't make you a loser!"

"That's exactly what losing does!" Homer didn't like the shouting and padded into the kitchen to lie down next to his food dish.

"Marley." Jake took a deep breath and pinched the bridge of his nose like he was trying to ward off an aneurysm. I loved him so much it hurt to look at him.

"Marley," he said again. "This is some midlife crisis deal, isn't it? You're scared. So you think leaving's the answer. You're just painting a pretty picture about seeking your destiny. But spoiler alert, sweetheart. Hard losses don't mean you're in the wrong place."

"Every job I've had. Every relationship I've had has ended. Badly. I've had the rug pulled out from under me so many times that it makes more sense to stay on the floor than stand back up."

"What does that have to do with you and me?"

"I'm not supposed to be here, Jake. This isn't what I want."

"What do you want, Mars. Tell me. Enunciate clearly so I can get it through my thick head."

"I don't know! How does anyone know?"

"Then how do you know that this isn't exactly what you want? Exactly where you're supposed to be? How do you know that every shitty job, every crappy relationship, every mistake wasn't leading you here to me? To those girls. To this town."

I didn't know what to say to that. I was suddenly bone weary. My muscles ached, and the anger, the frustration I felt bubbled up and out, evaporating into the air between us. This wasn't a choice I'd made. A job I'd earned. A relationship that started with boy meets girl. This was just another mess I'd created.

"This wasn't even supposed to be real," I said quietly.

"Bullshit. Maybe you fell for the fake label, but I knew from the start this was going to get real."

"You did not!" I argued.

"Don't tell me what I feel, Mars! I used to watch you in English class. You'd tuck your hair behind your ear, and I couldn't stop staring at your neck, your ear, your fingers. As soon as I saw you again, it was still there."

"Then why did you change your mind about Homecoming?" I shouted.

He blinked. "What the fuck are you talking about Homecoming?"

I held up my hands. "You know what? It doesn't matter."

"You know what I wanna know?" Jake demanded. "I wanna know when you're going to stop acting like high school ruined your entire life. When are you going to step up and be brave enough to find out what you really want? Not what your seventeen-year-old self wanted. Not what your sister wants or what you think your parents want. What the hell do *you* want, Mars?"

All I could cling to in this moment was what I'd been chasing my entire life. The important job. The necessary role. Making a difference. That's what I held on to when things got rough. When things went from bad to worse. Every new start felt like it had the potential to be that thing that I needed.

But this wasn't a new start. This was a crash landing, an agreement, a mutually beneficial, temporary arrangement.

How would I ever be important and needed here? In the town that I'd left in my dust twenty years ago. What would I be here? A gym teacher? A coach? A girlfriend? A daughter?

It wasn't enough. I wouldn't be enough. I was looking for the right role that would help me grow. Force me to shed my bad habits and finally become the strong, powerful, problem-solving woman I was destined to be. I would *matter*.

"Jake." I said his name wearily. "I'm sorry. But this isn't what I want."

I saw his jaw muscle clench and release. Clench and release.

"I'm not what you want?"

"None of this is what I want. I need something different. I'm not going to become a better person here. I'm just constantly reminded of all my shortcomings over and over again. I want more."

"I love you, Mars. I want more of this. More of you. You've made me a better person. Just look at what you've done for me. Look at this house."

I couldn't stand hurting him like this. He didn't love me. He couldn't. He was just confused.

"You cleaned your kitchen and got new curtains. That doesn't mean you're in love with me," I said softly.

"You are so damn pigheaded," he complained. "Do you think you're unlovable? Unworthy as is?"

That's exactly what I was.

CHAPTER 76

Marley

I spent all day Saturday and Sunday on a blow-up mattress on the floor in Zinnia's room. It was exactly what she hadn't wanted. And judging by the twinge in my lower back every time I rolled over to cry on the other side of my face, she'd been right about the consequences. Then again, Zinnia was always right.

Lying on that mattress with my Harry Potter pillow for two days was my purgatory. I didn't deserve to be comfortable. I deserved to hear fart noises every time I rolled over, trying to find a better position.

I kept my phone turned off and didn't log into the team message board. I couldn't face anyone. I couldn't face anyone's disappointment in me.

Vicky stopped by with tequila and chicken soup. Neither of which I deserved.

I missed Jake so much I slept in his T-shirt and wore his sweatpants around the house.

Zinnia, to her credit, didn't try to make me talk about it. My parents retreated to "my teenage daughter is emotionally unstable" survival mode, doling out junk food and pats on the head. But I overheard the whispered conversation about what we were going to do about Thanksgiving now that I'd blown things up with Jake.

I didn't sleep at all Sunday night. It was a school day tomorrow. The last one before Thanksgiving break. And as much as I wanted to take a sick day and avoid it all, I knew I needed to face the music.

By Monday morning, the snow had melted, leaving behind piles of gray slush that matched my cold, messy mood. I dragged myself into the shower then bided my time until I knew I'd be five minutes late to school just in case anyone was hanging out around the locker room wanting to talk to me. I couldn't see Jake. I would shatter like a wineglass on Amie Jo's patio.

Feeling sneaky, I let myself in the emergency exit of the locker room and tiptoed toward my office. I'd be free to wallow pathetically for the entire first period if Floyd didn't know I was here.

"It's about time."

I jumped, my wet sneakers nearly losing their grip on the concrete.

"Principal Eccles," I said, holding on to the bookcase closest to the door. "What brings you here?" Oh, God. She'd heard that I broke up with Jake, officially voiding my ethical behavior contract. She was here to fire me. I wasn't going to get to leave town quietly. Culpepper would probably line up to throw stones of judgment at me as I crawled out of town in shame.

"Your office is dingy and creepy. I'm wondering if we can find a few hundred dollars in the budget for some paint and new furniture," she mused, eyeing my dungeonlike abode.

She'd fix it up for the permanent gym teacher. Oh, God. What if she was smart and beautiful and a long-distance runner? Jake would fall hard, and they'd get married, and he'd be having Christmas brunch with her. I hated the new pretend gym teacher. Hated her with the passion of a thousand suns.

"I hope you're feeling better," Principal Eccles said as I

trudged into the office and dropped down onto a folding chair. "I heard you caught a cold after the game Friday."

More like a cloud of depression.

"Much better," I lied and pretended to cough.

She interlaced her fingers on my desk. "Good. Now, for the fun part. What are your plans for next year?"

I blinked. "Next year?"

"January."

"I'm interviewing for other jobs," I said hesitantly.

"Have you considered staying on here?"

Was I aurally hallucinating? Maybe she'd actually asked me if I'd considered joining a traveling circus or caring for our basketball donkeys.

"Staying here?" I croaked.

"Becoming a permanent member of the faculty," she explained. "You've done more here in a semester than most teachers have done in their entire career. Students are raving about gym class for the first time since parachute day in elementary school."

"I'm flattered, but—"

"And I don't even need to tell you what a wonderful job you've done with the girls' team. I've never seen a team turn around so quickly. I think next year will be even better," Principal Eccles continued.

She had it wrong. I'd lost. I'd trampled my players' spirit. I was no better than Steffi Lynn Hitler. I just came in a different package. "Thank you," I said flatly. "But I don't have a teaching license."

"You could get one. I looked into it. You'd have to pass the Praxis," she explained. "But there are ways to teach without having a teaching degree. The point is, you're an excellent fit. And I would be thrilled to recommend to the board that we make your position permanent."

I had a job interview on Wednesday. My next chance at a new start. I couldn't stay here. I couldn't stay me.

"Principal Eccles, I'm flattered. Really. But I think you can find a candidate better suited to the position. Someone with experience."

Someone who won't ruin everything.

The principal blinked rapidly as if she wasn't sure she'd heard me correctly. "I assumed you'd be interested in the position."

"It's a great job," I told her weakly, not wanting to disappoint yet another person. Though I couldn't understand why she'd still want me on the faculty. I'd been in her office more times than the worst troublemakers. I'd had more complaints against me than any other teacher. And I'd single-handedly crushed the spirit of an entire team. "It's just not something I see myself doing. I'm sure there are other candidates that would do a better job than I would."

Principal Eccles sighed. "Well, I can't say I'm not disappointed. I've been very happy with the way you've done your job, and I'll be sorry to see you go."

I didn't know what to say, so I just gave her a weak smile.

She pushed away from my desk and stood. "You'd tell me if Amie Jo chased you off, wouldn't you?"

The woman was dead serious, but I laughed. "I promise." For once, Amie Jo had nothing to do with this decision.

She sighed again and nodded. "Well, I'll wish you good luck in your future endeavors then."

She left the locker room, leaving behind a whiff of her disappointment.

I flopped down behind my desk and dropped my head to the desktop. Bitterly disappointed. Depressed. Hot mess. I ran through all the terms that could describe my current emotional state. My desk phone rang. I didn't want to answer it. It was just someone who wanted something from me. But it was the last day of school before Thanksgiving break. I could muster the energy to be kicked in the teeth a few more times today.

"Marley, how are you feeling today?" Andrea's voice was full of sympathy on the other end.

"Terrible. Awful. Like a big, dumb loser."

"I had a feeling," she said.

At least Andrea wasn't trying to silver-lining everything. *"At least you made it to districts... At least you had a winning season... At least Jake thought he loved you."* She knew I had something to be upset over.

"You're not just saying that to make me feel better, are you?"

"Your feelings are valid," she said, skirting the line of answer and nonanswer.

"I feel like this loss is the big neon sign I was waiting for from the universe to tell me that I'm not in the right place. I let a lot of people down, and now it's time for me to move on."

"What about Jake?" she asked. I could hear her clicking a pen. Open. Closed. Open. Closed. It was her nervous tell. She was about to blow.

"Jake and I have come to an agreement that we will be better off apart," I said evasively.

"Did you both come to that agreement, or did you break up with him?" she asked, sidestepping my bullshit.

"Oh, look at the time. I have to go disinfect the shower shoes. I have to go, Andrea."

"Listen, as your part-time therapist and full-time friend, I feel like I need to tell you when you're being an idi—"

I hung up the phone then took it off the hook and put my head back down on the desk. But it wasn't the cool metal I felt. It was thick paper.

I sat up again with an envelope stuck to my head.

Coach.

I ripped it up, sending ragged slivers of paper across my desk. Inside, I found a "We're Sorry" greeting card.

Dear Coach,

We're sorry for disappointing you.

> *Love Always,*
> *Your Team*

Oh, for fuck's sake. Why couldn't anyone understand? I'd disappointed *them*. They'd given me their all, and I'd let *them* down.

A second smaller envelope shoved under my phone caught my eye.

It was addressed to *Kidnapper*.

Dear Coach,

My mom died of cancer when I was six. My dad made a series of poor life choices and has been in and out of prison ever since. I've been moved from foster home to foster home for ten years. But Culpepper, this school, this team was the first time I felt like I ever belonged.

You made me feel like I belonged.

I say this to make you feel like epic shit for going off the "woe is me" deep end. We lost a game. Big fucking deal. Win some, lose some. You in your selfish downward spiral are forgetting about all the good you did this season. You didn't disappoint me.

You forced me to join your weird team, make friends,

and start living up to my potential. I don't have parents who can thank you for guiding their kid. So I'll thank you. Thanks.

Now, get your head out of your ass and apologize to the team for losing your damn mind.

Sincerely,
Morticia

P.S. I found the emergency snack cakes you stashed in your desk drawer and ate them. You're welcome.

CHAPTER 77

Marley

I made the three-hour-and-thirty-minute drive to Pittsburgh in complete silence. The Pennsylvania Turnpike was a monotonous stretch of rest stops, tunnels, and trucks. I'd survived Monday, using the locker room as my personal fortress of solitude. I'd ducked out the back when Jake had pounded on the door after the final bell rang.

My watch had vibrated as I jumped into my car and sped from the lot.

Jake: You can run, but you can't hide. We need to talk. Stop being a chickenshit.

But I didn't have anything to say. I was still sad, still broken, and I felt like an asshole for making an entire team of girls think that they'd disappointed me. I didn't know how to apologize. How to make it clear that I was the one to blame.

Tuesday, I spent the entire day on my air mattress while my mom and sister shopped for our Thanksgiving meal. I felt like an ass.

By Wednesday morning, I was sick of myself, and the only thing I could think to do was actually go to the job interview.

Outreach was a nonprofit startup that matched families in need with available social services while also recruiting individuals to make monetary donations.

Just the kind of thing the me from this summer would have been looking for. The current me, though, couldn't be bothered to get excited about it. All I could think about was Jake looking devastated, the girls getting off the bus crying. An endless loop of disappointment.

I found the office in a cool, renovated warehouse and sat on a couch shaped like a pair of red lips. The walls were painted in bright primary colors. All employees were dressed casually in jeans and hoodies. They were walking around with iPads in one hand and lattes in the other.

No one was even close to my age.

Normally, by this point, my palms would be so sweaty I'd have to wipe them before shaking hands. But I sat here stiffly on overstuffed lips and wished it was all over so I could curl up on my air mattress at home.

Thad appeared and introduced himself. He wore skinny jeans and a hoodie and large blue-framed glasses. The rest of the team was a collection of hipsters, slobs, and people too young and optimistic to know that a startup this cool was destined for some serious growing pains.

Numbly I answered the standard interview questions in their glassed-in conference room. The table was an oversized surfboard. The art on the walls was colorful and confusing. Someone rolled past the door on a skateboard.

It was exactly the kind of place I would have been looking for prior to my stint as a Barn Owl.

Thad explained the work schedule ("Come and go as you please; just get your work done"), the role (a stepping stone to head my own team in a year or two), and the mission statement before launching into the interview questions.

I'd done this often enough that I could almost predict the next question.

What do you see as your top strengths?

My ability to fail over and over again.

Where do you see yourself in five years?

Unemployed and single. History tends to repeat itself.

I wasn't even nervous. Usually, I was interviewing in a panic. I needed the job. I was desperate not just for gainful employment but for a bright future.

This time, though? I couldn't even rouse myself to care. I hoped it made me seem cool.

They turned me over to a chipper HR assistant who gave me the grand tour. Everything was open work spaces and primary colors. There was an espresso station and a yoga room. They were a startup that was growing like gangbusters.

It was exactly what I was looking for. I'd be busy. There was room for growth. There were benefits and a casual dress code.

And I couldn't for the life of me get excited about it.

They took me out for lunch, and I pushed my chicken salad around on my plate. Someone asked me about my coaching experience, and I told them about the girls on the team. Told them about our season, leaving out the devastating end.

After lunch, they showed me my potential office. A glorified cubicle but with a view of the river. They were growing, they assured me. Rapidly. They needed a data mining team in place as soon as possible. And within a year, I could be heading it.

All I could think about was how I had ten to fifteen years of life experience on the team. How would I be a better fit here than in my own hometown?

They liked me. I could tell. Like I said, I was practically an interview professional. But did I like them? Did I want to be the team elder? Did I want to spend my working hours explaining what CDs were and who Dan Aykroyd was?

Why did everything I'd always wanted feel so damn wrong?

They promised to call me after the holiday. I shook hands all around, threw in some fist bumps for the knuckle-preferring crowd, and returned to my car in the parking garage.

I got behind the wheel and thumped my forehead against it. What the hell was I doing with my life?

———

Me: I had my interview.

Vicky: Oh, you're emerging from your self-loathing to talk to me again? Goodie.

Me: I deserve that.

Vicky: Stop it. It's no fun when you act like a kicked puppy.

Me: Arf arf.

Vicky: How did it go? Did they offer you a million dollars and stock options?

Me: I think they're going to offer me the job.

Vicky: Are you going to take it?

Me: I don't feel like I'm in the position to make any life-altering decisions. I really let our girls down. I don't know how to make it better.

Vicky: Swing by my house. We'll get loaded and write apology notes.

Me: I'll be there in four hours.

CHAPTER 78

Marley

Thanksgiving was depressing. *I* was depressing. Every damn thing in this house was depressing. We were supposed to be celebrating with the Westons in Jake's house with his nice, roomy kitchen and big dining table. His sweet, doofy dog.

Instead, we were asses to elbows falling over each other in Mom and Dad's cramped kitchen, scrambling to prepare a feast that we hadn't planned for.

All because I was a chickenshit dumbass.

The turkey and the broccoli casserole were smashed into the oven while Zinnia did her best to steam more healthy vegetable sides in the microwave and on the stovetop.

The kids were running through the house, screaming and shouting, waggling zombies and giant insects at each other. Mom and Dad were sneaking wine in the garage, pretending to look for Christmas decorations. It was Cicero family tradition for the Christmas decor to go missing for at least a week or two after Thanksgiving.

And here I was alone, scraping gelled cranberry sauce out of the can.

I'd gone to Vicky's last night, and with the help of a bottle of bourbon, I'd written heartfelt cards to every girl on my team. Then, since we were wasted, we'd paid Vicky's mother-in-law twenty dollars to drive us around to every girl's house so we could stuff the note in the mailbox and then scream, "Go, go, go!"

In the light of morning, I was hungover and still miserable. But I'd woken up to over a dozen heart emoji messages from the team.

Jake was probably having a great day. Hell, he'd probably found a new girlfriend since we'd broken up. She was probably helping him in the kitchen, wearing an apron, and letting him kiss her on the neck while she whisked cornstarch into the gravy. I squeezed the cranberry sauce can so hard it dented on both sides.

The timer on the oven beeped shrilly, and I wrestled the door open, knocking over a kitchen chair in the process. Smoke billowed out.

"Fuck!" I waved a dish towel at the smoking mess. The turkey looked extra crispy and not in the delicious KFC way.

The smoke detector wailed to life, and all three kids came running, hands clamped over their ears. "MOMMY!"

"That's it," Zinnia said calmly. "I give up. I give up on everything." She neatly folded her tea towel on the counter and stormed out the back door.

My mom rushed in and pulled a chair under the smoke detector. She climbed up and ripped it off the ceiling. "There! That's better," she said cheerfully. She had a red wine mustache.

"Mom, can you take care of this?" I asked, gesturing at the blackened bird and the rapidly blackening broccoli casserole.

"Sure, sweetie. Ned! I need wine STAT," she called.

I headed out the front, stopping at the coat closet to grab my jacket and Zinnia's cashmere wool trench. It was cool and crisp outside, not smoky and hot like our indoor inferno. I let myself into the backyard through the gate.

"Zin?" My sister, the health nut perfectionist, was sitting

in the tree, smoking a cigarette and shivering. "What the hell is going on?" I demanded.

She ignored me, and I climbed up next to her, praying the branch could hold our combined adult weight. "Here." I shoved her coat at her.

Zinnia eyed it and then handed me her cigarette.

"Since when do you smoke?"

"Since I can't take a deep breath without one."

She took the cigarette back and drew in a sharp breath. "My life is a fucking disaster, Marley. I'm such a failure."

The confession shook me so hard I wobbled on the tree branch and nearly fell over backward. I grabbed on to the trunk and righted myself.

"A failure? You? Have you met me?" I squeaked. "Give me that." I took the cigarette from her again and took a drag.

I choked and gasped and passed it back. It had been a long time since my Diet Coke and cigarette days.

"Look at me and tell me what you see," she said.

I did as I was told. "My beautiful, insanely smart genius of a sister, who has the perfect husband, a great family, and an important job."

She laughed without humor. "That's what everyone sees. You know what I see when I look in the mirror?"

"What?"

She took another drag and blew out a slow stream of smoke. "An exhausted woman whose husband stopped being interested in sex six months ago. Whose children don't have any fun at all except the one time of year they're at Grandma and Grandpa's. My job—I work seven days a week. Because if I miss something, if I take a day off and turn off my phone, some baby somewhere could die because I didn't connect them to the right resources. People die when I don't do my job."

"Zin, why didn't you say anything?"

"What am I supposed to say? Complain about my perfect life and my perfect family. Whine about how hard it is to make a difference?"

"Yes! How else am I supposed to know that your life isn't perfect? Zin, I would have showed up on your doorstep. I would have helped."

"No one can help me," she said, and I heard the familiar stone wall in her voice. Zinnia was harder headed than any one of those basketball donkeys. "No one can do everything that needs to be done the way I want it done."

I was reeling. The woman I wanted to be was sitting next to me on the verge of a nervous breakdown.

"Where is Ralph?" I asked her.

She gave another bitter laugh. "Probably sitting with his feet up on the coffee table in his underwear enjoying the peace and quiet. 'Heart surgeons need downtime,'" she parroted in a baritone. "He's so busy saving lives he has zero time for family. For me. He blanked on our anniversary. He can't remember Rose's name half the time. We go days without seeing each other."

"But you two always seem so good," I pressed.

"Good?" She sniffled. "We're at a place where *everything* is more important to us than our relationship, our family. That's not good, M."

A single tear rolled gracefully down her cheek.

She took a shuddering breath. "It's like we're already separated. Even though we live together. I didn't even tell him I was coming. He didn't notice we were gone for two days because he was traveling for a consortium."

"Zin, I'm so sorry." I squeezed her shoulder, wishing there was something I could do to take the pain away.

I didn't want to appropriate Zinnia's midlife crisis, but if this is what being important produced, did I really want it?

"What are you going to do?" I asked. The woman who had everything I wanted was as miserable as I was.

"I have no idea. I thought I'd come home and regroup. I don't know who I am without a job that sucks the life out of me. I don't know what kind of a mother I am without overscheduling and smothering the creativity and fun out of my kids' childhood. I micromanage them because I'm afraid if I don't take care of every tiny detail, they'll turn into bullies, or get sick, or turn to a life of drugs." She took another drag on the cigarette. "I've always envied you, you know."

"Me?" I squeaked. "Why?"

"You're just free to be. If something isn't the right fit, you move on, and you try something else. I'm stuck. I've dug myself into a hole so deep in this job that I can't leave or people will literally die."

We heard a noise next door. From our vantage point in the tree, we spotted Amie Jo, in plaid ankle trousers and a glamorous red sweater, slam the sliding patio door shut. She had an open bottle of wine in one hand. She stood staring at the pool cover, her body rigid. And then she screamed.

It wasn't the cry of a wounded animal. It was a battle cry.

CHAPTER 79

Marley

E verything okay over there?" I called to her.

She jerked around and found us in the tree.

"Want a cigarette?" Zinnia offered, holding up the pack.

"What I want is to burn this house down with everyone in it," Amie Jo seethed.

"Well, why don't you bring your wine over here, and we'll start with a cigarette. Then if burning the house down is still the right answer, we'll help you," I offered.

She thought about it for a minute and then held up a finger. She disappeared back inside her house and reappeared on the back porch a minute later. She had two bottles of wine and a puffy winter coat. Amie Jo jogged to the fence separating our yards and dropped the wine bottles over into the grass one at a time.

She took a running start at the fence and scrambled over.

Zinnia and I scooted farther out on the limb, and Amie Jo handed up the wine. I pulled her up, and she settled on the branch next to me. It creaked a little.

"Rough Thanksgiving?" I asked.

Zinnia lit another cigarette and handed it to Amie Jo.

She accepted it and pulled the stopper from the first bottle of wine. "My sister just announced she's getting married for the fourth time. Her daughter, Lisabeth, is pregnant with some dropout's baby. And worst of all, my in-laws hate me," Amie Jo announced.

"What? You and Travis have been together since senior year."

"And they've hated me since then. They think I got pregnant on purpose in college so Travis had to marry me. To them, I'm just a gold-digging prom queen."

Zinnia and I shared a glance.

"Well, that's not fair to you," I said to Amie Jo.

"I know! I've done everything I can to make those horrible people like me! I gave them beautiful grandsons. I make sure their son has a home he can be proud of. A wife he can show off. We're upstanding members of the community, and the turkey is still too dry, and the house is still too drafty, and maybe I shouldn't show so much cleavage at a family dinner!"

Amie Jo took a gasping breath and a swig of wine before passing me the bottle.

"I'm having an out-of-body experience here," I admitted. "I thought both of you had the perfect lives."

Zinnia and Amie Jo shared a slightly hysterical laugh.

"Out of all of us, you're the happy one," Amie Jo said accusingly.

"Happy? I'm not happy. I'm fucking miserable. My life is one failure after another!"

Zinnia snorted. "I forgot Chandler's birthday this year. I packed him up and sent him off to a friend's for a sleepover because I had a grant I needed to finish. His little friend's mom told me the next day when I picked him up that Chandler told them it was his birthday. I'm regularly a not-good-enough mother."

"My kids learned from me that appearances are much more important than actually being happy," Amie Jo announced.

"I've taught them that great selfies on Instagram are more important than being a good person."

"Yesterday, Edith told me she hated me because I let Rose watch two movies back-to-back because I couldn't stand to hear another word come out of her sassy little mouth. And the grant proposal that I spent three months of my life on was denied, and I had to call the Mobile Surgical Organization and tell them that they wouldn't be getting the two hundred thousand dollars they were counting on next year."

"It takes me two hours in the morning to get ready because I don't want my husband cheating on me the way his father cheats on his mother," Amie Jo confessed, looking over her shoulder at her house.

"Do you lock yourself in the bathroom to cry?" Zinnia asked.

"Once a week. For twenty minutes," Amie Jo said.

"I sit in the empty bathtub."

I looked back and forth at these women and wondered how the hell I never knew any of this.

"I don't get it. From the outside, everything looks so perfect. What about your hashtag blessed post today on Facebook?" I asked Amie Jo.

"That's social media," Zinnia scoffed, taking a swig of wine.

"Exactly. That's a highlight reel. Social media is how you fantasize your life should be. Not the reality of it." Amie Jo looked at me like I was an idiot. "No one actually wants to know how you really feel."

I helped myself to more wine. I couldn't wrap my head around this. "You guys aren't happy? Even with money and husbands and kids?"

"I'm exhausted," Zinnia said.

"I'm miserable. The amount of attention I need just to be okay is terrifying," Amie Jo said.

"You had something real with Jake," Zinnia told me.

"Had? You didn't do something stupid, did you, Marley?" Amie Jo was horrified.

"I kinda broke up with him," I confessed.

Amie Jo gasped so hard the branch creaked. "That is asinine! Who wouldn't want Jake Weston? Hell, I want Jake Weston, and I'm married."

"I was only supposed to be here until the end of the semester. It was a temporary position! I wanted to do something bigger, more important than teaching gym class."

"What about your team?" Zinnia asked.

"Those girls had the longest losing record in school history. You taught them how to work together and trust each other," Amie Jo pointed out.

"Do you know how epically impossible that is to do at this age? Teach women that they're sisters, not enemies fighting over the last damn piece of fine pie?" Zinnia asked as she swung the bottle of wine wildly.

"I wanted to do something like you do. Something that makes a real difference," I told her, still trying to explain my hopes and dreams.

"I hate my job, Marley. I hate it," Zinnia enunciated carefully. "My desk and inbox are full of pictures of what landmines and gunshot wounds and poor medical care do to people. Every day I am drowning in them."

She took another drag on her cigarette. I drank deeply from the Chardonnay.

"What about that goth princess Libby? Look what you did for her this semester," Amie Jo said, breaking the silence. "You made a difference to her. You made her popular!"

"What you and Jake had together? That doesn't come around often, and you're my sister, and I love you, but you are a complete dumbass for ruining it," Zinnia said, poking me in the shoulder.

"Hey!"

"You were happy, M," my sister said. "Like really happy. And I kinda just want to push you out of this tree for not recognizing it."

"Ugh. You push her out of the tree, and I'll throw a wine bottle at her," Amie Jo interjected. "He loves her for who she is. She doesn't even bother with makeup or brushing her hair half the time, and Jake looks at her like she's Gisele Bündchen in front of a camera. It's disgusting."

"Well, this is fun and all, but let's focus on you two," I suggested.

"You know, I think that's the thing I hate about you most," Amie Jo mused. "You don't have to try. You don't have to wear extensions and shoes that make you lose your toenails. You don't have to spend six hours a week in a tanning bed afraid that your husband will leave you if you're not tan enough. They all genuinely like you just for being you."

"Yeah, no one is inviting you to black-tie affairs because you helped with their fundraising or raised their political profile," Zinnia said, getting into the spirit.

"But you're doing great things. Important things," I reminded her.

"Ninety percent of what I do is ass-kissing. Is that great? Is that important? I've never had one person in my office look up to me the way all of those girls on your team look at you. They adore you. They respect you."

"Just like Jake," Amie Jo complained. "Do you know how hard I had to work senior year to make sure you two didn't get together?"

"What?" I snapped.

"Remember how he asked you to Homecoming and changed his mind?" she said.

"He told you? Of course he told you. He said he changed his mind and was taking you. You were more his type." My voice was two octaves higher than usual.

"Jake didn't ask you to Homecoming. I did. And then I pretended to dump you for me," Amie Jo insisted.

"You diabolical little—"

"I know, right?" she said, shimmying her shoulders. "People always underestimate a pretty face and nice boobs."

Zinnia snort-laughed. I'd never heard her do that before.

"Good thing you gave up so fast," Amie Jo continued. "Otherwise you would have figured it out, started dating, fallen in love, and gotten married. Barf."

It hit me in a wave of nausea and truth. How many times had I turned my back on what was good in life because I didn't feel like I was good enough for it? How many times had I reminded myself that Jake was just going to change his mind about me again?

I'd been happy and loved. And then I'd fucked it all up. Big time. I loved Jake. I loved his arrogant confidence. His slovenly lifestyle. His commitment to his students. His doofy dog. His family. I loved that he made life better every day for someone.

"You had what we all want," Amie Jo told me.

"And then you threw it away," Zinnia sighed. "If you weren't my sister, I'd hate you."

"You waltz into town, all mysterious and interesting," Amie Jo complained. "And then you shit on everything that's important to me."

"Well, that's a little uncalled for—"

"Popularity is a privilege. I was popular, and I've done everything in my power to make my boys popular. I've been picking their friends, overseeing their activities, and making sure everything they do cements their position in this world. And along comes Marley Cicero to ruin everything again just like Homecoming!" She opened the second wine bottle and swung it wildly.

"I'm not trying to ruin your life or your sons' lives. I

promise. I'm just trying to show everyone that respecting each other is more important than proving you're better than everyone else."

"But if everyone is popular and accepted, where does that leave my boys?"

"I don't know. Happy? Well adjusted? Ready to face the adult world with kind hearts?"

"Pfft! When you're a mother—well, it's too late for you. Your ovaries probably shut down years ago," Amie Jo sniffed.

"Probably," I agreed.

"But when you're a mother, the only thing that matters is how well your kids turn out. They are a direct reflection of who you are as a human being. My kids are dumber than a box of rocks. All they have are their looks and their popularity."

Not sure what to say, I patted her awkwardly on the shoulder as she swigged wine.

"I know what people say about me behind my back. I got knocked up in college. I married a man who could take care of me. I dress like I'm an off-duty stripper."

"I never heard anyone say that," I lied.

"They don't understand how hard it is. Being a mom and a wife and working. I am hanging on by my damn fingernails here! And I don't know why I'm telling you any of this. It's not like you have any worries in life," she complained.

"Amie Jo, I think a lot of women are in the same place you are, feeling the same things you're feeling," I told her.

"I drink a bottle of chardonnay every night." Zinnia's confession was given like a balloon releasing its air.

"The highlight of my life was being crowned prom queen. It's been all downhill from there," Amie Jo responded.

"I'm really sorry about Homecoming," I said, starting to grasp just how important that crown had been to her.

"I probably deserved it."

"Maybe a little," I agreed.

"You need to go beg Jake for forgiveness," Amie Jo said, taking another swig from the bottle.

"Yeah, you do," Zinnia agreed.

It was then that the branch broke with a splintering crack, and we were all falling.

CHAPTER 80

Jake

I was not in the mood to entertain. Yet here I was, plating up Uncle Max's bacon-wrapped scallops on a serving dish. The whole family was spread out in my house watching TV, puttering in the kitchen, setting the table in the dining room.

And I still felt completely alone.

Marley should have been here. I felt her damn presence all over the damn house.

Not only was I being haunted by my grandmother, but now I had Marley's ghost in the new dishes she'd helped me pick out. In the rearranged furniture in the living room. The new curtains. The lack of clutter and dust and old takeout containers.

She'd swept it all out, making Grams's house mine. *Ours.* And now she wasn't here. Our new beginning was already over.

I liked the anger. It felt better than the hurt that kept trying to bubble to the surface. She'd never even tried. She hadn't returned my calls, my texts. She hadn't shown up on my doorstep begging for forgiveness. None of it had been real to her. I felt used and discarded and stupid.

"You're mangling the appetizers," Uncle Lewis observed.

"Sorry," I said, taking a deep breath and trying to gentle my grip on the scallops.

"I know we're not supposed to talk about You-Know-Who or You-Know-What," Uncle Lewis began.

I was already shaking my head. "I don't want to talk about it," I said for the nineteenth time.

"Do you love the guy? I mean the girl," Lewis said. "Sorry, force of habit."

I slammed the last scallop down on the plate. "I did."

"Whoa, what's with the past tense there, Grumpy Gus?" Max asked.

"I told her I loved her. I asked her to stay in Culpepper. And she dumped my ass. Reminded me we had a deal and that all this was only temporary. She wants '*more*.'"

"More what?" Lewis asked.

"That's what I said! I refuse to be in love with a dumbass."

Lewis and Max exchanged a glance.

The doorbell rang.

I stomped to the front door and yanked it open. Marley stood on my welcome mat. She had a split lip and a butterfly bandage over one eyebrow. Her arm was in a sling.

"What the hell happened to you?" I demanded. I couldn't stop the reflexive rush of concern, but I could hide it behind a bad temper.

"Fell out of a tree," she said quickly. "But that's not why I'm here."

"You thought of a few other ways to destroy my confidence?"

Homer, the traitor, shoved his face between my leg and the door and wriggled his way out to Marley. She leaned down to pet him with her good arm.

"I came to tell you you were right," she said, still looking at Homer.

"Great. Thanks. Happy to hear it," I said dryly. I started to shut the door. She could keep my jerk of a dog. She already had my heart. Why not take my dog too?

"Jake! Wait!" She slapped her good hand on the door. "I'm trying to apologize here."

"Try kissing him!"

I poked my head out the door and spotted Zinnia and Amie Jo hanging out the back window of Ned Cicero's car. Ned was in the driver's seat and waved to me.

I waved back. "What the hell is going on?"

"I don't want what I thought I wanted," she said in a rush. "I want you and Culpepper and Homer. I want to teach gym and coach soccer. I want to sleep late with you on Sundays. I want to run a half-marathon and spend my summers road-tripping with you."

Hope stirred in my chest, and I tried to squash it. But it was a slippery sucker. "I thought you wanted more," I reminded her.

"There is no *more* than what I found with you. I was happy with you, and it scared me, Jake. I've spent my whole life trying to be good enough. And you come along and don't even demand that I prove myself. You just love me as the hot mess that I am."

"What about that job in Pittsburgh?" I asked.

Her eyes widened.

"Yeah, small town. Remember?" I said.

If they hadn't made an offer and I was second fiddle…well, I'd take it, but I wouldn't be happy about it.

Homer spotted the women hanging out of the car window and bolted off the porch to greet them. He dove in through the open window and settled himself on the passenger seat.

"I have a confession to make. You're my second stop today," she said with a small smile.

"What was your first?"

"I crashed Principal Eccles's family luncheon and asked if she would consider me for a permanent position. Spoiler alert:

Even though I was bleeding and a little buzzed on chardonnay, she said yes. So you should know that I'll be sticking around here even if you aren't magnanimous enough to take me back. You'll be seeing me every single day of your life."

I stroked a hand over my mouth to cover the smile that was trying to appear. "You don't say?"

She nodded. "And I'm still going to be running. So I'll probably be bumping into you in the mornings before school. And asking for your help to study for the Praxis, since I'm going to be a real teacher in a permanent position."

"I guess it would be real awkward for everyone if you were still here and we were broken up," I mused, running a finger down her neck and hooking it in her sweater. I tugged her a step closer.

"Very," she nodded, eyes serious. "You'd be doing a service to your community by taking me back."

"And I suppose my uncles would be grateful to you for turning my pigsty into a home."

"Hi, Marley!" my uncles chorused behind me.

She waved over my shoulder before turning her attention back to me. "Look, Jake. I know that I screwed up big-time. I know that I hurt you. And I'm so sorry. I'll do better if you just give me a chance. You've made me realize something. I'm not a disaster or a loser. And just because things don't go exactly the way I think they should doesn't mean that they aren't perfect the way they are."

I held silent for a beat, not trusting my voice.

"There's something else," she said, taking a deep breath. "Read these." She held up two aged pieces of notebook paper. The folds were so deep they were practically canyons on the paper.

I opened the first one.

Marley,

You and me. Homecoming. Don't tell anyone. We need to play it cool since you just broke up with Travis. See you at the dance.

Jake

Horrified, I searched her face. "Mars, do I look like the kind of guy to ask a girl to be my secret date in a *note*?" I demanded.

"No, you do not. And I'm sorry for ever thinking that you did. Read the next one."

I read, flinched.

Marley,

I decided to take Amie Jo to Homecoming instead. She's obviously more my type. Good luck with everything.

Jake

"You spent twenty years thinking I dumped you for Amie Jo?" So many things clicked into place. Her worry that I'd just move on and forget about her. Her reluctance to trust me. Hell, I couldn't believe she'd let me anywhere near her after thinking I was capable of such a dick move.

She nodded.

"Hell, I was a dumbass in high school, but I wasn't that big of a dumbass."

"Sorry, Jake," Amie Jo called in a singsong voice, hanging out of the backseat window.

"I'm sorry for holding something you didn't do against you for two decades," Marley said, drawing my attention back to her.

My head was spinning. It was a lot to take in for a guy who'd spent the last several days in misery.

"So I just have to ask one question. Why *didn't* you ask me to Homecoming?" she asked. "You kissed me. You seemed interested."

"I had one weekend a month when I'd go visit my mom back in Jersey. That was the weekend. Besides, didn't you have some secret boyfriend—oh, shit." Realization washed over me. *Amie Jo, that diabolical teenage puppet master.*

Marley's head snapped around in the direction of the car so fast I thought she might add whiplash to her list of injuries.

"Oops! Forgot to mention that part," Amie Jo said cheerfully. "Sorry!" Homer licked her in the face.

Marley rolled her eyes and turned her attention back to me.

"She's basically Machiavelli," Marley sighed.

"Did you all hit your heads?" I asked.

Marley ignored me while I tried to get a good look at her pupils. "I love you," she said. "So much. So big and wide and more. You're the 'more' I've been looking for my entire life. And I love you, and I hope you still love me even though I was a jerk and told you that you didn't know what love was."

Homer barked from the car as if he were answering for me.

"Do you think there's a chance you could forgive me?" she whispered.

"That depends. Do you think you could be happy living here with me?" I asked, running my finger over her collarbone.

She nodded. "Yeah." Her voice cracked. "Really happy. Like, really, really happy."

"Baby." I swiped the hot tears off her cheeks and leaned down to kiss her.

"Ouch," she said when I touched her swollen lip.

"Sorry." I kissed the corner of her mouth.

"Woo-hoo!" Amie Jo and Zinnia celebrated from the back seat.

Ned beeped the horn. "Don't forget to ask him," he screeched.

"Oh, uh, yeah. If we're made up and everything, would you mind if my family came for dinner tonight? We burned our turkey."

"The more, the merrier," I told her. "Now what the hell happened to you?"

"I told you. Zinnia and Amie Jo and I got drunk and fell out of a tree."

CHAPTER 81

Marley

The lights were low. The kids, including my nieces and nephew, Jake's nieces and nephews, and Libby and her foster siblings were watching a Christmas movie in the living room on the floor while Homer snored on the couch. My pants were unbuttoned after thirds of everything.

Lewis was opening our ninth bottle of wine, and Jake was holding my hand under the table while he grilled his mom's boyfriend on his background.

Everything was just about perfect. Amie Jo and my sister were shit-faced and commiserating in the corner about how hard perfection was to maintain.

My mother was enjoying a lively debate with Max and Adeline about the education system. Dad and Jake's mom were in the kitchen doing dishes and talking about Louisa's water-coloring hobby. Rob, who'd been up with one of the kids last night, was asleep at the dining table.

My aches and pains from the fall were comfortably numbed by too much food, too much wine, and too much love.

I didn't have to be out there making a difference for thousands of people in order to matter. I could make my difference one person at a time. Starting with me. There was nowhere else in the world I'd rather be. And that was the secret,

I realized. It didn't matter what my salary was. Whether or not I had a corner office and an assistant. This feeling, this content-ment, was what mattered most.

I loved and was loved. And that was the most important thing in the world.

Jake leaned over and whispered in my ear, "What do you say we sneak upstairs for some very quiet makeup sex?"

"I say as long as I don't have to move around too much, you're on. I'd hate to throw up gravy on you."

"Let's pop some antacids first just to be safe," he said with a wink.

I followed him into the kitchen where he rifled through the cabinets. I poked my head into the living room and looked at the little bodies scattered on the floor, their attention glued to the TV.

Libby smiled and waved from the end of the couch. Homer's head was in her lap, and Rose was squished up against her side.

I waved back, feeling warm and fuzzy. Her foster mom was working a double today, so we'd picked up the entire clan of kids and brought them to Jake's.

Jake rattled the bottle of Tums. "Who wants?"

I heard adults from all corners say "Me!"

Jake was busy doling out antacids when the doorbell rang.

"I'll get it," I volunteered.

Homer grumbled and reluctantly crawled off the couch to join me. I opened the door and blinked.

My sister's husband, Ralph, and Travis stood on the porch looking uncomfortable.

"Um. Hi," I said.

"Hi. Are our wives here?" Ralph asked. "And before you feel like you need to lie for Zinnia, you should know I tracked her phone here."

"Uh. Well, maybe?" My sense of loyalty told me I needed to check with Zinnia and Amie Jo first before admitting that they were here. And shitfaced.

"Hi, Daddy!" Edith peeked around me and waved at her father.

Ralph's face softened, and he leaned down to pick her up. "Hi, sweetheart."

"Why don't you two come in, and I'll see if I can find your wives?" I suggested. "Wait right here."

I beelined into the dining room where Zinnia and Amie Jo were laughing hysterically over nothing. "Your husbands are here," I hissed.

"Who?" Amie Jo asked. She had an abrasion on her cheek, a black eye, and a broken middle finger.

"Your husband, Travis, and your husband, Ralph," I said, pointing to each of them in turn.

"What about them?" Zinnia asked. She had a cut on her forehead and a raw scrape on her neck. Her shoulder had been dislocated and popped back into place.

"They're heeere." I enunciated carefully, hoping my words would make it to them through the river of wine they'd ingested.

"Where?" Amie Jo asked.

"Oh, for the love of—your wives are in here," I bellowed. The men appeared in the doorway, and I bolted for safety, taking the last of the utensils with me. Amie Jo was more of a schemer. But angry Zinnia was new to me. I didn't know if she'd get stabby.

"What's going on in there?" Jake asked, nodding in the direction of the dining room.

"They're either making up or breaking up."

"It's the perfect distraction," he said, dragging me by the good arm toward the stairs.

We snuck upstairs, giggling. It was dark on the second

floor, and Jake fumbled with the light switch as he pushed me into the bedroom. Our bedroom, I thought. He flicked the switch, and the sconces on the wall glowed to life. The bed was made with…were those new linens?

"What do you think?" he asked, rubbing my shoulder.

The duvet was a nice, manly navy. Plain, simple, and a thousand times better than the scratchy comforter he'd had before. The pillows, well, there was a mountain of them. In blues and grays.

I crawled onto the mattress and flopped back against them. "Ahhh. This is really nice," I whispered.

He slid in next to me and carefully rolled me to the side so he could spoon me. His body against mine was the "more" I'd been looking for. This room. This bed. This house. This life. I was sure. And it had only taken a fractured radius, an honest sister, and a miserable nemesis for me to get the message.

"I love you, Jake Weston," I whispered.

He brushed his hand through my hair. "I love you, Marley Cicero." His lips tickled my ear. I felt him go hard against me, but he didn't make a move to tear my clothes off. He just held me like there was nothing else in the whole world he'd rather be doing.

"Where are we going to put the Christmas tree?" I asked, staring out the still-curtainless windows.

I felt him smile. "I think one in the living room and maybe a small one up here."

"I'd like that," I confessed.

Jake kissed my neck softly, sweetly, taking his time.

And I sank into that love, that goodness, that anticipation of all good things to come.

"Have you given any thought to whether you want to be Mrs. Cicero or Mrs. Weston?" he asked, sliding his hand under my sweater to cup my breast.

EPILOGUE

Marley

"Are you guys getting up?" the long-suffering voice demanded through the door.

"It's summer," I groaned. Next to me, Jake pulled the comforter over his head and snuggled closer.

"It's not summer. It's graduation. Tomorrow it's summer."

"Being a teacher is hard," I moaned into the pillow. I'd survived an entire school year as a gym teacher. Okay, admittedly, I had it easier than most of the faculty. But still. I'd been getting up early since August. I felt that I deserved a late morning with my handsome boyfriend.

"It's noon. You guys have two hours to eat, shower, and make yourselves presentable."

"She's not going to go away," Jake yawned.

"Do you ever feel like she's more our legal guardian than we are hers?" I asked him.

"Only every day," he said with a sleepy laugh before pulling a pillow over his head.

Grumbling, I stumbled out of bed, pulled on pajama pants and a T-shirt, and opened the door.

Libby smirked at me. "Look at you, all picture-perfect."

"Shut your face, smarty-pants. What are you so excited

about, anyhow? You still have an entire year of the horrors of high school left."

"My friends that you forced me to make are graduating today. So, really, my excitement and your 12:05 p.m. wake-up call are your own fault." She pushed a mug of coffee into my hands.

"Bless you, child. You don't by chance have five or six other siblings we could foster, do you? The lawn's getting a little tall, and it would be nice to have a designated kid for garbage takeout," I mused.

I followed her downstairs and paused to give Homer a sloppy good morning kiss. "I'll walk you tonight, buddy, and we'll stop for ice cream," I promised him.

He grumbled his excitement at me.

Libby grabbed her laptop that Jake had bought her for her birthday in the spring. "Now that one of you is vertical, I'm going to hang out on the porch for a bit."

"Obsessing about colleges again?" I teased. One of the best things about becoming Libby's legal guardians was telling her that college was on the table if she wanted it to be. Our normally cool and collected kid had squealed her girlish delight and hugged us off and on for three days straight. Since then, she'd researched every college and university on the East Coast. Libby had narrowed her list down to twelve schools.

"Maybe," she grinned.

"I'll make you a sandwich." I waved her off and rummaged through the fridge and crafted three delectable Lebanon bologna sandwiches. I delivered Libby's sandwich to her and jogged upstairs with the other two.

Jake was snoring softly in our bed so I helpfully whipped open the curtains, flooding the room with light.

"Lunch delivery," I said cheerfully, sliding his plate onto the nightstand. "If you don't wake up and eat it in two minutes, Homer will take care of it for you."

"Mmph," Jake said. But his hand snaked out from the covers and grabbed my wrist. "Come back to bed."

Was there anything sexier than bed-headed sex god Jake Weston beckoning me under the covers? No. Was I falling for it when I had an hour and a half to get myself ready for my first high school graduation ceremony as an adult? Apparently yes.

I let him tow me under the covers, let him wrap me in his inked arms. I relished the heat of his body against mine. The feel of his skin as it stroked over mine. The taste of his mouth. The rough of his jaw as it abraded my neck and shoulder.

He cupped my breasts as I straddled him. Together we were two lovers lost and found. His eyes, that bright, hard green, glinted as he drove into me. I was always ready for him, always wanting him. I marveled at the thought that I almost missed out on this. That I almost chose a sad apartment and a stressful job over Jake. Over this home. This family we cobbled together.

"I love you, Mars," Jake said as he leisurely thrust into me. He savored me. Worshiped me. Loved me.

And I welcomed it. Welcomed him into me so we were as close as two people could be.

"Jake," I breathed.

"Come, Marley," he ordered. The cords in his neck stood out as he held on to control while I rocked against him.

We linked fingers on the mattress. We were in this together. Coming apart together.

———

We were late enough that we drove the five blocks to the high school. Jake and I were decked out in our college caps and gowns, and Libby was rocking a little black dress that she and my mom had found on their monthly shopping spree to the outlets.

I'd rushed through the hair and makeup tutorial the girls

had posted for me on the message board. Even in the off-season, they'd made a sport out of pushing me to make an effort. And I enjoyed it. Thanks to my team, I regularly turned up in public as a reasonably put-together woman.

Jake didn't have a preference for Made-Up Me vs. Just-Rolled-Out-of-Bed Me. But I had fun making the effort on occasion.

We parked and funneled into the stadium with the better part of Culpepper. Good weather dictated an outdoor ceremony, and today was good. Balmy and sunny. Students were lining up in caps and gowns, sporting heels and sunglasses. It was a good day. I could almost smell the promise of the future on the late-spring breeze.

Libby ducked off to sit with friends while Jake and I headed to the teachers' section on the field next to the graduating class. We took our seats in the back row like the rebels we still aspired to be. Floyd grabbed the seat next to me. Amie Jo turned around from the front row and waved.

"Bet you never thought you two would be making nice on this field," Jake teased.

I elbowed him. "We've all grown up a lot since high school."

"Some of us more than others."

"Hey, what are my parents and your uncles doing here?" I asked, spotting the foursome in the audience. They'd become fast friends since Thanksgiving. Mom had joined Jake's poker nights, and Dad had been a regular attendee of Lewis's book club. They were planning a cruise with Jake's mom and Walter in the new year.

"Are you kidding?" Floyd said. "This is the social event of the year."

The first bars of "Pomp and Circumstance" crackled over the loudspeaker, and we all rose.

Culpepper liked to keep commencement short. No one in

town had time to sit through three hours of speakers. I tuned out Principal Eccles's remarks on past and future and relaxed against Jake's arm on the back of my chair.

Not so long ago, my future had been a lonely, anxiety-inducing mystery. Now it was an adventure.

"I'd like to take this moment to invite Jake Weston to the podium," Principal Eccles said.

"What's going on?" I whispered. Jake hadn't mentioned that he was part of the program.

"I gotta do this thing quick," he said with a wink.

I watched him walk to the podium and shake hands with the principal.

She stepped aside and let him have the microphone. "Ladies and gentlemen, it's my great honor this year to present the Teacher of the Year award. This year's recipient has not only been an exemplary member of the faculty but an integral part of the Culpepper community. The only thing more impressive than her bravery is the capacity of her heart. She set out to make every student feel like they belonged in this school, on her team, in this town." His voice tightened, and he cleared his throat.

Uh-oh. Jake was getting emotional. Could he possibly be talking about—

"Marley Cicero, if you'd join me up here," Jake said.

"Me?" I pointed at myself.

Jake grinned. Floyd elbowed me. "Get your ass up there, Cicero!"

I only vaguely heard the applause from the students or the faculty or the crowd. I was too busy wading through molasses. This wasn't happening. I hadn't even been a real teacher for half the year.

My feet moved of their own accord, carrying me closer to Jake. My Jake.

Principal Eccles handed me the award. It was heavy and

glass and had my name engraved in gold. Marley Cicero, Teacher of the Year. At least, that's what I think it said. My eyes were a little blurry. It was probably pollen.

"I'd also like to take this moment to ask Marley something in private," Jake said into the microphone.

I distinctly heard several of my senior girls scream, and when I glanced their way, they were standing on their chairs to get a better view.

"Marley?"

I looked back at Jake and found him in front of me, down on one knee.

"Holy shit."

"What do you say, Mars? You and me? Forever. We'll take Libby and Homer along for the ride."

He was holding a black box, but I couldn't see what was in it because my stupid wet eyes were geysering off my face. Why hadn't I done the waterproof mascara Natalee mentioned?

I didn't trust my voice. But I trusted my heart. I nodded so hard the cap fell off my head, and then Jake was picking me up and swinging me around to the wild cheers of the crowd.

"Oh, for Pete's sake, you amateurs." Amie Jo elbowed her way up to us and picked up the box I'd knocked out of Jake's grasp. She grabbed my hand, wrestled the ring onto it, then turned and smiled pretty for the crowd.

The deal sealed, I kissed Jake in an entirely unprofessional, unteacherly way. Some students probably had to bleach their eyes afterward. But I didn't care. We'd started in the shadows under the bleachers. And here we were, twenty years later, standing in the sun.

We resumed our seats, and the rest of the ceremony was a blur. So were the congratulations and celebrations afterward. I got so many hugs from my players my neck was sore by the time we got back to the parking lot.

Libby was waiting for us at the car, a grin on her face. "So my legal guardians are getting married. Guess that means I won't be an illegitimate bastard anymore," she said cheerfully.

"Show her the rest of the surprise, Libs," Jake said, ruffling her hair.

She punched a button on the car remote, and the hatch rose.

"Why is your SUV full of suitcases?" I demanded.

Jake slung an arm around Libby's shoulder. "We've got ourselves a three-week road trip planned to check out some of those colleges on our list."

"No freaking way!"

Libby nodded. "We're staying at all dog-friendly Airbnbs starting in Maine."

"But aren't you leaning toward Shippensburg University?" I asked. It was close by, and I had to admit I was hoping Libby would want to stay nearby. I was new to this kinda mom thing and wasn't ready to send her off to start a life far, far away.

Libby and Jake rolled their eyes. "That doesn't mean we can't have a little summer adventure!"

"I love you guys," I sniffed, grabbing them both close for a hug.

"Now she's crying again," Libby complained.

"No! I'm not, jerks," I cried and squeezed them tighter.

BONUS EPILOGUE

Jake/Marley

August
Jake

The tie was cutting off my oxygen. Uncle Lew must have tied the damn thing too tight, I surmised, pacing the confines of the kitchen. Our backyard was overflowing with happy guests. Homer was making the rounds in a new bow tie, trying to scam appetizers off of untended plates. Homer and Libby's rescue dog, Ruth Bader Ginsburg, was dancing at his heels in a sparkly tutu, enjoying the attention.

The shame page of the *Culpepper Courier* had struck again.

And here I was, guzzling a beer trying to drown the anticipation that was killing me.

This was a *big* day. The biggest.

I tugged at my collar for the nine hundredth time waiting for my bride. My wife-to-be. The fucking love of my life.

"Gusset strangling you?" Libby asked, popping into the kitchen from the stairs looking slightly less goth than usual in navy blue.

"What the hell is a gusset?" I demanded.

She attacked my tie, righting the damage I'd inflicted. "You're going to be fine. She's gorgeous. You're not hideous. The caterers opened the bar early, and everyone out there is celebratorily blitzed already. It's gonna be a great day," she promised.

"Gorgeous. Hideous. Blitzed." I nodded vigorously.

I know what you're thinking. The perma-bachelor turned willing fiancé was having second thoughts. Ha. Joke's on you jerks. I was in the throes of a panic attack stemming from the fact there was no way Marley Cicero would come down those stairs in some fluffy white dress and still agree to marry me.

She was too smart for that. I was a mess. A sweaty, manly mess.

I just needed to get her down the aisle and seal the deal before she came to her senses.

"She's not having second thoughts, is she?" I wheezed.

Libby raised an eyebrow piercing. "She might when she sees you turning green."

I slapped some color into my cheeks. Maybe a little too hard.

"Repeat after me," she insisted. "I will not vomit on the bride."

"I will not vomit on—Marley! Get your ass down here!" I bellowed. The need to drag her shapely ass outside and up the aisle to justice of the peace Tamra Hiebert was officially dire. If I didn't see her in the next thirty seconds, I'd have an aneurysm or a heart attack or irritable bowel. Or all three at the same time.

"Is Libby with you?" Marley called down from the second floor where she was probably knotting bath towels together to escape.

"Yes," I shouted back. I'd forgotten. We had a plan. The first-look thing. This wasn't just our day.

"Okay. Here I come," Marley warned.

"Isn't it bad luck?" Libby asked, sliding up on the kitchen counter and swinging her red Chuck Taylors.

"I saw her this morning before you estrogen-based beings kicked my ass out of the house," I pointed out.

"Fair enough. I'll give you guys a minute and check on the crowd outside," she offered.

I stopped her with a hand in the air. "Stay right there. This is a first look for all of us."

She rolled her eyes. "I've already seen both of you."

"Yeah, but you haven't seen us both together. We need to make sure we're breathtaking and shit."

The photographer, some swank Lancaster artsy-fartsy dude named JeMarcus that both Uncle Lewis and Amie Jo squealed over, poked his dreadlocks into the kitchen and pointed his camera at me.

"Ready to see your bride?" he trilled.

"Yes." It came out kind of a snarl.

I was desperate to see her.

I was convinced she'd climbed off the porch roof and was Ubering to the airport.

I was...*breathless*.

Marley stepped into the room, and my vision went keyhole on me. People were talking, but it sounded like Charlie Brown's teacher. The only thing I could hear clearly was the staccato beat of my heart. Definitely heart attack.

She was beautiful. Gorgeous. Sexy as hell. And I hadn't even looked at the dress. I didn't care what she was wearing. I didn't care that I was messing up her hair when I grabbed her in a hard hug and breathed her in. All I cared about was that she was here, grinning, holding me hard enough to convince me that she wasn't going to *Runaway Bride* on me.

"You're here."

She wrestled her arms up and cupped my face in her hands. "Of course I'm here. Where else would I be?"

"Halfway to Tijuana by now."

I kissed her on her mouth. Her cheek. Her temple. Her white gauzy thing. I realized she was wearing a veil. She looked so bridal it had me by the throat.

"You're ridiculous," she teased. Her eyes were bright. At least I thought they were. She was getting blurry on me. It was probably the aneurysm. "There's nowhere else I'd rather be."

"We're really doing this? You didn't change your mind? Because even if you did, I'm still forcing you to marry me. This is Pennsylvania. There's probably a rule on the books somewhere making it legal."

"Relax," Marley ordered with a laugh. "Take a breath."

"You're so fucking beautiful."

"You haven't even looked at my dress."

"Have so. It's white and poufy and perfect." She was swimming before me now, and my throat felt like I'd swallowed an entire jar of peanut butter.

"Don't you dare," she hissed. "The team spent forty-five minutes on this makeup, and if you make me cry one single tear, the entire day will be ruined."

"I don't care if you have snot bubbles in the pictures. We are doing this," I insisted.

"You guys look...nice." Libby sounded like she had the same peanut buttery throat problem.

Marley squeezed my arms. "You ready for this?" she whispered softly.

I wanted to answer but had to settle for a brisk nod.

Fingers linked, we turned to face Libby. The kid had brought more joy, more adventure, more fear into our lives than I thought possible. And today we were all going to make it official.

You see, guys. I met two special women, and they changed my entire life. And I wasn't letting either one of them go.

"So, Libby," Marley began, clearing her throat. Now it

sounded like she was being strangled by her gusset. "There was a little more paperwork to making this whole thing official."

I yanked the document off the kitchen table and shoved it at Libby.

"If you're cool with it, of course," I croaked. Great, my stomach felt like butterflies were punching me in it. Here came the irritable bowel. Libby could say no just as easily as Marley could decide she'd rather be a vice president of snack cakes in Europe. I was locking them down today.

Libby frowned and looked at the top page.

Marley was gripping my hand so hard I heard bone crack. I was too nervous to feel pain.

No one moved a muscle.

I heard the rapid click of the shutter, the laughter from somewhere in the backyard where half the town of Culpepper was doing shots of prosecco. *What could I say? We were classy AF.*

"Is she reading the whole damn thing?" I hissed at Marley.

"How should I know? Oh, God. What if she's trying to let us down easy?"

"I can hear you," Libby said dryly.

"Then put us out of our misery, you little punk," I said, choking the words out.

She looked up, nodded. Her eyes were filled to the brim, and I had to turn away to take a breath.

"These are adoption papers," Libby said softly.

"We know you're practically an adult," Marley began, forcing me to turn back around. "And God knows you're probably the most mature person in the house. But Jake and I would be honored if you would be our—"

We lost her. Marley was suddenly crying silently. Deep, shoulder-shaking sobs that wrecked the shit out of her makeup. I'd never seen anything more beautiful in my entire life.

"Daughter," I choked out the word. Mars and me, we were

a team. When we weren't finishing each other's sandwiches, we were finishing each other's sentences. And we wanted to bring Libby into the game.

Libby slid off the counter and grabbed us both in a hug fiercer than any gusset.

"Is that a yes?" Marley sobbed.

"Yes, it's a yes!" Libby hiccupped.

I didn't say anything seeing as how my brain was leaking out of my eyes in the form of salt water, I just squeezed them both as tight as I could.

"Is now a good time to give you guys your present?" Libby asked.

"Gimme!" Marley lunged for the envelope.

I pulled my fingers back just in time. I'd learned over Christmas never to get between this woman and presents.

"I know you're going to Puerto Rico for your honeymoon. So I kind of wrote this essay about me and you guys and how we all ended up together. And—"

Marley triumphantly yanked two tickets out of the mangled paper. She froze. "Holy shit. Holy. Shit."

I elbowed the photographer out of my way and peered over my almost wife's shoulder. "Ham—" I couldn't get the word out. It stuck in my throat. "Ham—" I tried again, but my voice broke.

"Lin-Manuel Miranda is performing as Hamilton in *Hamilton* in Puerto Rico next week," Libby said.

"Lin-Manuel," I breathed. I was hyperventilating. "Hamilton."

"You have tickets and backstage passes. And he sent a cool video to you guys. He even raps in it a little," Libby continued, wiping her nose on the back of her hand.

I couldn't respond. I was too busy bawling like a fucking baby. Marley was rubbing my back, and Libby was laughing.

"Way to show up your new mother, jerk," Marley teased. "All I got him was a stupid grill for the patio."

"Let's go, Cicero!" The chant started outside with hand claps. Family and friends were ready to celebrate.

"I'm gonna win some awards with these freaking pictures," Artsy-Fartsy sang, clicking away to capture the greatest day of my entire life.

Marley

You didn't think you'd get through my wedding day without hearing from me, the bride, did you? Let me tell you the highlights. My dress was amazing. A simple white crepe sheath that hugged all of my favorite body parts and generously skimmed over the ones I was only marginally fond of. I found it at a little boutique in Lancaster when I joined Libby and my mom on one of their shopping trips. We'd all gotten teary-eyed when I tried it on.

Guidance counselor Andrea showed up to the wedding with Bill Beerman as her official date. He had hives on his neck and couldn't stop smiling. They danced to every song the DJ played after the ceremony, including the Electric Slide.

My parents were so excited when justice of the peace Tamra Hiebert interrupted the ceremony to make Libby's adoption official that my dad bolted up the aisle and demanded that his new granddaughter start calling him Pop-Pop on the spot.

Zinnia and Ralph took advantage of their kids being distracted with wedding cake and snuck off. Vicky discovered them in the laundry room making out like teenagers. Since her meltdown at Thanksgiving, my sister went part-time at her job and insisted that her husband start working more human hours. They brought Jake and me a bottle of Dom and nine-million-thread-count sheets to celebrate today.

Travis and Amie Jo—two people I never thought would be invited to my wedding—were there in their small-town king and queen glory. Amie Jo, who of course tried to steal the show in a floor-length, barely off-white dress, organized the entire event for me as a sort of "sorry for being a monster to you" apology. I had to admit, it was a great day. I drew the line at swans, but the ice sculpture on the patio buffet really classed the day up. Until Uncle Max accidentally bumped the table while discussing Barbra Streisand's greatest hits with Jake's mom and the gigantic heart tipped over, smashing to bits on the patio. I chose not to view it as a sign of things to come.

Floyd and Vicky performed an imaginative and sometimes disturbing dance mash-up while Vicky's husband, Rich, dragged little Tyler away from the Boone's Farm fountain that we had borrowed from Amie Jo.

Libby and the rest of my inaugural soccer team dug out a ball, and we played barefoot in the front yard until the ice cream bar opened.

I had so many favorite people now. And they were all here. Especially the big, tattooed guy in half a tux. Jake had stripped out of his tie and jacket shortly after the ceremony. And he was beckoning me with the crook of a finger from the center of the dance floor. I ran to him. He caught me and lifted me up, spinning me around like he had at Homecoming. I felt like a winner. Like I was loved. Like I was just starting the best part of my life yet. And I got to share it with Jake Weston.

"I didn't give you your present yet," he said as he lowered me slowly and somewhat inappropriately against his hard body.

"Is it in your pants?" I guessed as he tugged my hips against his. Our gazes slid to the exquisitely wrapped box in front of my plate at our sweetheart table. Homer and Ruth Bader Ginsburg were sitting in our chairs and licking our empty plates.

Behind us at a long table, his cross-country team was mainlining cake and ice cream like it was fuel.

"I'm going to say something completely out of character here," I warned him. "I don't think I can take one more good thing today."

"You can't?" he rolled his hips against me to the beat of the music and I felt him pressing his hard-on into me.

"Not *that* good thing. I'm already counting on *that* good thing."

"Come on," he urged. "I promise it'll be the cherry on top of the perfect day."

"It really is the perfect day, isn't it?" I asked him, dreamy-eyed.

"Any day that I marry you, that I get to call you my wife, that I get to team up with you against Libby when she says she wants to shave her head and connect her nose ring to her eyebrow ring with a bedazzled chain is the perfect day," he insisted.

"I love you so freaking much," I said, my voice a little bit shaky.

"I've been waiting my whole life for you, Mars. I love you. Now, go open your damn present."

We wiggled our way through drunk couples canoodling on the dance floor. The DJ was going to have to drop some "Cotton Eye Joe" before people started making babies in our backyard. We reached the table, gave the dogs a good scruffing, and Jake handed me the box.

"I wanted to give you something that would make your life better."

"Better than *Hamilton* tickets?" I teased.

"Yeah, sorry. Nothing is ever going to beat that in a thousand million years. My man crush on Lin-Manuel knows no bounds. But hopefully this will rank up there somewhere."

I tore off the paper, half smashing the box to get it open. It was a gift certificate or coupon of some sort. Had Jake Weston finally failed? Was this for a half-assed massage or an "I'll wash your car four times for you" deal?

I read it. And couldn't stifle my gasp.

He was grinning at me, proud of himself.

Neat & Tidy Home Cleaning Service.

"You got me a cleaning service?"

Don't get me wrong. Jake had made great strides in cleanliness. But add Libby with her fifty shades of black wardrobe exploding all over the house and twice the usual dog hair, and there were days when I just wanted to move into the garden shed and not let anyone else in.

"Twice a month, top to bottom," he said proudly.

I wouldn't have to spend every Sunday with a cleaning bucket singing "Cinderelly" under my breath anymore and flipping off my small, messy family.

"This is the greatest gift you could have ever given me, Jake," I said.

"Yeah. I know. I'm awesome. Happy wedding day, Mars."

**Read ahead for a sneak peek
at another steamy Lucy Score
standalone, *Forever Never***

B rick Callan had no idea that he was one grocery aisle away
from his worst nightmare.

Had he bothered straightening to his full six feet four
inches and looked up from the canned goods, he would have
caught that telltale flash of red. The color of forest fires and the
temptations of hell.

Instead, he weighed the options between diced tomatoes
with or without green peppers while shopkeeper Bill House
complained to him.

"I'm telling you, Brick. That Rathbun kid spent half the
afternoon gunning his snowmobile down Market Street like a
maniac," Bill hissed, crossing his skinny arms over his chest.

Brick tucked the tomatoes with peppers into the cart next
to a bag of yellow onions, two cartons of beef broth, and the
pack of batteries.

"Kid scared the hell out of the horses on delivery yesterday," Bill continued. "*And* he came this close to sideswiping
Mulvaney's new Arctic Cat last week. You know we'd never hear
the end of that."

Brick bit back a sigh. Just once it would be nice to do his
shopping without small talk. "I'll talk to him," he promised. He
happened to know a thing or two about the dumb shit boys did
to impress teenage girls.

Bill blew out a sigh and adjusted the Doud's Market ski cap he used to keep his bald head warm from November through April. "Appreciate it, Brick."

There was a delicate balance to their little island community, and Brick's job was to help maintain that balance even in the dead of the Michigan winter when only the most hardy of residents remained on Mackinac. It was the same reason he'd promised Mrs. Sopp he'd change the batteries in the smoke detectors of her rental when she'd called from the back nine of a golf course in Florida.

The door to Doud's opened with a jangle of the bell.

Mira Rathbun—mother of said "Rathbun kid"—blew into the little store with a bone-chilling lake wind. Bill clammed up, looking as if he'd swallowed his tongue. The man didn't mind tattling to the off-duty cops on his neighbors, but he was more comfortable doing so behind their backs.

"Shut the damn door!" The order came from the cashier and two customers closest to the entrance.

When the last full ferry of tourists left Mackinac Island back in October, it also took the polite courtesy required for a summer resort with it. The town's five-hundred-ish year-round residents hunkered down for another bone-chilling off-season in the middle of Lake Huron with a charming surliness.

"Yeah, yeah. Sorry," Mira said, impatiently brushing a layer of powder off her bright-orange snowsuit. The woman was a mile-a-minute whirlwind, which stressed Brick out. It was unfortunate for the community that she'd been the one to teach Travis to drive his thirdhand snowmobile.

This was Brick's fourteenth winter on the island. He perversely looked forward to the frigid temperatures and the seasonal closures of most of the businesses. Winter was quiet. Low-key. Predictable.

Bill peered into Brick's cart, eyebrows disappearing under

the edge of his hat. "Beef stew again? Don't you know any other recipes? I bet there's a single gal or two on the island who wouldn't mind cooking up a nice pasty for ya."

"I like beef stew." He also liked not being forced to be social while eating it.

Brick made a batch of beef stew every week and ate it for four or five days straight because it was easy and familiar. As for the social aspect, he'd earned his solitary winters and wasn't inclined to set a second place at the table.

"Didja hear the news?" Mira demanded, bustling over and crowbarring herself into the conversation.

Brick was skeptical. News didn't happen on Mackinac in the winter. Which meant this was gossip. Something he preferred to avoid despite the fact that both his jobs constantly put him on the receiving end of it.

"This have to do with the plane that came in late last night?" Bill asked, temporarily forgetting his problem with Mira's kid's accelerator hand.

Her eyes sparkled with the rare nugget of novelty in the middle of a season when every day looked a hell of a lot like the day before. Brick had a sudden desire to walk right out into the cold and avoid whatever bomb Mira was about to drop. Instinct told him something bad was about to happen, and he'd left his gun at home.

"Now, keep this under your hats because rumor has it her family doesn't know yet," she said, leaning in and dropping her voice to a whisper.

Brick had a very bad feeling about this.

"Whose family?" Bill asked, looking bewildered. "I'm not following."

"I'm drawing it out for effect. Jeez. This is the longest conversation I've had with someone I didn't marry or give birth to in three months. Let me have this," she insisted.

Brick nudged his cart forward, hoping to escape the news. But Mira grabbed on tight, stalling his progress. "Remi Ford!" she announced.

His knuckles went white on the handle.

Remington Honeysuckle Ford.

Remi Honey to family. Trouble to him. *Hell.*

"Well, I'll be damned," Bill crowed. "What's she doing back here in the dead of winter without telling her folks?"

Their hushed voices melded beneath the steady hum in his ears. Brick did his best to keep his face expressionless while his insides detonated. The exit was only twenty feet away, but his feet rooted to the floor, knees locked. Over the deafening thump of his heart, he stared at Mira's mouth while she spilled the dirt.

She couldn't be here. Not without a heads-up.

It took him weeks to prepare mentally, to gird himself before being forced to exchange casual greetings across the dinner table.

"Psst!" The cashier, Bill's nephew, waved his arms from behind the register and silently pointed to the next aisle. Brick's stomach dropped into his boots.

No. This was definitely not happening.

Mira and Bill made a mad dash for the cereal aisle. Brick charged in the opposite direction toward the cashier, deciding now was as good a time as any to escape before—

His cart T-boned another just as it peeked around the corner. The momentum took both carts into a tower of oatmeal boxes, sending them toppling.

Fuck. He knew it before he looked up from the vanilla almond and maple bacon massacre on the floor.

And there she was. All five feet two inches of mischievous pixie. She wore her red hair in a long, loose braid over one shoulder of her magenta parka. Ear buds peeked out from the yellow wool cap crammed on her head. Her eyes were the color of the green antique glass his grandmother had once collected. Her mouth was full and wide, and when she turned that smile on a man, he couldn't help but feel just a little dazzled...at least until he got to know her. The smattering of freckles across her nose and cheeks stood out against the ivory of her skin.

She looked different. Pale, tired, almost fragile. The energy that usually crackled off her, raining down like sparks on her unsuspecting victims, was only a dull buzz. As someone who'd spent half a lifetime cataloging everything there was to know about Remi, Brick knew something was wrong.

Their gazes held for one long beat. He couldn't decide if he should say hello or if he could get away with running for his life. Before he could choose, she abandoned her cart and walked straight into him.

Instinct had him wrapping his arms around her even though it was the last thing in the world he wanted to do. She slid her hands under his coat and melted into him. Her scent was still agitating. It always reminded him of a meadow...right after a lightning strike. Without thinking, he rested his chin on the top of her head, his beard scraping over the soft knit of her hat. Something dug into his side, but before he could figure it out, she distracted him by letting out a long, slow breath, and some tension left her. This was not the Remi he knew. That girl would have teased him with a loud, smacking kiss on the mouth just to piss him off before whirling away again to wreak havoc.

He pushed her back, holding on to her upper arms. "What's wrong?" he demanded, keeping his voice low.

"Well, if it isn't little Remi Ford!" Bill declared as he skidded to a stop, Mira on his heels.

"What are you doing home in February?" Mira asked.

Remi slipped out of his grasp and plucked the ear buds from her ears. The smile she sent them wasn't up to her usual wattage, but he was the only one who noticed. "What can I say? I missed the winters here," she said brightly.

That raspy voice was so familiar even after all this time it almost hurt.

Bill hooted. "Now, that's a dirty lie!"

Mira rushed in to give the prodigal a hug. "Are you surprising your parents?" she asked. "I know they missed you at Christmas this year."

Remi avoided looking directly at Brick when she answered. "I felt bad about missing the holidays with them and thought I'd make up for it now with a nice, long visit."

She was lying. He was sure of it. Whatever had put those shadows under her eyes wasn't guilt over a missed holiday.

"You're such a good daughter. How's big city living?" Mira pressed. The woman would drain Remi of every detail if she let her. Then it would be served up to other islanders over school pickups and to-go orders.

"It's…good," Remi said.

Brick's eyes narrowed on the hesitation.

"Quick! What's my aura color?" Bill asked.

Remi's cheeks pinked up. "You're looking a nice bright green today just like always," she told him.

There were a lot of things that made Remi different from the average girl. Synesthesia was one of them.

The story went that little Remi Ford caused a fuss in kindergarten when she demanded a pink crayon to write her E's because everyone knew E's were pink. It took a few years, but her parents finally got an answer from a specialist. Their daughter's brain created extra connections, tying colors to things like letters, words, people.

But the thing he found most fascinating was the fact that she could see music. Back in the day, before things got complicated, he used to quiz her about the colors she saw for songs.

"Are you still at the museum?" Mira asked.

"Actually, I'm painting full-time now," Remi said.

That was news. He was surprised her parents hadn't mentioned it.

Brick glanced into her cart and spotted three boxes of Marshmallow Munchies cereal, coffee, sugary creamer, and a package of honey buns. Not a protein or a vegetable in sight. The woman was stress eating.

"Houses or paintings?" Bill teased.

"Mostly just paintings," Remi said with a wink. "But I'd paint a house for you, Bill."

The man turned a shade of scarlet Brick had never seen. Such was the power of Remi's charm.

She tucked a stray hair behind her ear, an old nervous habit, and that's when he caught a glimpse of pale-orange plaster between her thumb and index finger. Her right arm was in a cast.

Brick's gut clenched as questions revolved through his mind.

It wasn't any of his business. And he knew what would happen if he let himself get curious. Remi Ford was no longer his concern.

"Are you seeing anyone?" Mira asked. "Did you bring a boyfriend for Valentine's Day?"

Brick clenched his jaw. "Excuse me," he said, gripping the handle of his cart. "I've got to get going. Welcome home, Remi."

"Thanks. It was nice to see you, Brick," she said with a sad little smile.

He gave her a tight nod. With heroic effort, he walked instead of ran to the checkout, leaving her, the rest of the items on his grocery list, and his unanswered questions behind.

Author's Note

Dear Reader,

Whew! This book was so cathartic to write! Just like our heroine Marley, I *did not* thrive in high school. I had a couple of mean older girls on my soccer team (That being chosen last thing? That happened. And I obviously haven't gotten over it!), made the usual questionable teenage decisions, and generally suffered through being in a highly structured environment.

I loved writing a character who just kept getting back up no matter how many times she was knocked down. Like Marley, I bounced from job to job after college, never finding the right fit. Thankfully, I found where I'm supposed to be. At home, in leggings with greasy hair, chugging coffee while writing romance novels. However, I wasn't as charming or positive as Marley was in her quest. But Mr. Lucy *is* as dreamy and supportive as Jake Weston.

I hope you loved *Rock Bottom Girl*, and I hope you saw a little bit of yourself in the story—perhaps you kissed a Jake Weston under the bleachers? Or maybe you had an Amie Jo who made your school life less pleasant.

If you loved Jake, Marley, Libby, and Homer, please consider leaving a review. That's super nice of you!

If you're madly in love with my awesome writing skills, let's stay in touch:

- Sign up for my hilarious newsletter on my web page.
- Follow me on BookBub.

Hungover from this fabulous love story? Check out my hilarious madcap rom-com *The Worst Best Man* about a destination wedding gone awry. Or pick up *No More Secrets* for more small-town loving!

Xoxo,
Lucy Score

Acknowledgments

I'd like to thank the Academy. Oh, sorry. I just watched five seconds of the Oscars.

Special thanks to (in no particular order because I am incapable of prioritizing):

- Boo and Bex T-Rex for beta-ing this book and reassuring me that Jake and Marley deserved to be on your bookshelf.
- Dawn, Amanda, and Jessica for your editorial abilities to make me look not stupid.
- Taco Bell for bringing back Nacho Fries.
- Nora Roberts, Laura, and everyone at Turn the Page Bookstore for making my first book signing the best day ever. #LucyCon
- My Binge Readers Anonymous. You crazy BRAs make my life. End of story.
- Kari March Designs for this cover!
- Oreo Thins

About the Author

Lucy Score is a *New York Times*, *USA Today*, and *Wall Street Journal* bestselling author. She grew up in a literary family who insisted that the dinner table was for reading and earned a degree in journalism. She writes full-time from the Pennsylvania home she and Mr. Lucy share with their obnoxious cat, Cleo. When not spending hours crafting heartbreaker heroes and kick-ass heroines, Lucy can be found on the couch, in the kitchen, or at the gym. She hopes to someday write from a sailboat, or ocean-front condo, or tropical island with reliable Wi-Fi.

Sign up for her newsletter and stay up on all the latest Lucy book news. And follow her on:

Website: lucyscore.net
Facebook: lucyscorewrites
Instagram: @scorelucy
Readers Group: facebook.com/groups/BingeReadersAnonymous/